Secrets She Left Behind

DIANE CHAMBERLAIN

Secrets She Left Behind

MIRA®

MIRA®

ISBN-13: 978-1-61523-062-4

SECRETS SHE LEFT BEHIND

Printed in U.S.A.

For the families of the missing

Chapter One

Andy

I SAT ON MISS SARA'S COUCH AND KILLED ALL THE MEGA Warriors. I could usually kill them better, but her TV was way littler than ours and I was sick. That's why I was in Miss Sara's trailer. Only I wasn't supposed to call it a trailer. "It's a mobile home," Mom reminded me when she brought me here this morning. Even though she sometimes called it a trailer, too.

Things were different since the fire. Mom said I should call Sara "Miss Sara" like I did when I was little. It's politer. Miss Sara used to hug me and be real nice and Mom's best friend. Since the fire, Mom and her hardly even talk. The only reason I was in the mobile home was because Mom was desperate. That's what she said to Uncle Marcus this morning.

I was still in bed, tired from getting sick from both ends all night long. Uncle Marcus slept over, like he does a lot. I heard Mom say, "I've tried everybody. I'm desperate. I'll have to ask Sara." Uncle Marcus said he could stay home with me and Mom said, "No! Please, Marcus. I need you with me."

"I can stay alone," I called, but it came out quiet on account of being sick. I was sixteen; I didn't need a babysitter. I was sure I was done barfing, too. I couldn't be sick anymore because Maggie was coming home today. I wanted to jump up and down and yell

"Maggie's coming home!" but I was too tired. I could only jump up and down in my imagination.

I heard Mom on the phone with Miss Sara. "Please, Sara. I'm sure it's just a twenty-four-hour bug. I know it's a huge favor to ask, but I can't leave him alone. It'll only be for a few hours." In the before-the-fire days, Mom would say, "Can you watch Andy today?" and Miss Sara would say, "Sure! No problem!" But this wasn't those days anymore.

After a minute, Mom said, "Thank you! Oh, thank you so much! We'll drop him at your house about ten-thirty."

I pulled the blanket over my head. I didn't want to get up and get dressed and go to Miss Sara's trailer. I just wanted to go back to sleep till Maggie got home.

I brought my own pillow with me to the trailer. In the car, I leaned against the window with my head on it. Mom kept turning around from her seat. "Are you okay, Andy?"

"Mmm," I said. That meant yes, but I was too tired to open my mouth. I knew she wanted to reach back and touch my forehead. She was a nurse and she could tell if you had a fever by touching your forehead. Nurses are very smart like that.

"Just think, Andy," Uncle Marcus said. "When we pick you up at Sara...Miss Sara's this afternoon, Maggie will be with us."

Free, I thought. Maggie would finally be free. I hated visiting her at that stupid prison.

At the trailer, I laid down on Miss Sara's couch with my pillow. Miss Sara got a blanket and Mom covered me over. She got to put her hand on my forehead then. She gave Miss Sara ginger ale and crackers for me. I started falling asleep as Mom said, "I can't thank you enough, Sara," and things like that.

Then she left and I fell asleep for a long time. I woke up and Miss Sara was walking across the living room. She looked right at me. She was carrying a big box with a picture of a pot on it. She stopped walking and put it on the floor.

"How are you feeling?" she asked. She had some lines on her forehead and by her eyes. So did Mom, but not as many.

"'Kay," I said. My mouth tasted icky.

"You ready for some ginger ale and crackers? Think you can keep them down?"

I nodded. Except for feeling tired and kind of shaky, I was fine. I could've stayed home alone, no problem.

I sat up and Miss Sara brought me ginger ale in a glass with ice and crackers on a plate. Her eyes looked like she'd been crying. They were red how your eyes got. She smiled a funny smile at me. I smiled one back at her. People sometimes cried when they were happy and I knew that's what was going on. Mom had red eyes all week. Miss Sara was probably as happy about Maggie coming home as we all were.

I drank some ginger ale, which tasted good. Miss Sara carried the box outside. When she came back in, she said, "Do you want to play some of Keith's video games?" Which is how I started playing Mega Warrior.

Now I shot another Mega Warrior and then a Super Mega Warrior, which are the ones with the arrow things on their heads. At least it was a school day and Keith wasn't home. Keith was one of the people I couldn't save at the fire. Mom said he could actually die at first, but he didn't. He got scars, though. His hands and his arms look like they have maps on them, only without the country names. One of his hands is scrunched up, kind of. Part of his face has that map look on it, too. He got held back and now we're both juniors. He hated me even before I couldn't save him. I felt sorry for him, though, because of his scars.

The phone rang in the kitchen. I could see Miss Sara pick it up. She made a face.

"You said no later than one-thirty, Laurel!" she said. Laurel was my mom.

One of the regular warriors killed my littlest man. That happened when you forgot to concentrate, like I was doing because I wanted to know what Mom was saying.

"All right," Miss Sara said. She hung up the phone without saying goodbye, which was rude.

I wasn't doing so good at Mega Warriors now, but I had good determination and kept trying.

Miss Sara came in the room again. "Your mom said she won't be back till around four-thirty," she said.

"Okay." I killed two Super Mega Warriors in a row. Bang! Bang! Then one killed me.

"Andy? Look at me."

I looked at her face even though I didn't stop pushing the controller buttons.

"I need to run to the store," she said. "Keith'll be home soon. When he arrives, I need you to give him this envelope, all right?"

She put one of those long white envelopes on the coffee table. It said *Keith* on it.

"Okay."

She was in my way. I had to move my head to see the TV.

"Andy!" Miss Sara said. "Look at me!"

I stopped pushing the buttons. She was using an I-mean-business voice.

"Did you hear me?" she asked. "What did I just say?"

"Mom won't be here until…later." I couldn't remember the time she said.

"And what else?" Miss Sara used to be so nice. She'd turned into another lady this year.

"You're going to the store."

"And *this,* Andy." She picked up the envelope and kind of shook it in front of my face. "What did I say about this?"

"Give the mail to Keith," I said.

"It's very important."

"I'll give it to him."

She looked at her watch. "Oh, never mind. I'll put it where he'll see it."

"Okay," I said.

She walked in the kitchen, then came back again. "All right," she said. "I'm going now."

"Goodbye." I wished she would just *go.*

I started playing again when she left. Then I got thirsty and my glass was empty. I walked into the kitchen to get more ginger ale. I saw the mail that said *Keith* on it on the table. She said it was important. What if Keith didn't see it there?

I took the envelope back in the living room and stuck it in my book bag so I couldn't forget to give it to him. Then I sat down again to kill some more warriors.

Chapter Two

Maggie

THEY MOVED ME FROM MY CELL HOURS LATER THAN I'D expected because of some paperwork issue Mom had to straighten out. I was afraid they weren't going to let me go. There'd been some mistake, I thought. A prison official would show up at my cell door and say, *Oh, we thought you were in prison for twelve months, but we read the order wrong. It's really twelve years.* It's amazing the things you can imagine when you're alone in a cell.

I sat on my skinny bed with my hands folded in my lap and my heart pounding, waiting. An hour. Two hours. I couldn't budge. Couldn't open the book I was reading. Just sat there waiting for them to come tell me how twelve months was a mistake and I couldn't get out today. I deserved the twelve years. Everyone knew that, including me.

But finally, Letitia, my favorite guard, came to get me. I let out my breath like I'd been holding it in for those two hours and started to cry. Outside the bars of my cell, Letitia's face was nothing more than a dark, wavy blur.

She shook her head at me, and I knew she was wearing that half sneer it took me a few months to recognize as a kind of affection.

"You crying?" she asked. "Girl, you cried the day you come in here and now you crying the day you leave. Make up your mind."

I tried laughing but it came out more like a whimper.

"Let's go," she said, unlocking the door, sliding the bars to the left, and I thought, *that's the last time I'll ever have to hear that door scrape open.* I walked next to Letitia as we started down the broad central hall between the rows of cells, side by side like equals. Two free women. *Free.* I needed a tissue, but didn't have one. I wiped my nose with the back of my hand.

"You'll be back!" one of the women called to me from her cell. Others hooted and hollered. Cussed and shouted. "Yo, bitch! Gonna burn some more kiddies, huh?" *BB* they called me. Baby Burner, even though the people who died in the fire were two teenagers and an adult. I didn't fit in. It wasn't just that I was white. There were plenty of white women in the prison. It wasn't that I was young. Sixteen was the age at which you were tried as an adult in North Carolina, so there were plenty younger than me. It was, as Letitia told me the first week I got there, that "they can smell the money on you, girl." I didn't see how. I didn't look any different from them, but I guessed everybody knew my story. How I'd laid a fire around a church to let my firefighter boyfriend shine in the department. How I didn't set the fire when I realized kids would be in the church, but how Keith Weston lit a cigarette, tossing the match on the fuel I'd poured without realizing it was there. How people died and burned and had their lives totally screwed up. They all knew the details, and even though some of them had murdered people, maybe sticking a knife in their best friend's heart, or they sold drugs to junior-high kids or robbed a store or whatever, they stuck together and I was the outcast.

At the beginning of the year I'd thought about Martha Stewart a lot, how even though she was a rich white woman, she made all these friends in prison and they loved her. Adored her, even. How she came out on top. I told myself maybe that's how it could be with me.

As Letitia and I went down the wide corridor between the cells, I remembered the first time I'd made that long walk. The hooting and name-calling. I didn't think of the women as people then. They seemed like wild dogs and I was afraid one of them would break loose and run after me. Now I knew better. They couldn't get out. I learned it wasn't when they were in their cells that they could hurt me, but out in the yard. I was beaten up twice, and for someone like me who'd never even been hit, it was terrible. Both times, it was a girl named Lizard. She was six feet tall with thin, straggly, almost colorless hair. She was skinny and her body seemed out of proportion to the long arms and legs she could wrap around you like strands of wire. She let me have it, for no reason I could think of except that she hated me, like so many of the others hated me. I wasn't good at getting beaten up. I didn't fight back well. I cowered, covering my face with my hands, while she pounded my ribs and tore handfuls of my dark hair out by the roots. I had one thought running through my mind: *I deserve this.* You see people getting beaten up in the movies and TV all the time. There'll be cuts and some blood, but you don't get to feel the fear while it's happening. The not-knowing-how-bad-it'll-get kind of fear. Or the pain that goes on for days. Letitia saved me both times. Then I was "Letitia's pretty baby." LPB. They had initials for everything. A lot of the initials I never did figure out because I wasn't part of the in crowd. I wasn't the only outsider, though. Not the only one getting picked on. I wasn't the weakest by far. They'd find the ones who were least able to defend themselves and move in for the kill. All I could think was, thank God Andy wasn't the one to land in prison. He would never have survived.

I got over the whole Martha Stewart fantasy real fast. After the first couple of days, I didn't even try to make friends. I kept to myself, reading, thinking about how I was supposed to be in college at UNC Wilmington this year. Maybe a business major, which seemed totally ridiculous to me now. Business? What did that matter, really? Who could I help with a degree in business? What good could I do for anybody but myself and maybe some bloodsucking company? I tried to keep a journal, but I threw it away after a couple of months because I couldn't stand rereading what I'd written in the first few days about Ben and how I still loved him even though he betrayed me. How I did something so stupid out of love for him. How I killed people. *I took lives.* I wrote those words over and over on four or five pages of the journal like some third-grade punishment. I'd touch the latest cut on my lip from Lizard or the bruises that crisscrossed my legs and think *these are nothing.*

Letitia led me into a room that was the closest thing to freedom I'd seen in a year. It was the room where I'd checked into the prison, but it didn't look the same to me now that I was facing the windows instead of the door that led to the cells. There was a long counter, a few people working at desks behind it. There were orange plastic chairs along one wall. The windows looked out on a sky so blue I barely noticed the rows of barbed wire at the top of a tall chain-link fence. There was something else out there, too: a crowd on the other side of the fence. News vans. People with microphones. People carrying signs I couldn't read from inside the room. People yelling words I couldn't hear, punching the signs in the air. I knew that the crowd was there for me, and they weren't there to welcome me home.

"Yo, girl," Letitia said when she saw them. "Sure you don' wanna stay here wit' the devil you know?"

Letitia was a mind reader. I was shaking so hard my teeth chattered. There was a kind of protection I had in my cell that I wouldn't have once I walked through the prison gate.

"You sign over here, Lockwood." A man behind the counter handed me a sheet of paper. I didn't bother reading it. Just scribbled my name. My hand jerked all over the place.

I spotted my mother and Uncle Marcus on the sidewalk leading up to the building. Delia Martinez, my tiny but tough lawyer, was with them, along with two guards, helping them push through the crowd. I reached for the doorknob.

"It's locked, girl," Letitia said. "They goin' buzz 'em through. Just hold on."

I heard the buzzer. One of the guards opened the door, and Mom and Uncle Marcus burst into the room, Delia behind them.

"Mama!" I said, though I'd never called her "mama" before in my life. We crashed into each other's arms, and then I started crying for real. I held on to her, sobbing, my eyes squinched shut, and I couldn't let go. I didn't care who was watching or if anyone thought I was holding on to her for too long. I didn't care if I seemed nine instead of nineteen. I didn't care if Mom had had enough—though I could tell she didn't care about anything either. It felt awesome, knowing that. Knowing she'd hold me as long as I needed to be held.

Uncle Marcus hugged me when Mom and I finally let go of each other. He smelled so good! If anyone had asked me how Uncle Marcus smelled, I would have said I didn't have a clue. But now that I could breathe in his aftershave or shampoo or whatever it was, I knew I'd been smelling that scent all my life. His hand squeezed my neck through my hair and he whispered in my ear, "I'm so glad you're coming home, babe," which started me crying all over again.

"When we go out there, Maggie," Delia said when I finally let go of Uncle Marcus, "you don't say a word. Okay? Eyes straight ahead.

No matter what you hear. What anybody says. No matter what questions they throw at you. Not a word. Got it?"

"Got it." I looked over my shoulder at Letitia, and she gave me her weird sneer.

"Don't ever wanna see you in here again, hear?" she said.

I nodded.

"Okay," Delia said. "Let's go."

The guards led us out, and the moment my feet hit the sidewalk, the people went crazy. I could see some of the signs now: Life for Lockwood. Murderer Maggie.

"Eyes straight ahead," Delia repeated, her hand on my elbow.

Mom's car was parked right outside the gate so I wouldn't have to walk very far through the crowd. Still, when we got close to the car, the camera crews threw microphones toward us on long poles. They shouted so many questions I couldn't separate one from another, not that I planned to answer any of them. I nearly dived into the car, Mom right behind me. Delia got in front, and Uncle Marcus jumped in the driver's seat.

People pressed against the car as Uncle Marcus slowly drove through the crowd. The car swayed and shook, and I pictured the mob of people lifting up one side of it and rolling it over, crushing us. I put my head down on my knees and protected it with my arms—the crash position for flying. I felt Mom lean over me, covering me like a blanket.

"All clear," Uncle Marcus called as we turned onto the road.

I lifted my head and the angry shouts of the crowd faded away. Would they follow us to our dead-end street in North Topsail? Surround our house? Who would protect me then?

I could hear Delia and Uncle Marcus talking quietly, but not what they were saying. After about a mile, we pulled to the side of the road behind a black Audi.

Delia turned around and reached for my hand. "I'm getting out here," she said. "Call if you need me. You stay tough."

"Okay," I whispered, thinking that I wasn't the tough one in the car. Delia was, and I owed my puny twelve-month sentence to her. She'd gotten a bunch of charges against me dismissed or reduced. I had mandatory counseling ahead of me, where I guess I was supposed to figure out why I did what I did so I never did it again. The fire had been a one-time deal. No question there. I didn't feel like talking to anyone about the whole frickin' mess. I wasn't sure *what* I needed, but I knew it had to be some kind of total overhaul, not a few sessions with a shrink. Then I had three hundred hours of community service. No college for me for a while. Restitution to the families, but Mom was managing that by taking money out of my inheritance from Daddy. How did you pay families for their dead kids?

You'd think after a year in prison, we'd have a lot to talk about, but it was quiet in the car. Sometimes there's so much to say that you don't know where to begin.

I'd seen my mother and Uncle Marcus a couple of times a month while I was in prison. Each time, they sat closer together on their side of the table. I knew Uncle Marcus had loved my mother for a long time and I was glad she'd stopped with the ice-queen routine. They were probably lovers by now, but I didn't want to go there. It was strange enough that my mother was dating my father's brother.

"How's Andy?" I asked. I saw my brother about once a month, enough to know he'd grown at least an inch this year, which only made him about five-one. He was filling out a little more, though. He was swimming with the Special Olympics team in Wilmington now and he had a girlfriend named Kimmie. I hadn't met her, but

I was nervous about anyone who could possibly hurt my brother, who had fetal alcohol syndrome.

"Actually," Mom said, "he had a stomach bug all night."

"Oh, no." I hated to think of him sick.

"I hope we don't all catch it now," Uncle Marcus said. "Especially you, Mags. Nice homecoming that'd be."

"Is he home alone?" I asked.

"I left him at Sara's," Mom said. "We'll have to stop there and pick him up."

Could that be any more bizarre? Sara babysitting Andy while Mom picked me up? Mom's words just hung there in the car. "You and Sara are friends again?" I asked finally.

Mom sighed. "It's a little better between us," she said, "though I wouldn't use the word 'friends' to describe our relationship. I couldn't find anyone else this morning and he was really so sick I didn't want to leave him alone. Sara wasn't thrilled about it, but she said yes."

Mom looked older than I remembered. I hadn't noticed it during her visits, but now I could see that the skin above her eyes sagged a little. She'd cut her dark hair short, though, and it looked good. Actually kind of cool. Our hair was the same color, but mine was much thicker and wilder, like Daddy's had been. I had it in a long ponytail, which is how I wore it the whole year in prison.

"I don't think it'll ever be the same between Sara and me," Mom said. "I've let it go, though. My end of it." I knew she meant the part about Sara having an affair with my father while he was married to Mom. It turned out that my father was also Keith's father. Surprise, surprise. Andy didn't know that, though.

"But she's still upset," Mom said. "You know."

Yeah, I knew. Upset about Keith getting burned in the fire. I didn't blame her. I cried every time I thought about how I'd hurt him. "I won't go in when we stop there. Okay?" I didn't want to see Sara and I sure didn't want to see Keith.

"That's fine." Mom sounded relieved, or maybe it was just my imagination.

We drove over the swing bridge that crossed the Intracoastal Waterway.

"Oh, the ocean!" I said, looking toward the horizon. The water was a blue-gray, the sky a bit overcast, but it was beautiful. I'd never take living on the island for granted again.

We were practically the only car on the bridge. Although I usually liked September on Topsail, when most of the tourists were gone and it felt more like home, the lack of cars—of *people*—suddenly made me realize I would stand out. If the summer crowds had still been there, I could blend in with them. Now, I would know everyone and everyone would know me. I felt sick thinking about the girl I'd been a year ago. The girl who hid out in the Sea Tender and who did crazy things for love. Who led a secret life.

"Mom?" I said.

She rested her hand on mine. "What, sweetie?"

"I'm going to drive you nuts at first," I said. "I mean, I'm going to tell you everything that I think, okay? I need someone to tell me if I start thinking like a crazy person again."

"You can tell me anything you like," she said.

"Remember—" Uncle Marcus looked at me in the rearview mirror "—you'll have a counselor, too, Mags. You can be completely open with her."

We pulled into the trailer park and I scrunched down in the seat when Uncle Marcus stopped in front of the Westons' faded gold double-wide.

"I'll stay here with Mags," Uncle Marcus said.

"I'll just be a minute," Mom said as she got out of the car.

Uncle Marcus turned in his seat to smile at me. "It's going to be all right," he said. His brown hair was really short. Shorter than I'd ever seen it, and he had amazing blue eyes that I'd loved my whole life. He was one of the best people I knew. I could always trust him to be in my corner no matter how I screwed up, and that thought made my eyes prickle.

I bit my lip. "I hope so," I said.

"Here he comes."

I sat up to see my brother fly down the steps from the trailer's small deck and run across the sand. He pulled open the back door and flung himself toward me. I caught him, laughing.

"You're free!" he said.

"Yup, Panda Bear," I said. He seemed so much bigger. I brushed his thick hair off his forehead. "Now you're stuck with me."

Mom got back in the car, this time in the front passenger seat. "Everything okay with Sara?" Uncle Marcus asked her.

"She wasn't there," Mom said.

"She had to go to the store," Andy said.

"I left a note, thanking her," Mom said.

No one said it, but I knew why Sara wasn't there: she didn't want to see me any more than I wanted to see her.

Chapter Three

Keith

BRIDGET HAMMETT WAS SITTING NEXT TO ME IN ALGEBRA. TO
my *left*. That mattered. I didn't like anybody sitting on my left side.
In most of my classes, I made sure to get the seat next to the
window so nobody was on my left, but the first day of algebra, I
was late to sixth period and all those seats were taken. So now,
Bridget, who was the hottest junior—maybe the hottest girl in all
of Douglas High School—was sitting on my left side and texting
Sophie Tapper who sat on my right. I knew the text message was
about me. It was like I could feel when people were talking about
me.

My left arm was killing me and I needed another Percocet. Ten
minutes till the bell rang. I needed to get out of there. Not just out
of algebra—out of the whole damn school. I came in early today
to do this stupid makeup exam, and now I was wiped. I used to leave
after seventh period. These days, it was after sixth. Soon it would
probably be after fifth. I couldn't stand being there. Being a fucking
junior again. A seventeen-year-old junior. The guy everybody pretended not to stare at. Before the fire, girls were always staring at
me. I liked it back then, feeling them watch me in class, knowing
they were texting their friends about me. I'd get these e-mails about
how they wanted to do it with me. Lots of details in them. Now it

was different. I got, like, no e-mails at all. I knew what the girls were saying about me now. How if they looked at me from the right side—as long as they didn't see my hands and arms—I looked hot. If they looked at me from the left side, I was like something out of a horror flick. There was only so much of that kind of staring I could take before I wanted to toss all the desks out the windows.

The bell finally rang and I was outta there without looking back. I walked straight to my car and got in. Some dealership in Jacksonville donated the car to me after I got out of the hospital. It was a total dork of a car and I wanted to sell it and get a motorcycle, but my mother said that would be an insult and I needed to be grateful and blah blah blah.

I took a Percocet with what was left in a can of Dr Pepper I had stuck in my cup holder that morning. Then I laid rubber pulling out of the parking lot, heading toward the bridge and the beach. I wasn't going home, though. First, because Mom would be there and I never let her know I was cutting. I didn't want any grief from her. Second, today, for some total crap reason, Andy was at our house. Today! The day Maggie was getting sprung. The day I'd really like to forget the Lockwood family existed. Mom left a message on my cell about Andy being there, but said he'd be gone by the time I got home. She also said I should come straight home from school, probably because she knew I'd be freaking about Maggie getting out. "If you see any reporters," she said, "walk right past them. Don't engage them. You owe them nothing." Reporters? Shit. They'd better just stay out of my way.

No way was I going home until I was sure Andy was outta there. I wasn't taking any chances of seeing any Lockwood. Not Andy or Laurel or the bitch who burned my face. It was for her own sake. I might kill her if I saw her. Money could buy you anything, including a get-out-of-jail-free card. She visited me in the hospital before she went to jail and I swear, if I'd known then what I knew now, I would've found a way to kill her even with my arms bandaged up to my shoulders. I had this really tasty fantasy of setting her on fire— only someone else would have to light the match. I wasn't big on flames of any kind these days. But I liked to imagine her getting burned at a stake, like they used to do to witches. She was a witch all right. It was a sick fantasy, but not as sick as burning a church full of kids.

I parked by the pier where the surfers hung out, though the surf was so lame only three other guys were there. I didn't really know them. The cool thing about surfing was you could be with other people but not really have to *be* with them. Like talk to them or be close enough so they could stare at your face. The water was still warm enough that I really didn't need my wet suit, but I put on the top half anyway because I wasn't supposed to get sun on my arms. I spread sunscreen over my screwed-up face. Then I paddled out and waited for a wave worth riding in. My physical therapist thought surfing was good for me, as long as I could "do it safely." He meant, as long as I could manage the board with my screwed-up left hand and had enough flexibility in my arms. We worked on that in PT. Talk about pain! But if I skipped the exercises for even one day, I paid big-time.

From the water, I could see our trailer park, though I couldn't get a good look at our double-wide. It was three back from the road and I could just make out one pale yellow corner of it. Was Andy still there? My half brother? Not that I'd ever let anyone know I was related to that loser.

The three other surfers started talking to each other. Their voices bounced around on the water, but I couldn't really hear what they said. Then they started paddling toward shore, so I guessed they'd had enough of waiting for a decent wave. I wondered if they'd go somewhere together. Maybe get a burger. Talk about girls. While I just sat alone in the water paddling in place, looking at the corner of our trailer, wishing I had someplace to go myself.

Chapter Four

THE FIRST THING I NOTICED WAS THE SIMPLE BEAUTY OF THE small, pentagonal building. The scent of wood was so strong, it made me woozy. I felt grounded by it, connected to the earth, as if the smell triggered a primitive memory in me. Through the huge, panoramic windows, I saw the sea surrounding the tiny chapel and I felt as if I were on a five-sided ship, bonded together with twelve fellow sailors.

The second thing I noticed was the man in jeans and a leather jacket. Even though he hadn't said a word, I could tell he was in charge. Physically, he was imposing in both height and mass, but it was more than that. He was a sorcerer. A magician. Even now, writing about him all these years later, my heart is pounding harder. Without so much as a glance in my direction, he cast a spell over me that was both mystical and intoxicating and—if I'm being completely honest—sexual. In that moment, I realized I'd been missing two things for a long time: I had nothing in the way of a spiritual life, and nearly as empty a sensual life. And really, when those two things are taken away, what's left?

I sat with the others in an awed silence; then the man got to his feet. Morning sun spilled from the long window nearest the ocean, pooling on his face and in his dark, gentle eyes. He looked around the room, his gaze moving from person to person, until it landed on me. I couldn't look away. I didn't want to. He looked inside me to the vast emptiness of my soul. *Fill it for me,* I was thinking. *Help me.*

After a moment, he shifted his gaze away from me and back to the others in the chapel. "Where did you experience God this week?" he asked.

Nowhere, I thought. I wasn't even sure what he meant. All I knew was that I felt at home for the first time since Steve dragged me from Michigan to Camp Lejeune. I didn't belong in this little Southern enclave, with its hundreds of churches and its thousands of church-goers with whom I had nothing in common. I didn't know a grit from a tomato, a moon pie from a potato chip. I felt completely lost when I tried to connect with the other military wives. They missed their husbands who were on temporary duty assignment, while I guiltily looked forward to Steve's absences. Many of the women were my age—twenty-one—yet I couldn't seem to breach the gulf between myself and them as they gushed about their men while shopping for groceries at the commissary. I felt as though something was terribly wrong with me. Terribly lacking. Suddenly, though, there I was in an actual church—of sorts—and I felt at home.

There was a long silence after the man asked the question about God, but it wasn't at all uncomfortable, at least not to me. Finally, the woman next to him stood up. I saw the glitter of the ring on her left hand and thought: *his very lucky wife.*

"I was lying on the beach last night," she said, "and I suddenly felt a sense of peace come over me."

She was pretty. Not beautiful. There is a difference. She was thin in a reedy way. Her hair was incredible in that wash of sunlight. It hung well past her shoulders, and had the slightest wave to it—just enough to keep it from being straight. It was very dark and nearly Asian in its shininess, the polar opposite of my short blond cap of hair. She was fair-skinned with plain brown eyes—nothing like her husband's—and her face was the shape of a heart. When she looked at the man, though, her eyes lit up. I was jealous. Not of the woman, specifically, but of *any* woman who could feel what she clearly felt. Total love. An adoration a man like that would return ten times over.

I tried to picture Steve standing up like the man had done, asking about God. Caring so passionately about something. Creating that tiny masterpiece of a building. I assumed, correctly, that the man was the one everyone talked about—the crazy, motorcycle-riding guy who'd built his own chapel. I couldn't imagine Steve doing anything like that. I couldn't picture him smiling at me the way the man smiled at his wife as she sat down again. Frankly, I had no idea what went on inside Steve's mind. I'd married a near stranger because I felt like I had no choice. When you're young, you have more choices than you'll ever again have in your life, yet sometimes you can't see them. I'd truly been blind.

Steve had been so handsome in his uniform on the day of our wedding. I'd convinced myself he was a fine man for offering to marry me when I told him about the baby. I'd accepted his offer, although neither of us talked about love, only about responsibility. I told myself that love would come later.

But that morning, the man with the sun in his eyes made me doubt that loving Steve would ever be possible. Maybe if I'd never set foot in the chapel, everything would have turned out okay. I would have learned to be satisfied with what I had. As I got to my feet after the service, though, I knew it was already too late. The seed was planted for everything that would follow. The damage was already done.

Chapter Five

Maggie

WHEN WE TURNED ONTO OUR SHORT STREET THAT DEAD-ended at the sound, I saw the news vans parked all over the place and people running around, and I suddenly knew what my life was going to be like for the next few days. Or maybe forever.

"Oh, no," Mom said.

Uncle Marcus let out a noisy, angry breath. "Don't worry, Mags," he said. "We'll pull right into the garage. You won't have to talk to anyone."

I scrunched low in my seat, thinking of the prisoners I'd seen on TV hiding their faces with jackets as they walked past the reporters. I always thought they were trying to protect their privacy. Now I understood. It was humiliation that made them want to hide.

Inside the house, I walked from room to room, smoothing my hand over the sofa, the china cabinet, the dining-room table. I loved how familiar everything was. Andy followed me around, talking constantly, like he was trying to make up for all our lost conversations.

In the kitchen, I recognized Uncle Marcus's Crock-Pot on the counter. I could tell by the smell that Mom was cooking chili. I was glad they weren't making a big deal out of me coming home. No party or anything like that, where I'd have to see a lot of people. I was totally overjoyed to be home, but it didn't seem like something we should celebrate.

My room was exactly as I'd left it, with the blue-and-green-striped bedspread on the double bed and framed photographs of Daddy and Andy and some—former—friends on my dresser. There was a white teddy bear I'd never seen before on my pillow, and I picked it up. It was the softest thing! It held a little card that read, *Welcome Home! Love, Uncle Marcus.* The label on its leg said it was made of angora. A teddy bear might have seemed like a silly present for a nineteen-year-old, but it was totally perfect. How did Uncle Marcus know I needed something exactly like the bear? Something I could hold on to that made me feel kind of innocent, like a little kid who hadn't meant to do something so wrong.

I carried the bear around with me as I walked through the rest of the house.

Mom's room was a little different, mostly because of Uncle Marcus. His slippers were on the floor next to the bed. In her bathroom, his shaving stuff and toothbrush and deodorant and everything had taken over the counter around one of the sinks. While I was in her room, the doorbell rang a couple of times. I heard Uncle Marcus talking to whoever it was. I couldn't make out what he was saying, but I figured he was telling them to get lost. Leave us alone.

Andy's room was exactly the same in every way except one: it smelled different. The air seemed thicker or something. I'd been in the bedrooms of my male friends before I hooked up with Ben, and Andy's room smelled like theirs did. No longer a little-boy smell. Slightly dirty socks. A little sweat. A little aftershave. It felt weird to be in there.

"Do you want to see pictures?" Andy asked, sitting down at his computer.

"Sure." I pulled his desk chair next to him and hugged my arms across the teddy bear. "Do you have one of Kimmie?"

"Yeah," he said, clicking his mouse. He pulled up a bunch of pictures. "This is my Special Olympics team," he said.

There were ten of them, six boys and four girls, lined up in their bathing suits against a wall. At least seven of them looked like they had Down syndrome. Two of the boys looked totally normal. Then there was Andy. Cute, but much tinier than the rest.

"That's Matt." Andy pointed to one of the boys with Down syndrome. "He's Kimmie's brother."

It was coming back to me. Mom had told me Kimmie was one of five kids, all adopted, all special needs. Kimmie wasn't on the swim team herself, though. Just her brother.

"And this is me and Kimmie." Andy clicked on another picture.

"She's so cute!" I said. Kimmie stood a couple of inches taller than Andy. Her dark hair was coming loose from a long ponytail. Ethnically, I couldn't even guess. Her eyes were sort of Asian. Her skin was nearly as dark as Letitia's, but she didn't really look African-American. She wore rectangular glasses and behind them, her eyes were very green. She was beyond cute, actually. She was beautiful. I wondered what her special needs were.

"One of her legs is short," Andy said as if he knew what I was thinking, which I knew he didn't. "She was born with a funny foot. They did an operation but it made her limp."

"Are you in love?" I grinned.

The tops of Andy's ears turned red and I put my arm around him, hugging him with a giggle.

"Yes," he said.

"Does she love you back?" She'd better.

"Yes. She helps me. She keeps my stuff in her calendar in case I forget."

Mom had told me Kimmie'd taken on a sort of second-mother role with Andy, keeping track of his schedule, making sure he remembered things. That used to be my job.

"I can't wait to meet her, Panda," I said.

"Don't call me Panda anymore," he said. "It's a baby name."

For a second, I felt like he was stealing something from me. But I got it. Panda *was* a baby name.

"Okay, Andrew," I said, and he laughed.

Suddenly, there was a loud crash from downstairs, followed by a thud. Andy and I looked at each other, frozen like statues.

"Laurel!" Uncle Marcus shouted from somewhere downstairs. "Call the police!"

Andy raced out of the room before I could stop him. I followed him into the hallway, trying to grab his arm.

"Don't go down!" I said. He was too fast for me, though, and he went flying down the stairs.

"Stay out of there!" I heard Mom yell at him. "There's glass everywhere."

"Mom?" I called from the top of the stairs. "What happened?"

"Stay up there, Maggie." Mom came into view in the downstairs foyer. She was holding the phone to her ear and looking toward the family room. "Someone threw a... I don't know what it is. A rock, Marcus?"

Uncle Marcus answered her, but I couldn't hear what he said.

"A chunk of concrete or something," Mom said. "Someone threw... Yes. Hello?" She spoke into the phone, and her voice was shaking. "This is Laurel Lockwood," she said. "Someone just threw a piece of concrete through our front window."

I walked into my bedroom, the teddy bear clutched in my arms. Maybe I should have gone downstairs to help clean up, but I was too freaked out. Things like this didn't happen on Topsail Island, and I knew it wasn't any random act of violence. It was me they were after, but it was my family getting hurt.

From my bedroom window after dinner, I could see two of the news vans still outside. What were they going to do, sit there all night? All week? I bet they loved seeing the cops arrive and watching Uncle Marcus put the storm shutters over the broken window.

I closed my blinds. After a while, I got up the courage to turn on my TV and put on the news. Then I sat on my bed, waiting, my chin resting on the teddy bear in my arms. I didn't have to wait long. Suddenly the screen was full of the people outside the prison, the ones shouting and holding signs.

"Amid protests," a woman reporter who looked no older than me said, "Maggie Lockwood was released from Kawatchee Women's Correctional Institution today after serving a twelve-month sentence for the attempted burning of Drury Memorial Church in Surf City." She went on for a minute about who I was and what I'd done. Then she started interviewing people in the crowd. The first was a dark-haired man who was so angry, little bits of spit flew out of his mouth when he spoke.

"She gets twelve short months in prison and then goes on with her life like nothing happened!" he said.

"*I wish,*" I said out loud.

"My uncle is *dead,*" a young woman said. Her face was twisted into a mask of hatred. For *me.* "He was such a good man. And that girl just scoots out of here with her slick lawyer and everything," she said. She had to be Mr. Eggles's niece, since he was the only adult killed in the fire. I thought of my own uncle. Imagined him dead, the victim of someone like me. *No!* I shuddered, waving my hand in front of my face to erase the thought.

Reverend Bill was on the screen then. I gasped. I so didn't want to have to look at him! He stood in front of a brick church. The new Drury Memorial? Wow. Totally different. "Many people are angry," he said. "We've managed to rebuild Drury Memorial. We're nearly finished. But we can't rebuild those lives that were lost or shattered, and that's hard for a lot of people. I hope, though, that this can be an opportunity to practice forgiveness."

Forgiveness? *Reverend Bill?* What a hypocrite. He hated me. Hated my whole family.

Someone knocked on my bedroom door.

"Come in," I said.

Mom poked her head inside, glanced at the TV.

"Oh, Maggie. Don't watch that."

"It's all right," I said.

"Come downstairs and have some ice cream with us. Chocolate-chip mint."

I shook my head. My stomach hurt. "Stay away from the windows down there," I said. I was afraid that first chunk of concrete wouldn't be the last.

"Come on," Mom insisted. "We want to be with you tonight."

It was weird in the family room with all the draperies pulled shut. We never closed those draperies, but we didn't want anyone to be able to look at us while we sat—away from the windows—eating ice cream. At least everyone *else* was eating, while I pushed the melting green stuff around in my bowl. The phone rang, and Mom picked it up. She looked at the caller ID and shrugged as she handed the phone to Uncle Marcus. I guessed he was the family spokesperson.

"Hello?" he said, then, "Hey. Is everything okay?" I watched a line appear between his eyebrows and wondered who he was talking to. "Okay," he said. "She's right here."

I was afraid he meant me, but he covered the mouthpiece and looked at Laurel. "It's Keith. He sounds shaken up."

We were all quiet as Mom took the phone. I tried to picture how Keith looked now. The last time I saw him was in the hospital, when his arms looked like giant white tree stumps, thin steel rods sticking out of the bandages covering the fingers of his left hand. More bandages had covered half his face. I knew he was scarred. No one had told me exactly how bad it was. I could guess, though.

Mom held the phone away from her ear and looked at Andy.

"When Sara...Miss Sara said she was going to the store, did she say when she planned on getting home?" she asked.

Andy licked his spoon. "I don't think so."

"Did she say what store? What kind of shopping?"

"I don't remember."

She spoke into the phone again. "He doesn't know anything, Keith," she said. She stood up, turned her back toward us and walked toward the kitchen. She lowered her voice, but I could still hear her. "Why don't you try Dawn?" she asked. "Maybe she'll know something."

Dawn Reynolds was the woman Ben had cheated on me with. Or, as I admitted to myself this past year, I was the woman—the *girl,* really—Ben cheated on Dawn with. He'd lived with her, after all. Thank God he'd gone back to his wife in Charlotte and I wouldn't have to worry about bumping into him. Oh my God. That would be the worst.

"What's up?" Uncle Marcus asked as Mom hung up the phone and sat down again.

"Keith got home around five, and Sara wasn't there and she's still not home." She picked up her empty ice-cream bowl like she was going to get up and carry it to the kitchen, but she didn't budge from her seat. "He saw the note I left, thanking her for watching Andy."

"She probably told him she'd be out and he forgot," Uncle Marcus said.

"Kind of strange, though." Mom frowned. "What time did she leave, Andy?"

"Leave where?" Andy asked.

"The trailer. Their mobile home."

Andy shrugged. "I was killing Mega Warriors," he said.

Uncle Marcus laughed. "What was your score?"

"My best was 52,341," Andy said proudly.

Uncle Marcus smiled at my mother. "The boy has his priorities when it comes to what he remembers and what he doesn't," he said. "I'm sure Sara's fine."

I listened to the conversation, feeling apart from them all of a sudden. I felt as though I wasn't really there. Like I was only dreaming that I was home. It was a dream I'd been longing to have all year.

Around ten-thirty, Uncle Marcus went upstairs and I realized he was staying over. I was glad. I didn't feel safe in our house, and I liked having him there. I thought the news vans were finally gone, but I still felt as though people were sneaking around outside, maybe looking in the windows, maybe carrying something to throw. Oh,

God! What if someone torched the house with all of us inside? They might think that perfectly fit my crime.

I went upstairs myself, and for the first time in a year, put on the soft old drawstring shorts and T-shirt I liked to sleep in. The shorts just about fell off me. Wow, I'd lost weight this year. Big-time.

Before I went to prison, I used to always watch some TV from my bed at night, but I'd had it with TV for today. I lay in the darkness for a half hour, imagining I was hearing sounds outside. If someone set fire to our house and it blocked the stairs, what would we do? Andy and I both had these roll-up ladders in our closets that we could hook onto our windowsills, but there was nothing like that in Mom's room. I started to cry just thinking about how awful it would be.

Finally, I went downstairs, teddy bear in my arms, to make sure everything was locked up tight. I walked barefoot into the dark kitchen. Through the glass door, I could see the moonlight on the sound and our pier. I wanted to go out on the pier and breathe in the smell of the water and feel the salty air on my skin and in my hair. No way did I dare go outside, though.

I walked into the family room and saw that the door to the porch was open, and I froze. I tiptoed toward the porch and peeked around the door frame to see my mother sitting on the glider in the darkness.

"Hi," I said.

"Can't sleep?"

"Uh-uh."

"Come sit with me."

I glanced toward the street.

"No one's there," she said. "Even if they were, they couldn't see us here, it's so dark. Sit." She patted the cushion next to her on the glider.

I sat down. It felt strange to sit next to her like that. I bet I hadn't sat so close to her since I was a kid. Maybe not even then.

"I'm just biding my time until midnight," Mom said.

"What's happening at midnight?"

"I decided if I haven't heard from Keith by then, I'm calling him to be sure Sara got home all right."

"She probably did."

"Probably."

"Do you know if he talked to Dawn?" I wanted to say her name out loud to let Mom know I could take it. She didn't need to get weird about it.

"I don't know. I hope so." She rocked the glider a little. "You know, Maggie, I've gotten to know Dawn better this year."

"What do you mean?"

"Just…she and I had to clear the air after everything that happened. She was hurt, too, by the situation with…by the triangle between you and her and Ben."

"I know." I still felt some leftover hatred for Dawn. It wasn't her fault, but I couldn't help it.

"She's a decent person," Mom said. "She has a new man in her life now. Frankie. He works at this boat-rental place, and he moved in with her last month. I don't know him well, but he seems nice."

I hugged the teddy bear tighter.

"She's worked very hard to help the victims and their families, getting financial support for them and making sure they had counseling or whatever else they needed."

"I know," I whispered. "I saw some of them on the news. Mr. Eggles's niece was…" I shook my head, not wanting to remember the ugly look on the woman's face.

"Mr. Eggles's family is very angry," Mom said. "A *lot* of people are still angry. Marcus got a call from the police a little while ago and they said they caught the boy who threw the concrete through our window. It turns out he was a friend of Henderson Wright's."

I remembered the poster of Henderson Wright at the memorial service for the fire victims, how he looked like a scared little rabbit. I remembered Reverend Bill saying his family lived in a car.

"Henderson's *family,* though, has been more understanding," Mom said. "They've been quite forgiving."

"Really?"

"Dawn was able to get them into an apartment, and they're the kind of people who just..." She rocked the glider a little more. "They're religious. They have a way of accepting what happened that I can't even imagine."

I shook my head. I couldn't imagine it either.

Mom sighed. "I need to tell you about Jordy Matthews's mother," she said. "I don't want you to hear about it through the grapevine."

Oh, no. Jordy Matthews was the third death in the fire. A really cute blue-eyed blonde with the future ahead of her. I had those posters memorized. I still saw them when I closed my eyes at night. "What about her mother?" I asked.

Mom looked toward the moonlit sound. "She couldn't get over her grief," she said. "Not that I blame her for an instant. She tried to kill herself after Jordy died and they put her in a psych hospital for a few months. I guess she seemed better when she got out, but a few weeks ago, she was killed when she flipped her car off the high-rise bridge."

I sucked in my breath. "She was—" I pictured the bridge, how incredibly hard it would be to drive a car off it. That couldn't happen by accident. "Suicide?" I asked.

Mom nodded. "It was all too much for her. She was a single mom.

She had another daughter in college, but I don't think she had a good relationship with her, so I guess she felt like she didn't have anyone or anything else to live for."

I rested my chin on the teddy bear. "It just goes on and on, doesn't it?" I said. "What I did."

Mom put her arm around me. "I know you feel terrible," she said. "And I didn't tell you about Ellen—Jordy's mother—to make you feel worse. But I wanted you to hear it from me."

I leaned close to her until my head rested on her shoulder. "I'm glad you told me," I said.

She touched the teddy bear. "Isn't that the softest thing?"

"You must think I'm nuts, carrying it around."

"Not nuts at all. I thought it was sweet Marcus got it for you."

"It was."

"Is it uncomfortable for you?" she asked. "Having him stay over?"

I sat up straight again. "It's *awesome,*" I said. "It's like this family's the way it should be, finally." I ran my fingers through the angora on the back of the teddy bear. "Are you going to get married?"

"Probably. Would you like that?"

"Yes," I said. "Definitely."

She squeezed my shoulder. "Oh, sweetheart, do you have any idea how happy I am to have you home again?" I heard tears in her voice.

"Not as happy as I am to *be* home."

"I worry about how this year's changed you. Hardened you."

The last thing I felt was hard. "I think it *softened* me," I said. "I'm nervous about what happens now, though." I couldn't remember the last time I'd confided in my mother. It felt both strange and good.

"We'll take it one step at a time," she said. "And I'll be by your side every minute." She ran her hand over my cheek. "I forgot to tell you that I made an appointment for you for Thursday with the court-ordered therapist."

"Already?" I didn't feel like talking to anyone. Not yet.

"They said you needed your first appointment within a week of your release. And I have an idea for your community service. Do you want to hear it now or maybe tomorrow or later this—"

"Now." I hadn't thought about where I would do my community service. Topsail Island wasn't exactly crawling with opportunities. Plus, the idea of maybe running into all those hurt and pissed-off people was enough to make me nauseous.

"My school," Mom said. "Douglas Elementary. I spoke to Ms. Terrell—you know, the principal?—and she said you could help out in one of the classrooms. She's already talked to the first-grade teacher, Mrs. Hadley, who you'll love, and she said she'd like to have you."

"Really? I'm an ex-con, Mom."

"Don't use that term. You don't really think of yourself that way, do you?"

Yeah, actually, I did, even though the word made me think of disgusting old men. "That's what I am," I said.

"Well, Ms. Terrell didn't seem to think it would be a problem. She and I have talked a lot this past year and I think she understands who you really are and what led you to do what you did. Would you like that? Working at the school?"

"Yes," I said. "As long as the teacher, you know, thinks it's okay."

I loved that my mother had figured it out for me. Made all the arrangements. She'd left me to take care of myself for most of my life, and this felt good. Plus, she'd made a good choice for me. I wanted to make up to everyone for the fire, but how could I do that when I was afraid to walk out my front door? Little first graders had to be the safest possible choice. They wouldn't know who I was or what I'd done.

The next best thing to a stuffed teddy bear.

Chapter Six

Keith

MY MOTHER COULD ANNOY THE CRAP OUT OF ME SOMETIMES.
She hovered over me, like I was going to die if she didn't keep her
eye on me every second. I almost did kick the bucket after the fire,
so I guess that gave her the right to freak out, but it could really get
to me. So when I came home from the beach and she wasn't there,
I was glad. And after a couple hours, when I could heat up my own
mac and cheese for dinner and eat it in front of a *Simpsons* rerun
without her giving me grief about it, I was still liking it.

The Simpsons was still on when I heard someone on our deck and
then a knock on the door. I opened it and saw a couple of guys out there.
One was on the other side of our screen door, the other back a ways,
holding a camera. The sun was starting to go down behind his head.

"Keith?" the guy closest to me said. "Today Maggie Lockwood was
released from prison. As one of the fire victims, can you tell us how
you feel about that?"

It took me a couple of seconds to realize what was going on. Reporters!

"No fuckin' way!" I slammed the door shut in his face, then
walked around the trailer yanking down the shades. Like I needed
this! Where was my mother? She would've answered the door and
told those bastards to take a hike off the end of a pier.

When *The Simpsons* was over, the news came on. I never watched the news, but I wanted to make sure they didn't say anything about me. They didn't. Not by name, anyway. But the first thing they showed was this mob outside the prison and Maggie coming out the door, looking pale and scared. The crowd was vicious, shouting and holding these protest signs and everything. I loved it.

"You deserve it, bitch!" I shouted at the TV.

I watched the news awhile longer, then looked at the clock on the stove, which I could see from the couch. Almost seven-thirty. Where was my mother? She probably told me she was going out with Dawn or something and I forgot. I didn't listen all that much when she talked. But by eight o'clock, which was when she always helped me with my physical-therapy exercises, and she still wasn't home, I got…*worried* is the wrong word. *Mad.* I was mad she hadn't left a note or anything. She knew I forgot things she told me, and if she was going to miss eight o'clock, then she should have left a note or a message on my cell or something.

I sat in the living room and dialed her cell number. It rang and rang and finally cut to her voice mail.

"It's eight o'clock," I said. "Where are you?"

So I called Laurel to see if my mother had said anything to Andy. A sign of total desperation—me calling Laurel. After I talked to her, I called Dawn. Frankie answered the phone and tried to make chitchat with me.

"Just put Dawn on," I said. I didn't know what Dawn saw in that dude.

She sounded worried when I said Mom wasn't home. Dawn'd had no plans with her, and my mother didn't have much in the way of friends, really. She'd been best friends with Laurel all those years and then this last year she'd been glued to my hip, so she didn't get out much. Dawn said she hadn't talked to my mother since the day before at Jabeen's Java, where they worked together.

I tried to do my exercises by myself. I got out the exercise bands. My mother would pull against them while I pulled back, working all the muscles in my arms and trying to keep the scar tissue from tightening up. It was brutal shit. Without my mother there, I wrapped the bands around the leg of the heaviest chair in the living room, but every time I pulled on the band, the chair moved. My mother would always kind of cheer me on. *You can do it. I know it hurts. Keep going.* I hated her rah-rah stuff, but without it I wasn't doing all that good.

I sat like I was supposed to, with my legs stretched out wide on the floor, and got the red band into position on my left arm. I pulled, leaning way back, and the damn chair flipped over on my ankle.

"Goddamn it!" I managed to push the chair off my foot. I threw the band to the floor and stood up, grabbing my cell phone again, punching the number for my mother's phone.

"Where the hell are you?" I shouted, then rammed the phone into my pocket. Screw the exercises. Screw them. Now my ankle was killing me on top of the whole arm agony. I took a Percocet even though it was a couple of hours before I was supposed to.

I went outside and ran down the deck stairs to my car, moving fast in case the reporters were still hanging around. *She went to the store,* Andy'd said. Not that I trusted Andy to remember things right, but what else did I have to go on? I couldn't believe Andy and I were now in the same year when he was dumb as a toad. What did I care, really? School was a waste of time. My mother kept pressuring me, like, what do you want to do when you graduate? I didn't know the answer to that question before the fire. Now it was as if my choices had been reduced by thousands. Everyone at school was talking about college and how they were going to visit different ones this year, and since so many kids were poor—like us—how they'd get loans or try to get scholarships and all that crap. My counselor said if I could get my grades up, I might be able to get a scholarship myself, but the whole time he was talking to me, he was looking at my right eye so he could avoid the left side of my face. Didn't want to be caught staring at the freak. Pretending it was a normal dude he was talking to. I was thinking, *oh sure, buddy.* Once I was out of Douglas High, the last thing I wanted was *more* school with *more* kids staring at me. I didn't bother telling him that if I wanted to go to college, I didn't need a scholarship. I had a college fund. Guilt money given to me by Marcus Lockwood after Jamie Lockwood—my *real* father—died. I could only use the money for college, but if I didn't do college, I could have it when I was twenty-five. Twenty-five! What was I supposed to do till then?

So I headed toward the Food Lion in Hampstead where my mother usually shopped, checking the ditches along the side of the road for her car. It was dark and I had to use a flashlight and I thought, *this is so lame.* So fucking dramatic. Like what did I think, I was in some movie or something? But then I kept coming back to the fact that it didn't make sense she was gone. I called her, like, fifteen times. Maybe her cell battery was shot, but still, couldn't she find a phone somewhere?

Her car wasn't in the Food Lion parking lot. Then I drove back to the island and checked out the parking lots at Jabeen's and the restaurants and anyplace else I could think of, mostly because I didn't know what else to do. I wondered if I should call the police, but that seemed like even more drama. I went home after a while and sat in front of my computer and got online. We didn't have high-speed Internet, but I could piggyback on someone else's connection nearly every time I tried. I did what I usually did online. I Googled stuff like suicide and burns and ostracism and grief and all that shit. Sometimes I went to porn sites, but that was so pathetic. I didn't like thinking about how those sites would probably be the only place I'd get any for the rest of my life. Instead, I liked reading about how burn victims like me felt. Most of them were older. Some of their wives and husbands left them. Couldn't take the stress, they said, but I bet it was more like the embarrassment of having a partner who looked like a monster.

Most of the burn victims I read about took antidepressants. So did I. If I didn't, I probably would have offed myself months ago. I still thought about suicide, but not like I used to. Back then, I thought about how I could do it. Get a gun. Hang myself. OD on meds. Every time I thought about my mother finding me dead, though, I'd start crying. Pathetic. I'd turned into a sissy this year. Then I got on the Zoloft and stopped feeling like I wanted to die, but I still wasn't sure why I should want to live. My mother was worried because they said some kids on antidepressants were more likely to kill themselves. I thought that was interesting and paid attention to how I felt. The truth was, I *wanted* the Zoloft to push me over the edge. To give me the guts to do it. I started thinking that I could hang myself from this tree over by the police station. I could do it at night so no one would see me until it was too late, and then the cops would be first to find me and they'd cut me down before my mother could see me like that. But on the Zoloft, I started losing the urge. I got more pissed than sad. I felt more like hanging other people than hanging myself. It was Maggie Lockwood I wanted to see dead. Not myself.

I was still surfing the Net around midnight when the phone rang.

The caller ID said it was the Lockwoods' house and I stared at the number for a few seconds, worried it might be Maggie calling to say she was sorry or something. But around the fourth ring, I thought maybe it was Laurel and she knew where my mother was, so I picked it up.

"Did your mom get home okay?" Laurel asked.

"No," I said. "I don't know where she is. Dawn doesn't know either."

Laurel was quiet. "Did you try her other friends?"

I wasn't going to let her know there *were* no other friends. "Nobody knows where she is," I said.

"Keith, you should call the police. Or if you want, I'll call them for you."

"No." I didn't want Laurel Lockwood to do anything for me.

"Will you call them, then? Please? I'm worried."

"Yeah, I'll call," I said. It was like she was giving me permission to dive into the drama. Like it wasn't just me overreacting.

"Let me know what happens, Keith," she said. "Do you want me to come over there and stay with you?"

Right, I thought. *That's just what I want.*

"No. I'm good. I'm getting off so I can call the police."

A cop showed up half an hour after I called. Must've been a slow night in Surf City.

"Hey, Keith," he said when I opened the door. "I'm Officer Pryor." His name didn't register. He was an old guy, and he seemed to know me. But then, everyone knew who I was: the most damaged living victim of the fire. My claim to fame. "Okay if I come in?" he asked.

We sat in the kitchen. He took off his hat, leaving ridges in his gray hair. He knew my mother from Jabeen's, he told me. Nice lady. Where did I think she was?

"If I knew, I wouldn't've called you," I said.

He asked me the expected stuff about her description, even though he knew her. A couple of inches shorter than me, I told him. Blue eyes. Short blond hair. Tan. She had that kind of skin that went dark just from walking between the trailer and her car. She'd looked exactly the same my whole life. Never changed that hair or the way she dressed or her routine or anything. *She never changed anything.* That thought freaked me out. Made me realize how serious this was.

"She's always home at night to do my exercises with me," I said. "My physical therapy. And she always makes dinner, unless she's working and she didn't work today. Makes no sense."

He wrote things down on a notepad as I talked. He had fat hands and a gold band on his ring finger.

"Does she have any medical conditions?" he asked.

"No. I mean, except for some arthritis in her knees." She groaned like an old lady when she got down on the floor with me to do the exercises.

"No seizures or anything like that? Diabetes? Heart problems?"

"No."

"Did she take any medication?"

I couldn't ever remember seeing my mother take anything, except maybe cough syrup or vitamins.

"Nothing."

"How about mental-health problems? Been a hard year for her and you both, with the fire and all. Do you know if she was depressed?"

"Nah," I said, but I wondered. How would I know? I didn't think much about what this year had been like for her. "She's not the depressed type."

"What does that mean?"

"You know. She's tough. If she went on one of those *Survivor* shows, she'd win."

"Some of those tough survivor types are cream puffs inside."

"Not my mother."

"Did you call any of her friends?"

"Dawn Reynolds and Laurel Lockwood."

He raised his eyebrows when I mentioned the name Lockwood. Probably because of Maggie getting out of prison.

I explained about Andy being sick and staying in our trailer while Laurel went to get Maggie. How Mom told him she was going to the store and just didn't come back.

"What store would she go to?"

"I guess the Food Lion in Hampstead. I mean, I guess she meant food shopping. I don't know where else she'd go."

He had his eyes on his notepad even though he wasn't writing, and I figured he'd had enough of looking at my face.

"Can you tell me the names of her other friends?"

"She didn't have a lot," I said. I didn't want her to seem totally pathetic, so I named some ladies she used to be in a book club with.

"What church does she go to?"

"She doesn't."

"How about men? Was she dating anyone?"

"No." My mother didn't date. I couldn't even imagine it. I couldn't even imagine her getting close enough to Jamie Lockwood to get pregnant with me.

"Are you sure? Did you ever suspect she was—"

"Trust me," I said. "Especially this year. *I've* been her date. She made me her full-time job."

"You angry about that?" he asked. "You sound angry about it."

"Not angry," I said. "Just…I don't want to be babysat." I noticed him looking into the living room, where the chair that had fallen on me was still on its side. I realized he might suspect *me* of something. Foul play. Whatever. Like if I was angry at her, maybe I'd hurt her. That pissed me off even more.

"Have you looked around to see if anything's missing?" he asked.

"You mean, like someone broke in and stole something and she caught them and—"

"It's just a general question." He stopped me. "Did she have a suitcase?"

I didn't know the answer. "She never went anywhere," I said.

"Well, everyone has a suitcase."

Actually, I didn't have one. But, I supposed with all that time my mother spent in Chapel Hill when I was in the hospital, she must have owned a suitcase.

"Can we take a look in her room?" he asked, getting to his feet.

"Sure." I tried to sound more cooperative, now that I thought he might be suspicious of me.

We had to walk through the living room to get to her bedroom, and he whipped out a camera and took a picture of the chair on its side.

"I was trying to do my exercises," I said, reaching for the red exercise band I'd tossed on the sofa.

"Leave that there," he said. I dropped my hand and he snapped a picture of the band.

"Like I said, she always helped me with the exercises, so I put the band around the leg of the chair and when I pulled on it, the chair fell over."

"Uh-huh."

We reached my mother's room. It was small and neat. The bed

was made—she was one of those people who made their bed the second they got up in the morning. She tried to get me to do the same, but gave up a long time ago.

The cop stood in the doorway and looked around. My mother would've known if I'd moved my comb from one side of my bathroom counter to the other. But in her room, I was totally lost. I never went in there. I had no reason to.

Officer Pryor opened her closet door. "Does this look like more or fewer clothes than she usually has in here?" he asked me.

I leaned around him to look in the closet. "No clue," I said. "I never... I don't pay attention to her clothes."

He walked into her bathroom. "Toothbrush is here," he said. "Did she have more than one?"

"I don't know." Why would she have more than one toothbrush?

"I don't see any makeup bag," he said.

Makeup bag? "She didn't wear much."

"How about a hair dryer?" he asked. "Did she have one?"

"Nah. Her hair was really short."

He took a few pictures while I stood in the doorway, then he walked back in her bedroom and started opening the drawers of her dresser, one after the other.

"Really not a lot in here," he said. "Most women, especially if they live in a small space like your double-wide, have their dresser drawers so full you can't get them open."

It bothered me that I was letting this guy paw through her stuff. Through her underwear drawer, for Christ's sake. I was making way too much out of this. I expected her to come home any minute and say, "What are you *doing*? I told you I'd be out late tonight."

"I don't see a suitcase anywhere." He was still going through her dresser, like he might find a suitcase in there.

"Maybe she told me she was going away for the night and I forgot or something," I said. Though, where would she go?

He headed back toward the living room and I followed him. He was looking all around the room while he walked. Taking everything in. "You're what?" he said. "Eighteen?"

"Yeah," I said, though I wouldn't be eighteen for a few months.

"So, she didn't abandon a minor." He stood between the kitchen and the living room, his arms folded over his chest. He was staring at the couch. At the red exercise band. Did he think I tried to choke her with it or what? "It looks to me like she left of her own volition," he said, "since there's no suitcase—"

"I told you. I'm not even sure she had one." *And she wouldn't leave me!* Did I have to club him over the head with it?

"Look." He reached into his pocket. Handed me a card. "I'm going to get someone out here to do a more thorough search. Don't touch anything, all right? Don't move that chair back upright."

"The chair doesn't have anything to do with—"

"Just don't touch anything," he said. "Do yourself a favor. Meanwhile, we'll put a BOLO on her car."

"What's a BOLO?"

"A 'Be on the Lookout' bulletin. That'll get authorities to keep an eye out for her. We'll get Pender County to check the Food Lion parking lot and contact the hospitals."

"I already checked the Food Lion parking lot."

"You did? When?"

"A while ago."

"We'll be checking it, too," he said. "We'll subpoena her phone records and put a tracer on her car, but most likely, she's out with a friend and lost track of time and forgot to turn her cell on. By the time I get an officer back out here, she'll be home safe and sound."

"Right," I said, trying to calm myself down. I was making a mountain out of a molehill.

I watched him get into his cruiser and drive out to the main road. Then I looked next to my car, to where her car should have been. Where her car always was. And I knew something was very, very wrong.

Chapter Seven

Andy

I WAS STILL IN BED WHEN MY CELL PHONE RANG. KIMMIE! I got out of bed quick and ran over to my desk to get my phone.

"Hi!" I said, probably too loud.

"You better be up," she said.

"I'm up." I smiled even though she couldn't see me.

"Just checking." She checked on me every morning. "Do you feel better today?"

I had to think. I almost forgot I was sick yesterday. "It was only a twenty-four-hour bug." That's what Mom called it. I felt pretty good now.

"I'll text you later," she said. "Or you can text me."

"Okay!"

I hung up and went into the bathroom to take my shower. That was what the chart on my corkboard said for me to do first, but I didn't need to look at it for every little thing anymore. I was getting smarter.

I met Kimmie at a Special Olympics party. We started out just friends. She was pretty, but not the kind of pretty of any other girl I knew. We danced at the party. Special Olympics people dance really good and are nice. We played games and ate cake and things. The next time I saw Kimmie was at a swim-team practice. She came with her mother and father to watch my friend Matt swim. Her mother was a white lady with yellow hair and her father had brown hair like mine. After swim practice me and Kimmie went in the corner and talked. I made sure to stand four shoe lengths away, which was hard because I had bare feet. And she kept moving closer to me. I didn't care, though.

"How come you're America Africa and your parents are white?" I asked her.

"I'm adopted," she said. "My birth mother is black and I don't know about my birth father, except they think he was probably part Caucasian and part Japanese or maybe Indian."

"What does birth mother mean?"

"The woman who gave birth to me. You know, *had* me. Like your mother had you." She pointed to Mom, who was talking to my coach.

"Who's that lady, then?" I pointed to her mother.

"She's my adoptive mother," she said. "And the man is my adoptive father."

"You're complicated!" I smiled to let her know that wasn't a bad thing.

"I know." She smiled back at me.

I knew a lot about Indians. Like she shouldn't really have said Indian. She should have said "Native American." "Is your Indian part Cherokee?" I asked.

"No," she said. "*Indian.* Like from the country India. But they don't really know exactly where my birth father was from. I just am who I am."

"I am who I am, too," I said.

"I think you're cute," she said.

I got an instant hard-on. That happened sometimes. I wrapped my towel over my bathing suit so Kimmie couldn't see how it poked up. I started thinking maybe I didn't like her as just a friend anymore.

Now, she's almost the only thing I think about.

After I got all ready, I went downstairs. I hoped Maggie was up. I was so happy she was home!

When I got to the bottom stair, I saw Mom talking to a policeman in the family room. *No, no, no!* Not again! I didn't know if I should run back upstairs or what to do. It was like this: first I was a hero, then I wasn't a hero, then I was a hero again. Sometimes I couldn't remember which I really was. That's why I freaked. I decided to sneak into the kitchen so I could get cereal, but Mom saw me.

"Andy, come here, sweetie."

I didn't want to turn around. I stayed where I was, looking at the kitchen door.

"It's okay, Andy," Mom said. "Remember Officer Cates? He just wants to ask you a few questions about Miss Sara."

I turned around real slow. I recognized him. He was nice. But I answered three hundred questions after the fire. I knew over a whole year had went by, but I was tired of questions. "I don't know anything," I said.

"Hi, Andy," Officer Cates said. I all of a sudden remembered his first name was Flip. Funny.

"Come sit down," Mom said.

Her voice told me I had to do it. I sat down on the couch near her. She put her hand on my forehead.

"How are you feeling?" she asked.

"Fine."

"He had a stomach virus yesterday," she said to Officer Cates, who made an icky face. "Do you want to stay home again today?" Mom asked me. "It might be good to take it easy."

"I'm okay," I said. "Is Maggie up yet?"

"Not yet," she said. "Listen, Andy. I'm very worried. No one's seen Miss Sara since she left while she was watching you yesterday."

"Maybe Keith saw her," I said.

"No, he hasn't," Mom said.

"Can you help me out, Andy?" Officer Cates asked. He had a pad and a pen. Police always had them.

"I don't want to go to jail," I said. Jail had a little room with a window in the door and mean boys. I would never forget it.

"You won't be going to jail," Mom said. "This has nothing to do with you."

She didn't think I was going to jail that other time either.

"Tell me exactly what Mrs. Weston said when she left the trailer yesterday," Officer Cates asked. Mrs. Weston was Miss Sara.

"She was going shopping." I wasn't sure about the "exactly" part, but she said something like that.

"Did she say when she'd be back?" he asked.

Mostly what I remembered was the Mega Warriors.

"I don't think so," I said.

"Did she say *where* she was going shopping?"

I shook my head.

"Did she say grocery shopping or some other kind of store?"

"Grocery shopping, maybe." Maybe not. I should've paid better attention. My leg started jiggling up and down. Officer Cates wrote something on his pad.

"Did you see Keith yesterday?" he asked.

"At his house?"

"Yes."

"He wasn't there."

"Not at all?"

I shook my head. I was sure I didn't see Keith there.

"What was Mrs. Weston doing while you were there?"

"I don't know. She was in another room mostly. I was asleep part of the time."

"Did you see her do anything at all?"

"She got me soda and crackers."

Mom put her hand on my knee to stop the jiggling.

"Did she talk to anyone on the phone?" Officer Cates asked.

I shook my head. "Oh. Mom," I remembered. "Mom called."

He looked at Mom. She nodded. "I called to tell her we'd be late picking Andy up," she said.

"How did she sound?"

"Annoyed, actually," Mom said. "I didn't blame her. She probably wanted to go shopping and was worried about leaving Andy alone. We were three hours later than we thought we'd be."

"Do you remember exactly what she said?" I liked that he was asking Mom questions and not me.

Mom shook her head. "Something like, 'you said you'd be home by one-thirty.' Something like that. I felt terrible. She...we haven't been close this year and I know it was a big favor to ask her to watch Andy."

"I could've stayed home alone okay," I said.

"Did she seem angry to you, Andy?" Officer Cates asked.

"No."

"When she got off the phone with your mom?"

I waited for him to finish the question. He looked at me funny.

"I mean, did she seem angry at all?" he asked. "About anything?"

I shook my head. "She was happy."

"Happy?" He and Mom both said it at the same time, and I laughed.

"Happy Maggie was coming home," I said.

"She *was?*" Mom asked.

"Like how you cried yesterday morning 'cause Maggie was coming home," I explained. "She kind of did that, too."

"She was crying?" Officer Cates asked.

"Not exactly." I knew I had to be very truthful talking to the police. "I didn't see her cry, but her eyes were red like they get when you cry." I suddenly remembered the box. "I remember something else she did," I said.

"What's that?" he asked.

"She carried a box with a pot on it outside."

"A pot *in* a box or on *top* of a box?" Mom asked.

"No. A picture of a pot. The box had a picture of a pot on it."

Officer Cates wrote something down. Then he chewed the end of his pen.

"Maybe she was going to return a pot she bought," Mom said to him. "That's what she meant when she said she was going to the store."

Officer Cates nodded. "Possibly," he said. "So where did she usually shop?"

"She liked the Wal-Mart in Jacksonville, but it could've been just about anywhere. I can't imagine she'd leave Andy that long, though."

All of a sudden, I heard a brake-screech sound at the end of our street. I jumped up.

"Mom!" I said. "The bus!"

She looked at her watch. "Oh, no. We made you late." She put her hand around my wrist. "I think we're done here for now, aren't we?" She looked at Officer Cates.

He closed his little pad. "For now," he said.

"You go get some breakfast." Mom let go of me. "Then I'll drive you to school."

I ran into the kitchen and stuck some cinnamon-swirl bread in the toaster. I couldn't wait to tell Kimmie I was late to school and it wasn't even my fault.

Chapter Eight

Sara
Stepping into Jamie's World
1989

I HELD STEVE'S HAND AS WE SLIPPED INTO ONE OF THE PEWS at the Free Seekers Chapel. With Steve home and not interested in going to the chapel, months had passed since my last visit, and the congregation had swollen to thirty people. I spotted Jamie sitting in his usual pew, but Laurel wasn't with him.

Steve let out one of his long, weary sighs that told me he was already bored, and my chest tightened up at the sound. I'd struggled to explain to him why I wanted to return to the chapel. It was the sense of community, I told him. Being part of something.

"What are you talking about?" he'd asked. "You're surrounded by military wives. You have a built-in community."

"This is a *spiritual* community."

He stared at me with those steel-gray eyes. "One of the things we had in common is that we weren't into religion," he said.

"This is different," I said. "You'll see. Please come with me. Otherwise, I'll go alone." I felt nervous talking to him that way. Steve wasn't a mean man, but sometimes I remembered how it felt when he pried my legs apart in the backseat of his car. It hurt, and the animal that took him over didn't seem to care. I remembered that, and I was always a little afraid to stand up to him. But I needed what I'd found at the chapel. Was it the pull of the beautiful setting or the pull of Jamie Lockwood? I didn't even want to think about that question.

Steve finally said he would go to the chapel with me, just one time. I felt intimidated by his presence, though, so I didn't stand up to say where I'd experienced God that week. It would embarrass him. Or maybe I was afraid he'd think I'd been brainwashed. He kept up with the sighing. A few times he shifted in the pew as if longing to get up and stretch his legs. It wasn't working out as I'd hoped. He wasn't getting it at all.

After the service was over, Jamie greeted people as he usually did by the exit of the chapel.

"Is there any other way out of here?" Steve whispered as we moved toward the front door.

"I don't know." I didn't care, either. I was already smiling at Jamie, stretching my hand out to shake his.

"It's good to see you back, Sara," he said.

"This is my husband, Steve," I said. "Steve, this is Jamie Lockwood."

Steve shook his hand. "Nice building," he said, and I was grateful to him for making the effort to be sociable.

"You have a new baby by now, don't you?" I asked. The last time I came to the chapel, many months earlier, Laurel had announced her pregnancy. Saying the word *baby* out loud made my breasts ache.

"I *do.*" Jamie glowed. "She's a month old. Her name's Maggie."

"Congratulations!" I said. "How's Laurel?"

He hesitated just long enough to let me know that all was not well with his wife, and I wished I hadn't asked.

"She's doing okay," he said finally. "We're both a little over-whelmed right now, but I guess that's to be expected."

"Let me know if I can help somehow," I said. "I have plenty of free time."

Steve nudged me, so I walked forward, making way for the people behind us to talk to Jamie. My offer to help was genuine. I longed to get out of the house, but Steve didn't want me to work. "None of the guys' wives work," he'd said. Anyway, jobs were few, especially for a military wife who might have to move at a moment's notice.

Jamie caught up to us in the small, sandy parking lot in front of the chapel.

"Were you serious, Sara?" He shaded his eyes from the sun. "About wanting to help?"

"Oh, yes," I said.

"We can really use it," he said. "I'll pay you, of course."

"No! Please. Let me just help out. Like I said, I have loads of free time."

I gave him our number, and he wrote it on a small notepad he pulled from the pocket of his jeans.

I felt so happy as I got into the car. I could do something useful for a change. I could help Jamie, touching his life in a positive way, the way he'd touched mine by building his chapel.

Steve and I were nearly to the high-rise bridge before either of us spoke.

"You think that's a wise thing for you to do?" he asked.

"What do you mean?" I asked, although I knew.

"You know. Taking care of a baby."

"I want to," I said.

It was the closest we'd ever come to discussing Sam. I bit my lip, feeling anxious. Finally, Steve was giving me an invitation to talk about him.

"Do you ever think about him?" I asked.

"Who?" he replied.

"Sam."

He was quiet for so long I thought he was going to ignore the question.

"Doesn't do any good to think about him," he said. Then he pointed to a speed-limit sign. Thirty-five miles per hour. "Is that new?" he asked. "I thought it was forty-five along this stretch."

Jamie suggested I come to the real-estate office where he worked. I supposed he wanted to interview me before accepting my offer of help, but when I walked into his small office, I found him holding the baby. I sat down and he walked around his desk to hand the infant to me.

Every baby looked beautiful to me, even those with cone-shaped heads and scrunched-up faces and homely features. All of them, staggeringly beautiful. Yet Maggie Lockwood was extraordinary even at a month old. She had Jamie's enormous brown eyes, and they were wide open, already taking in her world. She had a thick crop of dark curls and tiny features carved in pale, flawless porcelain.

"She's a little colicky," Jamie said. "But she's a good baby."

It was like holding feathers, she was so light. Like holding a miracle. *Experiencing God.* The thought slipped into my mind, and tears filled my eyes. Could I bear it? Helping to care for this child?

"Are you all right?" Jamie asked.

"She's just so beautiful." I felt one tear slip down my cheek, but managed to stop the rest. He'd think I was deranged. Maybe the sort of woman who would steal a baby. I looked up at him, clearing my throat as I grounded myself again in my surroundings. "Is this her first visit to your office?" I asked. "Your coworkers must have flipped over her."

He tapped his fingers on his desk, not answering right away. "Actually," he said, "I've brought her here all this week." Leaning forward, he studied his new daughter where she rested quietly in my arms. "Laurel's having a hard time."

Was he confiding in me? "I'm so sorry to hear that," I said.

"She had a very rough start," he said. "She hemorrhaged during the delivery and is anemic and I think she feels isolated and...unsure of herself."

"Oh. Poor thing." I felt sympathy for the woman I'd met only a couple of times. How hard to have a new baby and not feel up to taking care of her. "I hope she feels better soon."

"Thanks. Me, too."

I looked at the stack of real-estate brochures on Jamie's desk. "It's strange, seeing you here in an office," I said. "Seeing you look human."

He laughed. "I'm very human," he said. "That's all I am. All I want to be. A good human."

"I..." I wanted to tell him what my few visits to the chapel had meant to me. I knew I would be going back, with or without Steve. I looked down at Maggie, whose long-lashed eyes were now closed, the lids twitching a little as if she was dreaming. "I don't know how to explain to you how I feel in your chapel," I said, raising my gaze to him again. "I'm not religious, so it's strange. It's hard to put into words."

"It's bigger than words?" he suggested.

I nodded.

"Oh, Sara," he said. "Welcome to my world."

Jamie and Laurel lived in a round cottage called the Sea Tender, right on the beach. I didn't want to feel envy when I walked inside the cottage and took in the ocean view from the living-room windows, yet how could I help it? Clearly, the Lockwoods had money, something I doubted I'd ever have myself.

"Oh, this is fabulous!" I said as Jamie led me through the room to the sofa, Maggie sleeping against his chest. He'd asked me to stop by to "reconnect with Laurel," since I'd be helping out with the baby. "Have a seat," he said. He handed Maggie to me. "I'll let Laurel know you're here."

I settled down on the sofa, the sleeping baby on my knees. A few minutes later, Laurel walked into the room. She moved slowly, as though her legs were made of concrete, and I honestly wasn't certain I would have recognized her. Her hair was long and stringy and dull, her eyes lifeless. Her face was not pale as much as jaundiced, like a tan that was fading in uneven patches. She wore a yellow robe that needed a good washing.

Seeing her, I felt deep concern that the pretty woman from the chapel had been replaced by a ghost. I could see that she had a long recovery ahead of her. Maggie's delivery must have been horrendous.

"You have a gorgeous baby." I lowered my eyes to Maggie to hide my shock at Laurel's appearance.

"Thank you." Laurel sat down in a rocking chair.

Jamie brought me a glass of iced tea I knew I wouldn't touch. It would be sweet, no doubt. That Southern abomination.

"You two remember each other, of course," Jamie said as he sat down on the other end of the sofa.

"Of course," I said. "Your house is beautiful, Laurel."

"Thanks."

"I...Jamie and I thought I should meet with you to see if you have any special instructions about Maggie."

Laurel shrugged as though she didn't really care how I took care of her daughter. "Just don't kill her," she said.

"Laurel!" Jamie said.

My body must have jerked at Laurel's words because Maggie started to whimper.

"Shh, honey." I tightened the blanket around the baby, wondering if Laurel could possibly know about Sam. Who could have told her? I was afraid to look up. I didn't want to meet her eyes.

Laurel laughed, breaking the tension in the room. "You know what I mean," she said.

"Well, okay." I attempted a laugh myself. "I think I can manage that."

Jamie had a tiny office in the chapel, and that's where I spent most of my time with Maggie because Laurel didn't want me in the house.

"It's not you," Jamie reassured me. "It's anyone right now. She's too tired to have someone around."

Or the baby around, I thought. It was unspoken between us, but Jamie and I both knew there was something more going on with Laurel than tiredness. Laurel wanted Maggie out of the house. Out of her sight.

The chapel had electricity and Jamie installed a small refrigerator and a hot plate in the little office so I could heat Maggie's formula. There was also an old-fashioned wooden cradle and a lightweight stroller. I spent my days there with Maggie, reading and teaching myself to knit when I wasn't feeding, cuddling or changing diapers. I couldn't believe my luck at being able to spend so much time in the beautiful, simple building. I was drawn to the panoramic windows, and I watched the sea for dolphins and the sky for pelicans. In a way, I finally had beachfront property.

When the weather was mild enough, I took Maggie for walks in the stroller. I'd push the little girl right past the Sea Tender, learning quickly there was no point in stopping in for a visit. Neither Maggie nor I would be welcome.

On Sundays, I sat next to Jamie in the chapel with Maggie on my lap. The first time, Jamie briefly explained to the thirty or so people there that I was helping him and Laurel out with Maggie. When new people came during the summer, though, I wondered if some of them thought I was Jamie's wife.

It fascinated me to feel Maggie melt into my arms when she heard her father speak. He had a hypnotic quality in his voice that soothed not only Maggie and myself but most of the other people in the chapel as well. With the influx of tourists, the fifty seats were nearly full each week. People stood one after another to say where they recently experienced God, but I rarely stood myself. I felt too raw with emotion in the chapel during the service. In just a couple of months' time, I'd filled up with such a painful sort of joy that I knew if I tried to speak during the service, I would lose all control. God—Jamie's God—was with me nearly every minute of every day by then. I had a purpose: I was able to hold a tiny life in my arms. I was able to help Jamie when he so clearly needed my help. Even at home, I caught myself smiling as I made dinner or pressed Steve's uniform or cleaned the small house we rented. I had enough joy inside myself that the sorrow over Sam, over my loveless marriage, didn't have a chance to come through.

A few months later, Jamie told me he thought Laurel needed a friend.

"She doesn't have any friends with babies," he said. "Not that *you* have a baby. But you're so warm and nice and kind." He looked away from me, as though he'd said more than he meant to. "She's depressed. She's not taking care of herself. You know. Grooming. Hygiene."

"Maybe she needs more help than a friend can give her," I suggested gently. The truth was, Laurel was unpleasant to be around, and I avoided her as much as possible. There was nothing of the starry-eyed young woman left in her.

Jamie sighed. "You're probably right." He sounded tired. "Her doctor thinks she needs that new Prozac medication, but neither of us likes the idea of her taking drugs. I think she just needs a girlfriend."

He looked so lost. I would have done anything to bring a smile back to his face.

"I'll visit her one day while you have Maggie," I said. "Then maybe she and I can have a good talk."

It had sounded possible when I said it, but I'd had no idea how bad things had gotten with Laurel. She was incapable of having a "good talk" with anyone.

I visited her under the guise of taking over a chicken-and-rice casserole. I found her lying under a thin blanket on the sofa watching a rerun of *I Dream of Jeannie*. The air in the cottage smelled stale in spite of all the windows being open.

"I brought you a casserole for dinner." I headed for the kitchen after letting myself in through the unlocked door. "I'll just put it in the fridge, okay? It should last you at least a couple of nights."

"Where's the baby?" Laurel asked.

I looked at her across the breakfast bar. "With Jamie. He's doing some paperwork in the chapel office. I thought I'd just bring this over and say hi."

Laurel actually wrinkled her nose as though visiting with me was the last thing she felt like doing.

Tough, I thought. Someone needed to get through to her. She was hurting her husband, not to mention her baby.

I sat down in the rocker near the sofa. "How are you?" I asked.

"Okay." Laurel kept her gaze glued to the TV.

I leaned toward her. "Seriously, Laurel. How are you feeling?"

She sighed. "Tired."

"Jamie said your doctor suggested Prozac." I thought Jamie was wrong to discourage antidepressants.

"That's none of your business," Laurel said.

Was she right? Maybe. But I was taking care of her baby and that *did* make it my business in a way.

"I have a really good friend in Michigan who takes Prozac and it's made a world of difference for her," I said.

"I'm not depressed," Laurel said. "I'm tired. You'd be tired, too, if you had to be up all night with a screaming baby."

"You're a nurse," I said. "You must know depression can be a medical problem. Jamie said you don't care about anything. Not even Maggie." I worried I might be going too far. "You were excited about having a baby. I saw that when you announced your pregnancy in the chapel. I think it's a definite sign of depression that you're so...disinterested in her."

Laurel looked at me. "I want you to leave," she said.

I was blowing it, handling it all wrong. The last thing I wanted to do was make things worse for Jamie, but I couldn't seem to stop myself. "You're not being fair to Jamie," I said. "It's like he's a single parent. He's great with Maggie, but she's not even going to know who you are."

I turned at the creaking of the screen door. A young guy walked into the living room and it took me a second to remember that Jamie's brother, Marcus, lived with them. *The rebel,* Jamie had called him. He looked harmless. Slender, tan and messy-haired, wearing a T-shirt and green bathing suit.

"You must be Marcus." I stood up. "I'm Sara Weston."

"The babysitter." He'd been drinking, and it was not even noon. I could smell it on him.

"Right. I wanted to stop in to see Laurel."

"She came over to tell me I'm a shitty mother and a shitty wife," Laurel said.

"Laurel!" I was stunned. "That's not what I meant. I'm sorry if I—"

"I told her to leave but she won't," Laurel said to Marcus.

I felt my cheeks blaze.

"If she wants you to go, you'd better go," Marcus said.

"All right." I raised my hands in surrender. "I'm sorry," I said, walking to the door. "I didn't mean to upset you."

In the chapel office, Jamie looked up from his small, wooden desk.

"How'd it go?" he whispered so he wouldn't wake Maggie, asleep in the cradle.

I was embarrassed when I started to cry. "I didn't handle it well at all." I sank into the only other chair in the office. "She kicked me out, and I don't blame her."

"*Why?* What happened?"

I told him about the conversation, grappling in my diaper bag— yes, I had come to think of the diaper bag as *mine*—for a tissue. I pressed it to my eyes.

"Sara." Jamie's chair was on wheels and he moved it closer to take both my hands in his. "It's not your fault, all right? I set you up for failure. You worked such miracles for Maggie and me that I guess I hoped you could work them for Laurel, too." He smoothed his thumbs over the back of my hands as he spoke. I curled my own hands involuntarily around his, gripping his fingers.

How do you stand it? I wanted to ask him. *How do you stand* her? I'd wanted to feel sympathy for Laurel because clearly the woman was ill. But my sympathy could reach only so far. Laurel had a live, beautiful child and she was doing nothing to mother her.

"I didn't realize what you were coping with at home," I said. "How bad it is."

"I hope it'll pass," he said. "It's just going to take more time than I thought."

"Maybe she *does* need antidepressants," I said.

"Maybe," he acknowledged.

"What keeps you going?" I asked.

"Oh, Sara." He smiled. "Silly question. I have so much to keep me going. The chapel, to begin with. And her." He nodded toward Maggie in her cradle. "And the fact that I *love* Laurel." He looked at me as if reminding me that he and I were only friends, nothing more.

But the way his thumbs stroked the back of my hands told me something completely different.

Chapter Nine

Keith

DAWN PARKED AT THE END OF THE ROAD BY THE LOCKWOODS' house so that Stump Sound was right smack in front of us. You could drive straight into it if you wanted. No guardrail or anything. I thought about Jordy Matthews's mother flying off the high-rise bridge. What would it be like to be inside a car with water pouring in through the windows? If you wanted to die, would you panic or could you peacefully let yourself drown?

The Lockwoods' house was on our left. There were a few other cars parked nearby, and I wondered how many people would be at this thing, whatever it was.

Dawn looked at me. "You all right, sugar?" she asked. "You look a little green."

"Never better." This was the last place I wanted to be. Maggie Lockwood's house. I was doing it for my mother. Otherwise, no way in hell I'd be there.

The past two mornings, the second I woke up, I looked out the window above my bed, hoping to see my mother's car. Hoping it had miraculously reappeared overnight. When I saw that it hadn't, I felt this *panic* building inside me. It was like when I woke up in the hospital with that effing breathing tube down my throat. I'd never wanted to have that feeling again.

"Okay." Dawn unsnapped her seat belt. "Let's go."

We walked up the sidewalk to the house, which was yellow, the only thing it had in common with our trailer. The house was big for Topsail. *Grand,* my mother called it. I wouldn't have gone that far, but having the sound in your yard was nothing to sneeze at.

I'd been there plenty of times back before Maggie torched me and my mother and Laurel'd been friends, but not since then. Not since I found out that I was a Lockwood, too.

"I don't want to see Maggie." I didn't mean to say it out loud, but it came out of my mouth anyway. I sounded like a kid. Like I was asking Dawn to protect me or something.

She was a step ahead of me, but she stopped and put an arm around me so we were walking together. Her long red hair brushed my cheek. The smell of her hair reminded me of my mother, like maybe they used the same shampoo or something. I turned my head so I could pull in another whiff of it.

"I'm not that wild about seeing Maggie either, Keith," she said. "But look. You don't have to talk to her. Don't even have to look at her. We just need to think about your mom, okay?"

It wasn't looking at Maggie that would piss me off as much as her looking at me. It would be massive humiliation, letting her see how she'd screwed up my life.

"Keith Weston!"

I turned to see a man and a woman running toward us from the street. The dude had a camera, the woman, a microphone. Reporters, again! I could not fucking believe it! Were they trailing me or what?

"Do you have any idea where your mother is?" the woman asked.

I turned away so fast I whacked my head into Dawn's chin. She gave me a shove toward the Lockwoods' front porch. "Go on," she said to me.

I headed for the porch and heard her shout from behind me, "Keep the hell away from him! Don't you think he's been through enough?"

I was shaking by the time she caught up to me on the porch, but I made like the whole thing had been no big deal.

"Total assholes," I said, nodding toward the reporters. They were walking toward a white van parked on the street.

"No kidding," Dawn said.

Trish Delphy—Surf City's mayor—opened the front door for us.

"Dawn." She hugged Dawn, then reached for me. "Keith, dear," she said. "How are you holding up?"

"All right." I let her hug me. I was surprised she was there. The *mayor*. Maybe people were finally taking this seriously. As far as I could tell, the cops weren't doing much. They told me the first forty-eight hours were critical, and tonight made it about forty-nine.

Miss Trish changed places with Dawn, putting her arm around me as she led me toward the kitchen. I saw the bright lights in there. Saw Laurel and Emily Carmichael's mother and another lady I didn't know yammering with each other while they did something with food on the island. I didn't want to go in.

I stopped walking. "I'll just wait over there," I said to Miss Trish, pointing to the empty family room, where it wasn't as bright. One of the windows had no glass and was shuttered from the outside. I liked that it was a little dim in the room. In the kitchen, I'd stand out like a lightbulb.

"Sure, dear," Miss Trish said.

"I'll come with you," Dawn said.

"You don't need to babysit me," I told her.

"Don't you think I know that?" She grinned, mussing up my hair with her hand. Then she leaned close to my ear. "I'd rather hang out with you than those people in there," she said.

Yeah, right, I thought. But it was nice of her, so I wasn't going to give her any grief.

We sat next to each other by the fireplace with its fake-o gas logs. I remembered the house had three fireplaces in it. One in here, one in Laurel's bedroom and one on the porch. The Lockwoods had more money than God.

Marcus came out of the kitchen carrying a plate of food. "Hey, Dawn. Keith," he said as he sat down on the other side of me. "Frankie with you, Dawn?"

"He's still at work," she said.

I was glad Frankie wasn't there. Dawn had been seeing him for a while now, but I thought he was an asshole. He was always staring at my face.

"We'll get some action going today, Keith," Marcus said to me.

I nodded. My eyes were on the kitchen door. I figured Maggie was in there, and I wanted to prepare myself for seeing her. I'd pretend I *didn't* see her. I'd look right through her like she didn't exist. That's how I'd handle it.

Dawn stood up. "I'm going to get us some food," she said to me. "You stay."

Like I was going anywhere.

"How's the PT?" Marcus dug his fork into the macaroni salad on his plate.

I shrugged. Marcus was all right. Of the Lockwoods, he was the only one I could stand, and not just because he started that college fund for me years ago with a honkin' chunk of his own money. But I didn't want to talk about the PT. I'd skipped this morning. PT was the last thing on my mind. I wasn't keeping up with the exercises and my arms and shoulders were killing me. I'd popped an extra half a Percocet before Dawn picked me up, but it hadn't kicked in yet.

"Who all's here?" I asked.

"Well, let's see." He chewed some. Swallowed. "Flip Cates, for starters."

Yeah. The whole point of this meeting was for the cops to update us and tell us how we could help.

"Who else?"

"Laurel, of course. Robin Carmichael. Sue Charles. You know her?"

I nodded. Sue was one of my mother's old book-club friends, so it made sense she was there. I didn't realize Emily's mother cared much about mine, though. Emily had been in the fire, too, so I guessed that was the connection. Emily'd gotten a few cuts and bruises, but she was basically okay. Or at least as okay as she'd been before the fire, which wasn't saying much.

"Is Maggie here?" I couldn't take the suspense anymore.

"She's upstairs," Marcus said. "She's only been home a couple of days and isn't ready to face the world."

Chickenshit, I thought. But I knew how it felt, not wanting to face the world, and her staying upstairs was fine with me.

"And Andy's at school," Marcus said.

"Right." Where I was supposed to be. Fuck school.

Dawn came back and handed me a plate covered with food. "Here you go," she said.

I looked down at the ham-and-biscuit sandwich and five different kinds of salad—macaroni and potato and egg and who knew what else—and my stomach lurched. I should've told Dawn not to bother. I hadn't eaten anything since Monday night. I had the feeling the Percocet were doing a nice job carving out a hole in my stomach.

Everyone else came in. They all said hi to me, and Laurel leaned down to hug me, which just pissed me off. Nothing was really her fault, but she was, like, an extension of Maggie and that was enough to get to me.

"So." Flip sat down on the sofa with Miss Trish and put his plate on the coffee table. Everyone turned to look at him. "Keith," he said, "we all share your concern about your mother. As you know, we've put out a BOLO bulletin on her. We checked her bank records this morning. There were no large recent withdrawals or anything out of the ordinary there. We put a tracer on her car." He yammered on about what they'd done. I already knew everything he was talking about. They'd even searched the trailer for blood and semen, which freaked me out. I mean, I was a teenage guy who hadn't gotten any in more than a year. There was definitely semen in that trailer. But nobody said anything to me about what they found.

"That's why Laurel and Dawn put together this meeting," Flip was saying, "and they asked me to help you all figure out what the community can do. So, that's the purpose of our get-together here."

The Perc was starting to kick in, but not the way I wanted it to. It wasn't taking away the pain as much as making my head fuzzy, the way it did when I took too much. I ate the corner of one of the biscuits Dawn'd brought me to maybe take the edge off the drug, but I could hardly get it down. The smell of the food was making me feel worse. I leaned over and stuck my full plate under my chair.

"We've interviewed a few of you who know Sara well," Flip said, "and there's no clear-cut reason to suspect foul play. At least nothing that's leaping out at us. There's no mental or physical illness that could affect her judgment. And there's no suitcase in her home, which suggests she left of her own volition. Keith's not a minor, so he's able to be on his own."

"This is so screwed up." I slumped down in my chair and stuck my hands in my pockets. "What are you saying? We just forget she's gone?"

"Not at all," Flip said, "and I understand your frustration. That's why we're here—to see what more we can do to find her."

Laurel put her plate on the coffee table and leaned forward. "Flip, doesn't the fact that Sara's not mentally ill make her disappearance even *more* suspicious? There's no reason for it. No explanation for it."

"I know it's hard to hear," Flip said, "but something we need to consider is this—adults in her age range who are not mentally ill usually disappear to escape from something. Younger women disappear, you think about kidnapping and rape. Older, you think about cognitive problems. In Sara's age range, where she may have chosen to leave on her own, you think about escaping from financial or relationship problems, maybe an abusive relationship. That sort of thing." He looked around the room. "Do any of you know if she was struggling with financial problems?"

Everyone looked at me. "Well, we're not exactly swimming in bucks," I said. "Gimme a break."

"She never complained about it," Dawn said. "The money we collected last year after the fire, along with the restitution money...we were able to pay most of what Keith's military insurance didn't cover." She put her hand on my shoulder. "I know you and your mom didn't have a lot, but she never made it sound like you were going without. Oh!" She suddenly looked surprised. "I just thought of something, Flip. This probably won't help, but...I think Sara was sort of writing a memoir. Did you find anything like that when you searched the trailer?"

"A memoir?" Laurel sounded surprised. No more surprised than me, though. Didn't you have to have an interesting life to write a memoir?

"Yes," Dawn said. "I talked her into taking a writing class with me at the Methodist church in Jacksonville last year. She really got into it and I think she stuck with it. More than I did."

Flip leaned forward. "Do you know anything about this, Keith?"

She was always writing this year, carrying a notebook around with her. I never thought much about it. I was into *my* life, not hers. "I don't know anything about a memoir," I said. The spot between my shoulder and neck was seizing up something fierce, and I rubbed it. "She wrote stuff down in a notebook a lot of times, but I don't have any idea what she was writing."

"That's it!" Dawn sounded excited. "She wrote by hand. Drove the teacher crazy the one time he tried to read something she wrote."

"This teacher," Flip said, "he might know what was in the...memoir?"

Dawn shook her head. "I think he only read her first chapter, or whatever you'd call it. Everyone else in the class would read aloud, but Sara was shy about it. She let Sean—that was the teacher—read that first bit and she told me he said she was a really good writer...something like that. She didn't care about typing it. She said it was just for her own eyes."

"The notebook or notebooks or whatever," I said to Flip, "they're not in the trailer. I haven't seen them and you would've found them, right?"

"Think if there might be a place she could have hidden something like that," Flip said to me. "If she was feeling secretive about them, maybe she really squirreled them away."

"I don't know if she was feeling *secretive*," Dawn said. "She was just self-conscious about reading aloud to the class."

"You'll get me the name and a number for that teacher, Dawn?" Flip asked.

Dawn nodded, and I tried to think where in the trailer my mother might have hidden something like that. The cops went over that place with a fine-tooth comb, though. If they couldn't find a notebook, I didn't know how I could.

"We've checked her cell-phone records," Flip said. "Her last call was to you, Dawn, Sunday afternoon."

Dawn frowned, then nodded. "Oh, right. We just talked for a few minutes. Nothing important, that I can remember."

"What about tracing her by her cell phone?" Marcus asked.

"No luck there," Flip said. "Her phone model's a dinosaur, but the towers still should've been able to pick it up. She may have ditched it or the battery may've run out."

"She wouldn't 'ditch it,'" I said. It was pissing me off, the way he made her sound like she wanted to run away. "She never keeps that thing charged, though. She always forgets."

"Maybe she bought a new phone?" Miss Trish looked at Flip. "I know this doesn't sound like Sara, but could she have known you'd try to trace her by her old phone and…if she didn't want to be found for some reason, she could have—"

"Christ's sake!" My voice came out a lot louder than I expected. "She didn't buy a new phone, don't you get it?"

"We're just trying to puzzle this all out, Keith," Sue Charles said.

"She wouldn't leave me," I said. "She *wouldn't*." It felt like somebody was hitting my shoulder with a meat cleaver. The Percocet wasn't working at all.

"He's right," Dawn said. "She really wouldn't, Flip."

He nodded. "Well, that's even more reason we have to do all we can to figure out what happened."

"You mean *we* have to figure it out." I sat up straight. "Me and her friends." The cops said they were doing all this stuff, but I wasn't convinced. How much did they care about someone they thought took off "of her own volition"? I'd spent practically all the day before searching for my mother's car in the daylight, driving the same streets I'd driven the night she disappeared. My neck ached from turning my head back and forth, searching every inch of road and every space in every parking lot for her old black Honda. Must've put a hundred miles on my car. Fifteen bucks' worth of gas. I couldn't keep that up. I had, like, a hundred bucks in my bank account. My mother'd let me keep the donations that trickled in from strangers in my name alone instead of to the fund Dawn had set up. I'd sped through it. After what I'd been through, I *deserved* that new cell phone, I'd told myself. I *deserved* the latest-generation iPod and the stereo for my wheels. Stupid. How was I going to eat when that hundred bucks ran out if she didn't come back? My eyes suddenly burned. *Shit.* She *had* to come back.

"It's a team effort, Keith," Laurel said. "What can *we* do, Flip?" She picked up a yellow notepad from the table and set it on her knees, ready to write.

"There are some Web sites where you can put up a page for a missing person," he said. "Not many legit ones for missing adults, so you need to be careful. Try ProjectJason.org." He named a couple others, and Laurel wrote them down.

"Maggie said she could do any of the Internet stuff we need," she said.

I looked at the toe of my sneaker at the mention of Maggie. Was everybody staring at me? I didn't want to know.

"You can make up flyers with her picture on it," Flip said. "Along with her vital statistics, etcetera. Then hand them out."

"Hand them out where?" Sue Charles asked.

"Everywhere," Robin's mother said. "Stores. Restaurants. The street."

"We've called the nearby hospitals," Flip said, "but you can call all the hospitals around the interstates."

"She wouldn't be on the interstates," I said, but everybody ignored me.

"Put my name down for calling hospitals, Laurel," Dawn said.

"Did we decide who'll make the flyer?" Trish asked.

"Maggie'll do it," Laurel said. "Then we can give each of you stacks of them to distribute."

"How about contacting the media?" Marcus asked.

Oh, shit. Now the reporters would really be after me, but he was right. They had to get word out.

"We've sent out a press release," Flip said, "but any media contacts y'all have will help."

"This is so fucked up!" I said. "You hear about other missing people on the news all the time. Did their *friends* take care of getting them on TV? I don't think so. I think the cops had something to do with it."

"Keith, hon." Dawn put her hand on my shoulder.

"Again, Keith—" Flip was so damn calm sounding "—the police are on this, but the more we can all work together, the better. In those instances where a missing person's all over the news? Most times the families have hired a private investigator to generate a lot of media buzz for them."

"Like I can afford that!" I'd had enough. Everybody was staring at me. I couldn't take it anymore. "Quit looking at me!" I stood up and walked to the door.

"Keith!" Dawn said, but I ignored her. I needed to go outside. Get into the fresh air. I was just about to turn the door knob when I saw the news van still parked on the street. *Damn.*

Everyone in the living room was calling to me by then, but no one was coming after me, and I was glad. My head spun, and I turned around and leaned against the wall, and that's when I saw a pair of bare feet disappear into the upstairs hallway. *Maggie?* She'd been sitting up there listening the whole time? The thought creeped me out and I thought I was seriously going to puke. I headed for the bathroom under the stairs and locked the door behind me. I closed my eyes and leaned back against the door and this picture of a machete chopping off Maggie's feet flashed into my mind. I breathed long and steady through my mouth so I wouldn't get sick.

Where was my mother?

I pounded my fist against the door behind me.

Where the hell was she?

I started to cry like a total jerk-off, and I turned on the water so no one could hear me. In the mirror above the sink, I saw this kid who didn't look like me. Half his face was tight and red and the skin was twisted into smooth planes and deep gullies and his hairline was all screwed up and it was all so damn unfair!

"Keith?" It was Dawn. Right outside the bathroom. "You okay?"

I knew if I tried to talk, my voice would crack, so I just grunted.

"Flip wants to know if you have a more recent picture of your mom than the one you gave him at the trailer. Trish is going to do up another press release and she needs one."

I got a grip on myself. "Be out in a minute," I said.

"Okay."

I heard her walk away. I splashed water on my cheeks until I felt settled down enough to face them all again.

Walking back to the family room, I thought of the pictures in the trailer. My mother had pictures of me—the pre-fire me—framed on the bookcases and her dresser, but the one I gave Flip was of both of us, taken on my twelfth birthday. Not exactly recent.

"Keith," Miss Trish said when I walked into the room. "Do you have a more recent picture of—"

"No." I cut her off. Then I felt like an asshole. She was only trying to help. "Sorry," I said. "That was the only one."

"I might have a picture somewhere," Laurel said. Good ol' Laurel, coming to the rescue.

"Me, too," said Dawn. "I'll look when I get home."

"You'll need a good one for the flyer and the Web sites," Flip said. He looked at me again. "How about your father?"

My *father?* The question caught me totally off guard. I glanced at Laurel as I sat down again. I knew she knew about her two-timing dead husband. Marcus knew, of course. Probably Dawn, too. But did Flip?

"What do you mean?" I asked.

"Steven Weston."

Oh. *That* father.

"I know your parents split up a long time ago, but did your mother stay in touch with him? Or did he stay in touch with you?"

"No, man." I rammed my hands into my pockets. I still felt kind of shaky and I didn't want everyone looking at my jittery hands. "He was out of our lives."

"Do you know his whereabouts?"

"No clue." Steven Weston deserted me and my mother when I was a baby. I had military insurance because of him, but that was it. I'd never met him and never wanted to. "Me and my mother've always been on our own."

"Is it possible your mother was still in touch with him?" Flip was barking up the wrong tree. "Or maybe just recently got back in touch with him?"

"Why would she?" I asked. "Believe me. He wanted nothing to do with us and we wanted nothing to do with him."

"I think Keith's right," Dawn said. "Sara never mentioned him at all."

The meeting went on like that awhile longer, with Flip saying what the cops would do and Laurel making her notes and divvying up the workload. I was tired when it was over. Tired and so damn frustrated, because my mother was somewhere out there and we'd been talking and arguing and getting nowhere except further and further from finding her.

And the whole time, nobody said what they were all thinking. What I refused to think, myself. That my mother was probably dead. Nobody said a word about that at all.

Chapter Ten

Maggie

"Do you want me to drive you to the therapist?" mom looked at me across the kitchen table. It was just her and me. Uncle Marcus had left for work at the fire station and Andy'd caught the school bus an hour ago. I knew Mom had made his breakfast and probably eaten with him, but she was drinking coffee while I ate my cereal. To be with me. Just to be with me.

Yes, I wanted her to drive me. I knew how all those stars felt with the paparazzi following them around. The reporters were in front of the house again. I'd heard Uncle Marcus out there when I first woke up, telling them to leave Andy alone as he walked to the bus stop. It was one thing for them to hound me, another for them to go after Andy, and I hoped Uncle Marcus walked with him to the corner. Andy wouldn't know what to say to the vultures, or else he'd say too much. You never knew with him.

If Mom drove me, I could lie down in the backseat until we were past the news vans. But I had to face this mess sooner or later, and it was my mess. Not Mom's.

"I'll be okay," I said. I wasn't just dreading getting past the reporters, but the appointment itself. What was I supposed to say to a shrink? Open up with my deep dark secrets? Everyone already knew mine. I was an arsonist. A murderer.

"Can you work on the flyer this afternoon?" Mom asked.

"I'm almost done with it already," I said.

"You *are?*"

I'd gotten to work on my "assigned tasks" right after the meeting, before Mom even came upstairs to tell me what they were. I'd been sitting at the top of the stairs during the whole meeting, taking my own notes. I'd heard how angry Keith sounded. I got a glimpse of him storming out of the family room, but didn't see any of his face. I couldn't blame him for being totally pissed off. He probably had plenty of anger to go around ever since the fire, most of it aimed at me. The least I could do was my part to help find Sara. "I just need a picture of Sara. Did you find one?"

"I did." Mom stood up and walked over to the refrigerator. She pulled a photograph from behind a magnet. "Will this do?" she asked, handing it to me. It was of Sara and Dawn at Jabeen's, both of them smiling from behind the counter.

"Yeah." I wondered if she thought it bothered me to see Dawn in the picture. "I can crop Dawn out and blow Sara up bigger," I said, like it was no big deal. God, Dawn was so pretty and so mature looking! How could I have thought Ben would be seriously interested in me? I'd been such an idiot.

We still had my white Jetta, only now Andy was learning to drive it. I couldn't picture it. Andy, behind the wheel of a car? Watch out. Today, though, the car was mine. I got into the Jetta inside our garage. I'd missed driving and that sense of freedom it could give you, but I felt kind of nervous since I hadn't driven in a year. I had to go through a mental checklist, like a pilot. *The car's in Park. Press the button on the remote to raise the garage door. Turn the key. Give it a little gas. Put it in Reverse.* I started backing out of the garage.

Suddenly, there they were in my rearview mirror—the reporters with their cameras, jumping out of their vans. *Oh, God.* I took my foot off the gas, letting the car come to a stop. *Exactly* the wrong thing to do. The faster I got past them, the better off I'd be. I floored it. I'd had a few frightening moments in the last couple of years, but flying backward down my driveway toward a bunch of reporters was one of the scariest. I was totally out of control. People jumped out of the way. *The crazy girl's coming!* I hit the brake when I got into the street, shifted into Drive and took off with a squeal of my tires.

I raced down our short street and turned onto the main road, glad now that the summer traffic was gone and I could go fast. I'd driven a half mile before I slowed down. Another half mile before my heart did the same.

I wasn't free at all. Not even a little bit.

I was driving into Hampstead when I noticed the white van behind me. I couldn't believe it! I should have been more careful. No way was I letting them follow me to the therapist's office. *Maggie Lockwood was seen walking into psychologist Marion Jakes's office for her court-mandated counseling.* I zigzagged all over Hampstead until I was a hundred percent sure I'd lost the van. I spotted the little parking lot behind the therapist's building, but I drove past it to a nearby veterinarian's office, where I hid the Jetta between a van and a pickup. I felt like I was in a movie. A thriller. By the time I walked into the therapist's office, I was sweating.

The small waiting room was empty. I sat down in one of the eight chairs and picked up an old copy of *Us* from the coffee table, but I didn't open it. I was thinking about the Web sites where I could post Sara's information. Wow, so many missing people on those sites! It was discouraging, and I wondered if everything I was doing was for nothing. The whole situation didn't make sense. Sara wasn't the type of woman to just take off. At least, the Sara I knew before the fire wasn't. But who knew how this year had changed her? It had changed me plenty.

An enormous man walked through the office door, and I figured he was another patient, maybe waiting for a different therapist. I glanced up just long enough to catch his eggplant-shaped body before quickly lowering my eyes to the magazine cover again.

"Miss Lockwood?" he said.

I was confused. *Oh, God.* I hoped he wasn't one of the reporters. "Yes," I said.

"I'm Dr. Jakes."

"No," I said. "Dr. Jakes is a—"

"A woman?" He smiled, and his eyes nearly disappeared above his round cheeks. "I'm Marion Jakes."

Oh, no. I didn't budge. The only thing that had made the idea of counseling tolerable was imagining a kindly, maternal sort of woman, maybe my mother's age, as my shrink. This guy was not only obscenely fat, but he was ancient. The small amount of hair he had on his round head was gray. The buttons of his blue shirt strained at their buttonholes, and he wore ridiculous red, white and blue striped glasses.

"Come in," he said.

What choice did I have? I got up and followed him into a room even smaller than the waiting room. This one had four leather chairs facing each other, and I sat down in the one closest to the door.

Dr. Jakes took up most of the space in the room. "How are you today?" He dropped into one of the big leather chairs. It creaked beneath him.

"Fine," I said.

He looked like he didn't believe me. "You're very pale," he said.

"I...I'm fine."

"Well—" he folded his hands across his belly "—I know why you're here, of course, since this is court-ordered psychotherapy. I know what you were convicted of doing and that you were released Monday after twelve months in prison. What I *don't* know is how you feel about being here."

He waited for me to speak, but I looked past him, out the window. I wanted to be outside again. I wanted to be *home*.

"Okay."

"Just okay?"

"I don't know what I'm supposed to say," I said.

"Have you ever been in therapy before?"

I shook my head. "Just...you know, the high-school counselor about college, but that's not therapy, I guess."

"You had college plans?"

"I was going to go to UNC Wilmington," I said. "Before...everything happened."

"Well," he said, "here's the way this goes." He leaned forward and I was afraid he might roll right out of his chair. "We'll be a team, you and me. Together, we'll figure out what we should be working on. Set some goals."

"I don't really have anything to work on."

"No?"

I shook my head. "I'm basically a normal person. I just got...sidetracked."

"I don't doubt that you're normal," he said. "But what you did was not, and it would be good for us to explore why you did what you did so you understand it. So you see the parts of yourself you need to pay attention to in order to prevent something like that from ever happening again."

"It won't," I said.

He smiled, his eyes disappearing again behind his striped glasses. "I'm not a cop," he said. "You don't have to give me the answers you think you should be giving. What we talk about in this room stays in this room. The only time I would ever break confidentiality is if I believe you're going to harm yourself or someone else. I'll need to let your case manager know that you've kept your appointments with me, but not what our sessions are about. All right?"

He had to have some hefty psychological problems himself to be so fat. I couldn't see how someone like him could help me, but I nodded. I would just nod my way through these sessions.

"What's it been like for you since Monday?" he asked.

"What do you mean?"

"Being out of prison? Being free?"

"Okay."

He waited for me to go on. I stared out the window with its view of the parking lot until my eyes watered. Then I looked at my ragged fingernails. He wasn't going to talk until I did. It was like a standoff. A war, but I had the feeling he could take the silence longer than I could.

"The reporters are everywhere," I said finally.

"Ah," he said. "What's that like for you?"

I shrugged. "I hate it," I said. "It's not fair to my family, either. If it was just me...well, that's bad enough, but I get why they have to be after me. I'm the story. But I want them to leave my brother and mother alone."

"Tell me about your family."

"You probably know all about them already. You know about Andy, for sure."

"I know what everyone else who followed the news about the fire knows, Maggie," he said. "But even when I listened to the news back then and heard all the details, I couldn't help but wonder… It's being in this business, you see." He smiled. "I couldn't help but wonder what it was like for *you*. For the young woman at the center of it all. So, yes. I know about Andy as he was presented by the news media. I want to hear about him—and the rest of your family—from *you*."

I sighed. "Okay," I said, giving in. "Andy's very sweet and cute and a perfect brother. He's… You know about the fetal alcohol syndrome?"

He nodded.

I twisted my watchband around and around on my wrist. I was thinking, *I almost killed my baby brother.* But I wasn't going to give this guy that much of a peek inside me. "So," I said, "Andy's learning to drive and he's got a girlfriend. He's really grown up while I've been away. And my mother…she's nice. She looks older than I remember her looking. She and my uncle Marcus… He was my father's brother—"

"The fire marshal."

"Right. He and my mother have gotten together."

"How do you feel about that?"

"Good." I nodded. "Really good. He still has his own place. One of the Operation Bumblebee towers."

"Ah." He smiled. You couldn't think about the houses made from the old towers without smiling.

"Yeah." I almost smiled myself. "But he stays over our house sometimes. I guess he's been there a lot this last year."

"And how do you—"

"Feel about it?" I finished the sentence for him. "I told you. Good. Especially with the reporters around." I thought again about Andy walking to the school bus that morning, maybe trying to make sense of the reporters and their questions. Struggling to figure out how to answer them. Before I knew what was happening, my eyes filled with tears.

"You love your family very much," Dr. Jakes said.

I nodded.

He motioned to the box of tissues on the table next to my chair and I took one and pressed it to my eyes. I did *not* want to cry here. I didn't want to give this old sloppy fat man the satisfaction of making me cry. But suddenly, that was all I could do. I cried, and he let me. That's about all I did for the rest of the session. He said that was okay. Good, even. I had a lot of pain inside me, he said, and we'd have plenty of time together to talk it all through.

"Our session's nearly up," he said when I'd gone through half the tissues in the box. "But before you leave, I wanted to ask what your plans are for community service. You have three hundred hours, is that correct?"

I let out a long, shivery breath. I needed to pull myself together in case the reporters had tracked me here and were waiting in the veterinarian's parking lot.

"My mother…she's a nurse at Douglas Elementary in Sneads Ferry," I said. "I'm going to help one of the teachers there. I start Monday."

"Did you arrange this or did your mother?" he asked.

"My mother," I said.

He looked like he wanted to say something else, but just nodded. "Okay then." He pushed himself out of the chair with his hands. "We'll be meeting twice a week," he said.

"Right." Mom had scheduled appointments for me into infinity. I didn't want to have to cry my eyes out twice a week, but it wasn't like I had a choice. I stood up and gave him what felt like a dopey smile as I walked past him to the door.

It would have been going too far to say I liked him, but I could have sworn he didn't look as fat when I left as he did when I arrived.

Chapter Eleven

Andy

I HATED POLICE CARS. MOM SAID I WAS JUST SCARED OF THEM because one night a police car took me to jail. So when the police lady wanted me to ride with her to Wal-Mart, I said no. Mom told her I should practice driving, so we'd take our car instead. Mom was being a quick thinker!

I had a cushion thing I put on the driver seat so I could see good through the window. I kept waiting to get taller but it wasn't happening. Kimmie was taller than me, but she didn't care. Some girls cared about that but Uncle Marcus said who'd want a girl who cared about something so trivial? Which meant not very important.

I was an excellent driver. We were supposed to follow the police car, so I tried to keep looking at it, but I had trouble.

"You're losing her, sweetie," Mom said.

My speedometer thing said thirty-five. "She's going too fast."

Mom laughed. "You're right. You take your time. We'll catch up to her at the Wal-Mart."

We came to the corner I hated. There was no light but a lot of cars. I had to look a lot of different ways and wait and wait. A car behind me honked.

"Take your time," Mom said.

The car honked again. I didn't know whether to stay stopped or go.

"Brain," I said. "You gotta stay focused!"

"That's right," Mom said. "Ignore that silly horn."

Finally, when I was really, really sure it was safe, I drove across the street. Then we were at the Wal-Mart, where I got to practice parking between the lines. I was good at that, except for Mom couldn't get out and I had to do it again.

The police lady leaned against a brick thing with her arms folded. "Thought I lost you," she said. She was pretty old. She had on a hat, but I saw her gray hair underneath it.

"You went over the speed limit," I said.

She laughed. "I probably did. Better write myself a ticket."

"Yup," I said. "We can wait."

But she didn't write herself a ticket at all. Police can get away with things regular people can't.

Inside, we walked to the place where the pots and pans were. The police lady told me to look at all the boxes to see if any of them looked like the one Miss Sara carried. I thought I remembered it perfect. It was red with a big silver pot on it. But when I saw all the different boxes, I got confused.

"Maybe it was blue." I pointed to a blue box. Then I saw a yellowy one with a funny pan on it, and my memory said that was it. "I think it was this one," I said.

"That's an electric wok," the police lady said. "I thought you said it was a big pot?"

"What's an electric rock?" I asked Mom.

"Wok," she said. "It's a kind of pan. Is that what it looked like?"

I moved my mouth back and forth like I did when I was thinking hard. I felt so mixed up with all those boxes. Maybe it wasn't even a pot at all. I pointed to a red box that had a white square bowl thing on it. "Maybe it was that one," I said.

"A casserole?" Mom asked.

I shook my head, because casseroles had lots of different food in them. I didn't like them. I didn't like food to touch.

"Memories can play tricks on you sometimes, can't they?" Mom said. It was her patient voice.

"Can you narrow it down, Andy?" the police lady asked.

I wasn't sure what "narrow it down" meant.

"Are there any you're absolutely sure were *not* the box she was carrying?" Mom asked.

"The little ones," I said. "It wasn't little."

The police lady's cell phone rang. Mom and me waited while she talked. Mom winked at me.

"Are you excited about Kimmie coming to dinner?" She used a quiet voice because of the police lady talking on the phone.

"Yes!"

Mom put her finger on her lips.

"Yes," I whispered. I wanted Maggie to meet Kimmie. Maggie wouldn't come to swim practice because she didn't like seeing people yet. That was why Mom said Kimmie could come to dinner.

Kimmie told me, "I used to hate going to Matt's swim practices, but now I can't wait so I can see you."

When she said that, I hugged her. I wasn't supposed to hug people besides my family, but I had to hug Kimmie then. She didn't mind. She really didn't. But she said I smelled like cigarettes. She said, "Please don't smoke." I threw my cigarettes away.

"Mom?" I said now. She was looking at a can-opener thing.

"What?"

"Me and Kimmie hug sometimes, but she doesn't mind so it's okay. Right?"

Mom kept looking at the can opener. It had a handle and she made it go up and down.

"Where are you when you hug?" she asked.

"The pool and her house and our house."

"In your room?" She looked at me in a way that told me I better say no, even though we *did* hug in my room once.

"No," I said. We were allowed in my room with the door open.

"Hugging's nice," Mom said. "And Kimmie's your girlfriend, right?" I nodded.

"It's okay to hug your girlfriend."

The police lady turned off her phone. "That was the manager," she said. "No pots or pans have been returned in the last few days."

"So maybe it wasn't from this store?" Mom asked.

"Right. Or it wasn't a pot or pan." She tipped her head funny and looked at me. "Maybe it was actually a wok or a casserole or a potato peeler," she said.

"What?" I laughed. She was making a joke.

"Or she never made it to the store," she said.

"Oh, don't even say that." Mom had on her worried look. She had it on a lot since Miss Sara went missing.

Everybody was worried about Miss Sara. I got asked a lot of questions by the police and Mom and Uncle Marcus. Even Maggie asked me questions on account of the Web site thing she's making. Everybody wanted to know what clothes Miss Sara had on. Things like that. I kept telling them I was too sick that day to remember.

I told my friend Max about the questions and he said it was 'cause I was the last person who saw her. He said the police maybe thought I killed her and cut her up in bags. Like her head in a bag and her arm in a different bag. That was stupid. I told Uncle Marcus what Max said and he said, "Max is just yankin' your chain."

The police lady looked at her watch. "I'm out of time," she said. "Can you two go to some more stores on your own? Maybe the Bed Bath and Beyond and the Target?"

Mom nodded. "Of course," she said. I wished she said no so we could go home and wait for Kimmie.

But we left the Wal-Mart and went to some more stores. I got more confused in every one of them.

"I can't do this anymore," I told Mom when we walked outside from the Bed and Beyond store. It wasn't just because I wanted to go home. My head hurt. Maybe I never even saw a box. Maybe I dreamed I saw it.

"Okay," she said. "You've been a good sport."

"You be the one to drive home," I said. I didn't feel like driving. I felt bad I messed up about the box.

"Okay," Mom said.

We got in the car. Mom was an excellent driver. She could go real fast in the parking lot around all the cars and everything.

"I'm sorry, Mom," I said when we got to the road. "I lost the picture of the box in my head. You know my brain."

Mom smiled at me. "I love your brain, Andy," she said. "Don't worry about it."

But I *was* worried. Miss Sara could be chopped up in bags and I couldn't even remember if she was carrying a pot or a pan.

Chapter Twelve

Keith

I PARKED IN THE LOT OF THE HARRIS TEETER IN OGDEN. STUPID to go all the way there with gas prices like they were, but I couldn't face seeing people in the Food Lion. People would know me there. Want to talk. They'd ask if I knew any more about my mother's disappearance, because now it was all over the news. All the time they'd be staring at me. It wasn't like the people in Ogden wouldn't recognize me—I wore my ID on my face. But at least there, they wouldn't try to talk to me.

I got out of the car, grabbed a cart and pushed it into the store, which was pretty crowded. I didn't have a plan. No list. My mother always had a list and she stuck to it like it was the law. Man, I hated this. I bet it'd been five years since I'd been in a grocery store, and then only because I had to tag along with my mother. If I needed to pick up a snack or something, I did it at the gas station. But our refrigerator was almost empty now, and I was finally starting to get hungry even though thinking about that plate of food at Laurel's still made me gag.

That was another reason the cops thought my mother left on purpose. "Looks like your mom cleaned out the fridge before she disappeared," one of them said to me. Screw him. I told him we never had much in the fridge to begin with, but I got the feeling he didn't believe me.

"She cleans out the fridge, but not her bank account?" I'd asked him. If I needed proof something terrible had happened to my mother, that was it. She never used credit cards, so she wouldn't take off on purpose without cash. When I started thinking about that, the breathing-tube sort of panic would start again.

The cops had a couple of new theories they were playing with now. First theory: She left on purpose because she couldn't handle the burden of me anymore. Gimme a break. I was less of a burden now than I'd ever been in my life. I'd had all the fight taken out of me. I knew that wasn't it, and Dawn and Laurel and Marcus all told them that was crazy. They said how much my mother loved me and how devoted she was to me and all that, which made me feel like a shit for how I treated her sometimes, like she was my maid. I'd be different when she came back.

Second theory: I had something to do with her going missing. They didn't say that, but I didn't have to be a genius to know what was going through their heads. A couple of them—a guy named De-tective Wiley, and I couldn't remember the other dude's name— came to the trailer this morning and went through it again, looking for the diary or memoir or whatever. I'd already looked everywhere I could think of. After they tore the place apart, they talked to me for a couple more hours. Their questions started in one spot and then spun out like a spiderweb, looping all over the place until they had me good and confused. I got angry and told them they were wasting their time, and Wiley said, "Settle down, Keith," which pissed me off more. Like *he* could settle down if his mother went missing.

They asked me where I was the afternoon she disappeared.

"In school," I said. *Stupid.* I knew the minute I said it, I'd screwed up. Right in front of me, Wiley called over to Douglas High to check the attendance records. "Uh-huh," he said into the phone, but he was looking at me with these half-closed, suspicious eyes. "Uh-huh. Right. Thanks." He turned off his phone and talked to the other guy like I wasn't even there. "She says he left after sixth period," he said, and they both looked at me, like, what d'you have to say for yourself now, kid?

"All right," I said. "I went surfing. By the pier. You can ask anybody." But I knew the dudes who hung out there wouldn't be able to say if I was there or not. You could be invisible out in the water. That's why I liked going there in the first place.

The cops finally left, and I spent the next few hours waiting for them to come back with handcuffs—or worse, with a social worker. I couldn't believe they still hadn't figured out I was only seventeen. No one at Laurel's meeting had ratted on me about it, either. Maybe no one knew? Or cared? That was all right with me. The last thing I needed was to end up in a foster home or something. If the cops thought I was eighteen, I'd be eighteen.

I'd managed to get one of those grocery carts with a squeaky wheel, just so the other shoppers would be sure to notice the burned guy. The wheel made the cart tough to push and probably would have killed my shoulder if I hadn't doubled up on the Perc again that afternoon. The good news was that, even though I was out of food, I had plenty of Percocet. I got them through the mail and my mother must have just re-upped before she disappeared, because three beautiful bottles arrived that afternoon. When it came to pain meds, at least, I was golden.

I lowered my head as I raced through the store, tossing stuff in the cart, not looking at anybody. I just wanted to make it fast, but I didn't know where anything was. I found the bread and then got some of those packages of ham and cheese. The cart was getting to me, so I traded it in for a smoother ride. Then I got some toilet paper. Some Coke. I pulled one of the cans from the carton, popped it open and drank it warm as I tooled around the store. I passed the cold beer. Oh, man, what I wouldn't give for a six-pack! I knew this guy at the gas station who'd buy some for me. He got burned in Iraq, so he knew what it was like. I found the cereal and threw a couple boxes in the cart. Then I noticed the price on the shelf below the Honey Nut Cheerios: $4.49? No way. I put the boxes back on the shelf and started looking through the other stuff I'd stuck in the cart. No prices on anything. How were you supposed to figure this out? I'd planned to get out of there for ten bucks. If everything was as expensive as the cereal, I was screwed. How did my mother do it? She was always cutting coupons, so maybe that was the secret to getting by on the crappy money she made at Jabeen's. I didn't want to think about her while I was in the store or I'd end up with another crying fit like I'd had in Laurel's bathroom. That'd be really smooth in the middle of Harris Teeter.

I stared at the meat counter for a long time. I'd had steak maybe four times in my life, and my mouth actually watered, staring at it. I wasn't even sure how you cooked it. We had this old charcoal grill, but you needed lighter fluid to grill stuff. Just the thought of spraying the coals with lighter fluid and tossing a match on them made me hyperventilate. I was never going to be one of those guys who got his rocks off cooking things on a grill.

I looked up from the meat counter to see this old lady. She was holding a package of ground beef, and she was staring at me. At my face. I'd let down my guard while I was salivating over the steak.

"What are you lookin' at?" I asked, shoving my cart past her. I had to get out of there.

I whipped down the first aisle I came to. Canned chili was on sale and I tossed four cans in my cart. Then I saw some rice, which was cheap and had directions on the back, so I couldn't screw it up. That was enough. I headed for the checkout, wishing I could just steal the stuff and not have to face a checker and count out money and everything. I had twenty dollars in my pocket. What if I had more than twenty dollars' worth in the cart? Crap.

I spotted boxes of chocolate-covered doughnuts at the end of the cereal aisle for half price. A lot cheaper than cereal. My mother never bought doughnuts, but they looked good. I reached toward one of the boxes.

"I can't resist them either."

I looked up to see this totally, *totally* hot girl smiling at me.

I lowered my head again, fast. "'Scuse me," I said, trying to push my cart past her, but her cart sort of had me blocked in. Shit. I started moving backward to get around her.

"Aren't you going to get the doughnuts?" she asked. Like, what the hell did she care?

"Oh. Right." I grabbed one of the boxes.

"They're so yummy," she said.

I turned my head so the right side of my face was toward her. "Yeah," I said. I hoped it seemed natural for me to talk to her with my head turned, but it probably just made me look weird. Whatever.

"I totally love Entenmann's," she said, and it took me a minute to realize she was talking about the brand. "You put those doughnuts and chocolate together, and I'm powerless." She looked like she'd never eat a speck of chocolate or anything else that could pack on the pounds, but she was skinny in a good way. Not like one of those anorexic actresses. She had small breasts, the way I liked them, and an inch of flat stomach between her white top and brown pants. Those pants fit her like the chocolate coated the doughnuts. She still had a tan and I could picture her on the beach in a string bikini. Her hair was nearly black and her eyes blue and— Oh, shit! I'd let down my guard again. Turned my head toward her while I was salivating over her. She was still smiling, though. I slipped my bad left hand into my pocket.

"You don't look like you indulge." That was out of my mouth before I thought about it. It was the kind of thing I would've said to a girl before the fire.

"Well, like I said, chocolate's my weakness."

I took my hand out of my pocket long enough to flip open the doughnut box and offer her one. "Your *only* weakness?" I asked. *Whoa.* All the way, dude. I felt my smile freeze on my face, waiting for the rejection.

She laughed. Reached for a doughnut. "I've got others," she said. "How about you?"

Was she *blind?* "Too many to count," I said.

"So." She nibbled the doughnut. Licked the chocolate from her lips. "What're you buying today?" She leaned on my cart to peer inside. Her top wasn't all that low-cut, but I liked what I could see.

"Shopping cheap," I said.

"I'm the queen of shopping cheap." She picked up one of the cans of chili. "Need a little nutrition here, though," she said.

"That's good protein," I said.

"Need some veggies. And fruit."

"Too expensive."

"Uh-uh," she said. "Come with me."

I followed her, both of us pushing our carts, back to the place where all the fresh stuff was. Her ass was perfectamundo. I had her undressed, legs wrapped around me in a death grip, by the time we reached the apples.

"What do you like?" she asked.

I looked at the stacks of vegetables. "Asparagus," I said.

"Okay, that *is* too expensive. How about spinach?"

"I don't know how to cook it."

"Just zap it in a little water in the microwave. Covered. Not with plastic, though. That's toxic. Just stick a paper towel over it. But wash it real well first." She wrinkled her nose. "It's gritty."

It sounded like too much work, but I didn't complain when she picked up a bag of spinach and handed it to me.

We went through the stacks of fruit and she put a few things in my cart, a few in hers. I started feeling weird. She was being way too sweet, like Dawn or somebody hired her to be nice to me. Something felt off about the whole thing.

"So where do you live?" she asked.

"Surf City."

"Really? I'm staying in Topsail Beach."

We were practically neighbors. "Why are you shopping way out here?"

"On my way from an appointment," she said. "How about you?"

"Same," I lied.

"Listen—" she suddenly stopped her cart in front of the eggs "—I'm from Asheville and I don't know people around here. How about I cook you something tonight? Make you dinner?"

"Why?"

She shrugged. "I don't have many friends here," she said. "Like none, really."

"I don't think so, thanks." The old me would have given anything for a few hours with a babe like her.

"Oh, come on. Please?" she said. "I don't usually have to beg guys to spend time with me."

She didn't have friends in Topsail, so I'd do for now. Then she'd meet some good-lookin' dude and sayonara Keith. I could skip the pain. I had bigger things on my mind, anyhow.

"Thanks. I'm just not in a great place right now."

She tipped her head to one side. "Excuse me for prying," she said, "but were you one of the people in that fire I heard about?"

I looked away. "Depends on what fire you heard about." I sounded mean.

"Sorry," she said. "That was way too personal."

"No, it's okay. Yeah. The lock-in fire."

"You're still really good-looking," she said. "I don't think you know that, but I mean it."

Oh, man, did I want to believe her, but I had a mirror in the trailer. I knew the truth. What the hell was her game?

"Going through something like that...like a fire and all the recovery and stuff. It's got to be hard."

"I really gotta check out." I started to push my cart past hers.

"I did this all wrong," she said.

I stopped walking. Couldn't help myself. "What do you mean?" I asked.

"I came on too strong. Made you feel uncomfortable."

"I'm not uncomfortable."

"See? I did it again."

"Don't give yourself so much credit." I started pushing my cart again. "You're not all that powerful."

She grabbed the corner of my cart. "I've been hurt, too." She had the kind of blue eyes you could go swimming in. "Only difference is my scars are on the inside," she said. "But I know what it's like."

"You don't have a fucking clue."

Her cheeks turned red. "All right," she said. "Sorry I upset you."
She let go of my cart and began pushing her own away. Why was I
being such a prick? She scared me. She could look right at my face
and not freak, and that just seemed too damn weird.

"Wait," I said.

She turned around. Her hair swept through the air like she was
in a shampoo commercial. "Sorry," I said. "You can cook me something. Not tonight, though. I feel like crap today." Not really the
truth. I was nicely medicated, but I needed some time to adjust to
a girl like her being interested in me.

"Soon?" she asked. "Can I have your cell number?"

She pulled a scrap of paper from a tiny purse and wrote down
my number. She wrote hers down, too, then tore the sheet in two
pieces and gave me the half with her number on it.

"What's your name?" she asked.

"Keith."

"Well, hey, Keith," she said, sticking her hand out toward me.
"I'm Jen."

Chapter Thirteen

Sara
Angel's Wings
1990

SOMETIME DURING THE FIRST YEAR THAT I BABYSAT MAGGIE, I began leading my double life. It crept up on me gradually until, before I knew it, it had me by the throat. By then it was too late for me to change a thing.

I hadn't given up trying to help Laurel, despite being so rudely kicked out of the house the first time I visited. Or, I supposed, it was really Jamie I was trying to help. I'd pick up groceries for the Lockwoods when I went to the commissary and I brought over the occasional meal. Laurel tolerated me. She was nearly always on the couch when I arrived, her expression flat as she watched TV. If Maggie was with me, Laurel barely seemed to notice her. I sometimes felt as though *I* was Maggie's mother instead of Laurel.

In early January, Jamie's father was hospitalized with pneumonia. Since Steve was in Monterey studying Arabic, I kept Maggie at our small rental house outside Camp Lejeune while Jamie spent most of his time at the hospital in Wilmington. Jamie called often, ostensibly to check on Maggie, but the conversations quickly began to shift to something deeper. He told me how afraid he was that his father might die. I had lost my father when I was sixteen and it was easy for me to sympathize with him.

"I can't talk to Laurel about any of this," he said at the end of one of our phone conversations. "I... It's not her fault. She loves my father, and I know she's worried about him, but it's as though she can't really see outside herself right now. It's like she has nothing to give me anymore." He hesitated. "Or Maggie. Or anyone."

"I know." I was sitting in a rattan rocker in the third tiny bedroom of my house—the room that had become Maggie's nursery away from home. Jamie'd furnished it with a crib, the rocker and a changing table. "It must be so hard for you," I said.

"I keep reminding myself that she's sick," Jamie said. "If she had a physical illness, I'd take care of her, so this shouldn't be any different. But you're right. It *is* hard. I sometimes feel like I'm losing my ability to empathize with people."

"Oh, no, Jamie," I said. "I watch what happens when you're in the chapel on Sundays." People would file into the small five-sided building, talking quietly among themselves as though the morning was nothing special. Then Jamie would walk into the chapel, and the atmosphere would shift to a higher plane. I could see the change in the faces of the people. I could *feel* it happening inside my own skin. "Think of how many lives you touch there."

"Yeah. The lives of strangers." He sounded annoyed with himself. "Yet Marcus pisses me off, and now I'm scared I'm losing it with Laurel. She doesn't take care of herself. We have...no physical life anymore. I look at her sometimes and don't even know who she is."

I decided to take him into my confidence, the way he was taking me into his.

"It's not great with Steve and me either," I admitted.

Jamie hesitated. "I haven't gotten to know Steve," he said finally, "but you two do seem like a mismatch. You're friendly and warm and positive and he's very…reserved."

That was putting it mildly. "I'm not sure I've ever been in love with him," I said.

"But you married him," Jamie said. "There must have been something there."

I looked over at the crib where Maggie was sleeping. "There was a baby there," I said finally.

"A baby…?"

"It was so stupid," I said. "I got pregnant on our second date. We barely knew each other. I was so naive." *And a virgin,* I thought, but I was already saying more than I should. "I let things go too far and then it was too late for him to stop."

"It's never too late to stop," Jamie said.

"I let it go too far," I repeated, remembering the sudden pressure of Steve's penis pushing against me. Into me. "I asked him to stop, but he was…you know. He was so far gone he couldn't hear me."

"He heard you," Jamie said. "Don't make excuses for him."

"He said he didn't. I believe him. He was—"

"You were date-raped."

"*No.*" That was too extreme a description of what had happened. "It was my fault."

Jamie hesitated again. "But…what happened to the baby?" he asked.

Gripping the phone hard, I started to cry the tears I'd learned to hide from Steve. "He died," I said. "He was born at thirty weeks. He only lived a few hours." I could remember the shape of his fingernails and the narrow bridge of his tiny nose as clearly as if I'd given birth to him only a moment before.

"Sara," Jamie said quietly. "I'm so sorry. Why didn't you tell me? And here you've been taking care of Maggie. I never would have asked you to if I'd known."

"Taking care of her has helped." I wiped my tears away, thinking, so *this* is what it feels like to unburden yourself to a man. I hadn't even known it was possible.

"Well," Jamie said after a moment. "At least Steve married you. He took responsibility. A lot of men wouldn't, especially after dating for such a short time. You two barely knew each other."

"You're right. But I had to marry him."

Jamie was quiet. "You don't have to *stay* married to him," he said finally.

I bit my lip. "And you don't have to stay married to Laurel."

"I do," he answered. "It's like I said, Sara. She's sick. That's different."

My phone conversations with Steve during that same period were very different from those I had with Jamie. Steve called nearly every day from Monterey. He told me about the other guys in his classes and how hard the work was, but he was always talking about nuts and bolts. Never about his feelings.

"Will that baby be gone by the time I get back?" he asked one time when he heard Maggie crying in the background.

"Would it bother you, having her here?" Maybe having a baby around would remind him of Sam, even though I was quite sure Steve had put Sam completely out of his mind. I imagined the sort of father he would have made. He wouldn't be like Jamie, that was certain. Where Jamie was open, expansive and uninhibited with his daughter, Steve would have been wooden and mechanical. Jamie cuddled Maggie, cooing to her, telling her flat-out that he loved her, while Steve had never even spoken those words to me.

"It's just...weird," Steve said. "It's like he's turned that kid over to you to raise. I don't like it."

"Well, it's just while Jamie's father's in the hospital," I said.

"What's with that whole situation?" Steve asked. "What's with his wife?"

"They...the baby put a lot of strain on their marriage," I said. "Especially on Laurel. She's depressed and not managing things well."

"Hey!" Steve said abruptly. "If they split up, one of them could rent our spare room. For some extra money, they could even bring the baby. She's practically living with us for free as it is." He was always talking about renting out the extra room to one of the guys in his unit. We could use the cash. But Jamie and Laurel split up? I couldn't imagine it.

The day after that conversation with Steve, Jamie showed up at my house while Maggie was napping. His eyes were red, and I knew before he said a word that his father had died. Without thinking, I wrapped my arms around him while he wept. He clung to me, and I felt the comfortable bulk of him against my body. I wanted to take the hurt away, even though I knew it was one of those hurts that would never disappear completely. I was glad he'd come to me. Laurel didn't have the capacity to comfort him the way he needed comforting.

After a few minutes, I drew away. "Can you eat?" I asked. "I made beef stew yesterday. I can heat some up."

He reached for my hand as he sat down at the kitchen table. "Just sit with me awhile," he said. "Okay?"

I sat across the corner of the table from him while he told me about his father. How smart he was. Tolerant and good-hearted. People called him Daddy L, even those outside the family. Jamie wished I could have met him. He'd been so shrewd, buying up the Topsail Island property when it was cheap, making money that would keep the Lockwoods wealthy for generations.

We sat that way for a long time, Jamie holding my hand while he talked. I focused on the sensation of his skin against mine, so I could remember later exactly how it felt. That's when my double life truly began to take hold. I pretended to care about Laurel, wanting her to get better for the sake of her husband and daughter, yet at the same time hoping she didn't, so I could hang on to the part of Jamie and Maggie that I had. Without them, my life would have been too empty to bear.

I was shocked when I realized I was fantasizing about both Steve and Laurel dying. It was easy enough to picture with Laurel. She'd starve herself to death. Maybe even kill herself. Then there was that whole big Iran and Iraq mess heating up in the Middle East and maybe Steve would be deployed there and maybe he would be killed. Then Jamie and I would gradually get closer and closer, comforting each other in our grief until we finally realized we belonged together. We'd get married, and I would adopt Maggie. Maybe we'd go on to have kids of our own.

The fantasy came with a terrible, gut-wrenching guilt, but it was hard to control. I could be sitting in the living room with Steve while he studied for an exam, and I'd be knitting a scarf and killing him off in my mind at the same time.

And then, everything changed.

One day, while Maggie was with Jamie at the chapel, I took

some groceries to the Sea Tender. I knocked on the door and when I didn't get an answer, I went inside to find Laurel sitting on the kitchen floor. It was so unusual to see her off the sofa that I dropped the groceries on the counter and rushed to her side.

"Laurel!" I said. "Are you okay?"

She looked up at me. There was an electric drill in her hand.

"What are you doing?" I asked.

"Screwing up," Laurel said with a small laugh. She looked at the drill. "In a couple of months, Maggie'll be crawling and then walking, and I got worried she could get into the things under the sink here and in the bathroom."

I saw the small plastic clip in Laurel's left hand and realized she was trying to childproof the cabinets. Trying to protect her daughter. The brittle part of my heart that I'd reserved for Laurel cracked into slivers like a broken window.

I sank down next to her. "Can I help?"

Laurel stared at the drill. "I think I did it wrong," she said. "I don't think the part on the door is exactly in the right place to match up with this piece."

"Let me see." I checked the plastic piece she'd screwed into place on the door. It was off just slightly. In the plastic latch and the small crooked screw and the cumbersome drill, I saw the love of a mother for her child. The love that Laurel's stubborn depression—her stubborn *mental illness*—could not extinguish.

My eyes suddenly filled with tears. "It'll be okay," I said. "We can just put this one a little to the right." I considered taking the drill from Laurel's hand and making the hole in the door myself, but it would be better if she did it. With a pencil, I marked the spot for her to drill. I held the door steady and Laurel, biting her lip in concentration, drilled the hole. When she screwed the plastic hook in place, she sighed with exhaustion, as if she'd swum a few laps in a pool.

"Beautiful, Laurel!" I said.

Laurel closed the cabinet door and saw that it hooked. She unhooked it. Hooked it again.

"Ta-da," she said in a very small voice. She set the drill on the floor. "I'll do the bathroom cabinet tomorrow." Then she looked at me. "Thank you," she said. "You've done a lot for us. Don't think I don't know how much. And I haven't thanked you."

"You're welcome." I put my arm around her, the gesture automatic, although it felt strange. It felt even stranger when Laurel rested her head against my shoulder. Her hair smelled musty. Her lethargy was nearly palpable, and I felt tired myself all of a sudden, as though the exhaustion was catching. "I'm glad to do it," I said. "I love taking care of Maggie. She's a joy."

"She always cries with me."

"Maybe she picks up on your...your sadness," I said. "I know you don't want to think about it, but you really *may* need some, you know, professional help to pull out of this."

Laurel's body stiffened beneath my arm. She grabbed the counter and stood up, and I knew the spell was broken for both of us.

"I brought groceries," I said, getting to my own feet. "Can I make you some lunch?"

Laurel started for the couch. "Not hungry," she said.

She was so thin. I saw the long ridges of her shoulder blades beneath the back of her T-shirt, like the beginning of angel wings, and I knew that, no matter what happened from this day forward, I would no longer be able to wish her dead.

Chapter Fourteen

Maggie

UNCLE MARCUS WAS AT THE FIRE STATION, SO IT WOULD JUST be Mom, Andy, Kimmie and me at dinner. I wanted to meet this girl Andy was so nuts about. I still had trouble picturing him with a girlfriend.

Mom had asked me to grill the chicken while she made mashed potatoes and snap peas, but I didn't want to be out on the deck. There were still a couple of news vans in front of the house, plus anyone in a boat would be able to see me from the sound. I was getting paranoid. I'd already made the late-afternoon news. When I got home from my appointment, Mom said they'd showed film of me racing backward down the driveway like a maniac.

"Why did you do that, sweetie?" she'd asked me. "Were you scared?"

"Yeah, I guess," I said. She hugged me and I got teary all over again. I was a mess today, and I was mad at myself for giving the stupid reporters such a perfect opportunity to talk about me again. I wasn't going out on the deck to give them another Maggie Lockwood display.

Mom understood, and she grilled the chicken while I made the mashed potatoes and snap peas and Andy made the salad. I whipped Mom's potatoes without butter in a separate bowl. That part of

Mom hadn't changed—she was still a health freak. Still jogged all the time and took a dozen vitamins in the morning and watched every smidgen of trans-fat she put in her mouth. But she'd changed a lot in other ways. I could honestly say I never knew what it felt like to have a real mother before. Now I knew. It felt like a safety net, made out of self-healing fabric, that would always be there for me. I guessed I'd always loved her, but I never felt like she loved me back until now. Until this year. Bizarre. Screw up royally and suddenly I had a mother.

Kimmie's father dropped her off just as Mom finished grilling the chicken. Oh my God, I so got why Andy was gaga over this girl! In person, Kimmie's looks were even more intriguing than in the picture Andy showed me. Her thick dark hair hung nearly to her waist, and those green eyes were beautiful, though almost eerie, against her dark skin. I'd never seen anything like them before. She had a pronounced limp that I forgot the second I saw her wide, white smile. Her personality wasn't exactly typical, either. I loved my brother with every bit of my heart, but I never honestly thought a girl could love him, too. Kimmie did. I was sure of it. When she walked into the kitchen with Andy, I saw how she was looking at him. She could barely take her eyes off him to glance at me. I'd always thought of Andy, with his curly brown hair and big dark eyes, as cute. All of a sudden, I could see what a girl his age might see in him. He was very short, true, but he was good-looking. The right girl might even think he was hot.

"I'm making the salad," he told Kimmie after he finally got around to introducing me to her. He pointed to the cutting board. "I'm cutting the green pepper."

"I'll cut the tomato," she said, pulling a knife from the knife block near the stove.

I watched them as I covered the bowls of mashed potatoes with aluminum foil to keep them warm. Kimmie directed his chopping, and it was like she was half girlfriend, half mother to him. That was exactly the kind of girl he needed in his life.

When we sat down at the kitchen table to eat, Kimmie said grace, something we never bothered with, although I'm pretty sure we did when Daddy was alive.

"Thank you, heavenly father, for this beautiful food," she said, "and for bringing Andy's sister, Maggie, home safe and sound. Amen."

"Amen," Andy and Mom said. Clearly, they knew this new-to-me routine with Kimmie. As for me, I wasn't sure I'd be able to swallow any of the "beautiful food" around the lump in my throat.

"Thank you, Kimmie," I said. "That was really nice."

We started passing plates and bowls around the table.

"So," Kimmie said to Andy after we'd been eating awhile, "I don't understand why you had to look at all those boxes."

Andy remembered to swallow whatever he was chewing before he answered. "Because of Miss Sara going missing, and she had a box," he said.

Kimmie rolled her eyes. "That makes no sense," she said.

I wanted to come to his defense. I didn't like it when anyone put down my brother. I opened my mouth to say something, but Mom held up a hand to shush me.

"Yes, too, it makes sense," Andy said.

"Explain it better," Kimmie said. "I know Mrs. Weston went missing. Where did she have a box?"

"In the trailer."

Kimmie waited. If it had been up to me, I would have asked him another question, like *when* did she have the box? What was she doing with it? That's how Mom and Uncle Marcus and I always handled Andy. But Kimmie had her own way, and although I itched with discomfort that she wasn't doing it "right," Mom obviously didn't want me to jump in.

"I woke up and she carried a box with a pot on it," Andy said. "Outside. I think she carried it outside. But I got confused at the store."

"I can picture it now," Kimmie said. "The police wanted to find out if you saw a box at the store like the one she carried."

"Right." Andy looked at me. "Kimmie's real smart."

"Everybody's got things they're good at and things they're not good at," Kimmie said.

"Like I swim good," Andy said. "Even though not as good as I used to."

"You're an awesome swimmer," Kimmie said. She looked at me. "My father said I'm the brains and Andy's the brawn, and together we make a perfect person."

Oh, wow. I felt that lump in my throat again. What was with me? What she said was so sweet. At the same time, though, I wanted to reach over, clench her wrist in my hand and say, "Don't you ever, *ever* hurt him!"

I was trying to figure her out. She was not quite all there when it came to brainpower, but she was more all there than Andy. IQ-wise, she was probably somewhere around his low normal range, but she didn't have his developmental issues. His "concrete thinking," as Mom always called it. Kimmie didn't seem to have that burden. Plus, unlike Andy, she had some definite social skills.

"Andy said you're going to do community service at his school," she said to me, like an adult might say to start a conversation.

"Not at his school," I said. "At the elementary school right near his." I'd start there on Monday. Way too soon. I wished I had another week—better yet, another *month*—before I had to be so public.

"Why don't you do your commutity service at my school?" Andy asked.

"Community," Mom corrected.

"Because Mom already got the okay for me to do it at Douglas Elementary, since she works there."

Andy stuck his fork in a piece of green pepper. "My friend Max's sister goes there," he said, "and his father doesn't want you there. So you should come to my school."

I stopped my glass of water halfway to my mouth and looked at my mother. "Is it going to be a problem?" I asked.

"I don't think so," Mom said. "Not with Ms. Terrell's and Mrs. Hadley's blessings."

"We can watch a movie after dinner," Andy said to Kimmie, as if he'd already forgotten we were talking about my community service.

"You have some makeup work to do, Andy," Mom said.

"I'll help you with your homework and then we can watch," Kimmie said.

"Don't do it for him, Kimmie," Mom warned.

Kimmie rolled her eyes. She had that move perfected. "I never do, Miss Laurel," she said.

I started clearing the dishes once Kimmie and Andy'd left the room. "She's really cute," I said to Mom.

"She's good for him, I think." Mom opened the dishwasher.

"It's weird, though," I said.

"What is?"

I tried to find the words. "Seeing someone else talk to him like family."

"Well, it took a while. You've missed out on watching their relationship develop."

I scraped the leftover potatoes into a plastic container. I'd missed out on so much this year. Watching the relationship between Uncle Marcus and Mom develop, too, for example. So much had changed. Me, most of all.

I snapped the lid on the container. "Are they, like…physical?" I asked.

Mom stopped loading the dishwasher. "You mean, sexual?"

"Whatever," I said. I couldn't picture it.

"Oh, *please,* don't even think it!" Mom laughed. "Both Marcus and I have talked to him about…you know, not getting too close. We supervise them, and the rule is, when they're in his room—or Kimmie's—the door needs to be open. Her parents are on the same page. When we were at Wal-Mart today, though, Andy told me they've hugged a few times. I figure as long as he's so comfortable telling me what's going on, we're safe. I've seen them hold hands, but that's about it. It's cute."

"It's what they do when you *can't* see them that matters," I said.

"You sound like Marcus."

"Well, really, Mom. Did you think I was doing what I was doing?"

She didn't say anything. Just went back to loading dishes, and what I'd said hung there in the air.

"You haven't mentioned your therapy appointment," Mom said when I handed her a rinsed plate. "I don't want to pry, but were you pleased? Does she seem like someone you'll be able to connect to?"

I laughed. "Well, first of all, Marion Jakes is a man. He's old and he weighs about four hundred pounds."

"*No.*"

"Really. Well, three hundred, anyway."

She got the dishwasher soap from under the sink and poured some into the cup. "Aside from that, how was it?" she asked.

I thought about how much crying I'd done in his office. It embarrassed me now to remember it.

"It was okay," I said. "I think it's a waste of time, though. I've had a whole year to think about what happened with Ben and the fire and everything. But I have to go, so I'll go."

"I think it's important, Maggie," Mom said as she closed the dishwasher door. "There's a big difference between thinking about what happened on your own and talking it over with a therapist."

"I guess." It was easiest to just agree.

The phone rang and I dried my hands, then checked the caller ID.

"It's Uncle Marcus," I said, pressing the talk button. "Hey," I said.

"Hey, Maggie. How great it is to hear *you* answer the phone. I'm so glad you're home."

"Me, too," I said. "You have no idea. Did you want to talk to Mom?"

"I'll tell you first," he said. "I just heard from Flip that there was an anonymous call to the Crime Stoppers tip line about an hour ago."

"*Really?* What did they say?"

"The caller said that he—or she, I'm not sure which—saw a man and woman walk into the woods behind the Food Lion in Hampstead Monday afternoon. They didn't get a very good look, but the description of the woman could possibly match Sara."

"Oh, no." I repeated what he'd said to my mother. She pressed her hands to her mouth. "Did they say anything else?" I asked.

"The man was walking very close to the woman, so she was possibly being coerced."

"Oh, no," I said again.

"What?" Mom said.

I handed the phone to her. Suddenly, the whole bit about Sara disappearing felt real to me. Up until that moment, all the work I'd done—getting her profile up on the Internet, talking to the woman at the Project Jason Web site Officer Cates had mentioned, making the flyer and everything else—had felt like busywork. It hadn't really sunk in that something terrible might have happened to her. I couldn't stand the thought of her being forced into the woods by a man, much less what might have happened to her after that. And poor Keith. I remembered again how pissed off he'd sounded during the meeting the night before and thought of something Letitia told me the second time Lizard beat me up. "Her anger comes from her fear," she'd said. "You remember that." It had made no sense to me then. Lizard afraid? I didn't think so. But now I got it. I got that Keith sounded so pissed off because he was scared. Who wouldn't be scared when their mother went missing?

I sat down at the table, watching my own mother's worried face while she listened to Uncle Marcus. When she got off the phone, she was pale.

"He said it's probably a blind lead." She leaned back against the counter, one hand pressed against her cheek. "He said there are these people who are...serial anonymous tipsters, he called them. They get their jollies leading the police on a wild-goose chase and that's probably what this will turn out to be."

"But they can't just ignore it!" I said.

"No, they won't. Tomorrow morning, there'll be a search of the woods behind the Food Lion. Flip's calling a few searchers with dogs, and he asked if Dawn and I could make calls tonight to get volunteers out to help."

She opened the cabinet door where we kept a list of phone numbers for friends and neighbors. Then she reached for the phone.

I watched her, scared and ashamed, because I knew I wouldn't be one of those volunteers. No way could I be out in the open with other Topsail people all around me. I'd do anything I could to help from the safety of my house, but I wasn't ready to go out in public. Not for my half brother, or for Sara.

Not for anyone.

Chapter Fifteen

Keith

WE WERE SUPPOSED TO WALK NEXT TO EACH OTHER, JUST a few feet apart, as we moved slowly—and I *do* mean slowly—through the woods behind the Food Lion. We'd move forward ten feet at a time, then stop and examine every square inch of ground and rock and grass and weed and shrub around us. I never realized how much trash was in the woods. Soda and beer bottles all over the place. Food wrappers from Ding Dongs and Twinkies. Paper bags from McDonald's. Empty cardboard boxes, still soggy from the last rain. Somebody's shoe. *Oh, shit.* I nearly had a heart attack when one of the volunteers shouted out that he'd found a shoe. But it was a kid's shoe. A sneaker. Nothing that could've belonged to my mother.

Sue Charles, one of my mother's friends, was walking on my right side and she said she couldn't get over how calm I looked. Yeah, well, looks could be deceiving. First, I was in a shitload of pain. I'd only taken one Percocet that morning so my head would be clear. I'd been doubling up on them since Monday and now one just wasn't holding me. Plus, I ate a can of that chili the night before. Mistake. My gut was doing somersaults, and thoughts—none of them good—flew through my head a hundred miles a minute. I was afraid we wouldn't find anything, and more afraid that we would.

This search felt like too damn little too damn late. My mother went missing Monday and here it was Friday and the cops were only now getting around to doing an actual search. Of course, they didn't have that anonymous tipster until last night, but they could've done more by now than just badger me with questions. Marcus said it was all happening behind the scenes, but as far as I could tell, the volunteers were doing most of the work, taking the flyers all over the place and calling hospitals and stuff. I wished my mother could've seen what people were doing to try to find her. I knew she sometimes felt like she didn't have many friends. Like people didn't really care.

Now that the cops had this anonymous tip, here was their new theory: She made it to the parking lot of the Food Lion. The checkers working that day didn't see her, so she probably didn't make it inside. Instead, some guy got to her in the parking lot and forced her to go with him into the woods. Then he did whatever he did to her—I didn't want to think about it—and then stole her car, since it wasn't in the lot. Possibly, he took her with him. Like maybe he raped her in the woods and then forced her back into the car. By now they could be in Siberia.

So now we were searching, and I couldn't believe how many people had joined in. That was the one cool thing about the whole mess. The cops might've been twiddling their thumbs, but nobody else was. Some of the Food Lion employees were out here. A bunch of marines from Camp Lejeune. A couple of cops on horseback. Two volunteers with trained dogs. Strangers from as far away as Raleigh. Miss Trish had made sure the news about my mother was on TV stations all over the state, plus in Virginia and South Carolina. Her press release mentioned me, though, and I wished she'd left me out of it. TV stations talked about how my mother had almost lost me in the big Surf City fire, etcetera, etcetera. They wanted to interview me and I said forget it. If it would help, yeah, okay, I would've done it, but I couldn't see what difference it would make. It'd just give people a chance to look at the burned guy's screwed-up face. No thanks.

Way down at one end of the search line was this girl I swore looked like that Jen chick from Harris Teeter. She had on a blue cap and her black hair was in a ponytail, and she was skinny, but I couldn't get a good look at her. It probably wasn't her, anyway. She was just on my mind, so I thought I saw her everywhere. Besides, this search was about my mother, not about me, and definitely not about the Harris Teeter chick.

After a few hours, some people started peeling off from the search line. The girl who looked like Jen must have been one of them, because I didn't see her again. I didn't blame anyone for leaving. The going was so damn slow and boring and we were deep into the woods by then. The day was cloudy, and with all the trees, the ground was pretty dark and it was hard to tell a leaf from a Ding Dong wrapper. I had a killer headache and had stopped to rub my forehead when a man suddenly let out a holler.

"I found something!" he yelled. "I think it's a body!"

He was a long way from me, and even though we were supposed to stay in line no matter what, I took off in his direction.

"Keith!" Sue Charles called after me. "Stay here!"

I kept going, tripping over branches and rocks and dodging tree trunks. A bunch of people surrounded the guy, and leaves flew through the air as if he was digging through a pile of them to get at whatever he found.

Marcus Lockwood suddenly jumped in front of me, grabbing my shoulders and blocking me from going any farther.

"Let me go!" I was so winded from running, I could hardly get the words out as I tried to twist away from him. My lungs burned.

"Just hold on," Marcus said.

I pushed against him, but he wasn't budging. Man, the dude was strong. The pain in my left shoulder felt like a sword cutting through the muscle. "Let me go!" I shouted again. "It's not *your* mother. I want to see."

"Let the police find out what—"

"False alarm!" one of the marines shouted. "It's just a deer."

Marcus let go of my arms, and my legs suddenly gave out. I dropped to my butt on the ground, and before I knew what I was doing, I put my head in my hands and cried like a fucking baby.

Chapter Sixteen

Maggie

I FELT LIKE SUCH A FAKE WHEN I DROVE INTO THE FACULTY parking lot at Douglas Elementary. Mom swore that's where I was supposed to park and she even gave me a placard that said Faculty on it for me to hang from my rearview mirror. But I felt like, by parking there, I was asking for special treatment I didn't deserve.

Douglas had been my own elementary school years and years ago. As a kid, I'd imagined maybe returning someday as a teacher. I never imagined returning as an ex-con.

I leaned over the passenger seat in my car, pretending to be gathering up my purse and things in case anyone was watching. Really, though, I was gathering up the courage to walk through the parking lot and into the school. It hadn't scared me all that much when Mom suggested I do my community service there. I was picturing the first graders. I hadn't pictured the other teachers who would know who I was and why I was there. I'd once been so self-confident. Even a little conceited. Top of my class. Popular and all that. I'd really done a number on my life.

It had taken me just as long to get out of my car near the Food Lion on Friday. I hadn't planned to join the search for Sara, but I couldn't sleep Thursday night, thinking about her. I'd spent most of my life loving Sara, but when I found out she'd had an affair with

Daddy, I felt nearly as betrayed as Mom did. Sara probably felt just as betrayed by me and what I did, though. Which was more normal? Having an affair or burning kids to death? Right.

I'd wrecked Sara's and Keith's lives a year and a half ago. I owed her more than getting her picture up on the Internet and putting together a few flyers. She was in trouble. Maybe lying hurt in the woods. Maybe even dead. All I had to worry about was a little humiliation. Joining the search was the right thing to do.

Friday morning, though, I almost chickened out again. But I put my hair up under a hat and borrowed Mom's ugly big sunglasses, which I eventually had to take off anyway because it was so dark in the woods. Andy spent the day at the Carmichaels' house; Mom didn't think the search was such a great idea for him, not knowing what we'd find—which turned out to be exactly nothing. I told Mom and Uncle Marcus I'd drive myself to the Food Lion so no one would see me get out of Mom's car and know who I was. I just didn't want people to go "Hey! There's Maggie Lockwood. Home from jail."

By the time I got to the Food Lion parking lot, there were so many cars and so many people that I knew I would blend in without a problem. I saw Keith—oh my God, his poor face! He didn't look as if he'd stepped out of a horror movie or anything, but scars covered one whole side of his face and were impossible to miss. As soon as I saw him, I turned and walked in the other direction, getting into the search line as far from him as I possibly could.

I stayed with the search all morning. I saw a bunch of people I knew, including Amber Donnelly, who used to be my best friend back before Ben. I guessed she was home from college for a long weekend, and she was walking the search line with a few other girls from my high-school class. I was glad no one knew who I was. It was hard enough just seeing everybody, knowing I was no longer a part of them and their world and never would be again.

Now in the school parking lot, I looked at my watch. Seven forty-five, which was the time I was supposed to be in Mrs. Hadley's classroom.

"Grow up," I told myself, and got out of my car.

There were a lot of parents, both mothers and fathers, near the entrance to the school. Dropping their kids off, I figured, but then I realized they were standing in a line, all facing the parking lot. Facing *me*. There must have been twenty of them. What was going on?

I slowed down, unsure what to do. Turn around? Walk straight ahead like nothing was going on?

"Go home!" one of them shouted, and a few more joined in with the same words until it sounded like a chant. *Go home, go home, go home!*

I took another couple of steps forward.

"You're not going in there!" a woman shouted at me.

"I'm supposed to work in Mrs. Hadley's classroom today," I called out, like this whole thing was a misunderstanding and they were keeping me from helping a teacher.

"You're not getting anywheres near our children!" a man yelled. He had a bushy blond beard and a deep, gruff voice that sounded like he'd been smoking since he was in diapers. I suddenly felt truly afraid, and I froze at the curb of the parking lot.

"Get off school property!" one of the women shouted.

I felt a *thud* against my arm and looked down at the ground to see an apple lying by my feet. I lifted my purse in front of my face as another one whizzed past my head. That was it. I was out of there.

I was starting to turn around, when a tiny African-American woman suddenly pushed open the door from inside the school. The line of parents parted for her, and I knew she had to be the principal, Ms. Terrell. She marched over to me on high heels.

"Ms. Lockwood?" she said as she came closer.

My cheeks burned as I nodded. "I'm not sure what to do," I said.

She didn't stop walking. "Come with me," she said as she passed me, and I followed her nearly to the middle of the parking lot, where she turned to face me. Out on the street, I saw one of the dreaded white vans, this one with a colorful peacock logo on its side. Oh, no. I took a step to the left so my back was to it.

"This clearly isn't going to work out," she said. "When I gave your mother the green light and Mrs. Hadley said she was fine with it, I didn't count on this." She waved her hand toward the parents. "I had to let them know you'd be working in the classroom, and I got a few concerned phone calls over the weekend, but I thought I'd put out the fire."

I winced at her choice of words. "It's okay," I said. I just wanted to get back in my car and go home.

"This organization on the part of the parents was unexpected," she said. "I can't put *your* needs over those of the students, and since the parents are refusing to bring their children to school as long as you're here, this won't work out."

I glanced back at the determined faces. "It's okay," I said again.

"You understand my position," she said. It wasn't a question.

"They hate me," I said.

"It's not a matter of liking or hating. They feel as though they have to protect their children."

I'm harmless, I wanted to say. "Okay." I hiked the strap of my purse higher on my shoulder. "Sorry. I...I'm sorry about this whole thing."

* * *

No one was around when I got home. I made sure all the doors and windows were locked, then went up to my room and lay down on my bed, the teddy bear in my arms. When I shut my eyes, I saw the angry, ugly faces of the parents in front of the school entrance. We lived in a kind, softhearted part of the world, and they were probably kind, softhearted people most of the time. I brought out the mean side in them. How many of them knew me personally? Some did, I was sure of it. Some were probably the parents of my former friends—my friends from before I flipped out. They'd probably wanted their kids to hang out with me back then, hoping a little of me would rub off on their own children. Now they thought I was crazy or dangerous. Maybe both.

I couldn't do this community-service thing, I thought, running my fingers over the angora on the bear's back. You needed a *community* to do that in, and I'd lost mine a year and a half ago, destroying it myself in a plume of smoke.

Chapter Seventeen

Sara
Private and Deep
1990

THERE WERE EMOTIONAL AFFAIRS AND THEN THERE WERE physical affairs. Before meeting Jamie, I thought a physical affair would be the far more devastating, destructive and complicated of the two. Now I knew that an emotional affair was even more dangerous. It created a need to share every thought and feeling with another person. It seduced you into being entirely vulnerable while still feeling entirely safe. That was what I was having with Jamie: an emotional affair. It ran deeper and darker than I could ever have imagined.

I didn't even *want* a sexual affair with him. Sex was overrated. I'd never truly enjoyed it. I'd never even had an orgasm. When I watched an actress writhing with pleasure in a movie, I wondered if the problem rested in Steve's lovemaking or in myself. Steve seemed perfectly content. He was one of those men who would fall asleep two seconds after he came, while I lay awake, longing for conversation, for the closeness the sex hadn't given me.

I was finding that closeness in Jamie. I saw him nearly every day, sharing the care of a child with him, sharing the *love* of that child. Jamie and Maggie gave my life purpose and joy. It was impossible not to get close.

One afternoon when Maggie was fifteen months old, I was pushing her in a shopping cart at the commissary when I spotted a firefighter walking toward us. He was a big man, and although it was August, he was dressed in bulky tan-and-yellow turnout gear. Was there an emergency in the commissary? I looked over my shoulder to see if something was going on behind me.

"Hey!" he said, and I saw the smile. The eyes. *Jamie!* In the *commissary?*

Maggie heard his voice and twisted around in the seat of the cart. "Dada!" she cried, reaching for him.

"What are you doing here?" I asked as he scooped Maggie out of the cart and hugged her to him. "Is something wrong?" He wasn't supposed to pick up Maggie for another few hours after his shift as a volunteer firefighter ended.

"Everything's fine." He pressed his lips to Maggie's cheek. His soot-streaked face was damp with perspiration, and he smelled of smoke.

I felt a smile spread across my face. Anyone watching me was sure to know I loved this man, and I didn't care. "How did you get in?" I asked. He had no military ID.

"That's why I kept on my uniform." He nibbled Maggie's fingers and she giggled. "I figured they wouldn't turn me away. And they didn't."

"Did you come straight from a fire?" I still couldn't get over seeing him there. "Are you sure you're okay? You must be roasting in that jacket."

"Just needed to see my baby girl." He settled Maggie in his arms and she rested her head against his shoulder, her dark curly hair mixing with his. Jamie glanced in my cart. "Are you almost finished? Can we go back to your house so I can get a shower?"

I no longer cared about the groceries. "I've got everything I need," I said, and I meant those words in more ways than one.

In my little house, I put away the groceries while he showered. *This feels so right,* I thought, listening to the spray of water behind the bathroom door. *This is how a woman should feel when the man she cares about is in the house.* My happiness was so simple and pure. If only I felt that way when Steve was home. Right then, I was glad he was back in Monterey, three thousand miles away, this time for two weeks.

I was feeding Maggie in the high chair by the time Jamie came out of the shower.

"Dada!" Maggie said again, but she was too intent on the yogurt she was eating to raise her arms to him this time.

Jamie leaned against the doorjamb between the hallway and the kitchen, smiling, his arms folded.

"Are you going to tell me why you're here so early?" I asked. I'd almost said *home* so early.

"The fire was brutal," he said. "It was in a third-story apartment and there were these twin baby girls about Maggie's age."

"Oh, no." I set down the container of yogurt.

"No, it turned out okay," Jamie said.

"Ehh! Ehh!" Maggie reached for the yogurt and I gave her another spoonful.

"I was able to find them and get them out," Jamie said. "I had to give one of them CPR, but they're both okay. I just had a need to see my Maggie girl before I did anything else."

"Ah," I said. "Of course you did."

He crossed the room, took the spoon from me and gave me a gentle shove. "May I?"

"Da." Maggie showed off her tiny new teeth in a grin.

"I'll get her things ready," I said. I went into the nursery—Maggie's nursery, never Sam's—and packed the diaper bag. Where my heart had felt light only half an hour earlier, now it was weighed down. In a few minutes, they'd be gone. Both of them. I'd be alone again.

"Sara."

I turned to see Jamie holding Maggie in the nursery doorway.

"She's done already?" I asked.

"Yes. And I was wondering… I know it's too early, but if we put her in the crib right now, do you think she'd fuss or do you think she'd be quiet for a little while?"

I looked at him, and I knew what he was really asking. Why it didn't surprise me when we'd never talked about it before—had never even come *close* to talking about it—I couldn't say. I only knew that I loved him, and that he'd had no one to love him—not *that* way—in more than a year.

I stepped forward, reaching for Maggie, who came willingly into my arms. "Come here, Mags," I said. "How would you like your special fishbowl? The magic fishbowl?"

"Fiss," Maggie said.

"Dim the light, Jamie."

As he lowered the light switch, I reached over the crib rail and let Maggie slip from my arms to the mattress. She let out one small wail of alarm as she realized she was being put to bed way before it was time, but I quickly pressed the button on the magic fishbowl attached to the end of the crib.

"And here's your blankie, honey."

Maggie took the small flannel blanket from my hands, but her eyes were already so wide with wonder that I could see the reflection of the blue and yellow fish in them.

I walked toward Jamie. "That should give us a good half—"

He stopped my talking with a sudden kiss, his hands in my hair, and we stumbled from the nursery to the bedroom, where I discovered more—*much* more—of what I'd been missing with Steve.

"That was longer than a half hour," Jamie said after we'd been making love for close to two hours.

"You'll have hell to pay tonight." Instantly, I regretted what I'd said. I'd meant that Maggie wouldn't sleep well after this long, post-dinner nap, but the "you" in my sentence was plural, including both Jamie and Laurel. He and I both knew it.

"It was worth it," Jamie said. He lifted my hand to his lips, kissing my palm, then the backs of my fingers.

Don't go, I thought. *Please don't go.* Yet now Laurel was in my mind. I had struggled to befriend her, and she occasionally seemed to welcome my friendship. What was she doing right now? Right this minute? Was she thinking of the little girl in my nursery? The man in my arms?

"I love you," Jamie said suddenly.

They were words I'd never once heard from Steve. I raised myself on an elbow to look down at him. "I love you, too," I said.

He ran his fingers down my throat and over my collarbone. There was sadness in his face that I didn't want to see.

"Jamie," I said. "If you and Laurel split up, you and Maggie could live here."

"*What?* Sara—"

"It's Steve's idea. He wants to rent out our extra room. He said you and Maggie could live here. We'd have to charge you rent, but that way I could watch her all the time."

Jamie shook his head. "Sara, why are you saying this? Why are you bringing Steve and Laurel into this room right now?"

Why *was* I? I started to cry.

"Sara, Sara." He wrapped his arms around me and rocked me against his chest. "I'm sorry," he said. "I'm so sorry. But you know I can't leave Laurel."

"I know. I'm not asking you to. I wouldn't do that." I didn't want to be one of those women who grew clingy and needy during an affair. I didn't want to be one of those women who'd *have* an affair. Cheaters. Liars. Yet now I *was* one of them and although I couldn't deny the guilt I felt, I suddenly understood those women better. How many of them lived hollow lives like mine? "I just wanted you to know what Steve suggested," I said.

Jamie rocked me awhile longer, and I knew by the loud sound of his breathing that he was troubled. I wished I hadn't said anything about him moving in.

"This was a mistake," he said.

"No!" I raised my head to look at him again. "No. I didn't even know I wanted to do this, but now I realize that it was absolutely *necessary.*"

He laughed. "Necessary, huh?" He kissed the tip of my nose. "You're quite the romantic."

I laughed with him, hoping the lightness in his voice would last. It didn't.

"It was a mistake," he said again. "Steve's a good man and I bet if you tried, you could find some...common interests. You walk on eggshells around him. You need to communicate. To tell him what you want."

I rested my head on his chest again, breathing in the scent of him. Trying to memorize it, because I knew he was telling me there would be no other evenings like this one.

"And Laurel is—" he hesitated "—she *was* a wonderful wife and she will be again."

"I won't ever feel about Steve the way I feel about you," I whispered.

He swallowed loudly a couple of times. "Tonight was my fault," he said. "We can't always have what we want in life. I should know that by now." He let go of me, and the air was cool where it hit my bare skin. "Help me, okay?" he asked. "Let's never do this again."

Two weeks later, Steve came home from California. We made love the night of his homecoming, and I had the bizarre feeling that I was cheating on Jamie in spite of the fact that we hadn't made love again since that one time. I tried to capture with Steve the physical passion I'd felt with Jamie, but it was hopeless. I simply didn't feel it. I knew Jamie was right and that I needed to talk to Steve, to tell him what I wanted from our marriage, in bed and out, but the words wouldn't come. Steve was just Steve. Nothing I said would change him.

Late in September, Jamie did what he said he would never do: he left Laurel.

I arrived at the chapel office to take care of Maggie. I'd seen Jamie nearly every day since our "mistake," and although we acted as we always had with one another, I knew there was a difference. I felt him looking at me when I played with Maggie. He brushed his fingers over mine when he handed me a toy or the blankie. It was not my imagination. There was a hunger in him that he struggled to tamp down. I recognized it because I shared it.

"I need to talk to you," he said that morning as he poured a cup of coffee from his thermos.

"Missu!" Maggie lifted her arms in the air to be picked up, and I saw the huge bandage on her left hand.

"Maggie, honey!" I lifted her into my arms. "What happened to you?"

"Have a seat," Jamie said.

"Don't you need to get to the real-estate office?"

"I need to talk to you first." He motioned toward Maggie's hand. "This happened yesterday. I got called to a fire, so Laurel took her out on the beach and Maggie picked up a board with a rusty nail and cut her hand."

"Oh, no." I kissed the bandage. "Did you get a boo-boo, Maggie?"

"Laurel couldn't handle it," Jamie said.

"What do you mean?"

"I mean she lost it. Marcus heard Maggie screaming. Thank God he was there. Laurel was trying to run water over the cut, but she… Marcus said she just panicked. Freaked out. Started crying and let go of Maggie and didn't seem to know what to do."

"But she's a nurse," I said. It was extremely hard to picture Laurel as a nurse.

"Well, that was the old Laurel," Jamie said with a sigh. "I feel sad for her. She was trying to be a real mother to Maggie. Taking her out on the beach to play with her. You know what an effort that must have been for her."

I nodded.

"Anyway, we talked last night and she said…she said she wanted to leave. That Maggie and I would be better off without her."

"Oh, Jamie!" I hurt for him. I truly did. But I was also thinking, *what does this mean for me?*

Jamie looked out the window toward the inlet. "She doesn't want the responsibility of Maggie right now. She knows she can't handle being a mother, but she won't get help, and I don't know what I can do about it." Jamie had been able to talk Laurel into one appointment with a psychiatrist, but she'd refused to go back. "One thing I know is that I can't let *her* be the one to leave the Sea Tender. She'd be so lost."

I rested my hand on his. "You know you have a place to go," I said. "You and Maggie."

He nodded. Pressed his lips together. "If it's still okay with you and Steve, maybe we could try it for a while," he said.

"Of *course,*" I said.

"It'll just be temporary." Jamie sounded as if he was trying to warn me of something, but if he was, I didn't hear it. I was already making plans. I'd cook for them. Take care of them. And I'd erase the frown lines that were deepening by the day across Jamie's forehead.

Having Jamie and Maggie in the house worked out better than I could have imagined. Steve was gone so much, and I loved Jamie's company. When Steve *was* around, I got a kick out of watching a different side of Jamie emerge—the masculine side that could talk sports and cars. It was a facet of his personality I'd had no idea existed. He used to ride a motorcycle, he told Steve, and the two men even went to a motorcycle show together in Raleigh. Jamie and I kept careful distance from each other, even more so when Steve was out of town than when he was there. A witness would never guess we'd ever been lovers. But even though we didn't touch, the longer Jamie was there, the deeper in love I fell.

In September, I missed my period. I'd never been very regular, but when I missed it again in October and felt queasy two mornings in a row, I went to my gynecologist, who told me what I already knew: I was eight weeks pregnant. Eight weeks earlier, Steve had been in the middle of his training in California.

I was both excited and terrified. I was pregnant! No baby could ever replace Sam, but how I'd longed to try again! Yet it wasn't Steve's baby, and I had no idea what Jamie would say.

I called him at the real-estate office as soon as I got home from the doctor. I hated to tell him over the phone, but Steve would be home that night, and I'd have no privacy then to speak to him.

"I'm eight weeks pregnant," I said less than a second after he said hello.

He didn't respond right away and I twisted the phone cord in my hand, waiting.

"Hold on a minute," he said.

He spoke to someone, then I heard the sound of a door being closed. Finally, he was back on the line.

"How do you feel?" he asked.

"Do you mean physically or emotionally?"

"Is it mine?" he asked.

"Yes."

"Oh, God," he said. "I'm sorry. I should have been more careful."

"I'm *happy*," I said. "I want this baby so much, Jamie."

"Are you...will you let Steve think it's his?"

I paused, wishing, hoping, he would say the things I needed him to say. "Only if I have to," I said. "Only if you won't..." I squeezed the phone cord again. "I can divorce him," I said.

"Sara," Jamie said, "I can't leave Laurel."

For the first time in the nearly two years since I'd known him, I was angry with him.

"That's crazy, Jamie!" I said. "You've *already* left her. You left her emotionally a long time ago, and now you've left her physically. You *live* with us, remember? You live with *me.*" Although the truth was, he went to the Sea Tender often to check on Laurel. So did I, for that matter, building a friendship with her to ease my guilt over my feelings for Jamie. I pretended to myself as well as to the world that I cared for them both. God, what a sloppy, crazy, twisted life I was living!

Jamie responded with his usual calm. "I'll help you any way I can, but I don't think either Laurel or I expect our separation to be permanent, Sara," Jamie said. "I've told you that. She's still sick. Sicker than before, really. She needs me."

"I need you, too," I said.

"I know, but you have Steve. Laurel only has me."

My anger rose again. "I'm supposed to let this baby...this child...grow up thinking that Steve is his or her father?" I asked. "This baby can't possibly be Steve's."

"But he doesn't know that, does he?"

"But *I* do, and so do you!" I said. "What do you want me to do, Jamie? Just make this baby go away?" I wouldn't have an abortion no matter what he said.

"No, I don't want you to do that," he said. "Look, Sara. I'll support you whatever you choose to do."

"What does that *mean?*"

"I'll support you financially. Emotionally." He hesitated. "You know I love you."

Tears burned my eyes. Yes, I knew he loved me. That's what made this all the more painful.

"I'll love the baby, too," he said. "And I'm sorry this is so hard for you. But I have a commitment to Laurel and Maggie that I can't break."

"What about me?" I asked. "Where do I fit in?"

He hesitated. "Sara," he said finally, "what I have with Laurel is public and shallow. What I have with you is private and deep. Which part of me would you rather have?"

Chapter Eighteen

Keith

I PULLED INTO ONE OF THE TWO PARKING SPACES IN FRONT of Marcus's tower. His pickup was in the other space and I sat looking at it for a couple of minutes, trying to decide if I should go through with talking to him or just go home instead. I took another Percocet and washed it down with a swig from my water bottle. I was a little spacy from the extra Percs, but I needed them. I could swear the pain was worse every day. I wouldn't talk to Marcus until it eased off a bit. I was uptight enough to begin with.

I'd finally made it back to physical therapy a couple of days earlier. As soon as Gunnar, my therapist, stretched my left arm over my head, I broke out in a sweat.

"You've lost some of your mobility here," he said.

"No shit." I gritted my teeth together.

Gunnar looked like a Viking, tall and blond and ripped. He grew up in Alabama, though, and when he opened his mouth, it was weird to hear that drawl come out. "Have you been keeping up with your exercises?" he asked.

His question pissed me off more than the pain. "It's hard to do them alone," I said.

"Sorry," Gunnar said. "Still no word on your mother, huh?"

I shook my head. I didn't want to talk about it.

"You have to keep your appointments." Gunnar moved my arm out to the side and I squeezed my eyes shut. It felt like he was tearing the scar tissue apart. "It's bad enough about your mother. You don't want to backslide physically, too, now, do you?"

Yeah, that was exactly what I was after. Getting worse.

"We'll fix some way you can do the exercises alone," Gunnar said. He didn't get it. It was more than just having her hold the other end of the exercise band. It was the way she'd cheer me on. The *"you can do it, honey!"* and the *"just two more and I'll make you a banana split."* I hated how she treated me like I was ten years old. But if I got back to the trailer and found her waiting there for me, she could treat me any way she liked.

Today made it a full week. Those critical first forty-eight hours were long gone.

Between the Percocet and the fact that I'd hardly slept since she disappeared, I was wiped out. My mind kept torturing me with those horror stories about what might've happened to her. I just hoped that if some bastard killed her, he made it fast. That was the worst part—picturing her scared, 'cause she would be. I mean, who wouldn't? But being a woman, kind of defenseless like she was, she'd be scared shitless. I had to get up at night and turn on the TV to get those thoughts out of my head.

I thought I saw some movement in one of the second-story windows of Marcus's tower. I scrunched down in my seat, wishing the Percocet would kick in. If I didn't feel better in five minutes, I'd leave. I could hold out another couple of days before I had to talk to him. At least I hoped I could.

It wasn't just the PT appointments I'd been skipping; I wasn't going to school, either. Mrs. Wichewski, one of the guidance counselors, actually came to the trailer the day before. She didn't call

first with a warning or anything. Just showed up at the door. That's
how you knew you were either totally screwed or a charity case or
both. Did I need transportation? she asked. Did I need a tutor? She
shook me up. If she got into my school records, she'd figure out I
was seventeen and I'd be up shit's creek. Wouldn't she have to call
a social worker or something? Right now, I was slipping through the
cracks and that's how I wanted it. The cops weren't all that worried
about me. My mother was missing, but not dead—or at least not
confirmed dead. I was pushing eighteen, so nearly legal anyway.
There were plenty of younger kids who needed help more than I
did, so maybe someone knew I was seventeen and was just letting
me slide. Mrs. Wichewski, though. She could get it in her mind she
needed to save me or something and I'd end up in a foster home
after all.

"What about moving in with a friend's family for now?" she suggested. "You could come to school with your friend, then."

"Yeah, maybe," I said, trying to get her off my case. Like I still
had friends in school. Some graduated, but a lot dropped out. They
were probably spending their days getting high. Not that popping
Percocets was all that different.

The front door to Marcus's tower suddenly opened.

"Keith?" he called.

Busted. No turning back now. I got out of my car.

"Hey," I said.

"I saw your car out here. You all right?"

"Never better." Why did people keep asking me stupid questions
like that? How was I supposed to answer? My mother was gone. I
had a screwed-up face. My arms looked like they were covered in
pink Saran Wrap. I could end up in some group home who knew
where. And now—and this was my reason for coming to see

Marcus—I was almost out of money. My mother's savings account still had a little over a thousand in it—the same amount as when the cops first checked it—but I couldn't get at it. The day of the search, Marcus gave me two hundred bucks to keep me going. Just pulled out his wallet and peeled off ten twenties, like it was no big deal. That two hundred looked like a lot to me, but pizzas and Chinese ate it up, and every time I went to PT, I had to pay a copay. Marcus'd give me more money if I asked for it, but I didn't want to ask. I didn't want his money. I wanted *mine*.

"Come in." He held the door open for me.

I hadn't been inside Marcus's tower for a few years. Probably the last time had been for Andy's tenth or eleventh birthday party. Marcus's house was the coolest on the Island, or close to it, anyway. He'd taken one of the old Operation Bumblebee towers they used back in the forties and added to it, painted it light green and pimped it out with an awesome sound system on every floor. The rooms were small but every one of them had a major view of the ocean, so who cared? The only thing I didn't like about his house was his roof. It was flat, with no railing, and the one time I went up there, I had some kind of panic attack. I wasn't great with heights. And of course, I wasn't great with fire now, either. This week, I could add living alone to my list of phobias. I wasn't afraid someone was going to break in and kill me or anything like that, but I got this weird empty feeling in my chest at night, like maybe I was going to have a heart attack or something. The darker it got outside, the more I felt it. I'd take that feeling over living with a bunch of loser foster kids, though.

I followed Marcus into the living room/dining room/kitchen, and could see some surfers out on the waves. I hadn't surfed since the day my mother went missing.

Marcus stuck his hands in his pockets. "What can I get you to drink?" he asked.

"Beer?"

"Yeah, right. Second choice?"

"Nothing." I sat down on his leather couch. "I just need to ask you a question."

He pulled a bar stool out from beneath the kitchen counter and perched on it. "Shoot," he said.

"You know that college fund you gave my mother?" I'd never talked to him about that money. Never thanked him or anything.

He nodded.

"Well, like, with my mother gone, I need the money. She always told me I couldn't use it for anything except college, though. Is that true?"

He leaned back against the counter. "Here's how it worked, Keith," he said. "I set it up as a trust fund, with your mom as the trustee and with the—I guess they call them directives—that the money only be used for college. In that case, your mother would arrange to have the money paid directly to the school. Unless you were twenty-five. Then the money could go to you."

"But what if I need it now?"

He shook his head. "You can't get at it now." He sat forward, his elbows on his knees. "But listen," he said. "You don't need to worry about money, all right? You tell me what you need and I'll—"

"*You* set the fund up, though, right?" I was getting pissed.

"That's right."

"So why can't you change it now that the, like, the whole situation's different?"

"It's out of my hands. I had nothing to do with it once it was set up. I'm sorry."

I looked out at the surfers. Man, I envied them. Nothing to worry about except catching the next wave. I'd have to get a job. I could just picture going someplace, looking like I did, and asking for work.

"Keith," Marcus said, "you have to let people help you."

I stood up. "No, thanks." I walked toward his door. "I'll figure somethin' out."

"The restitution money!" Marcus said suddenly, getting to his feet. "You get that monthly from Maggie, don't you?"

"The fucking restitution money goes into my mother's account!" I shouted. "I never see it, and the bank won't let me touch it." I reached for his door and started to pull it open, but he grabbed my arm.

"*Shit!*" I squeezed my eyes shut. The pain was like a hot iron running up my arm and into my shoulder.

He let go quickly, his hands in the air. "Oh, buddy!" he said. "I'm sorry!"

"Go to hell." I pulled open the door and went outside, and this time he didn't try to stop me.

The needle on my damn gas gauge was on E as I drove home, and I drove right past a gas station without stopping. I couldn't. Here's how I'd been getting gas since the fire: either Mom would fill the tank for me, or I'd drive to the station in Sneads Ferry, where this burned dude—the one who bought me beer—would take care of it. It wasn't the money that was the problem. It was the smell of gas. I couldn't make myself take the cap off the gas tank, push the start button on the pump and then smell that explosive stuff running into my car. I kept picturing it catching on fire, wrapping me up in flames again. I had actual nightmares about it. I thought the vet from Iraq was the bravest guy I knew to work around something as flammable as gasoline. "It's how I deal with it, man," he told me once. "I decided I'd work in a place where I had to face my fear every damn day." Yeah, well, good for him. I wasn't doing it.

The needle was dropping below the E, actually, and I acted like I didn't notice as I pulled into the trailer park. I'd do something about it later. Just couldn't press that start button today.

Inside the trailer, I turned on the TV, then went into the kitchen to nuke a frozen thing of lasagna. From the living room, I heard those two words that made me want to barf: *Maggie Lockwood*. I went back to the living room to change the station, but I saw ol' Maggie outside what looked like the elementary school, getting pelted by rotten tomatoes or something. A woman news anchor was talking in the background while a line of pissed-off adults showed up on the screen.

"The parents wouldn't let Lockwood into the school," she said as ol' Maggie ducked behind her purse.

"Kill the bitch!" I shouted at the TV. This was the best thing I'd seen in a long time.

Then they interviewed this big blond dude who I figured was one of the parents.

"She can do her community service on the moon," he said. His face was totally red. "She can do it in *I-raq,* for all I care! But she ain't doing it anywhere near our kids."

"You tell 'em!" I said.

The news changed to something about beach erosion, and I went back into the kitchen to take the lasagna out of the microwave. For the first time in a week—hell, maybe the first time in a *year*—I was smiling.

Chapter Nineteen

Maggie

IN FRONT OF ME WAS A CARTFUL OF BOOKS WAITING TO BE shelved. Mom had pulled some of her never-ending strings to get me community-service work at a library in Jacksonville. My job was mainly to organize and shelve books. It was perfect. Hiding in the stacks, I felt anonymous. Of course, the staff knew about me and they weren't exactly friendly, but my supervisor, this middle-aged guy named Gary, didn't mention a thing about who I was or that this was court-mandated community service or anything like that.

Dr. Jakes had wanted me to find my community-service job on my own, but I felt paralyzed after facing that wall of parents at the school. "Your mother's rescuing you," he said when I told him about the library. I explained to him that in my whole life, she never rescued me; she was always too busy rescuing Andy. I was going to enjoy it for now.

I'd made the news again Monday night with film of the parents blocking my way into Douglas Elementary. Mom was totally furious, more with herself for setting me up like that than at the parents. I told her it wasn't her fault. She wasn't the one who just got out of prison. I didn't go anywhere for a few days after that except to sneak out to Dr. Jakes's office. Otherwise, I just hung out in the house. I updated Sara's information on the Internet and printed more flyers for people to hand out, but the whole situation was more upsetting every day. Mom talked about hiring a private investigator with her own money. I thought she should. Keith couldn't afford it, and the police seemed convinced Sara'd just taken off on her own, so how much more would they do?

Yesterday was my first day at the library, and I kept looking through the books as I shelved them. First, I was in the cookbook section, then crafts and knitting and that kind of thing. When I'd finished shelving, I looked up books on finding people who'd gone missing. I ended up checking out eight books, some about missing persons, some about building your self-esteem, since mine was at an all-time low, and a couple of novels.

Gary laughed when he saw me carrying the stack of books out the door. "You're a library gal, all right," he said. It was such a simple thing to say, but it made me feel normal for a change, like he saw me as a nineteen-year-old girl instead of a nineteen-year-old felon.

Today, the cart in front of me had a bunch of books with the call number 133. I couldn't believe it. Of all the books in the library, was it just a coincidence that I had a cartful of books on psychics and life after death and talking to the dead? I got a chill up my spine looking at their covers.

I could still remember feeling Daddy's spirit next to me on the deck of the Sea Tender. I didn't like thinking about it because remembering how *real* his visits felt to me made me feel borderline insane. So most of the time, I blocked those thoughts from my mind. Twice in prison, though, I felt like he was in my cell with me. After the first time Lizard beat the crap out of me, I took the pain pills they gave me and fell asleep on my hard-as-a-rock bed. When I woke up, he was there, sitting next to me and wiping tears from my eyes with his big hands. If someone else told me they experienced something like that, I would have said it was the meds or just a dream, but I knew it wasn't. Which either meant Daddy was truly there or I was truly a fruitcake. The second time, though, I wasn't drugged and I wasn't just waking up. Instead, I was sitting at the little table in my cell, writing in my journal, and I heard him call my name, clear as day. *Maggie.* I turned around and there he was, standing against the bars of my cell. Smiling at me, like he always did. Then he was gone. I freaked out. Maybe I really *was* nuts. I thought I should write about it in my journal, but writing about it would make something concrete out of something mystical. Maybe ruin it for me. Crazy or not, I didn't want to lose the connection I sometimes felt to him.

I sat down on the rolling stool and flipped through some of the books. Of course, they all said it was possible to be in contact with the dead, which made me suspicious right there. I'd done it, and I still didn't believe it.

"Excuse me?"

I looked up from the stool to see a girl around my age peeking around the corner of the stacks.

"Do you work here?" she asked.

I stood up, putting the book I'd been reading back where it belonged in the cart. "I'm a volunteer," I said.

"Do you know how I can look up college information?" she asked.

It wasn't my job to help the patrons, but I sure knew how to look up college information. That had been the story of my life during my junior year—the year before things started up with Ben.

"Sure," I said. "What kind of information do you need?"

"I don't even know where to begin." She smiled, glancing at the stacks. She was incredibly pretty. Model kind of pretty. Really thin. She had almost jet-black hair, stick-straight to her shoulders, with long bangs above blue, blue eyes. And unlike me, she wore makeup. It looked natural, though. Just glossy nude lips and mascara and a tiny bit of eyeliner. A year in a women's prison had *not* turned me into a lesbian or anything close to it, but she was one of those girls you couldn't help staring at.

"Are you talking about how to apply to college or finding the right ones to apply to or financial aid or—"

"Finding the right ones," she said.

"Your high school probably has tons of information," I said. "Have you talked to your guidance counselor?"

She wrinkled her slightly freckled nose. "Damn," she said. "Do I look like I'm still in high school?"

"Oh," I said. "I just figured…"

"I'm nineteen. I just got my GED."

Wow. From the looks of her, I never would have guessed it. I was really curious about her now. She looked so together, like the prom queen who'd hooked up with the star football player. Why'd she drop out? Pregnant? Burned down a church? I was the wounded seeking the wounded. That had been the one and probably only comforting thing about prison. We were all wounded there.

"Congratulations," I said. I had my GED myself, earned behind bars. "So, okay." I led her to the bank of computers, looking over my shoulder for Gary. I hoped I wasn't crossing some invisible line in my volunteer job description. "You know how to use the Internet, right?"

"Sure."

We sat down side by side in front of one of the computers.

"Do you have any idea where you want to go?" I asked.

"Well, no, actually." She laughed. "I only just decided to get my GED a few months ago, so this is all new to me." We were using those quiet, not-quite-whispering library voices. Hers sounded embarrassed by her ignorance. I wanted to pump up her ego a little.

"That's great that you got your GED," I said.

"My mother thinks so. Most definitely."

"Do you live near here?"

"Right now I'm in a family friend's cottage in Topsail Beach," she said. "They're letting me use the cottage for the fall and winter, and then I want to go to college in the spring. I actually live in Asheville, but me and my mother needed some time apart." She laughed again. "You know what I mean."

"Yeah," I said, although I was happier than ever to live with my protective mother for a while. I hadn't always felt that way, though, so I got it. "Do you want to go someplace near Asheville?"

She shrugged. "Not really."

I chewed my lip, trying to remember the Web site I'd found most helpful when I was doing my own search. I typed in a few wrong URLs before hitting the right one.

"This site has everything," I said, moving the cursor across the screen. "You can figure out which colleges have your major, for starters. Do you know what you want to major in?"

"Not really," she said again.

"Have you been working since you left high school?" I just *had* to know her story.

"Well—" she chewed her own lip like she wasn't sure she wanted to answer "—I had this part-time job while I was in high school doing filing and answering phones for this lawyer firm. It was easy work and paid pretty good, so I thought I'd drop out of school and do it full-time. I hated school with a passion." She rolled her eyes. "But a couple of months after I dropped out, I got laid off."

"Oh, no."

"Right. I just didn't want to go back to school. I would've been in with kids a year younger and everything. So I got a job at Old Navy, which was very cool, except I didn't get along with my boss. So I left there, and—" She laughed. "This is way TMI, isn't it?"

"No, no," I said. "I'm just trying to see what your interests are. You know, what you might like to—"

"To be when I grow up?" She smiled. Her teeth were a little crooked, but very white.

I laughed. "Exactly. And you don't have to declare a major right away, so it's not a big deal if you don't know now." I was jealous. When would I get to go to college? I would have been a sophomore by now if my life hadn't gone off track. If I hadn't *made* my life go off track. Dr. Jakes was into me taking responsibility for what happened. He was irritating, but he was right. It was nobody's fault but my own.

"What were you good at in school?" I asked. "I mean, not just good at, but what did you get excited about?"

"Besides guys, you mean?"

I smiled. "Right. Besides guys."

She looked lost. "I don't know. Did you actually get excited about anything in high school?"

"I liked my psychology class," I said.

"So how come you're working in a library?"

I was going to have to learn how to answer that kind of question. No way she was getting the truth, though. I needed my cover story. Other women at the prison told me about making up a story to explain their time away from the real world. A favorite was the "I've been in Iraq" story, which was sure to get them sympathy. Others were more creative, like the woman who said she was going to tell people she'd been training to be an astronaut until she developed an inner-ear problem, or the one who'd say she was a trapeze artist in a circus until she took a terrible fall. But I hadn't given my own cover story a whole lot of thought until that moment.

"I'm taking some time off before college, too," I said. "I'll probably go in a year."

"Why are you taking time off? You seem so into this whole—" she waved her hand toward the monitor "—this whole college scene."

"Just...you know." I squirmed. "I had my fill of school for a while."

"Yeah, I get it."

"So back to you." I focused on the screen to avoid her eyes. "Seriously, about your interests. A law firm, maybe? You liked working there."

"Just because it was easy. I wasn't all that into it."

"You liked Old Navy. How about retail. Marketing, maybe?"

She wrinkled her nose again. "It was the *clothes* I liked. I wanted to design them. I liked helping people put together outfits. I could tell right away what they should be wearing."

I suddenly felt subconscious about my wrinkled tan capris and the navy blue shirt I'd owned since high school. I'd never been into clothes the way a lot of girls my age were. But I was not totally out of the loop. "Did you ever see that *Project Runway* show on TV?" I asked.

Her eyes lit up. "Exactly! Oh my God, I love that show. That would be, like, my dream, to be on a show like that."

"Well, girl," I said, realizing I sounded like Letitia. "There's your passion. We need to find some schools where you can study fashion design."

"They have schools for that?"

Maybe she wasn't the brightest bulb in the chandelier, but I liked her.

"Of course. Schools specifically *for* it, and schools where you can just major in it." I clicked on the computer screen, ran a search. "You can start here," I said. "The thing is, some of these places are probably hard to get into. You might have to start at a community college and take some art courses. Some of them probably even have fashion courses."

I glanced up and saw Gary standing at the end of the computer bank, watching me. "D'you think you're set for now?" I asked her, getting to my feet.

"Yeah, thanks. This is great."

I walked over to Gary. "I'm helping her with college research," I said. "Is that all right?"

"Sure." He looked pleased. "I just wanted to be sure you're okay."

My mother had probably told him to baby me a little. "Just don't let any reporters in here," I said, "and I'll be fine."

I was back to shelving books an hour later when the girl found me again.

"I've gotta go," she said. "I got a ton of info, but I'll probably be back again Friday."

"You don't have a computer where you're staying?"

"I have a laptop, but the cottage only has dial-up and it's torture getting online that way."

"Oh, yeah."

"My name's Jen Parker," she said.

"I'm Maggie."

"Will you be here Friday?"

I nodded. I'd be living in the library for the next three hundred hours.

"Great!" she said. "I'll probably see you then."

I watched her walk away, her hair catching stripes of light from the fluorescents overhead, wondering if I just might be able to have a friend.

Chapter Twenty

Keith

I WOKE UP AROUND ELEVEN IN THE MORNING, THE PAIN IN my left arm so bad I felt like cutting it off. The bottle of Percocet was on my nightstand and I took two of them with a swallow of water while I was still in bed. It was dark in the trailer. There was a window right above my bed, but I couldn't stomach the thought of stretching my arm high enough to pull the blind open.

Our trailer was always dark inside. I hated that rusty tin can. Lived in it practically my whole life. Of course, my tin can was less than a block from the ocean and not everyone who lived in a trailer park could say that. Maybe I'd surf today. Once the meds kicked in, that's what I'd do. Out there, I could ditch my problems. First, though, I'd drive to Sneads Ferry and get my buddy there to fill my tank and then I'd get him to buy me some brew, because I wasn't going to go through one more day without beer. For the first time ever, I could drink in my own house, whenever I wanted. Hell, if my mother had to be missing, I might as well get something good out of it.

When I got in my car, though, the needle in the gas gauge did a tiny little jump and then just sat there below the E. It was lower than I'd ever seen it before, and I'd run on fumes plenty of times. Sneads Ferry wasn't all that far, and maybe I could still make it, but what if I didn't? It was midweek in late September, so there wouldn't be that many cars on the road to begin with. I'd be stranded trying to hitch a ride with a face that'd scare off anybody who slowed down long enough to get a look at me.

There was a gas station less than a mile from the trailer park. I was going to have to bite the bullet. A zillion people filled up their tanks every day and never caught on fire, I thought as I pulled onto the main road. A zillion people.

There were no other cars at the pumps when I pulled into the station, but I could smell the gas already even though I hadn't opened my car door. It wasn't my imagination. Maybe the station had a leak going on or something. Maybe a car'd knocked one of the pumps a little off its base and no one knew about it yet.

Whatever, I thought. *Whatthefuckever.* I just needed to get this over with.

I got out of my car, then realized the tank was on the other side. Got back in. Turned the car around. Remembered to pop the door on the gas tank.

I looked at the pump. There was this little cardboard sign taped to the display. *Pay inside if using cash.* Crap. I didn't want to go inside and have to talk to somebody. Mom always took care of that. I dug into my pocket and pulled out my two last twenties, a five and three singles. I'd get ten bucks' worth. It wouldn't get me far, but it would have to do.

The blond guy behind the counter in the little market was talking on his cell. He didn't even look up when I put a twenty on the counter.

"I want ten dollars' worth," I said.

He laughed into the phone as he opened the register. "She was, like, totally wasted," he said, putting the twenty in the drawer and pulling out a ten. "Yeah, no kidding. I wasn't letting her in my car like that. She'd puke all over it."

He handed me the ten. "Thanks, man," he said. He finally looked right at me, and his eyes bugged out. *"Wow,"* he said. "What happened to your face, man?"

"Go to hell," I said, and I headed for the door. I pulled it open and could hear him saying into his cell, "I don't know. Guy looks like he walked into a propeller."

Back at the pump, I leaned against the side of my car, trying to get a grip on myself. I finally reached down and twisted off the cap on the gas tank, my hand jerking around like I was spastic or something. *Walked into a propeller?* I pushed the button above the cheapest gas, took down the nozzle and stuck it in the tank. All I had to do now was pull up the trigger or whatever you called it. I held my fingers on it. *Just pull it up. Pull it up.* Ten seconds passed. Thirty. Forty. I couldn't do it. The gas would come out, and it would be all over for me. That's how Maggie started the fire. Gas and diesel. Gas and diesel. One little spark and *wham!*

"You havin' trouble out here?"

I looked toward the door of the minimart, where the blond guy stood, half in the store and half out.

"You need some help?" he called.

"No, I've got it," I said. I squeezed my eyes shut, pulled up on the trigger and waited to die.

I was wiped out and shaky as I drove back to the trailer. I didn't feel like surfing now. I felt like going back to bed, so that's what I did. Crawled in. Pulled the covers up to my chin.

Guy looks like he walked into a propeller.

Effing son of a bitch.

I tossed off the covers and went into my mother's room, into the closet where she kept this box of pictures. They were mostly of me. She was always annoying me with the cheapo digital camera somebody gave her. *My handsome son,* she'd say. *C'mon, good-lookin'. Smile for your mom.* I'd sneer or turn away. Why did I do that? Why did I treat her like shit all the time?

I went through the pictures, pulling out every one that had me in it. Old school pictures from when I was a kid. A bunch with Andy and Maggie on the beach in front of the old Sea Tender. Maggie and I looked like brother and sister for sure. Andy not so much, but Maggie and I had those giant brown eyes and dark curly hair. Then there were those school pictures from over the years. I remembered the eighth-grade picture real well. When we got that picture from the photographer, I stared at it for about an hour, thinking I was turning into a hot-looking dude. There was a picture of me with Lindsey Shallcross. We were all decked out before some dance our freshman year of high school. There was a shot of me posing next to my surfboard in my wet suit, my eyes squinty and the sour look I reserved for my mother on my face.

I got a pair of scissors from my mother's desk, and started to cut the pictures up. I cut them into smaller and smaller pieces until my hand was sore. I would've liked to burn them, but I hadn't lit a match since the night of the fire. Instead I tossed the pictures, which looked practically like confetti by then, into the toilet and flushed it. About half the pieces went down. I flushed again. Then again. The pieces just circled the inside of the bowl, and I knew I'd screwed up.

We had a plunger and we had a snake because my mother never wanted the expense of calling in a plumber if she could help it, so I spent the rest of the day working on the damn toilet. By late afternoon, I had the thing working again. I took a shower, thinking about maybe driving to Sneads Ferry to get my buddy to buy me some beer, but if he wasn't working, it'd be a waste of gas. I couldn't face the evening without a beer, though. My shoulder and arm and left hand were totally wrecked from using the plunger. I thought the Perc would work better and quicker if I took them on an empty stomach. No food for them to cut through. Just straight into the bloodstream. I popped a couple, and I was right. I fell asleep on the sofa and didn't wake up until morning.

I put on my wet suit as soon as I got up. I was surfing, no matter what. I didn't care if we had a thunderstorm, I was going out there where I didn't have to deal with anyone or hear people talk about my face. My arm felt a lot better than the night before. Those drugs were brilliant. I opened my front door and nearly tripped over a pot of flowers. Crap. Some old lady sending me flowers like my mother was already dead. I carried them into the kitchen.

The flowers were in a dented old aluminum coffeepot, and they weren't anything fancy. They looked like someone grabbed them from a field or something and stuck them in whatever thing they could use for a pot.

I saw a folded piece of white paper stuck in the stems and pulled it out.

I've been thinking a lot about you. Sorry if I came on too strong in the grocery store last week. I'd really like to cook you dinner. Something chocolate for dessert! Tonight? Jen

She wrote her phone number again in case I'd lost that scrap of paper she gave me. I hadn't lost it. It was still in my jeans pocket, though I'd never planned to call it and sure didn't expect to hear from her either.

I leaned against the counter, remembering that hot bod and those pretty blue eyes. She was hurt inside, she'd said. Did she actually get it? Did she understand? I looked at her number. Picked up my cell.

Maybe I could get laid, at the very least.

Chapter Twenty-One

Maggie

ON FRIDAY NIGHT, MOM, ANDY, UNCLE MARCUS AND I ATE dinner at the picnic table on the deck. Pork chops and sweet potatoes we cooked on the grill, and collards Mom bought from the old woman on Route 17 who was the only person who really knew how to make them the way I liked them. Oh my God, it felt *so good* to be outside in my awesome yard on the awesome sound! The news vans were gone. *Finally.* The last one pulled out sometime that afternoon. Maybe it was just because it was the weekend and they weren't bothering to cover the news, but whatever the reason, I could finally go outside without hiding in the shadows.

Sitting at the picnic table, I felt really, truly happy for the first time in forever. God, I'd missed my family! I munched on my pork chop, smiling inside as Andy talked about Kimmie, Kimmie, Kimmie.

"Somebody's got Kimmie on the brain," Mom said after he'd been going on and on for about ten minutes straight.

Andy looked surprised. "Who does?" he asked, and we all cracked up.

At one point during dinner, Uncle Marcus brushed Mom's hair away from her forehead. She caught his hand. Squeezed it and smiled. I still couldn't get over watching them. I'd get tense every once in a while around them, the way I used to feel when they were in the same room together. I was waiting for my mother to say something cold to him, to freeze him out like she used to, but those days were gone. A couple of nights, I heard them making love. That was slightly creepy. My mother'd always been so not interested in sex—or at least, that's how I thought of her. What did I know, though? Daddy died when I was eight, and she never dated anyone. Maybe she craved it all that time. Well, she was getting it now. It was strange. I'd left a family that was screwed up and miserable, and I came home to people who were suddenly giving off all these romantic vibes. I hoped the vibes weren't catching, because I was done with romance for a while. Maybe forever.

It was nearly dark by the time we finished cleaning up, and I looked through the kitchen window toward our long pier. I hadn't felt safe enough to walk out on the pier since I got home, but tonight the reporters were gone, and in the darkness no one would be able to see me from the water.

"I'm going to go out on the pier," I said as I turned on the dishwasher.

"Beautiful night for it," Mom said.

"Can I come?" Andy asked.

"Sure." I'd really wanted to be alone, but I needed to make up for lost time with my baby brother.

The sand was cool under my bare feet as we crossed the yard to the pier. Fall was coming already. I'd missed summer while I was locked up. I never wanted to miss another one.

The good thing about fall, though, was that the tourists were gone and the island was dark, which meant you could see zillions of stars. As I walked down the long pier next to Andy, I felt so incredibly free. I put my arms out like I was flying.

"What are you doing?" Andy asked.

"Just feeling happy," I said.

He stretched his own arms out at his sides. "Me, too," he said.

At the end of the pier, we sat down and dangled our legs over the side, like we'd done thousands of times before. It was totally still on the water, and I could hear little waves lapping against the pilings. I loved that sound.

"Uncle Marcus is getting me a kayak," Andy said.

"Really? Mom's letting him?" Mom had been paranoid about any sort of boat ever since Daddy was killed on Uncle Marcus's.

"Yup. She said I'm old enough."

I leaned against the piling and watched the moonlight flicker on the water. For a quick, sickening moment, I remembered the last time I'd sat with Andy looking out over the water—in the Sea Tender during the nor'easter, on that stupid, stupid night when I'd lost every particle of sanity I'd ever had. The memory made me feel queasy. I hoped Andy wasn't thinking about the same thing.

I suddenly felt the rhythmic vibration of footsteps on the pier. I looked over my shoulder. If it was a reporter, I would jump into the sound before I'd talk to him.

But it was Mom and Uncle Marcus, walking toward us, holding hands.

"What a gorgeous night!" Mom said as they came close to the end of the pier.

"Yeah," I said.

"Can we sit with y'all?" Uncle Marcus asked, even though he was already lowering himself to the pier next to Andy.

Mom sat down next to him. "We wanted to talk with you both about something," she said.

"What?" Andy asked. I wondered if they were getting engaged.

"Well, first of all, I just wanted to let you know that I'm definitely going to hire a private investigator to help us find Sara," Mom said.

"Good idea," I said. Maybe a P.I. could do something the police hadn't thought of.

"Yeah, good," Andy said, like he had a clue what a private investigator did.

"But second," Mom said, "and this is the part that affects you two—Marcus and I think we should ask Keith to move in here while Sara's gone."

I looked down at the water beneath my feet. I couldn't imagine it. Not for a second.

"I don't know where Miss Sara can be," Andy said.

"No one does, And," Uncle Marcus said. "It's hard to know if she'll be gone for just another day or maybe forever, so—"

"She might be dead," Andy said.

"I hope not," Mom said, "but it's a possibility we have to face. We just don't know. But in the meantime, Keith is alone. He has no money. He can't legally get any of Sara's savings, so Marcus and I think it would be a kind thing to ask him if he'd like to stay with us."

I couldn't even face Keith at the search. How could I live in the same house with him? It would be like a whole new kind of prison for me, but I so understood where Mom and Uncle Marcus were coming from: Keith was a Lockwood. The world might not know it, but—except for Andy—*we* did and *Keith* did. How could we let him stay alone when we could help him? I thought it was amazing of my mother to suggest it. She'd forgiven my father and Sara for what they did. I wasn't sure I'd be able to in her shoes.

Still, I wasn't quite ready to say yes. And Andy, who didn't have a clue that Keith was related to us, didn't get it at all.

"He's always mean to me," he whined. "Maybe he could live with somebody else?"

"If he lived here," Mom said, "it would be with the understanding that he's not mean to *any* of us. That he follows the house rules and returns to school. He'd have to treat all of us with the same respect we'd treat him."

"What are you thinking, Maggie?" Uncle Marcus reached around Andy's shoulders to touch my arm. I hadn't said a word.

I tipped my head back and looked at the stars. I didn't feel like speaking. I finally felt peaceful and safe for the first time in more than a year, and having Keith there—the flesh-and-blood reminder of what I'd done—would practically be the worst thing I could imagine. How Mom and Uncle Marcus could even ask me to go along with the idea seemed so unfair. But could I be any more selfish? I totally messed up Keith's life. My *half brother's* life. He had some of Daddy in him. Hard to imagine, but somewhere inside that hotheaded, mean-spirited boy was a piece of my father.

"I guess it's the right thing to do," I said.

Uncle Marcus laughed. "A ringing endorsement," he said.

"What's that mean?" Andy asked.

"It means we all have reservations about it," Mom said in a voice that let me know she really *did* have reservations. "We all have concerns. But like Maggie said, it's the right thing to do."

Chapter Twenty-Two

Andy

"I CAN'T READ THIS ONE," KIMMIE SAID. SHE STOOD BY THE cork wall in my room. She was writing things from my calendar into her special phone that has a calendar in it. At night when we talk, she reminds me what I have to do tomorrow.

"What one?" I got up from my desk where I was doing organizing and walked to the cork wall.

"This one." She pointed at the October 2 square. It was Mom's handwriting. Usually I could understand it, but not when she wrote uphill. I turned my head sideways to try and read it.

"Shergletropskinder," I said.

Kimmie laughed. She thought I was funny a lot of times. "Say it again," she said.

"Shergletropskinder."

She giggled so hard she had to flop onto my bed. I loved when she laughed 'cause a lot of times she was serious. Like Mom. I flopped next to her and laughed, too. My ceiling had little stars on it that lit up at night from when I was a kid. I could see them now even though it wasn't dark.

I turned to see Kimmie. She was looking at the ceiling and I just stared at her because it wasn't impolite to stare if she didn't know I was doing it. She was so pretty. I wanted to hug and kiss her. She had on a green shirt like her eyes and I liked how it went over her breasts like hills. I would've really liked to touch them. I never did, except when I hugged her and could feel them on my chest. I had a hard-on again. I had one most of the time around Kimmie.

I knew a lot about sex even though I never did it. Uncle Marcus told me stuff a long time ago. Mom did, too, but she never explained about hard-ons and everything because of being a girl. I also seen magazines Max brought to school sometimes. Max called hard-ons boners. One thing I knew was that you weren't supposed to do sex unless you loved somebody and you were supposed to use a condom, too. So I started thinking about the condom Uncle Marcus gave me back when he did the sex-talk thing. I found it in my clutter drawer a few weeks ago, but the date on it said 10/07 which meant it was too old.

"Okay!" Kimmie all of a sudden sat up. "Back to work. Did you organize your desk?"

I sat up, too, so she wouldn't see my hard-on. "Almost all of it," I said.

Kimmie was a neat freak. Uncle Marcus called her that and Mom said, "Don't knock it."

"Okay," she said. "Then we can do our homework now." She walked over to my desk to get our book bags. She has a bad limp because of her foot, but it doesn't hurt her.

We were at the movies once and a girl called Kimmie a gimp. I didn't know what it meant, but I knew it was mean. Like when somebody called me retard. I wanted to hit the girl. I used to actually do it—hit people when they said things I didn't like. But now I had self-control. Instead, I just told Kimmie not to listen and about the sticks and stones and everything. Kimmie said the girl was just an igoramus. That was a funny word and made me laugh. So instead of hitting the girl and getting in trouble, I was laughing. My life was lots better with Kimmie in it.

Kimmie gave me my book bag and sat next to me on my bed. We both liked to do homework sitting on our beds. It was one of our things in common. I opened my book bag and pulled out a bunch of papers.

"Your book bag is a total mess," Kimmie said. "You should clean it out before you start."

"Yeah, you're right." I never cleaned it out. I wasn't even sure which papers were my homework and which were old.

Kimmie leaned against the wall and started reading her history book. I sat on the end of my bed and dumped all the things out of my book bag onto my dresser. It *was* a mess. I even had cigarettes in there that were so old I forgot about them. I got my trash can and started putting the old things in it. I found a card from Maggie. It was a thank-you card she made in prison, but I couldn't remember why she thanked me. She drew a picture of a big yellow flower on it. I didn't want to throw it away, so I pulled out the clutter drawer of my dresser and put it in there. I could hardly get my clutter drawer open. I'm allowed to keep it messy, though, so it was okay. Even Kimmie knew I was allowed to keep that drawer messy.

"Do you need help?" Kimmie asked.

"I'm good," I said.

I found some tests with B and C on them and put them in my clutter drawer, too. Then I found an envelope. I thought it was a note from a teacher I forgot to give Mom until I turned it over. *Keith,* it said on it. I was confused.

"We're going to invite Keith to move in with us," I said to Kimmie. I kept staring at the envelope, trying to remember.

"The boy whose mother is missing?"

"Yeah."

"That's so cool. Two more kids and your family'll be as big as mine."

Why did I have that envelope? Then I remembered it was mail for him from the day I was sick. That was so long ago. He'd make fun of me that I forgot to give it to him. I threw the envelope in my clutter drawer and pushed it all the way to the back.

Chapter Twenty-Three

Sara
His Wife
1990

IF I HAD TOLD ANYONE ABOUT MY LIFE, THEY WOULD HAVE thought I was out of my mind. I was married to a man I didn't love, expecting the baby of a man who was my soul mate—although not my lover; not since that one time—and I was nurturing a friend-ship with that man's barely functional wife. Why? Because I felt his love for me even though he could promise me nothing more than that. Because every time I was in the Free Seekers Chapel with him on Sundays, I still felt lifted up by the space, by the sound of his voice, by the way people responded to him. Because there was an honesty between us we couldn't have with anyone else. And because I made a decision to appreciate the richness of what he could give me instead of focusing on the limitations. Yet the longing would always be there. Always.

I worked out a schedule with Jamie to check on Laurel, bringing lunch over to the Sea Tender once a week, making sure she was at least out of bed. By then, Laurel had started drinking. Jamie wasn't sure how bad it had gotten. I hadn't actually witnessed her drinking, but I'd seen empty wine-cooler bottles in the kitchen.

"It's Marcus's influence," Jamie said. Marcus had moved out of the Sea Tender and now lived next door. "I appreciate that he's keeping an eye on her, but I think he brings booze over and encourages her to drink with him."

I was four months along when I decided it was time to tell Laurel about my pregnancy. It was a sparkling November afternoon, and we ate sandwiches I brought to the Sea Tender—or rather, I ate a sandwich, while Laurel picked at hers. Laurel didn't seem quite as down as she usually did, though, and I was amazed when she agreed to join me for a walk on the beach.

"Bare feet in November!" I said as we walked near the water's edge. "I'm *never* going back to Michigan."

"Good," Laurel said. "I'd hate for you to leave."

I looked out to the horizon. When Laurel said things like that, I felt the depth of my deception. What had happened to my self-respect? My integrity?

"Well, I'm not going anywhere," I said when I got my emotions under control, "but things *are* about to change." I rested my hand on my stomach. "I wanted to tell you before it became obvious," I said.

"You're *pregnant?*"

I nodded. "Due in May."

"Congratulations!" Laurel said. "Is Steve excited?"

I laughed. "Oh, you know Steve. Always cool, calm and collected." I had a sudden, almost irresistible urge to tell Laurel the baby was Jamie's. To finally bring this thing to a head. But I couldn't do that to him. I just couldn't.

I couldn't even do it to Laurel.

Chapter Twenty-Four

Keith

JEN LOOKED EVEN BETTER THAN I REMEMBERED HER FROM the grocery store. When she opened the door to the house where she was staying, she had on this short little strappy dress, one of those that made certain girls look pregnant even though you knew they weren't. On a girl like Jen, the way it hardly covered her ass, it just made her look hot. Her legs were long and curved just right, and her feet were bare.

"Hey," I said. I tried not to think about how I must look to her.

"Hey." Her smile was so sexy, but I hardly had a chance to take it in before she put her hand on the back of my neck, leaned forward and Frenched the hell out of me. *Damn.*

We were still kissing as I staggered into her house, thumping into the doorjamb with my knee, just managing to get the door closed behind me. Then I was devouring her. I was unstoppable, and she didn't want to stop, either. You could tell when a girl really wanted it and when she was just faking, and this one *wanted* it. She was every bit as hot as she looked. She had me flat on the living-room floor before I knew it, straddling me, tossing that hair around. I reached up to touch her breasts, braless beneath the slippery stuff her dress was made out of. Her nipples pressed against my palms, and I ran my thumbs over them.

It took me about twenty seconds to discover she had no panties on under that dress. I knew chicks liked sex slow, but damn. What was I supposed to do? It'd been way too long. She rubbed against me through my jeans. I finally held her hips still.

"I'm gonna come if you don't stop it," I said.

She laughed, leaning forward to kiss me, and I reached between us to touch her. She was wet, slippery as silk. I groaned, and she undid my zipper and whipped off my jeans like she did it every day of the week. Then she sank onto me. I tried to hold back, but two thrusts and it was over.

"Sorry," I said when I managed to catch my breath. I could usually hold out long enough to get girls to come. I used to be good at it.

She laughed in my ear. "That's okay, baby," she said. I felt her muscles tighten around my cock. "You needed it."

We lay like that awhile longer, with her head on my chest and my aching arms around her. Her hair smelled incredible, the scent just about making me drunk. I needed another Percocet, but I didn't want to move.

"Are you cold?" I asked, rubbing her left arm with my right. I felt my cock slip out of her.

"Not at all. You?"

"No." I twisted some of her hair around my fingers. "You smell like oranges. Orange and vanilla. Creamsicles."

She laughed. "Is that bad?"

"Uh-uh. It's excellent."

"Let's move to the bedroom." She got to her feet and reached down to help me up. I thought briefly about dinner—I could smell that she actually *had* cooked something—but right then I didn't care if I never ate again.

* * *

Her bedroom was massive, the bed bigger than my whole room in the trailer. We got naked and under the covers and she wrapped her arms around me.

"Are you in pain?" she asked.

"Uh-uh." I'd hesitated half a second too long before answering.

"Yes, you are, too," she said. "Can I get you some aspirin?"

"I have pain meds in my jeans pocket." My jeans were on her living-room floor and I didn't feel like letting go of her to get them.

But she hopped out of the bed before I could stop her, and in another minute was handing me my bottle of pills and a glass of water. I popped a couple of the Percocet. Any more action like we'd had in the living room, and I'd need every milligram.

She climbed back into bed again, wriggling over next to me.

"I'm sorry you have pain," she said.

I kissed her. "It's all right," I said.

"Are you angry?" she asked.

"*What?*" I thought she meant about attacking me at the front door before I'd even had a bite to eat. "About what?"

"Your…the pain."

"You mean the burns."

"Yeah."

Oh, yeah. I was angry.

"Do you know the whole story about the fire?" I asked.

"You mean, how that Maggie Lockwood girl was trying to help out her boyfriend by starting a fire so he could be some big hero, and—"

"She didn't actually *start* it." I interrupted her. "That's the thing. She—"

"I remember reading about it," Jen said. "She planned it and poured the gasoline around the building and then chickened out when she realized there would be kids in the building. But one of the kids lit a cigarette and tossed down the match and—"

"That was me," I said. Then I laughed. "Cured me of smoking, that's for damn sure."

"Oh, Keith," she said. "You don't blame yourself, do you?"

"Hell, no. I blame Maggie." I thought of telling her how Maggie and I were related, but just didn't feel like getting into all that. "I hate that bitch. Our mothers were friends when I was a kid, so I was always stuck playing with her and her brother." I could tell her about my mother going missing, but I didn't want to think about that tonight, either. "Her brother, Andy, was so weird," I said. "Turned out Maggie was even weirder, though she was good at putting on the normal act."

"Andy's the one they thought started the fire, right?"

"Right."

"How could she let him take the blame?" she asked. "Did she have a crappy relationship with him or what?"

"The opposite of crappy," I said. "She's really protective of him. She and her mother even tampered with evidence to try to get him off."

Jen suddenly sucked in her breath. "I think I just figured something out," she said. "Though I hope I'm wrong."

"About what?"

"Your mother's not that woman who just went missing, is she?"

"That's the one."

"Oh, no. How *awful*." She leaned up on an elbow. "I'm sorry. Have you heard anything? Does anyone know what happened?"

"The cops are supposedly looking for her, but they think she left by choice, which is bullshit. I feel like I should be doing something myself, but I don't know what."

"Like looking for her?"

"I don't know."

"It must be so terrible for you. I wish I could do something to help." She ran her fingers across the ruined half of my face. My muscles tightened up. Only my mother had touched those scars, and that was just because she was supposed to massage them to keep adhesions from forming.

"Did I hurt you?" she asked.

"No."

She touched my cheek again. Her eyes were on my skin and I tried not to pull away. To hide. She leaned over me, pressing her lips to my cheek. Kissing it. When she lifted her head away, I saw tears in her eyes. I touched one of them where it hung on her lower lashes. My throat tightened up.

"I'm all right," I said.

She smiled. "I know you are. And you're beautiful. You're a beautiful man. Do you know that?"

I laughed. "No, I don't know that at all," I said. If another girl had told me that, I would've thought she was mocking me. Not only wasn't I beautiful, I was only seventeen. Not exactly a man. But I had the feeling Jen was being totally real.

"You are," she said. "And you have the most amazing, big brown eyes. Don't let anyone tell you you're not beautiful. Not ever."

I kissed her again, nibbling her lower lip. No tongue. Not yet. I'd try not to rush this time. I'd make it as good for her as she'd made it for me.

Chapter Twenty-Five

Maggie

I WAS SHELVING BOOKS IN THE BIOGRAPHY SECTION WHEN JEN poked her head around the corner of the stacks.

"There you are!" she said. "I was looking for you."

"Hey, Jen." I was ridiculously happy to see her. She was the only person my age who didn't try to avoid me. Of course, that was because she didn't know who I was, but still. Plus, I'd been doing some research to help with her college plan. "I found out some things for you."

"Really?"

"About getting into schools with fashion design programs." I reached into my pocket and pulled out the little piece of paper where I'd written the URL. "Here's the Web site." I handed the paper to her.

"That's so cool of you!" She looked at the Internet address. "I want to narrow it down some more today. I don't know whether to go in-state or out or what. I thought I could apply, like, everywhere, but I didn't realize how expensive that would be."

"Oh, I know." I'd applied to several schools, but money had been no big deal for me. Once I met Ben, though, I knew I'd be going to UNC Wilmington. No way would I go any farther away from him than that. I was so stupid. I'd never ever *ever* again plan my life around a guy. Actually, I didn't think I'd ever fall for someone that way again. Trust someone like that. You couldn't totally know a guy, ever. They thought differently. They had a different kind of moral code or something, or maybe it just boiled down to testosterone. Even Daddy'd given in to it. I couldn't picture Uncle Marcus ever hurting my mother like that, though. He practically worshipped her.

Jen glanced at the books I was shelving. "Do you have a minute to help me get online? I do not *get* these library computers!"

"Sure." The library computers could be confusing the first couple of times you used them.

I sat down next to her like I did on Wednesday and showed her the Web site with the information on fashion design programs. Then I got caught up in helping her narrow down her choices. It was more like bringing her back down to earth. She was ready—in *her* mind, anyway—to apply to Parsons and the Fashion Institute of Technology.

"See how it says you need a portfolio to get into these schools?" I pointed to the Web site. "It's really best if you go to a community college or one of the state schools so you can get the experience and put a portfolio together. That'll be easier moneywise, too. Then maybe you could get into one of the fashion design schools later."

She bit her lip. "I would love to go to New York," she said. "How cool would that be?"

"But do you get what I'm saying?" I asked. "About starting out someplace where you can learn the basics? The sketching and sewing and…I don't know, the design jargon and theory or whatever it is in design." I felt overwhelmed for her. She had a GED. She had no experience. She probably had, like, zero extracurricular activities from when she was in high school. Could she write an admissions essay? I doubted it.

"Yeah, don't worry," she said. "I get it. I'm just dreaming."

"Dreaming's good," I said. "You just need to—"

"Are you Maggie Lockwood?"

I looked up to see a woman about Mom's age standing next to my chair. Her brown hair was in a ponytail and a little blond boy held on to her hand. She looked angry, and I wished I could lie.

"Yes," I said.

"They should have kept you locked up for the rest of your life," she said. "Or worse."

I didn't know what to say. It was like my mouth was paralyzed. I was so embarrassed that Jen heard her, and I suddenly realized that the other two women and one old man sitting with us at the computer bank were staring at me.

"I...I'm doing community service now," I finally managed to say. "That's the second part of my sen—"

She leaned forward, her eyes practically popping out of her head, and spit in my face. I felt the saliva hit my eye and start running down my cheek.

"Oh my God!" Jen knocked her chair over in her rush to get out of the way.

I jumped out of my own chair, wiping my face with my hand, horrified. People around us gasped. Whispered. I stared at the woman, but she was already walking away from me. I could hear her little boy ask, "Mommy, why did you spit at that lady?"

I ran to the restroom. I didn't look at my face in the mirror. I didn't want to see that disgusting wad of spit slipping down my cheek toward my mouth. I leaned over the sink and pooled water in my hands, washing my face over and over again. Then I scrubbed it with a rough paper towel.

Jen quietly opened the door and slipped inside. I caught her gaze in the mirror.

"Are you okay?" she asked.

I shut my eyes, pressing the wet paper towel to my face. "Sort of," I said.

"That was so disgusting. Why did she do that?"

"It's a long story." I was a little surprised Jen hadn't recognized my name, but then, she was from Asheville. The fire had been national news, though, thanks to Andy's appearance on the *Today* show.

"I've never seen anyone do something like that before," she said. "And she did it in front of her little boy. Gross."

I nodded. I felt so tired all of a sudden. "She had a reason, though."

"Why? What did she mean about you being locked up? Did she mean *prison?*"

I wanted to tell her. I needed a friend. I liked Jen, and we had something in common: she was the same age as me and, like me, had taken time off before college—even if it had been voluntary in her case. And if she said I should take a hike once I told her, what had I lost?

I looked around the cramped bathroom. "I don't want to talk about it here," I said.

There was a knock on the restroom door.

"Maggie?" It was Gary.

"Yes."

"Are you all right?"

"Yes."

"I need to talk with you when you come out. Just come into the office."

I couldn't imagine walking back through the library. No way.

"I just want to go home," I said through the door. "Can I call you? We can talk on the phone?"

He didn't answer right away. "All right," he said finally. "You sure you're okay?" He was a nice man.

"I'm okay," I said. "But I want to leave."

I realized Jen was holding my arm, like she thought I'd fall over if she let go of me.

"Okay," Gary said. "I'll be here until seven."

Jen let go of me and I looked in the mirror. My face was bright red from the rubbing I'd given it with the paper towel—and from being humiliated in front of half the world in the library. "What a total disaster," I said.

"Let's go get some coffee," Jen said.

I looked at her in the mirror. "You wanted to do research, though."

She shook her head like it was no big deal. "I can do that anytime."

I'd wanted to go home. I could already picture the safe haven of my room. My angora teddy bear. But the possibility of friendship was stronger.

I nodded. "Okay."

"Do you want to go out toward the beach?" she asked. "There's a cute little coffee place."

I knew she meant Jabeen's. I'd probably never go in Jabeen's again. I could picture Dawn whipping us up some lattes while I explained to Jen about my criminal past. It was almost enough to make me laugh. "Let's go closer," I said. "There's a coffee shop down the street."

"All right."

I suddenly remembered my purse. Damn.

"I have to go into the office to get my purse," I said.

"I'll get it for you. I'll ask them to give it to me. What does it look like?"

"Why are you being so nice?"

"'Cause you helped me."

"You might not feel that way once you hear why I was locked up."

She shrugged, like she couldn't imagine that what I'd done was such a major deal. "What does your purse look like?"

"It's small." I held my trembling hands about ten inches apart. "Brown-and-tan fabric, with a shoulder strap."

"Okay," she said. "I'll meet you in the parking lot."

I walked through the library as quickly as I could, not looking at anyone and hoping no one was looking at me. I didn't even know I was holding my breath until I got outside and gasped for air.

Jen followed my car to the coffee shop. I paid for our mocha lattes, and she didn't put up a fuss at that. I had the feeling she didn't have much money.

"So, all right," she said quietly once we sat down in a booth. "Out with the details. Why were you locked up?"

I tapped my fingers nervously on the lid of my cup. "Do you remember about a year and a half ago there was a fire in Surf City? I know you were in Asheville, but I'm sure it was on the news there. It was everywhere. There was a lock-in at one of the churches, basically a sleepover for their youth group, and…" My voice trailed off because I could see the puzzle pieces coming together in her head.

"Maggie Lockwood," she said. "Oh."

I wrinkled my nose. "Right."

I thought she leaned away from me a bit, but I might have imagined it.

"So…people are upset you didn't get a long enough prison term."

"Right."

"Wow."

I looked down at the lid of my cup, where I was making crisscross lines with my fingernail.

Jen frowned. "You don't seem… I just can't picture you being an arsonist," she said.

"I never actually *lit* the fire," I said. "I'd never intentionally hurt anyone."

"Yeah, I remember. Some kid tossed a lit cigarette on the gas or something, right?"

"A match."

"And wasn't there something about her…your…brother being blamed?"

"Andy," I said. "He saved a lot of people by finding a way out of the fire, but then the police started thinking he set it."

"Did you set them straight?"

"Not for way too long. I put my poor brother through a lot."

"And he could've gotten killed himself."

"Don't even say that," I said. "I can't stand to even think about it."

Jen sipped her latte. "Why did you do it?" she asked.

I told her. I told her all about Ben and how crazy I got. How I loved him so much and wanted to give him a chance to prove himself in the fire department. How the church was going to be demolished in a year or two anyway.

"The lock-in was supposed to be in the youth building," I said. "So when they moved it to the church, I decided—of *course* I decided—not to light the fuel."

"But that other kid dropped the match."

I nodded.

"How awful." She clutched her hands around her cup like she was trying to warm them. "Do you ever think about the people who were killed?" she asked. "I mean, do they, like, *haunt* you? Not literally...but you know what I mean."

I nodded. *Haunt* was nearly the *perfect* word to describe how I felt about Jordy Matthews, Henderson Wright and Mr. Eggles. "I think about them all the time," I said. "And the people who have to live with the scars, too."

"Are there a lot of them?" She took a sip from her cup.

I nodded. "The worst is... Have you heard about that woman who went missing? Sara Weston?"

"Yeah, I heard about her on the news. *Oh.*" She set her coffee cup down on the table. "Her son was in the fire, wasn't he?"

"Yes. Keith. And he's actually my half brother, which is a really long story."

"He *is?*"

I rolled my eyes to indicate just how long and convoluted that story was. "He has scars on his face and hands and arms. My mother's going to ask him to move in with us while Sara's... gone." Today. She was asking him today. And the more I thought about it, the more I knew she had to do it, even if I couldn't stand the thought of him living with us. With me. But I could only imagine what life was like for Keith, having to carry those scars around with him everywhere and now with Sara missing. Still, I wished I never had to see him again. How was I going to eat meals with him and pass him in the hallway and watch TV with him in the family room without totally losing it? I couldn't picture it.

"What do you think happened to his mother?"

"I just don't know. It's so weird. I just hope she's not...that she's not dead. It's unbelievable to think she might be, but she wouldn't just disappear. She's, like, the most responsible person I know."

"So how's her son your half brother?"

"Sara had an affair with my father. He died when I was eight."

"Wow. You mean, he had an affair with her while he was married to your mother?"

I nodded. "We didn't know anything about it until a year or so ago when it all came out."

"Your mom's amazing to ask him in."

"She's had time to adjust to the whole thing. She and Sara were totally best friends, but that changed after the fire and the bit about Sara and my father came out." I was spilling so much, it was embarrassing, but Jen was so attentive. And nothing I said seemed to freak her out.

"So whatever happened with Ben?" she asked. "Are you still hung up on him?"

"No way. I found out he was cheating on me the whole time."

"Ouch."

"Right."

Jen took a final sip from her cup. "I've done some crazy things because of guys myself," she said.

"As bad as setting a fire?" I asked.

"Well…" She laughed. "No. You've topped me there."

"Do you want to come over to my house tonight?" she asked when we walked out to our cars. "I like to cook. I'll make dinner."

"Are you kidding?" I asked. "You want to get together after everything I just told you?"

"It's okay, Maggie." She opened her car door and sat down inside. "Trust me," she said. "I haven't had the most mistake-free life either."

Chapter Twenty-Six

Keith

WHEN I LEFT JEN'S HOUSE THE NIGHT BEFORE, I TOLD HER THAT I'd call her, but now I wasn't so sure. I'd felt really good last night. Almost like the old, before-the-fire me. I was totally convinced she was glad I was there, and that she was into me big-time. Today, though, I had some doubts. Maybe she regretted inviting me over once she really got a look at me. Maybe she'd just been too nice— or too horny—to kick me out. I wished I'd gotten her e-mail address. E-mail would be safer. A piece of paper with her number on it was tucked under the saltshaker on my kitchen table. I stared at the number all morning, but I couldn't make myself pick up the phone. If I said let's get together, and she said no, I wouldn't be able to take it.

I was eating a bowl of ramen noodles for lunch when I heard footsteps on the deck, then a knock at the door. Ever since my mother disappeared, I'd been waiting for a cop to show up with bad news. So when the knock came, I got up slowly from the table, like I could put off getting that news for a few more seconds. I pulled open the door and found Laurel standing on the deck and instantly broke out in a sweat. Bad news, definitely. The cops would send her to deliver it, thinking I could handle it better from her than from them.

"Hi," she said. "I brought you some food. Can I come in?"

I finally noticed the plastic grocery bags she was carrying. I didn't want her inside, though. The trailer was a wreck. Probably stank, too, with the dishes in the sink and two-day-old leftover spaghetti on the counter.

"I'll come out there." I started to walk out on the deck, but she held out the bags to stop me.

"At least put these inside," she said. "And there're some things that should go in the fridge."

I looked down at the bags like I'd never seen groceries before. "Okay." I took them from her, put them on the floor inside the door and walked outside.

The trailer had a wooden deck a few feet off the ground and we sat at the round plastic table. I made sure the right side of my face was toward her. I didn't even think about it anymore. It was automatic.

"Do you know anything?" I asked. If she did, I wished she'd just spit it out.

She shook her head. "I was hoping maybe you did."

"How would I? It's not like anyone's looking for her."

"I know it must seem that way." She leaned her elbows on the table. There was, like, this layer of dirt on the table I'd never noticed before, but Laurel didn't seem to see it. I guessed my mother usually kept it cleaned off. "If the police had a good lead, that would be one thing," she said. "It's got to be very frustrating for you, Keith."

"Whatever." I didn't want to get in this big sympathy-for-Keith talk with her. Now that I knew she didn't know any more than I did, I wanted her to leave.

"I wanted to talk to you about hiring a private investigator," she said.

I started to open my mouth to tell her I hardly had money for food, much less a P.I., but she held up her hand to shut me up.

"My dime," she said. "I'll pay for it. I want to. I've done some research and found a man in Washington who has an eighty percent success rate finding people."

"Yes," I said. No question. She could afford it and I needed it. "Do it."

"Good. And I'm also here because we—Maggie, Andy and I—want you to stay with us until…while your mother is gone. We'd like you to move in."

She had to be kidding. I was supposed to actually live in the same house as Maggie? Give her a second chance to kill me?

"No, thanks," I said.

She seemed to notice the dirty tabletop all of a sudden. She sat back, brushing off her elbows, then folded her arms across her chest. "Marcus told me that money's a problem."

"It's not."

"I understand you don't want…charity," she said. "You're too proud for that and I would be, too, in your shoes."

"You don't know the first thing about my shoes."

She looked toward the beach. You could see the dunes and the beach grass from where we sat. "You know what I was thinking about while I picked up the food for you?" She faced me again.

I just stared at her. I didn't give a shit what she'd been thinking about.

"I was remembering that your mother did a lot of grocery shopping for me long ago. For a couple of years, actually. Did you know that?"

"Why?"

"Because I was depressed and an alcoholic and doing a bad job of taking care of myself and my family."

It wasn't like I didn't know Laurel'd been a basket case at one time. My mother'd told me that's why she and Jamie Lockwood hooked up. But it still jolted me, the way she said it. Straight out like that. No embarrassment or anything.

"I know you're not going to school," she said.

"You the truant officer now or something?"

She leaned forward, her elbows on the nasty table again. "I just care about you, Keith," she said. "I always have. You don't need to push me away."

"I'm your husband's bastard kid."

She flinched. She tried to cover it up, but I didn't miss it. "All the more reason for you to live with us. You have siblings. Andy doesn't know. I mean, I plan to tell him soon, but just…please let *me* be the one to tell him. Not you. But that doesn't matter. You and I know you're a…a Lockwood. And you should stay with us. Your mother would want it."

"Oh, you think so? Do you have any idea how much my mother hated Maggie? How shafted she felt by her?"

Laurel leaned away from the table. Away from me. "I don't believe your mother *hated* Maggie," she said, "but I know she felt terribly betrayed by her."

She was pissing me off. "I don't think you get it at all," I said. "My mother would rather see me *dead* than living in the same house with the person who left me like this." I lifted my arms in the air. Showed off the scars. I knew that was a lie about my mother, but I loved how much I was upsetting Laurel.

"Keith," she said. "Let's not say things we're going to regret, okay? I'm offering you a place to live. A roof over your head and food on the table. And friendship if you want it." She stood up. Dusted off the seat of her pants. "Think about it."

I watched her walk down the wooden steps to the sand and get in her car. As she drove away, I felt a weird kind of longing, like I didn't want her to leave. Like I wanted to call her back.

Just when I felt like I was going to sink straight into a black hole of depression, my cell phone rang. I ran back into the trailer and grabbed the phone from the kitchen counter. I checked the number on the caller ID, then looked at the number on the piece of paper Jen had given me. I let it ring a couple more times, grinning to myself, before I pressed the talk button.

"Hey," I said. "I was just about to call *you*."

Chapter Twenty-Seven

Maggie

"WHAT'S HURTING YOU EVEN MORE THAN YOUR GUILT," DR. JAKES said, "is your shame."

I hated when he was right. This was my third session with him and I didn't see how it was helping or ever would help. But every once in a while, he hit the nail on the head. Feeling guilty sounded kind of noble. Like I had deep remorse or something, which I did. Feeling *ashamed,* though, felt dirty. And he was right. That's how I truly felt. Dirty and sinful.

But so what? So I felt shame instead of guilt? What did it matter?

"You feel as though you deserve to be spit at."

I nodded. It had been five hours since the woman had accosted me in the library, but I could still feel her saliva on my face. "I guess," I said.

"And you feel as though you don't deserve to have a friend."

"Right." I'd told him about Jen. About how nice she was and how I was going to her house for dinner tonight.

"She apparently doesn't feel that way," he said.

"Yeah, well." I rested my head on the back of the big leather chair. "I don't think it's really sunk in to her what I did."

He waited for me to go on. I hated when he was quiet like that and all the burden was on me to fill up the silence. I stared up at his ceiling. He had recessed lights laid out in a pattern I couldn't figure out. No symmetry to them at all. One of them was burned out. I stared at its round brownish-gray bulb and suddenly, for no reason at all, I felt like crying.

"What's hurting you right now?" Dr. Jakes asked.

How did he know? I *wasn't* crying. I only felt like it. Sometimes he totally freaked me out, the way he knew exactly when I was ready to crack.

"I don't know how to get through this," I said. "This whole...shitty experience."

He shifted in his chair the way he did when he was about to say something he thought was important. I lowered my eyes from the ceiling to him.

"Let's reframe what you're going through, Maggie," he said. "I'd like you to think of it as grief."

"For the people who died?"

"No. For *yourself.* For the life you thought you had before the fire. Before Ben."

My eyes burned, and I blinked fast. I'd hold the tears back if it was the last thing I did.

"And grief is never quick and easy," he said. "It takes time to get through."

"I'll never get over it," I said.

"Not over, but *through.* That's the key word. You can't skip it. You have to go *through* it."

"Like, endure it."

"At the risk of sounding like a Pollyanna, *endure* is a very negative word. There are things to be gained from this grief."

"Oh, sure."

"Trust me on it. But you have to let yourself feel it. Embrace it even."

I rolled my eyes.

"Learn from it."

I looked at my watch. Twenty more minutes of this.

He smiled at me. "What are you thinking now?" he asked.

"You don't want to know."

He laughed. His belly bounced up and down.

"Will you continue at the library?"

"No way."

"What will you do about your community service if you leave?"

"You say that like you think I should stay there." I was never setting foot in that library again.

"I don't think there's a right or wrong decision with regard to the library," he said. "That's your choice."

"My mother's working on finding me something else."

"Your mother didn't commit the crime."

I felt a flash of hatred for him. "What do you want from me?"

"You're angry with me."

I looked away.

"I don't want anything *from* you," he said. "But I want a great deal *for* you. And one of the things I want is for you to take responsibility for your sentence."

"I just spent a year in prison! No one else did that for me."

"As you said yourself, that was part one. Your mother's not responsible for part two. No one is except you."

The cottage Jen was staying at was not at all what I'd expected. It was at the southernmost end of the island, right smack on the ocean near Serenity Point. So maybe *Jen* didn't have much money, but her friends were sitting on some pricey property. I was glad she had such a cool place to live while she was getting her act together about college.

"Come in!" she said when she opened the front door. She looked like one of those TV cooking-show hosts, a domestic goddess in a red-striped apron, her hair clipped back and a slotted spoon in her hand.

"It smells amazing in here," I said. I was in the living room, but could see into the open kitchen. "What are you making?"

"Chicken cacciatore. Hope that's okay. I didn't ask if you were a vegetarian or anything."

"It sounds perfect." I was no longer fussy about food after all the crap I'd eaten in prison. I wasn't sure what chicken cacciatore was, but by the smells coming from the stove, I was certain I'd like it.

"I'm so glad to have someone over," she said as I followed her into the kitchen. "Topsail's cool, but I'm, like, totally isolated here."

I looked out at the sea, feeling wistful. Yes, my family lived on the sound, but I couldn't help it—I still longed for the ocean view from the Sea Tender. I'd driven past that stretch of beach only once since getting home, and I doubted I'd ever drive past it again. All the condemned cottages were gone. Some of the pilings still jutted from the sand, but my stomach had turned just looking at them. My feelings about the Sea Tender were so jumbled up now. I had such great memories of Daddy there, mixed up with the nauseating memories of my illicit meetings with Ben, and the final, horrific hours with Andy, when I almost got us both killed.

An open bottle of white wine sat on the counter near the sink. Jen poured herself a glass, then started to pour one for me.

"None for me, thanks."

She raised her eyebrows. "Because you're not twenty-one?"

"Just don't like the taste," I lied. I didn't want to get into my reasons for not drinking. I decided while I was in prison not to smoke weed or drink anymore, and not just because alcoholism ran in both sides of my family. I didn't want to do anything that might cloud my judgment, which I wasn't sure I'd ever totally trust again. I'd already screwed up enough for a lifetime.

"You mind if I drink?" she asked, already raising the glass to her lips.

"No, that's cool." I didn't want to sound like a Goody Two-shoes. She knew I was an arsonist, though. I guessed I didn't have to worry about that.

With Jen's hair clipped up, I could see the faint shape of a heart on her jawbone, just below her ear. A tattoo? That would give us one more thing in common. But as she tipped back her head to sip from her glass, I could see that the heart was not quite symmetrical. It was nothing more than a pale grayish birthmark, and although half the world had tattoos, I decided to keep my own a secret from her. At least until I got to know her better. My tattoo always required more explaining than I felt like doing right then, and besides, she didn't seem like a tattoo kind of girl.

Jen turned off the flame beneath the skillet on the stove. "Well," she said, "I may be a good cook, but I can't time things worth a damn. This is already done. Are you hungry?"

"Sure."

We made up our plates and carried them to the table, which looked out on the ocean. It was still light outside, though the sky had turned that early-evening gray.

"I've got the perfect night planned for us," Jen said as she added another inch of wine to her glass.

Oh, God. I hoped she didn't want to go out somewhere. I really didn't know what this girl was like. What was her idea of a perfect night?

"What d'you have up your sleeve?" I asked. The chicken was tender and totally delicious. Someday I'd have to learn to cook.

"Well, after dinner, we'll fill a couple of plastic basins—I found some on the deck—with hot water and give ourselves pedicures while we watch a movie. They have shelves of movies upstairs in the family room and a big-screen TV."

I stared at her, speechless for a second, before I started laughing. I was so relieved she didn't want to go out. But *pedicures?*

"I've never had a pedicure," I said.

"Not even, you know, at home?"

"Not even."

"Oh, you are in for a treat, Maggie."

We ate in silence for a few minutes. Outside, the stars were beginning to pop out of the sky.

"So who owns this cottage?" I asked. "Not that the word *cottage* really fits this place."

"You're right. It's pretty incredible, isn't it?"

"It is."

"It belongs to some family friends. The Roscoes. They live in Chicago and don't use it at all off season, but they spend the whole summer here."

"Chicago." I didn't know anyone who came to Topsail Island from Chicago. "How does your family know them if you live in Asheville?"

"Oh—" she moved a slice of zucchini around on her plate "—Mrs. Roscoe and my mother went to college together." She set her fork down and raised her arms to take in the whole house. "Did I luck out, or what?"

"You really did."

"Where do *you* live, exactly?"

"On the sound in North Topsail," I said.

"Right on the sound? I bet you get great sunsets."

"Yeah, we do," I said, thinking how glad I was to be home, and—although I was ashamed of myself for feeling that way—how totally thrilled I was that Keith didn't want to live with us. Mom had left a message on my cell while I was driving to my appointment with Dr. Jakes, saying he turned down the offer. "I really lucked out, too," I said.

After dinner, we went upstairs to the huge family room. Jen turned on the TV while we looked through the shelves of movies. These Roscoe people had to be rolling in dough, especially if this was just their summer movie collection. Jen liked slasher flicks. Bad news. I used to like them, too, before I ended up living with a bunch of real-life slashers.

"You know—" I was going to have to be straight with her "—I'm just not in the horror mood these days. Any chance of a comedy?"

Her head was turned sideways as she looked at the movie titles. "You get nightmares?" she asked.

"Not really. I'm just into lighter stuff right now."

"Yeah, I guess you've had enough horror to last a while." She glanced at the TV screen where a commercial for Viagra was airing. She rolled her eyes at me. "Men," she said. "I swear."

I laughed.

"A comedy'd be cool," she said. "You pick, and I'll go get the stuff ready for our pedicures."

I'd pulled out a few movies and was waiting for Jen to return when another commercial came on the screen. *"Brier Glen Hospital needs you!"* a man's voice said. There were pictures of an old woman in a hospital bed. A man pushing another man in a wheelchair. A little girl smiling up from a coloring book. I sank onto the sectional, watching. I remembered seeing volunteers at New Hanover Hospital when I delivered cards to the fire victims. They'd all been elderly. Were the volunteers at Brier Glen old, too? Would they let someone my age volunteer? More specifically, would they let *me?* It was far enough from the island that patients probably wouldn't know who I was. Could that be my community service? I thought of Dr. Jakes pretty much telling me that I should find community service on my own. Ugh. I hated to please that man, but I felt excited. Maybe I could work with kids there. I smiled at the TV screen just as a man dressed in a white coat and stethoscope pointed his finger at me and repeated, "Brier Glen Hospital needs *you!*"

Jen came back into the room, carrying a basin of fragrant, bubbly water, along with two rolled-up towels under her arm. "I filled yours, too," she said. "It's in the master bath. Last door on the left."

I found the master bedroom. It was enormous, cut into two separate spaces that were connected by a big arched opening. The largest space had a bed and dresser and an armoire in it. The smaller space had a love seat and one of those long, luxurious lounge chairs. A huge painting of the ocean was on an easel in front of the window. I turned on the light for a better look. It was just the water and sky, but the colors were awesome.

In the main part of the bedroom, there were two huge windows and I envied Jen waking up with an ocean view in the morning. It was obvious that was the room she was staying in. For starters, why not? No one else was there and it was probably the best bedroom in the house. But also, her suitcase was in the corner, and her clothes were scattered across the bed. And it *smelled* like her. A citrusy smell that was strong and really nice. In the bathroom, with its sunken tub and glassed-in shower, her makeup covered the marble countertop. There was an eyelash curler, moisturizer, a tube of fake bronzer and a small tan rectangular case I recognized instantly as birth control pills. I touched the case lightly with my fingertip, remembering how careful I'd been about taking mine. How wise and responsible I thought I was being! I'd stopped taking them after everything ended with Ben. Who knew when I'd ever need them again?

So, I wondered as I picked up the basin of water from the closed toilet-bowl lid, did Jen have a boyfriend?

I carried the basin back into the family room. Jen had moved the coffee table aside and put her basin on a towel in front of the sectional. She was already soaking her feet. I lowered my tub to a second towel.

"I put on *In Her Shoes,*" Jen said. "I thought that was appropriate to watch during a pedicure."

"I love that one," I said.

"Me, too."

I sat down and rolled up the hem of my capris.

"Is one of the people who own this house an artist?" I asked.

"Why?" She held the remote toward the TV, pumping the volume button.

"I saw the painting in the bedroom."

"Oh. Yeah. Mrs. Roscoe paints, I think." She fiddled with the remote for a second. "You have great hair," she said suddenly.

"Are you kidding?" I lowered my feet into the warm, slippery water. "I'd give anything to have yours."

"Mine's so totally straight. You've got those amazing waves."

"I'd rather have straight," I said. This felt so high school, the two of us pampering ourselves and talking girl talk. I was loving it.

"Ready?" She pointed the remote toward the screen.

"Uh-huh."

She clicked the button, then groaned. "A preview," she said. "I hate previews."

"Me, too." The preview was for *The Holiday*, which I'd seen about five times.

"Oh, well." She hit the mute button, then reached for one of the throw pillows on the sectional, plumping it up behind her back. "So," she said, "what was it really like in prison?"

Huh? It was such a totally weird time to ask a question like that, that I was too surprised to answer right away. I guessed it was her idea of small talk while the preview was on, but there was nothing small about the subject.

"It was what you'd expect," I said finally. I stared straight ahead at the TV, where Jack Black was chatting with Kate Winslet. "It was scary. Lonely. A lot of really tough women." I so did not want to think about prison.

"You see those shows that make it seem not all that bad." Jen lifted one foot out of the basin and watched the water stream off her heel for a couple of seconds before submerging it again. "You get three meals a day and health care if you get sick and recreational stuff to do, right?"

She was so far off the mark that I didn't know what to say.

"You get all that for free," she said. "I mean, I know it's not like being on the outside, but how bad could it be? You don't have to have a job and go to work every day."

"Jen," I said. I felt like there was a huge animal inside my chest that was fighting to get out. "It's nothing like that. It's—"

"Shh, shh! It's starting!" She pressed the volume button on the remote, then suddenly laughed out loud. "Oh, God!" she said. "Cameron Diaz is such a hoot in this movie!"

I fantasized about grabbing the remote. Turning off the movie so

I could set her straight about the last year of my life, but Jen was smiling. Giggling. Totally absorbed in the movie, and I knew the animal in my chest would stay trapped in there for the rest of the night.

Maybe forever.

Chapter Twenty-Eight

Sara
A Hole in My Heart
1991

"Hey!" Jamie said as he walked into my hospital room, and I pressed my lips together to keep from crying. I felt as though I'd been waiting weeks instead of hours to see him. He didn't look at me as he reached toward Steve, who sat next to my bed. "Congratulations!"

"Thanks!" Steve stood up and shook his hand. "Did you get to see him?" He nodded toward the hallway and the nursery. "Nine pounds, four ounces."

"I saw him. He looks great." Jamie leaned down to kiss my cheek. "How're you doing, Mama?" he asked softly.

"Okay." I smiled, although I was not doing okay at all. My calm exterior was an act. Inside, I was falling apart.

"I think he has your lips," Jamie said to me.

No, I thought. *He has* your *lips.* Your *hair.* Your *eyes.*

"Listen." Steve stuck his hands in his pockets. "I'm going to take advantage of you being here to grab a bite in the cafeteria. Is that okay with you, Sara?"

I nodded. It was better than okay. I didn't know how I was going to hold it together with both men in the room.

We listened to Steve's footsteps receding down the hallway and when I knew he was far enough away that he couldn't hear me, I burst into tears. Jamie pulled the curtain around my bed—I had a sleeping roommate in her own curtained cubicle—then sat on my mattress and wrapped me in his arms.

"Shh," he said, "it's okay. It's okay."

"Oh, God, Jamie." I tried to keep my voice a whisper, but it was so hard. "I *needed* you here."

"I'm here now," he said.

My voice caught on a sob. "I wanted it to be *you* with me."

"I know." He rubbed my back. "I wish I could have been."

Steve had surprised me with how well he'd handled my labor and the delivery. I'd been afraid he wouldn't be able to get through it after what happened the last time with Sam, but he hardly left my side. I was grateful to him for that, but he wasn't Jamie.

"The baby's sick," I said as Jamie let go of me. I wasn't sure he knew.

"He's going to be all right."

"He has a *hole* in his heart!"

"I know, but it's small. I called Dr. Glaser, the pediatrician Laurel used to work for. He said it's not that uncommon and that it usually goes away on its own, and—"

"They said he might need surgery when he's older!" I grabbed his arm. In my mind, I was already burying another precious son.

"Dr. Glaser said that even if he needs surgery down the road, it's successful in ninety-nine percent of the cases."

Steve suddenly pulled back the curtain, and I jumped. "They told us more like ninety-nine-point-nine, didn't they, Sara," he said.

Jamie got to his feet. "Cafeteria closed?" He looked so guilty. As guilty as I felt.

"I didn't go to the cafeteria," Steve said. "I went to the nursery to have a chat with one of the nurses."

"About Keith's heart?" I asked.

Steve shook his head. "No, not about his heart." His voice sounded tight, and the cold-steel color of his eyes made my own heart start to pound.

"What do you mean?" Jamie asked.

Steve leaned against the wall by the window. "I was confused by something the pediatrician said when he was in here earlier." He looked at me. "About the baby being forty-one weeks."

Oh, God.

"I thought I must have heard wrong, because according to what you told me, you were only thirty-eight weeks along."

"Steve," Jamie said. "It's not an exact—"

"Science?" Steve finished his sentence. "Actually, it is. And I had the nurse check his chart and it said, yup. Forty-one weeks. You think I'm an idiot? I can count. I was in Monterey forty-one weeks ago. And forty weeks ago, and forty-two weeks ago, just in case you want to try the 'not an exact science' argument again."

"What are you *saying?*" I tried desperately to play dumb.

"How could you *do* that to me, Sara?" Steve looked so hurt, and for the first time—truly, the first time—I wondered if maybe he *did* love me after all.

"Look, Steve," Jamie said, "let's—"

Steve suddenly stepped away from the window and pushed Jamie *hard,* shoving him into the footboard of my bed.

"Steve! *Don't!*" I said.

"I opened my house to you, you son of a bitch!" Steve shouted as Jamie recovered his balance.

"Settle down." Jamie held his hands in the air, either in surrender or to ward off another blow. "Let's you and me go out in the hall—"

"That's supposed to be *my* son in there!" Steve pointed toward the hallway. "*My* son! I already lost one and now you're taking this one away from me, too!"

I saw the tears in his eyes, and my heart broke for him. "Steve." I leaned forward, reaching toward him, but he ignored me.

"Why couldn't you be like the other wives?" he asked me. "You never even try to fit in. They're just happy to have a man who cares about them and a roof over their heads. Do you think they screw around when their husbands are away?"

"C'mon, Steve." Jamie reached for Steve's shoulder.

"Get off me!" Steve shrugged his hand away.

"We need to talk, but not here," Jamie said. Suddenly, he shut his eyes, two deep lines between his eyebrows. His face was gray. "Let's get out of Sara's room," he said.

The way he looked frightened me. "Jamie, are you all right?" I asked.

"What's the point in talking?" Steve shouted. "The damage is done, isn't it?"

Jamie suddenly sucked his breath as if he were in pain. He bent over, his hand on his chest. "Oh, *shit!*" He grabbed the footboard of my bed. "Call someone, Sara!" he said. "I think I'm dying."

At first, the doctors in the emergency room thought Jamie was having a heart attack, but I guessed it was his guilt that finally brought him to his knees. Steve called Laurel to tell her Jamie was in the E.R., and I listened to his call to her in terror, afraid he would tell her the truth about the baby. But he didn't. And Laurel, who somehow managed to drive herself to the hospital in Jacksonville by herself, thought Jamie's chest pains were just his overdeveloped capacity for empathy acting up. Our baby had a heart problem, so Jamie's pain made perfect sense to her.

Late that night, Steve told me he'd made a decision: he wanted a divorce. Our marriage had been a mistake from the start, he said. He couldn't live with a woman who'd betrayed him the way I had, and he absolutely couldn't live with another man's child. He'd stay home for the next week, so my mother, who was coming to help out, wouldn't know anything was wrong. Jamie and Maggie would be gone anyway, since the plan all along had been for them to spend that week back in the Sea Tender.

I listened quietly. I was so tired. All I felt was relief that he was making all the decisions for me.

"And here's the deal," he said. "My name's on that birth certificate, so I know I'm legally responsible for child support for that…"

I watched him reach for and discard the word *bastard*.

"That boy," he said finally. "But I'm not paying it."

"I agree," I said. "You shouldn't have to." Yet I was scared. How would I manage with no money and a baby to take care of?

"I know you can come after me for it," Steve said as if I hadn't spoken, "but if you do, I'll make sure that *everyone* knows whose kid he is. Laurel Lockwood'll know. Your mother'll know. Jamie Lockwood's…*ridiculous* congregation will know."

I winced.

"Do you understand me?"

"Yes."

"The…baby will have health insurance through the military, but you'll lose yours. But don't think that means you can go on welfare. Not ever. Because then the government will come after me for child support, and then... Well, I've explained what will happen then."

I nodded.

"So when your mother leaves, I'm packing up and moving out. Then your minister buddy can move back in and you can live out your years together or whatever you want. At least until the end of the month when the rent is due. Because I won't be paying it anymore."

"I'm sorry, Steve." I remembered his emotional words about losing Sam. "I'm so sorry I hurt you."

"Yeah, well." He rubbed his hands together and looked out the window. "You should have thought about that forty-two weeks ago."

I was afraid Jamie might not return to my house once Steve was gone. Without Steve there, would he worry about how our living together might look? But the day after Steve moved out, Jamie and Maggie returned. If anyone talked about us, I never heard about it and I didn't really care. I had my family together. Jamie still slept in his room while I slept in mine, but that would change eventually, I thought. I would be patient.

"Laurel's worse than ever," Jamie said as he told me about his week back at the Sea Tender. "She's drinking. I mean, *seriously* drinking, now. She hangs out with Marcus. It's out of control and I can't tell you how glad I am to be back here with you and Mags and Keith."

Jamie paid the rent on the house so that I—*we*—didn't have to move. I was exhausted, taking care of the baby with a not-quite-two-year-old underfoot, but there was such joy in my heart when I saw Jamie interacting with Keith that my lack of energy was easy to bear. I was too tired to visit Laurel—too tired to keep up that pretense of friendship. Jamie had given Laurel every chance to get well, and now that she was starting to self-destruct, I felt little sympathy for her.

Finally, one evening when the children were in bed, he sat with me on the sofa. He was very close to me. We were physically closer than we'd been in a long time.

"A question for you," he said.

The way he held my hand and the easy tone of his voice told me I would like his question very much.

"Yes?" I asked.

"You and I have been saints, haven't we?"

I laughed. "You're not kidding."

"How would you feel about stopping the sainthood routine?" he asked. "Maybe going on the pill?"

"Yes!" I let go of his hand and nearly leaped on top of him, straddling him.

Jamie laughed at how out of character I was suddenly acting.

I leaned back to smile at him. "I'll make an appointment with my OB tomorrow," I said.

Jamie rubbed his palms over my thighs. "You've been so damn patient, Sara," he said. He tucked my hair behind my ear. "I love you, and I love our son."

I lowered my head, and for the first time since the night Keith was conceived, I kissed Jamie on the mouth. I loved how he groaned. I loved the way he tightened his hands on my thighs. But although I wanted to make love to him, this time I needed more. I leaned away from him again.

"Will you divorce Laurel?" I asked.

He hesitated long enough to let me know that was not necessarily a part of his plan.

"I'm still struggling with it, Sara," he said. "She's not well. And she's Maggie's mother."

I climbed off his lap. "And I'm Keith's, in case you've forgotten."

Jamie grabbed my hand. "I know," he said. "I'm moving in that direction. It's just… I worry about her getting even worse than she is."

"You still love her," I said.

He looked down at where our hands were knotted together, his silence giving me his answer.

"Why?" I asked.

"The past. The person she used to be."

I wanted to feel anger. I was *ready* to feel anger. Instead, I remembered seeing Laurel in the chapel long ago, looking up at Jamie with complete adoration. I could imagine how it felt for him to lose that. I rested my head on his shoulder.

"That person's dead, Jamie," I said. "She's been dead a long time."

We became lovers again, and I helped him formulate the words to tell Laurel he wanted a divorce. I knew, though, that he was still troubled about it. I'd find him in the living room late at night, studying financial statements, punching numbers into a calculator as he tried to figure out the best way to divvy up their assets so that Laurel would be taken care of. He read books about child custody, wanting to find a way to gain custody of Maggie without dragging Laurel through the mud.

Finally, he went to see Laurel, armed with his notes and determination. I waited anxiously at home with the children, trying my best not to think about the conversation taking place in the Sea Tender. I didn't want to think about Laurel being upset and Jamie comforting her.

He said he'd be home by dinnertime, but that hour came and

went. Seven o'clock ticked by. Eight. I grew worried, remembering the chest pains he'd suffered in my hospital room after the confrontational scene with Steve. Could that have happened again? How would I ever know what was going on? I could hardly call the Sea Tender to find out.

I was standing in the kitchen heating a bottle for Keith, who was screaming in the nursery, when I finally heard the car door slam in the driveway. A moment later, Jamie came in the back door.

"Jamie!" I turned off the burner on the stove. "I've been so worried!"

He looked too tired to speak. He stood in the doorway, shaking his head.

"What?" I asked. "What's going on?"

"She's pregnant," he said. "Seven months."

My mouth fell open. "How exactly can she be pregnant?" *No,* I thought. *No, no, no!*

"The week I was there after Keith was born."

"You *slept* with her?" I never imagined he would do that. "I thought she was so drunk and repulsive!"

Jamie ran both hands through his hair. "I'm sorry," he said. "It's...a terrible situation. Maggie and I are going to need to move back to the Sea Tender, Sara," he said. "She needs my help."

"No, Jamie! *Please.*" There was so much hurt inside me that my heart felt like a knot in my chest.

"I know it's not fair to you," he said. "I know that. But I don't feel like I have a choice."

I thought of Keith—*our* baby—crying in the nursery. Of Maggie, the little girl who felt like mine, asleep in the third bedroom. The little girl he wanted with him. More important to him than our son.

Before I could stop myself, I lifted the bottle from the water on the stove and threw it at him. He didn't even bother to duck.

Chapter Twenty-Nine

Andy

I MOVED THE POPCORN BOWL THING IN FRONT OF KIMMIE and she took some. We got the second-to-largest bowl of it, and it was almost gone even though the movie practically only started. We had sodas, too. I always got a soda at the movies because I liked putting it in that holder thing like you could in Mom's car.

"This popcorn is so much better than the popcorn my mother makes," Kimmie said.

"Shh!" somebody said, because you weren't supposed to talk at the movies.

"Shh, yourself!" Kimmie said back.

I laughed because Kimmie always did things like that. Mom said Kimmie didn't care what other people thought. She said that like it was a good thing, but when *I* did stuff she didn't like, Mom always told me, "Don't do that, Andy! People will think you weren't raised right!"

This was our third date at the movies. Her mom dropped us off and my mom was going to pick us up when it was over. In another year, I'd be able to drive us to the movies myself, although Uncle Marcus said "we'll see about that" when I told him.

The movie was named *Kit Kribbage,* and I knew right away it was a girl movie because the main person was a girl. Kimmie picked it out. I wanted to see *Star Wars and the Clone People* or some other name like that, but I didn't care that much. I just liked being at the movies with Kimmie.

The movies were crowded because it was Saturday night and we couldn't sit right in the middle where we liked. We had to sit in the side part, which was okay with me, but Kimmie said it wasn't as good as being in the middle. The movie was okay until they got to the hobo-jungle part. I didn't understand how a lady could be a hobo. I started not concentrating on the movie then. All I kept thinking about was that Kimmie smelled good. The smell came from her hair, which was always so long and fluffy and pretty. I thought about putting my arm around her like boys were supposed to do at the movies. That was kind of like a hug and she was my girlfriend, so when I got bored with all the hobo parts, I put my arm around her. I could tell she liked that I did it because she moved closer to me. She was so close, her hair tickled my nose and the corner of her glasses pressed on my cheek but it didn't hurt.

The girl in the movie was named Kit, which I kept thinking was too short. When somebody said her name, I wanted to say "meow," but knew that wasn't an appropriate thing. Kimmie laughed at something the Kit girl did, but I didn't laugh because I didn't know what she did because I wasn't paying any attention at all anymore. I was thinking about kissing Kimmie instead of watching the movie. My friend Max always made out with a girlfriend at the movies. He had a lot of girlfriends. "Made out" meant kissing and hugging and touching a girl's breasts, only Max called them hooters, which I wasn't supposed to do. Max said, "You been to the movies twice with Kimmie and you haven't even kissed her yet?" I told him I did, too, kiss her, but it was a lie.

I decided I would do it right now. I ate some more popcorn first, though, and drank some more soda. Then I was ready. *One, two, three.* I turned my head and did it. I kissed her! I sort of missed her mouth, or the whole part of her mouth at least, but I got some of her lips. It was cool.

I looked at her to see if she liked it. The movie light was on her face and the Kit girl walked around in Kimmie's glasses, but Kimmie was looking right at me and she smiled. Then all of a sudden, she kissed me back. This time our lips totally touched. We were getting better at it.

Kimmie stopped concentrating on the movie, too. We kept kissing and Kimmie stuck her tongue in my mouth, but only a little. That was a French kiss. I got a hard-on so fast. I put my tongue in her mouth, too. Our tongues slid around together and Kimmie started to giggle.

"Shh!" somebody in back of us said.

Kimmie stopped giggling but she didn't stop kissing me. My arm around her shoulder was going to sleep. I didn't care, though. Kimmie took my hand from where I was holding the popcorn bowl thing and put it right on her breast. It felt like a little pillow under my hand, only there was a hard thing that I thought was the nipple part. Girls' nipples poked up when they were hot, Max said. Hot like turned-on kind of hot. Not like weather hot. So I guessed Kimmie felt exactly like I did.

The popcorn thing suddenly fell off my lap and that made Kimmie laugh again even though my tongue was in her mouth.

I stopped kissing her just long enough to say "It's okay. It's practically empty."

"*God,* you two," a guy I couldn't see said, "get a room!"

"*Seriously,*" some girl said.

A whole lot of people said "shh!" to us now. Then a man with a flashlight came and told us we had to leave.

"We paid!" I said. I didn't think he could make us leave if we paid.

"Shh!" he said. "You're disturbing the other viewers. You'll have to go."

Kimmie grabbed my hand. "Come on," she said. "We don't need this ol' movie."

We got up and started walking to the door that said Exit. I felt strange. My arm that I'd put around Kimmie's shoulders felt all rubbery, like it wasn't really my arm, and my legs shook like after I rode the upside-down roller coaster at the state fair.

In the lobby, we sat down on a bench because my mother wasn't there yet.

"I'd like to still kiss you, but there's too many lights out here," I said.

"I know." She sat really close to me. She still held my hand. If my arm wasn't rubbery, I would've put it around her shoulders again.

"Andy?" she said.

"Yeah?"

"Do you want to have sex with me?"

Did she mean right here? With the lights and people around?

"I don't mean right now," she said. "But sometime. Do you want to?"

"Definitely!" I said. "Do you?"

"Yes. But I never did it before."

"Me neither. But I know how."

"Well, I know how, too."

"My condom is too old, though. I have to get a new one."

"What's a condom?"

I liked that I knew something she didn't. "Like a balloon for a penis," I said.

She laughed. "No!"

"Really."

"Why do you need a balloon?"

"The boy wears it so the girl doesn't get pregnant and so nobody gets a disease."

"Oh, you mean a rubber!"

That's what Max called condoms, too.

"Right."

"Where do you get a new one?"

"The store, I guess." I saw condoms at the Food Lion, but there were a lot of different kinds. When there were a lot of different kinds of a thing, I never knew which one to get.

Kimmie made a big long sighing noise. "Well," she said, "I sure hope my mom doesn't ask me how the movie was."

My arm felt normal again, so I put it back around her shoulders. "I'll just tell my mom it was the best movie I ever went to," I said. And I wouldn't be lying.

Chapter Thirty

Keith

JEN AND I WERE LYING IN MY BED THE MORNING AFTER ONE of the best nights of my life. Maybe it was terrible to feel that way, with my mother missing and everything, but damn, what a night! Jen was like an acrobat in bed. We were both wiped out now, naked and all twisted up in the sheets, with her head resting on my chest. My arm was killing me, the way we were lying, but there was this cost-benefit thing going on in my brain, and I liked having her lie like that more than I hated the pain. I was definitely falling for this chick. Except for my mother, she was all I thought about. I'd put up with the pain for now and pop some pills when I got up. I was going through the Percs faster than I was supposed to. I didn't want to think about what I'd do when they were gone.

She came over with Chinese food the night before. I was embarrassed about having her spend the night in my shoddy tin can, but she didn't seem to care. She reminded me she didn't own the beach house she was in. "It's not like I'm rich, either," she said while we were changing the sheets on my bed. I'd thought about us spending the night in my mother's double bed. That would have made sense, but the thought creeped me out. It just seemed wrong somehow, and I was glad Jen didn't suggest it. She understood me better than I understood myself.

The sunlight from the window above my bed was right on her hair, and I saw the skinniest stripe of roots showing. I thought maybe it was just her scalp, but it was too wide for that. The light wasn't perfect, but I could've sworn the roots of her hair were gray. Gray! I'd seen plenty of blond chicks with dark roots showing, and ladies my mother's age with gray roots coming in, but Jen was *nineteen*. How could she have gray hair? Was she really nineteen? I didn't want to have questions about her in my mind. She'd been perfect up till two minutes ago. I wanted her to stay perfect.

She shifted her head a little and rolled off me, leaving the scent of oranges in the air. I couldn't smell an orange these days without thinking of her. When she opened her eyes, she smiled at me.

"Good morning," she said.

The light was in her face now. In her crystal-clear blue eyes. I ran my fingers over her cheek.

"*Very* good morning," I said.

Her skin was still mostly golden. A little blotchy where her tan was starting to fade. But wrinkles? No way. She was nineteen, like she said. Maybe I could stretch it to twenty-one or -two. Even if her hair was totally gray, which I couldn't picture at all, she wouldn't look old. She said she had scars inside. People could go gray overnight when terrible things happened to them. I hadn't asked what she'd meant by those scars. I figured she'd tell me if she wanted to. Probably molested or something. That happened to girls all the time.

"I'm gonna make you breakfast." She sat up. Her breasts were small and totally perfect. Man, she was fine, and not one of those chicks who covered herself over with the sheet right away. My woody was back again. I'd lost track of how many times we did it last night. She finally said she wouldn't be able to walk today if we did it one more time. Last thing I wanted was to hurt her. Otherwise, I would've grabbed her again right then. "Do you have eggs?" she asked.

"Yeah." Only because they were part of the food Laurel'd left with me the other day. Yesterday, while I was racing around trying to clean up the trailer for Jen to come over, the P.I. Laurel hired showed up. Black dude named Mister Johnson. Seriously, his first name was Mister and he looked like that James Earl Jones guy. He went through the trailer like the police did, poking his nose in my mother's closet and drawers. He asked a lot more questions than the cops, though, mostly about my mother's so-called "personal life," which I realized I knew zilch about. I told him her life revolved around me, myself and I. He said there was probably a lot about her I didn't know, so I sent him to Dawn for that info. I had the feeling he was just covering the same territory as the police, and Laurel was wasting her piles of dough on him.

Jen leaned over to kiss me, then sat on the side of the bed and started pulling on her clothes. I watched her get dressed and walk out of the room. After a few minutes, I got up myself and that sinking feeling came over me again like it always did when reality hit. My mother was gone. I was just about out of money. Bills were showing up in the mail. My body was fucked up. And I needed a couple of Percocet.

I walked to the kitchen, gave Jen a little bite on her shoulder, popped open the bottle of pills, then took a beer from the refrigerator.

"How do you get beer?" Jen asked as she moved the frying pan from the dish drainer to the stove.

"Dude at the gas station buys it for me," I said, twisting off the top. I'd made a run the night before to stock up. "How d'you get the booze you have at your house?" *Are you really only nineteen?*

"Came with the property," she said. "I don't think they'll miss it. They have plenty, but I hope I'm not drinking wine from some special, exotic vineyard." She laughed. "Maybe they've been saving it for their fiftieth anniversary all these years." She pried the bottle from my hand and took a long pull on it. Then she tipped her head to the side and smiled at me. "Oh, hell," she said, wrapping her arms around my neck. "Let's skip breakfast and just go back to bed."

"Really?" I asked.

"For sure." She led me through the living room to my bedroom, dropping articles of clothing along the way.

Nineteen. Ninety. I really didn't care.

Chapter Thirty-One

Maggie

IT TURNED OUT THAT BRIER GLEN HOSPITAL HAD ALMOST doubled in size, which is why they were desperate for volunteers. They *had* to be desperate to let Maggie Lockwood work for them. That's what I kept thinking on my first day.

The pediatric unit, which is where I asked to volunteer, had expanded from eight beds to fifteen, and they were nearly all full. I spent my first day with a longtime volunteer named Helen Rogers—*Miss* Helen to me and the patients—who had to be at least eighty. She had one of those extremely thick, mouth-full-of-marbles accents that made me think she was from someplace a lot deeper south than North Carolina. She was such a sweet-grandma type, and she practically led me around by the hand, introducing me to everyone as "the little girl who'll be helpin' us out from now on." She obviously didn't have a clue who I really was.

"You'll spend a good half your time in here," Miss Helen said, walking me into the playroom. The room wasn't very large, but it was a wonderland, full of small chairs and tables, lots of toys and books and movies and a plastic slide. A couple of kids sat in beanbag chairs in front of a TV where *Finding Nemo* was playing. There were two adult-size rocking chairs, and another volunteer, an elderly man, sat in one of them, reading a book to a pale little bald girl on his lap.

"That's Mr. Jim," Miss Helen said. "He's here on Tuesdays and Thursdays. Mr. Jim, this is Maggie Lockwood. She'll be with us every single day. Isn't that grand?"

"Terrific!" Mr. Jim smiled at me before going right back to his reading. I wondered how long the listless girl on his lap had been a patient here. I imagined myself reading to a child that way. Holding her or him on my lap like that. My eyes got misty. What was *that* all about? I thought it had something to do with being trusted with these kids. I wasn't even sure I should be.

Saturday—the day after I saw the Brier Glen commercial at Jen's—I checked out the hospital's Web site and e-mailed the woman in charge of volunteers—without using my name, of course. The woman, Cathy Moody, e-mailed me back on Monday. She asked for my phone number and said she wanted to talk to me about my reasons for volunteering and have me fill out an application, etcetera. Oh, yeah—and sign a form letting them do a background check on me. *Scratch working in a hospital,* I thought.

But I kept going back to the Web site, where it talked about how much they needed help. They especially needed someone in pediatrics. There was a picture of a little boy sitting in the beautiful playroom making something out of clay, his tongue between his lips like he was concentrating hard. Forgetting he was sick for a few minutes. I stared at his picture for the longest time. Finally, I hit Reply to Cathy Moody's e-mail. What did I have to lose?

My name is Maggie Lockwood. My name might be familiar to you. I'm the person responsible for the fire at the Surf City lock-in a year and a half ago. I was released from prison two weeks ago and have to do three hundred hours of community service. I know I owe the community a lot more than three hundred hours. Like I said in my other e-mail, I saw your TV ad and knew working in a hospital was the right thing for me. It feels as though it fits my crime, since so many people were hurt because of what I did. I understand if you don't want someone who's served time, but I wish you'd give me a chance.

I typed my phone number and hit Send, and within minutes—*minutes,* which is how I knew they were totally desperate—Cathy Moody called me. We talked for half an hour, and I told her the truth about what happened when I tried volunteering at the school and the library.

"Would you allow me to speak with your therapist?" she asked.

I was surprised she didn't just tell me it was a no-go, but she sounded amazingly sympathetic.

"You mean…to be sure I'm sane and everything?"

"Well…" She laughed. "Something like that."

"I see him this afternoon," I said. "I'll make sure it's okay with him and call you back."

Dr. Jakes gave me two thumbs-up when I told him I was trying to volunteer at the hospital.

"Attagirl!" he said. "You took the bull by the horns."

I didn't like pleasing him all that much. I didn't get why I still had trouble letting him in. He was definitely in my corner. Maybe prison did that to me—made me just not trust people who were nice to me. Jen was the exception. She was so totally easygoing about all the stuff I told her that I felt safe opening up to her. She had some off-the-wall ideas about life behind bars, though. I told her whatever shows she'd watched about what it's like in prison had gotten it all wrong, and she apologized for making it seem like I'd been on a spa vacation instead of in jail.

"There's a snag, though," I said to Dr. Jakes. "I explained about...you know. My record. And the woman in charge of volunteers asked if she could talk to you."

"Ah," he said. "How do you feel about that?"

"It's okay with me. It's not like you know anything the rest of the world doesn't already know about me."

"Not true," he said.

"What do you mean?"

"From what you've told me, much of the rest of the world thinks you deserved more punishment than you received."

"You don't?"

He shook his head. "No, I don't, Maggie," he said. "You've already given *yourself* a life sentence."

I looked down at my hands. It was a sentence I needed to serve.

"Anyhow, I'd be pleased to speak with her." He leaned forward, his poor old chair creaking beneath him. "This is the first step in saving yourself," he said.

"What do you mean?" I asked.

"You took the initiative this time. Your mother didn't do it for you."

"Well, it's just that I saw the ad on TV and—"

"Discount it all you want, Maggie," he said. "You've taken a big step forward."

* * *

I called Jen after my first day at the hospital and told her every single detail about Miss Helen and the kids I'd met and what I'd be doing there. I was sitting on my bed, the angora teddy bear at my side, admiring the purple polish on my toenails.

"You sound totally psyched," she said when I finally stopped talking. "I'm still amazed they let you work there. With kids, I mean."

"Me, too, but I'm so glad." The library suddenly seemed ridiculously tame to me. "I think I'm going to love it."

"That's great." Jen sounded...I wasn't sure what. Distant, maybe? Or just tired? Had I bored her to bits? I suddenly realized that I was always talking about myself. When did I ever ask questions about *her?* It had been so long since I'd had an honest-to-God girlfriend, I didn't know how to be a good one anymore. She was such an excellent listener, and I was totally self-absorbed. "Sorry I talked your ear off about the hospital," I said.

"No, that's cool." Was she yawning? Maybe I'd caught her in the middle of a nap or something.

"Do you want to get together again soon?" I was already formulating questions I'd ask her about herself if she said yes.

"Definitely." She sounded a little more awake. "This weekend?"

"That'd be great." I was relieved by the enthusiasm in her voice. "I want to hear all about *you* this time."

The next day, Miss Helen sent me out on my own. I took the book cart around to the patients' rooms. I entertained a couple of kids in the E.R. while their little brother got stitches. I sat with a scared four-year-old boy in his room, giving his mother a chance to get something to eat. I helped a few kids color and make things out of clay in the playroom and I tried to keep two boys from clobbering each other over whose turn it was to go down the sliding board. And that was just the morning.

In the afternoon, I brought a new patient—a five-year-old boy named Jacob—into the playroom. He was in the hospital for asthma, like Andy'd been so many times at that age. Jacob clung hard to my hand as he looked around the room. There was so much to do in there, it could be overwhelming. He was probably already overwhelmed just by being in the hospital.

The only other kid in the room was that pale little bald girl I'd seen with Mr. Jim the day before. She looked so tired and very, very sick. She sat alone in the big rocker, watching TV. I knew her name was Madison, and Miss Helen had told me she had a rare cancer of the blood and that she was in the hospital more than she was out. "I think she likes it here better than she does at home," Miss Helen told me at the nurses' station. She cupped her hand around her mouth like she was telling me a dirty little secret. "Dysfunctional family," she whispered.

"Hi, Madison," I said to her as I pulled out a chair at the table for Jacob. She didn't answer me and there was no trace of a smile on her face. Her eyes reminded me of my own—huge and dark—except that she had no eyelashes or eyebrows. Her skin was so pale, I could see the blue-gray veins beneath the surface of her bare scalp. She had a capped-off tube strapped to her left arm with wide bands of green-and-blue dotted tape, and she held that arm gently cradled in her lap as if it hurt her.

"Do you want to join Jacob and me?" I asked her. "We're going to color."

She shook her head. "No, thanks," she whispered, and she closed her eyes.

* * *

At five o'clock, I went to the nurses' station to check out for the day. Two men and two women were behind the counter, busily writing notes and typing on keyboards. I'd already figured out that some of the men in the peds unit were nurses and some of the women were doctors and I didn't yet know which was which. They all looked preoccupied, but I knew I wouldn't be able to sleep that night unless I talked to someone about Madison.

"Excuse me," I said.

A young woman with short blond hair and too much mascara raised her head from her keyboard and smiled at me. "How'd your second day go, Maggie?" she asked.

"Good." I was surprised she knew my name before I remembered the name tag pinned to my blue vest, which was the uniform of the volunteers. "But I have a question about Madison…" I realized I didn't know the little girl's last name, but the woman—her name tag read Taffy Cruise—knew who I meant.

"Here's her doc right here," she said, motioning to a broad-shouldered, dark-haired man sitting in front of a computer screen. "Dr. Britten? You have a minute for the volunteer?"

He looked up at me, rubbing a hand across his chin and looking nearly as tired as Madison did. There was something familiar about him that I couldn't place. Maybe I'd seen him the day before and just didn't remember him.

"What's up?" he asked.

"I…" I felt intimidated all of a sudden. I was a nineteen-year-old ex-con brand-new volunteer. What did I know? "I noticed Madison holding her arm like it hurts her," I said. "The arm with the—" I rubbed the inside of my left arm "—the tube."

"It probably does hurt her," he said, like it was no big deal. "She's a tough cookie." He turned to the other man at the station. "You want to check on Madison's IV when you get a chance?" he asked.

The other guy nodded, although he kept tapping at a keyboard of his own.

"Okay," I said. "Thanks."

"No prob," Dr. Britten said. He lifted a cardboard coffee cup to his lips and looked at his computer screen again. There was a gold band on his ring finger, a dimple at the corner of his mouth when he sipped his coffee, and I had a sudden, truly terrible feeling of déjà vu. I knew why he looked familiar to me. He looked like Ben. Dark hair, like Ben. Thirtyish, the age Ben would be around now. Big, teddy-bear kind of build. Maybe not quite as massive as Ben, but still. He put down his cup and began typing, and I stared at his hands. I knew those hands. I knew them, and worse—*much* worse—I suddenly missed them. I missed *Ben*—the Ben I'd thought he was. The one who touched me with hands that looked a lot like Dr. Britten's. How could I even be *thinking* that way? I was so screwed up!

"We'll see you tomorrow, Maggie," Taffy said, and I realized I'd just been standing there like an idiot, staring at Dr. Britten.

"Right." I slipped my purse strap over my shoulder. "See you tomorrow."

I walked straight from the peds unit to the hospital exit. In the parking lot, I got into my car and rested my forehead on the steering wheel. I took a few long, deep breaths. Did he really look like Ben? He was a little older, wasn't he? And his eyes were not quite so dark.

"Stop it!" I punched my fist on the steering wheel. "Just stop it!"

I rested my head back against the car seat with a sigh.

There were no parents protesting outside the hospital. Nobody spitting at me in the halls. But there was still one big obstacle standing in the way of me doing my community service there—or *anywhere*—and it wasn't Dr. Britten. It wasn't a man at all. It was me—the weak-willed, easily seduced, insecure girl I'd become. I was the obstacle I'd be carrying around with me for the rest of my life.

Chapter Thirty-Two

Sara
Painting and Sewing
1991

JAMIE SPLIT HIMSELF IN TWO. THAT WAS THE WAY I SAW IT. IF I'd been stronger or tougher or meaner, I would have demanded more. Instead, I witnessed Jamie's struggle to be there for me and our beautiful son, as well as for Laurel and Maggie, and I couldn't bring myself to make things harder for him. The baby who was yet to be born would up the score on Laurel's side. Two to one. I didn't want to think that way, but sometimes I did.

I spent a lot of time in the comfort of the chapel. On Sundays, I often stood near the entrance with Keith and Maggie to keep them from disrupting the service. I was there during the week as well. The walls needed painting, and I talked to Jamie about painting them myself—a massive job. I asked him if I could bring color into the space I loved. He looked alarmed at first. His vision for the chapel had always been pure white walls, but when I talked about the view—how it looked outside the panoramic windows after a rain, with the sand that deep khaki color—he understood what I was saying. So I painted the inside of the chapel the color of wet sand, all by myself, in between feeding and changing Keith. Jamie'd found a nanny for Maggie, and although I missed the little girl, I had to admit it was a relief not to have both of them to care for. I loved Maggie, but I would have resented being asked to watch Laurel's child as well as my own now that Jamie seemed to have chosen between us. That was small of me, but I couldn't help it.

When I finished painting the chapel, I asked Jamie if I could make cushions for the pews. The task of making the long, foam-filled cushions would be grueling, but I pleaded, and Jamie finally agreed. I spread fabric on the floor of the chapel office and cut it into long rectangles. I brought in a sewing machine and sewed well into the evenings.

All my work served a purpose separate from making the chapel warmer and even more beautiful: it kept me from thinking about the Sea Tender. Laurel had stopped drinking, Jamie told me. She was doing much better. He'd made the right decision to go home, he said. All the while, I painted and sewed because I knew which home was ultimately Jamie's greatest love, and it was the one where I was working.

I was in the chapel when Jamie called me early one morning.

"The baby's here," he said, and I knew from the thick, tired tone of his voice that something was wrong. My heart dropped. As envious as I was of Laurel, I would never wish for anything to happen to her or the baby.

"What's wrong?" I asked. My first thought was that, like Keith, the baby had a hole in its heart, but that was not the problem.

"They took him away from us," Jamie said. "Laurel's been drinking all along. She just hid it from me somehow. She was smashed when she went into labor last night. Marcus drove her in so I wouldn't know. And the baby—" His voice broke.

"Oh, Jamie. Honey." I put down the fabric I'd been sewing. "What happened?"

"They think he has this...condition called fetal alcohol syndrome. He looks okay, except for being small. But it's something about his development or...I don't understand it all yet. I just..."

"What do you mean, they took him away from you?"

"Protective Services. They have custody of him, though he's still here at the hospital. The social worker said Laurel probably had severe postpartum depression after Maggie was born and that she's been drinking to...they called it self-medicate. I shouldn't have left her. I should have insisted she get help."

"You did everything you could," I said. "You couldn't force her. Even that psychiatrist you took her to told you that, remember?"

"This poor little guy," he said. "He's all tied up to machines. I can't take it, Sara. Laurel's upset. I know she feels terrible. But she doesn't really understand the whole thing. The social worker said our best chance of getting the baby back is for her to go into rehab, but she won't do it."

I turned off the sewing machine. "I'm coming to the hospital," I said.

On the drive to the hospital, I felt my anger toward Laurel building. Laurel had everything. Jamie. The money. Two children. And she was doing her best to throw it all away and hurt every single person who cared about her. Everyone treated her with kid gloves, and it wasn't working.

When I arrived in Laurel's hospital room, I found Jamie sitting next to her bed. Laurel looked ashen and tired, her eyes at half-mast.

"Go get a cup of coffee, Jamie," I said.

He looked at me. "I don't need a cup of coffee."

I grabbed his arm, tugged him out of the chair and pulled him physically to the door. He stopped in the doorway, trying to read my face, and I knew he was worried what I might say to Laurel in his absence. Tough.

"Go," I said.

Once he left, I sat down in the chair he'd vacated and skipped right over the pleasantries. "You need to go into rehab," I said, "for your family's sake if not for your own."

"I wish y'all would just leave me alone." Laurel's voice was so whiny and pathetic. I wanted to slap her face. Slap some sense into her.

I somehow managed to get control of my anger. I told Laurel about the first time I saw her. It was in the chapel, when she'd looked so pretty and so full of love for her husband. I told her how much Jamie loved her. How her children needed her to be whole and healthy for them. For a moment, I thought I was getting through to her.

Then she shook her head. "All I want right now is a drink," she said.

Furious, I sat forward and grabbed her wrist. "You've become a selfish, self-absorbed bitch, Laurel, you know that?" I stared hard into her eyes. "I know your hormones got screwed up," I said. "I understand you can't help the depression. But you can *fix it,* Laurel. You're the only one who can."

I got up, scraping the chair against the linoleum floor, and walked out of the room. In the hallway, I started to tremble, and I fought tears as I left the hospital and walked into the parking garage, knowing I'd done what no one else had dared to do: tell Laurel the truth.

Chapter Thirty-Three

Andy

I HAD A HARD TIME GETTING ALONE WITH UNCLE MARCUS. Mom and Maggie were always around, but finally it was just me and him at breakfast Saturday. I felt embarrassed all of a sudden, but I knew I had to do it.

I poked my cereal with my spoon. "My condom is too old," I said.

Coffee all of a sudden squirted out of Uncle Marcus's mouth and he started choking. He got up and leaned over the sink and coughed and coughed. Was he having an asthma attack?

"You need your inhaler?" I asked. I never saw Uncle Marcus's inhaler, so I didn't know where to get it.

He shook his head. "I don't have asthma, remember?" His voice was croaky like a frog. Finally he got a paper towel and wiped his mouth and then his eyes. He sat down again. I looked real hard at his face. He looked like he'd been crying, but he was smiling. "You just caught me off guard there, buddy. Sorry 'bout that."

"You spilled coffee on the table." I pointed to a place where the coffee came out of his mouth.

"Thanks." He pressed on the coffee spot with his paper towel. Then he looked at me. "What are you talking about, Andy?" he asked. "Do you mean the condom I gave you a while back?"

I nodded. "It says ten-oh-seven on it."

"Well, you're right, then. It's too old." He breathed out like he was real tired but he didn't look tired. "Are you saying you and Kimmie want to have sex?"

"Yes."

"Well—" he got up and poured some more coffee in his cup "—I'm proud of you for coming to me and for wanting to be careful," he said. "But let's talk about it a little first."

"Me and Kimmie already did."

His eyes got big. "Did what?"

"Talk about it."

"Oh." He sat down again. "Okay. And what did you say?"

"That we both want to do it but how we need a new condom. I saw them at Food Lion but I don't know which one to get."

"I'll get you some, And. Don't sweat it. But please. There's no rush. You're only—"

I just knew he was going to say I was only sixteen, but he looked out the window instead.

"There're some rules that come with having sex," he said.

"Never ever do it without a condom," I said. I remembered that's what he told me.

"That's right. That's rule number one. Number two is to always treat a girl with respect. That means you don't go telling other people that you had sex with her."

"It's private."

"*Very* private."

"I'm telling *you,* though. You just said you were proud of me about that."

"I mean you don't tell your friends."

"Like Max."

"Especially not Max."

"He tells me what he does with his girlfriends, though."

"Do you think he's treating them with respect?"

"I don't know. I'm not there when he's with them."

"No, I mean, by telling you what happens between him and them. That's disrespectful."

"Oh." I got it. "Right. So I won't tell Max."

"Or any other friends. It's between you and Kimmie."

"Yup. Can I have the condom now?"

Uncle Marcus shook his head. "I'm not done," he said.

"Okay." He had a lot of rules.

"Do you love Kimmie?" he asked, all serious.

"Totally."

He nodded. "Well, here's another rule. If she *ever* says no or she doesn't want to do it, you don't push her."

"I'd *never* push her." I was surprised he thought I'd do that.

"I mean, you don't try to talk her into it," he said. "When a girl says no, that's it. You stop. You won't want to stop, but you have to. Even if you have to get up and go in the bathroom and…"

"Jerk off," I said.

He laughed and twisted his mouth up funny. "You know more than I figured about this," he said.

"So does Kimmie. We both know how to do it." We'd been talking about it a *lot* since the movies. I couldn't wait to see her again, and not just at stupid swim practice when all the people were around. "We just haven't ever done it. Either of us."

Uncle Marcus rubbed his face with his hand. "It's a powerful urge, isn't it?" he asked, like he didn't know about it himself.

I nodded.

"D'you remember we talked last year about another powerful urge you have? Used to have?"

I shook my head.

"Hitting people?"

"Oh, yeah. When they call me a name."

"Right. And what was the rule for that?"

"Stop, think and act," I said. "Only it's atomic now."

He scrunched his eyebrows together. "What do you mean?"

That wasn't the right word. "You know. When you don't need to do all the steps in your head."

"Automatic?"

I smiled. "Yeah."

"That's great, Andy. But when it comes to sex, I want you to go back to the rules. When you feel like…getting close to Kimmie that way, stop and think first."

"About what?"

"About being safe, first of all. About how it might be better to wait."

"For *what?*" I was getting confused.

He blew out a *long* breath. "Too many rules, huh?" he asked.

I nodded.

"Just repeat the important ones back to me."

I just wanted the condom, but I knew he wouldn't give it to me unless I said the rules. "Always use a condom." I looked at the ceiling, remembering. "Don't push her if she says no. Jerk off instead. Don't tell other people." Then I looked back at him. He was smiling. "How'd I do?"

"Great, Andy," he said. "I'll get you some condoms today, okay?"

Chapter Thirty-Four

Keith

LAUREL CALLED ME A COUPLE OF DAYS AFTER THE P.I. PAID his visit to my trailer.

"I spoke to Mr. Johnson," she said, "and he's concerned you have some household bills coming in with no way to pay them."

Damn Mr. Mister Johnson, I thought. He'd asked me about the bills that were piling up, but what gave him the right to talk to Laurel about them? Maybe since she was paying for him, she got to know everything there was to know.

"And how is this your business?" I asked.

"Let me take care of them," Laurel said.

"Uh-uh," I said.

"Keith," she said, "please don't let your pride get in the way of letting people help you."

I would have hung up on her if I didn't know she was right. I needed help if I wanted to stay in the trailer. So far the phone and electric bills had shown up, along with medical bills that weren't covered by my insurance. I knew where my mother kept her checks and had thought of forging her signature, but the bank knew she was missing and I figured I'd just end up screwing myself. I didn't need the house phone as long as I had my cell. And I could get by without electricity until winter, but I would definitely need it then. I wished Dawn hadn't let Frankie move in with her. I could tolerate living with Dawn, but that was out of the question with him there now.

"If it makes it easier to swallow, I'll use the restitution money, okay?" Laurel said. "Instead of having that money automatically sent to your mom's bank account, I'll pay whatever bills come in."

All right, I thought. "I don't need the house phone," I said. "Just the cell."

"Well, the P.I. said for you to definitely keep the landline," she said. "Just in case someone tries to contact you about your mother."

Oh, man. I wished someone *would* contact me. Kidnapper. Extortionist. Mom herself. As long as it wasn't the school or Social Services, I'd love that phone to ring.

I decided to go over to Jen's that afternoon. I didn't call first and I guess it was kind of uncool of me to just drop in, but I felt like we were getting tight and she wouldn't mind. There was no answer when I knocked on the front door of her cottage, though, so I walked around back and saw her sitting alone out on the beach. Her back was to me, and even though the sky was overcast and gloomy, she had on a straw hat and she was bundled up in a big tan sweater.

"Hey!" I called as I walked toward her. The ocean was rough, and she didn't seem to hear me. "Hey!" I shouted again when I was practically on top of her.

She jumped to her feet suddenly, a hand to her chest. "You scared me!" she said.

"Sorry." I smiled, reaching for her, but she dodged my hands.

"Don't do that again," she said. "Don't sneak up on me, okay?"

"Okay." I raised my hands like I was showing her I was unarmed or something. "I said I'm sorry."

"It's all right." She flopped down on the sand again. "Didn't mean to overreact."

I sat next to her. "You want me to go?" I asked.

She shook her head. That's when I noticed that her eyes were red, her cheeks damp. I'd caught her crying.

"What's wrong?" I asked.

She shook her head. "Nothing."

"Then why are you crying?"

She didn't answer right away. Finally she smiled. "You know how girls get sometimes. PMS and all that. Anything can set us off." She pointed at a string of pelicans flying low over the rough gray water. "Like the pelicans, for example. See the one at the end? Why's he at the end? Is he sick or just slow? Is it some pelican pecking order? Does he always have to be last?"

Whoa. Weird. PMS could turn a perfectly sane chick into a lunatic.

"So you're sitting here crying over a pelican?" I asked.

"Not specifically. I'm just trying to explain how I get emotional sometimes. It doesn't need to make sense."

She had those scars inside. I couldn't make myself ask about them. I didn't want to get into a whole big heavy thing with her.

She wiped her cheeks with her hands like she was trying to erase her bad mood. "You want to watch a movie?"

"Yeah. Sure," I said, though I would have rather gone to bed with her. I had the feeling that wasn't going to happen.

"Okay." She stood up and brushed off the back of her shorts. Then she brushed off the back of my jeans, which only made me want to fuck her ten times more.

She suddenly stood on her tiptoes, leaned over and kissed me on the cheek. "I'm glad you're here, Keith," she said. "I really am." And she put her arm around my waist and kept it there as we walked back to her house.

Chapter Thirty-Five

Maggie

TAFFY BROUGHT MADISON INTO THE PLAYROOM THURSDAY afternoon. "I thought she could use a break from her room," she said.

"Great!" I reached out, and Madison moved her hand easily from Taffy's to mine, as if she was used to being transferred from one person to another.

"Thanks, Miss Maggie," Taffy said. "I'll see you later, Madison."

I walked with Madison toward the table in the middle of the playroom. We had the whole room to ourselves for the moment.

"What would you like to do, Madison?" I asked. "We can paint or color or I can read to you or you can watch a movie?" She looked sort of lost, and I thought I'd given her too many choices. Her dazed expression reminded me of the way Andy looked when someone asked him too many questions at once. "Would you like to paint or use clay?" I tried.

"Paint," she said so quietly I had to read her lips to understand her.

"Okay."

I put her in a corner of the room with the easel, but quickly realized she didn't have enough wind to stand and paint. I got her a chair and lowered the easel for her.

"How old are you?" I asked as I set up the paints for her.

"Almost seven." She looked much younger than that.

"Do you have any brothers or sisters?"

She stared at the blank paper in front of her, and I leaned close to hear her answer. "A brother," she said.

"Me, too." I said. "My brother's name is Andy."

"Mine's Devon."

"Younger?"

"Older." She *almost* smiled. "He's horrible."

I laughed. "How is he horrible?"

"He tells gross jokes."

"Wanna tell *me* one?"

She giggled, but shook her head.

"Well, okay," I said, moving the paints closer to her. "Do you know what you'd like to paint?"

She shook her head again.

"Maybe these pictures can give you some ideas." I pointed to the wall in front of her, where someone had hung photographs of animals. There were twelve of them, but we needed more. I'd find some stock images on the Internet and bring them in.

Madison began painting a lion, doing a not-bad job for a six-year-old. She wheezed a little when she breathed, but her arm with the tube taped to it didn't seem to be bothering her today.

I'd seen Dr. Britten in the hallway outside Madison's room that morning. I'd stared at him, separating which features were his and which were Ben's. I had to stop that. I knew perfectly well that my attraction to him was screwed up. Plus, the man was married, married, married! Yet that didn't prevent my insides from knotting up with longing when I looked at him. Sick.

But it was really *Madison* I was in danger of falling in love with. That had been one of Miss Helen's warnings to me on my first day.

"You'll want to love 'em up, honey," she'd told me, "but you have to keep a little bit outside their world to be able to help."

I thought of that now as I sat with Madison while she painted. She was pretty good at it, considering how sick she was and the goofy fat brushes we had for the kids to use. Maybe I could get some better ones. Madison painted the lion, an alligator and a bear. I got her to tell me a couple of her brother's gross jokes in her quiet little voice, and we giggled together. I kept feeling my eyes tear up, and could practically hear Miss Helen warning me to get a grip. It was just that I felt so *healthy,* sitting there. I tried to beam my health into Madison's tiny, weak body. For the first time in more than a year, I felt the *Empathy* tattoo on my hip burning.

"I'm tired," Madison said after a while. She set down the paintbrush.

"Okay," I said. "How 'bout I wheel you back to your room? Save you the walk?"

She nodded, and I pulled the kid-size wheelchair from the side of the room. Madison sat down in it, and I wheeled her out into the hallway.

I spent the rest of the morning and part of the afternoon reading to kids in their rooms, giving their mothers—and in a couple of cases, fathers—a break. I reached Madison's room last and her mother, Joanna, seemed relieved to see me.

"I'm dying for a smoke," she said. It bothered me that she used the word *dying* when that was exactly what her daughter was doing. She had Madison's brown eyes and small pouty mouth. Her strawberry-blond hair was clipped to the back of her head so that the ends spiked straight up like a crest. I wondered if Madison's hair was the same color.

"Go ahead," I said to her. "I brought a book to read to Madison, if she's up for it."

"I'm up for it," Madison said in her small voice.

Joanna leaned over and kissed her forehead. "I'll be back soon, cutie," she said.

Miss Helen had told me we weren't supposed to sit on the patients' beds, so I sat in the big recliner in the corner of her room, and Madison climbed willingly into my lap with a trust that made my heart ache. I could barely feel her weight on me, she was so thin. Her head rested against my chest while I read to her, and I could actually feel the air moving in and out of her lungs as she breathed.

Ten or fifteen minutes had passed when a man walked into the room.

"Hey, Madison!" he nearly shouted. He was around thirty, with a few days' growth of beard on his cheeks and blond hair to his shoulders. And he was, like, totally drunk. The stench of him reached all the way to the recliner. "How's my girl?"

Madison rolled her head against my chest to get a look at him. I thought I felt her stiffen beneath my arms.

"Can I help you?" I asked. I didn't like the boom of his voice.

Neither did Madison. "Go 'way, Rudy," she said.

He suddenly seemed to notice me. "Who the hell are you?" he asked. "Where's Joanna?"

"She's taking a break." I could see old sweat stains in the armpits of his T-shirt. "She should be back any minute. Maybe you could wait in the hall for her."

"Like hell!" He pointed at Madison. "*I* can read to her now," he said. "You can turn her over to me."

Madison shook her head, and I tightened my arms around her. "Sir... Could you wait in the hall until—"

"No, *damn it!*"

I cowered, sinking a little deeper into the chair.

"I'll be damned if I'm waiting in the hall!" he said. "I've made arrangements at Children's Hospital for her to go there. This here hospital's for kids they give up on!"

I spotted the call button attached to Madison's bed. Leaning forward, I grabbed it and pressed it hard, over and over again.

"What do you think you're doing?" He snatched the button out of my hand.

"Nurse!" I yelled. Madison curled into a ball on my lap, hiding her face in her arms.

"Who are you anyway?" the man asked. "You're nobody to her. Let me have her!"

What was I supposed to do? I knew the hospital had security guards, but I couldn't reach the phone from the recliner.

"Sir," I said as calmly as I could, which wasn't very. "Please go out in the hallway and see the nur—"

"Do you know who I am?" He leaned toward Madison, who turned her head against my neck and grabbed my arm.

"It's okay, Madison," I said. But it didn't feel okay at all. I slid even farther down in the recliner, trying to get away from the man's rank breath.

"Look at me!" he shouted at Madison. "Do you know who I *am*, little girl?"

"Rudy," she whispered.

He let out this half growl, half moan. "It's time you put an end to that Rudy shit. I'm your *daddy!* And I'm gettin' you outta here."

Madison cried quietly against my neck. "He's not my daddy," she whimpered.

The man folded his arms sloppily across his chest. "The hell I'm not!" he said.

Taffy suddenly appeared in the doorway. "Did you buzz..." She looked from me to the man and back again. "What's going on?"

"Call security." My voice shook, though I was practically whispering.

"We don't need no security!" The man flung his arms out at his sides, and even though he was still a few feet away from Madison and me, I ducked. I saw Taffy take off at a run down the hallway.

"You!" He shouted at me now. "Let go of her or I'll yank her outta your arms. I'm not joking."

I was totally confused as well as frightened. "Are you her father?" I asked. If he *was* her father, didn't I have to do what he said?

"Hell, yes, I'm her father! Now give her to me!" He reached for Madison, but I batted his hand away before I could think. He could probably sue me if he was really her father, but I didn't care. I wasn't turning her over to him until I knew for sure.

Instead, I stood up, still holding Madison, who had to be the world's lightest six-year-old, and turned my back on him.

"Rudy!"

I looked over my shoulder to see Joanna run into the room.

The man grabbed her shoulder. "You left Madison here with some stranger!" he shouted. He tried to hit her, but he was so drunk that he missed totally and fell to the floor. I climbed over him before he had a chance to get up, ran past Joanna and into the hallway, still clutching the little girl in my arms. Two security guards practically crashed into us.

"In there!" I nodded toward Madison's room. Then I carried her to the playroom, which was empty. Thank God. I sank with her into one of the rockers, shaking all over and totally winded from carrying her.

"Are you all right, Madison?" I asked as I started to rock the chair.

Her head was still pressed against my chest. "He's not my daddy," she said.

"Your mom and the security men will figure it all out," I said as I rocked her. "You're safe here." I hoped that was true. I hoped the security guards could arrest that guy or something. Mostly, I hoped he wasn't her father. What an asshole.

Madison slipped her thumb into her mouth. She sniffled, and I felt her heart beating hard against my ribs.

Or maybe it was my own heart I was feeling.

That night, after Andy went to his room to do his homework, I walked out to the porch where Mom and Uncle Marcus were sitting all lovey-dovey under an afghan on the glider.

"I need to talk to you two." I flopped into a wicker chair. I'd been waiting for the chance to talk to them ever since getting home from the hospital.

"What's wrong?" Mom asked. It was dark on the porch and I couldn't see her face, but I heard the worry in her voice.

"I'm fine," I said. "But…an incident happened at the hospital today, and it made me realize we need to talk about something." Damn, I'd been scared! That drunk Rudy guy bursting into the room, coming at me. It had reminded me of when Lizard would come after me in the prison yard. Only with Lizard, I just had myself to protect, not some helpless little kid.

"What happened?" Mom asked.

"This little six-year-old girl who has cancer… I was reading to her in her room and this guy came in, falling-down drunk and screaming that he was her father and I should hand her over to him."

"How frightening!" Mom said.

"What did you do?" Uncle Marcus asked.

I told them the whole story about how the cops eventually showed up and how I sat with Madison in the playroom while everything got sorted out.

"The thing is," I said, "he really *was* her father. Her biological father. Though Madison—the little girl—didn't know that. She thought he was some...I don't know...annoying family friend, I guess. He found out she was sick and wanted some other treatment for her." I wasn't sure of the facts. Once the nurse told me that the guy really was Madison's father, that's all I heard. "But I started thinking, what if Keith tells Andy that Daddy was...that he— Keith—is our half brother. You know Keith. He could blow at any minute. I'm amazed he hasn't already. I think Andy really needs to know the truth."

Mom and Uncle Marcus looked at each other. It was dark, but I knew they could see each other's eyes and they were communicating in a language I didn't know.

"What?" I asked. "I think it's important."

"You're right," Uncle Marcus said. "He should know."

Mom let out this long breath. "Maggie, there's more to it, though. There's something neither you or Andy—or Keith— knows. Marcus and I have been trying to figure out how to tell you and there's just no easy way."

Oh, crap. What more could there possibly be?

"Do you want me to leave?" Uncle Marcus asked Mom.

"Oh, you chicken." She actually laughed. It couldn't be too horribly serious. "You're not going anywhere."

"What's going on?" I asked.

Mom stopped laughing. "I'm sorry," she said. "I don't mean to make light of it, because it's not funny at all."

"*What's* not funny?"

"Back when I was drinking," Mom said, "after you were born—"

"You had postpartum depression." I wanted her to get to the point.

"Right. And you know Uncle Marcus was an alcoholic, too."

"Yeah."

"We spent a lot of time together, drinking. And we…one time we—"

I stood up. "I do *not* want to hear this!"

"Sit down, Mags," Uncle Marcus said.

I did. I looked at my mother. "So you and Daddy both cheated on each other." I felt sick. "This is totally too much information. Why do I need to know this?"

"Because I'm Andy's father," Uncle Marcus said.

I stared at him. "No way."

"Yes," Mom said. "It's true."

I rubbed my head. This was unbelievable. My family was a train wreck.

"Did Daddy know?" I asked.

"Yes," they said at the same time.

"Is that why he had the affair with Sara?"

"No, remember?" Mom said. "Keith is older than Andy."

"So did you know about them, and you were angry and—"

"No, Mags," Uncle Marcus said. "At the time, nobody knew anything about anybody. What happened with your mom and me was independent of what was happening with your dad and Sara."

"This is so fu—screwed up."

"Well," Mom said. "I admit things *were* very screwed up back then, but what we have to deal with now is how to tell Andy, because you're right. He's old enough to know. Especially now that Marcus and I are together."

"*No.* I don't want him to know." I was pissed off with both of them. "It's going to hurt him."

"I know it will confuse him," Mom said. "I know that and I'm so sorry for it, but you said it yourself...that it's time for the truth to come out."

"I didn't know about *this* truth, though," I said.

I thought of how Uncle Marcus treated Andy. For as long as I could remember, he was always around, even when Mom wasn't exactly putting out the welcome mat for him. He saw Andy whenever he could. Showing up at his swim meets. Taking him places. He did the same for me. I always thought he was being a dad to us because our own father was dead. I suddenly realized that not only was *Keith* my half brother, so was Andy. It felt like someone was twisting my heart in his fist.

"I think you're both underestimating Andy," Uncle Marcus said.

"I know you say that," Mom said to him, "but I'm just... I'm worried, that's all."

I could tell they'd talked about this a lot, that this was like a continuation of a conversation they'd been having a long time.

"Look. Am *I* your daughter?" I asked my mother. "Yours and Daddy's? Are there any more big skeletons going to pop out of the closet? Because I don't know if I can take any more."

"You're Jamie's and mine, Maggie," Mom said. "Absolutely."

"Let's all get on the same page about this, okay?" Uncle Marcus leaned toward me, elbows on his knees beneath the afghan. "Maggie, we need you behind us on this. If you and your mom are breaking down in front of him and everything, it's only going to make it worse for him."

"I don't want to be there when you tell him," I said.

"Please be there," Mom said. "He'll need you there."

"Your mom's right," Uncle Marcus said. "The easier *you* are with it, the easier it will be for him to hear it."

"Fine." Even to myself, I sounded stupidly immature and belligerent. I sighed, tipping my head back to look at the dark porch ceiling. "All right," I said. "I'll be there. When are you going to tell him?"

They looked at each other again with that weird silent communication.

"Tonight," Mom said. "Let's get it over with."

Chapter Thirty-Six

Sara
Part of the Family
1991

DURING LAUREL'S SIX-MONTH STAY IN REHAB, JAMIE MOVED
Keith and me into a double-wide trailer in the Persimmon Trailer
Park in Surf City, which it turned out he owned. I knew he'd inherited plenty of property from his father. Marcus, quite a bit less.
But I'd driven past that trailer park any number of times and never
knew it belonged to him. He told me I could live in the trailer—
rent-free, of course—for as long as I liked.

I had never even *been* in a trailer before and was surprised how
much I liked it. First of all, it was mere steps from the beach.
Second, Keith and I would nearly have the park to ourselves during
the winter months. The trailers were definitely summer rentals, yet
ours was cozy and warm, and it felt solid. Not as solid as a house
with a foundation, especially since it was raised up on stilts in case
of flooding, but it didn't feel as though it was going to topple over
in the next nor'easter. The rooms were small, though no smaller
than in the house Steve and I had rented outside Camp Lejeune.

Best of all, it was only a few miles from the Sea Tender and Jamie.

Not only did Jamie essentially "give" me the trailer, along with
two thousand dollars a month to live on, but he told me he

planned to make arrangements for Keith and me for the future. "I want to be sure you and Keith will be taken care of in case something happens to me," he said as he helped move my things into the trailer.

I should have asked him what he meant. I should have pushed him to "make those arrangements" as soon as possible. Instead, I simply laughed.

"Nothing's going to happen to you," I said with that sense of immortality only someone in her twenties could possess. "Don't talk like that."

I expected the months Laurel spent in rehab to be blissful, having Jamie all to myself, but even though we saw each other often, he was preoccupied with her progress and with the baby he was not even allowed to visit. He loved our sweet son, but he knew Keith was safe and adored, while his other son was on his own in a foster home.

Laurel got out of rehab on a Thursday, and I wasn't invited to visit the Lockwoods until the following Tuesday. It was a very lonely few days. It felt as though Keith and I had suddenly been cut out of Jamie's life. On that Tuesday, I tried not to feel bitter as I pulled up in front of the Sea Tender and got Keith out of his car seat. I'd put on my game face.

I could barely believe that the woman opening the front door of the Sea Tender was the same woman I'd chewed out in the hospital. Laurel looked vibrant and healthy and very, very pretty. So much so that I felt a wave of jealousy as I imagined Jamie holding this attractive woman in his arms. Worse—much worse—*sleeping* with her. Laurel the depressed drunk had been a weak adversary for me. This woman looked strong enough to take on the world.

"Laurel!" I hugged her, Keith squawking as he got crushed between us. "You look fantastic!"

"Thanks," she said. "I feel like I've come back from the dead." She grabbed my arm and drew me into the living room. "Come in. Come in."

"Miss Sara!" Maggie ran up to me.

"Let me take that little guy so you can say hi to Maggie," Laurel said. "She's been babbling about you all weekend."

I did as I was told, numbly handing Keith over to Laurel and squatting down to hug Maggie, the whole time knowing that my world was shifting beneath my feet.

Jamie had gone out to pick up a couple of pizzas, and once he arrived, we sat out on the deck in the spring weather, eating and talking. Laurel spoke openly about her months in rehab—how long it had taken her to accept that she was an alcoholic, how amazing the antidepressants were and what a fool she'd been to turn them down when her doctor suggested them after Maggie was born. The only time I saw sadness in her face was when she talked about Andy.

"We've started the process to get him back," she said. "They'll do a home study in a few weeks and then I hope it won't be long after that."

"I'm sure you'll get him back soon," I said.

"I hope so," Jamie said. If he was uncomfortable with me being there, he didn't show it. He seemed happy and at ease, more so than I had seen him in a while, and seeing him that way made me realize what a terrific strain he'd been under the past six months. I knew that Marcus had moved to Asheville just the day before, and that Jamie was hugely relieved he was gone, afraid of his negative influence over Laurel. This new Laurel, though, wasn't going to break, I thought to myself. She wasn't even going to bend.

* * *

They didn't get Andy back until he was a year old. By that time, I had allowed myself to be drawn into their family by deepening my friendship with Laurel, knowing it was the only way I could ever safely have Keith and his father together, as well as be with the man I loved on holidays and birthdays. My loneliness away from him was profound, and there was not a soul I could confide to about my grief and longing. So, I helped Laurel learn how to mother a year-old boy, a role she was suddenly thrust into with no real preparation since she'd mothered Maggie not at all. I thought she was far too over-protective with Andy because of her guilt over his rocky start in life. But aside from that, I had to admit she did well, and she and Jamie were both effusively grateful to me for my help.

My true feelings about Laurel vacillated between admiration and disdain, affection and animosity. I knew that she had fought hard to regain her sobriety and mental health, and that none of my situa-tion was her fault. Yet Laurel had what I wanted, and I couldn't simply will away my sense of envy and resentment.

Jamie seemed careful about showing Laurel too much affection when I was around, but that didn't stop me from imagining it. Sometimes, alone in my bed at the trailer, I'd picture him making love to Laurel, and I'd have to go outside and take in deep breaths of salty air to erase the image from my mind.

One evening, Laurel and I were cleaning up the kitchen after a celebratory dinner for Maggie's third birthday, when she suddenly stopped drying the dishes to smile at me.

"I just want you to know that, next to Jamie and my kids, you're the most important person in my life," she said.

I felt stunned. "I am?" I asked.

"I owe my happiness right now to you," she said with a laugh. "I never would have gone into rehab if you hadn't called me a self-absorbed bitch."

I laughed myself, and hugged her, knowing I'd never be able to use those words to describe her again.

Chapter Thirty-Seven

Andy

ME AND KIMMIE WERE IM'ING ABOUT A GIRL AT HER SCHOOL when Mom and Uncle Marcus and Maggie walked in my room.

"Hey, Andy," Uncle Marcus said. "We'd like to talk to you. Are you done with your homework yet?"

"Yup." I was totally done, which was why I could IM Kimmie. I wasn't allowed to IM or text her or call her when I still had homework. I didn't really want to talk to them, though. "Is this a good thing or a bad thing?" I asked.

"Neither," Mom said. "Just an important thing."

"Okay. Wait a minute."

I wrote in the IM to Kimmie, Gotta go. C U later.

I swirled my desk chair around. Mom and Maggie were on my bed. Uncle Marcus stood by Mom. His hand was on her shoulder. I wondered if this was going to be about sex. Uncle Marcus gave me four new condoms with good dates on them, even though he didn't want me to do it.

"This is going to be a little…shocking," Mom said.

I thought she meant like when you walked across a room and touched something and got a shock. Then I knew she meant like a surprise. My brain was thinking quicker as I got older.

"What are you talking about?"

"Andy," Uncle Marcus said. "I'm not really your uncle. I'm your dad. Your father."

I laughed. He was being silly. "No," I said. "You are, too, my uncle."

He shook his head. "There are some secrets your mom and I kept from you and Maggie because we didn't want to upset you, but we've decided it's time you know the truth."

All of a sudden, I got scared. Was this one of those things I just didn't know about? I thought Mom and Uncle Marcus had sex when he slept over sometimes. I tried not to think about it, but I was pretty sure they did it. Could him and Mom having sex *now* somehow make him my father?

I thought of how Kimmie was adopted.

"You adopted me?" I asked.

"No," Mom said. "It's that—"

"Panda...Andy." Maggie sat cross-legged on the bed. "Mom and Uncle Marcus had sex a long time ago. They weren't married to each other, so it was wrong, but something good came out of it and that was you. Mom got pregnant with you when she and Uncle Marcus had sex."

I looked at Mom. Her face was red.

"Uncle Marcus and I cared about each other," she said. "That's why we made love. Maggie is right that we shouldn't have because I was married to your dad...to the man you've always thought was your father...at the time."

"You didn't use a condom?" I asked Uncle Marcus.

He rubbed his hand over his mouth. I knew he was smiling. Sometimes you could see smiles in people's eyes even if you couldn't see what was happening with their mouths.

"We didn't," he said. "And that was very stupid of us."

"Totally," I said.

"But I love you," Uncle Marcus said. "I've always loved you, and I'm very proud that you're my son."

"Because of when I saved kids in the fire?"

"No. I mean I'm... I feel *lucky* that you're my son. You're very important to me."

"Do you get it, Andy?" Maggie asked. "Do you understand that Daddy wasn't your father and that Uncle Marcus is?"

"It's like with Kimmie," I said. "Daddy is my adopted father and Uncle Marcus is my birth father."

"That's right!" Mom clapped her hands. Just once. Not like at a play.

"Close enough," Uncle Marcus said. He walked over to hug me. "I love you," he said again.

"Me, too. Am I supposed to call you Darren?"

"Darren?" he asked.

"That's what Kimmie calls her birth father. She never met him, but she says Darren was America Africa and was a marine and things like that."

Maggie cracked up, so I must've said something funny. Uncle Marcus laughed, too. "She calls her...birth father Darren," he said, "because that must have been his name. You can keep calling me Uncle Marcus, okay?"

"Okay," I said. I swirled around to my computer. I couldn't wait to IM Kimmie to tell her I had an adopted father and birth father, just like her.

"Andy?" Mom said. "We're not finished talking."

"Maybe that's enough?" Maggie said.

"No, let's finish it," Mom said.

"I want to IM Kimmie that I have a birth father," I said.

"I know," Uncle Marcus said. "But there's one other thing we want you to know. Turn your chair around again, okay?"

I swirled it back again.

Uncle Marcus sat down on the bed, too. They reminded me of an audience, all looking at me and everything.

"Keith is your cousin," Uncle Marcus said.

"Keith?" He was wacko. "I don't have any cousins."

"I don't blame you a bit for being confused," Mom said. She leaned over and picked up a pad from my dresser. "Come sit here, Andy," she said.

Maggie got up so I could sit where she was, even though I didn't want to leave my computer. Mom was drawing something, though. Maybe a picture of Keith? I wanted to see, so I sat next to her on my bed.

She was drawing little people. "Okay," she said. She pointed to a stick man and a stick lady with a dress. She wrote *adopted Daddy* above the stick man and *Mom* above the lady. Then she drew a line from them to another stick lady that was Maggie. Pretty soon there were stick people and lines everywhere. She put a lady that was Miss Sara on the paper. Then I gave up.

"I don't get it," I said.

Mom laughed. We all looked at her crazy drawing. "It's a mess, all right," Mom said.

"Want me to try?" Maggie asked Mom.

"Be my guest," Mom said.

Maggie stood in front of me like a teacher. "All you need to know is that Keith is your cousin. Daddy—your adopted daddy—is his real birth father like Uncle Marcus is your birth father."

"Are you his mother?" I asked Mom.

"No," Maggie said. "*Sara* is his mom, like you always thought."

I wanted a cousin. Not Keith, though. "Can I have a different person to be a cousin?"

"It doesn't work that way, And," Uncle Marcus said. "*Keith* is your cousin. He's also Maggie's half brother."

I put my hands over my ears. "I'm Maggie's brother!" I wasn't angry, but I felt like when Mr. Krachwitz talked about A equals B equals X equals all that stuff.

"Like, here's the thing," Maggie said. "Keith is your cousin and that means he's technically a Lockwood. I mean, his last name is Weston like always, but he has...he's related to us. That's why Mom asked him to move in with us until Sara is found. Because he's part of our family and we should help him. And...like, you know how our family has a lot of money?"

"We're rich."

"Well," Mom said, "it's not that we're—"

"Yes," Maggie said. "We're rich, especially compared to Keith. And that's why Keith was upset the night of the fire. Remember he called you a little rich boy? He and Sara never had a lot of money, and because he had the same father, that seemed unfair to him."

I stared at her. I was almost as confused as when I looked at Mom's stick-people drawing.

"Do you understand any of this?" Mom asked.

"Of course I do. I'm not an imbecile."

But all I got was that we were rich. Keith was poor. And that was totally not fair.

Chapter Thirty-Eight

Keith

"DO YOU KNOW HOW TO DRIVE A BOAT?" JEN ASKED.

She was lying sideways on my bed, totally naked, with her long tan legs stretched up on my wall. She said it felt good on her back to lie like that. I was propped up against my pillow, a beer in my hand, enjoying the view. My shoulder was killing me, though.

"I don't know if you say 'drive,'" I said. "I think you pilot a boat or something like that."

She rolled her pretty, blue eyes. "Whatever. Do you?"

"Uh-uh." It seemed lame that I'd lived on an island all my life and never piloted a boat. "Why?"

She shrugged. "I thought it'd be fun to rent one, maybe. Go out in the sound." Her hair was spread out all around her head, and it was totally dark again. It made me wonder if I'd imagined that gray stripe. Maybe it *had* just been her scalp.

"Kayaks are best out there," I said. I didn't know much about boats, but I knew you could get stuck in the sound and the Intracoastal pretty easily. "My friend Dawn's boyfriend works for a boat-rental place. Maybe he could give us a discount."

"Really?" she said. "That'd be so cool."

I stood up and pulled on my jeans. "Need a Perc," I said.

She swung her legs off the wall and pulled on her thong. "How 'bout I make us an omelette." She followed me, still nine-tenths naked, into the kitchen.

"Sounds good," I said.

I had the bottle of Percocet in my hand when I heard a car door slam, then footsteps on the deck stairs. Crap. Who now? I held my breath as the screen door squeaked open, followed by a knock on the door.

Jen started to say something, but I put my finger to my lips.

"Keith?" It sounded like Marcus. I really didn't want him to meet Jen—especially not nine-tenths naked—and have to go through that whole conversation of who she was and all that. I wanted to keep her separate from the rest of my life. She was like my fantasy girl and Marcus was too much reality for me.

I managed to pull open the door in spite of the pill bottle in my hand.

"Hey," I said, walking onto the deck.

Marcus looked from one of my hands to the other. Bottle of pills to the bottle of beer. Then he nodded toward the trailer. "Company?" he asked.

I walked to the other side of the deck to get out of Jen's hearing.

"Just a friend," I said, putting the beer down on the dirty plastic patio table.

He smiled. "Great." He leaned against the creaky deck railing. "I've got something serious I wanted to talk to you—"

He stopped midsentence. He must've seen the color drain from my face.

"No, no," he said fast. "Sorry." He went to touch my arm, but I pulled it away, remembering the last time he did that. "This isn't about your mother," he said. "There's no news there. I just wasn't sure this was the time to talk to you about something serious with…you know—" he nodded toward the trailer again "—since you have company."

"I've got a minute." I sat down at the table, mostly because my legs were suddenly giving out.

"Well—" Marcus sat down across from me "—there're a couple of things. We—Laurel and Maggie and Andy and I—want to be sure there's no more family secrets between any of us. And since you're part of the family, I want to tell you something we talked about yesterday."

Shit. How many secrets could one family have?

"Here's the big one," he said. "I'm actually Andy's father."

"Whoa. You've gotta be shittin' me."

He shook his head. "We only told Andy and Maggie yesterday, but we thought you should know, too. Not find out in some half-assed way."

I tried to figure out what the news meant for me. "So I'm not related to Andy?" I asked.

"Yes, you're his cousin. Jamie and I were brothers, remember?"

"Damn, is there anybody who didn't screw somebody else in your family?"

He laughed, though I don't think he meant to. "Mistakes were definitely made," he said. "You can do stupid things when you're young. And it's *your* family, too, don't forget." He held out his hand. "Let me see the pills."

For some reason, maybe because I was still in shock over what he'd told me, I turned the bottle over to him. He opened it, poured the pills into his hand, checked the date. "You're taking too many, aren't you? And it's ten in the morning and you're drinking beer. What gives?"

"Oh, gee, I don't know." The question really pissed me off. "You think I might have some crap going on in my life or something?"

"This can only make it worse, Keith," he said, Mr. Serious now. "If you've got that much pain, maybe you need different meds, and you sure don't need beer to go along with them."

"You don't know anything about my pain."

"You're right." The sound of pans clanking together came from inside the trailer and he looked toward the door. "You know I'm a recovering alcoholic, right?"

"You are? Like, since when?"

"Fifteen years."

"You don't drink at all?"

He shook his head.

"Well, so why tell me this? I'm not an alcoholic."

"I'm just concerned about the pills and the booze. Creeps up on you."

"I'm fine." It *was* creeping up on me, but so what? The pills and the booze—and now Jen—were the only things keeping me going. "What was the other thing you wanted to tell me?"

"I get that you don't want to stay at Laurel's," he said, "but I'd like you to move in with me until your mother's found."

"No way."

"I know you're eighteen, Keith, but you're not used to being on your own."

I didn't want him looking over my shoulder every minute. Cracking down on my booze intake. Counting my pills. "I just want to stay here," I said.

He was looking at me funny all of a sudden. Head tipped to the side. Eyes narrowed. "Wait a minute," he said. "You're not... When's your birthday?"

Shit. "You going to send me a card, or what?"

"You're seventeen!" he said.

"What does it matter?" I asked.

"Why do *you* think it matters? You can't live alone."

"I'm *fine,*" I said.

He shook his head. "Look, I'm sorry," he said, "but I have to talk to DSS about this."

"No fucking way! They'll stick me in some group home."

"I have to," he said, like he'd go to prison or something if he didn't. "No choice. But I'll see if they'd let you live with me, since we're related."

"*Marcus.*" I was pleading with him. "Just let it go. I'll be eighteen in a few months, anyway."

"Then you can just move in until you turn eighteen. Or your mother's found." He shook his head, motioning toward the trailer. "This is no good, you living here by yourself, Keith," he said. "You can see that, can't you?"

I thought of Jen inside, making me a perfectly nutritious omelette. Taking care of me.

"I'm not moving in with you or anybody," I said. "I'll split first. Someplace they won't find me." He didn't say what we were both thinking. It would be pretty hard for me to blend in with a crowd.

"Sorry, Keith." He ran his hands through his hair. "I'll let you know what they say, all right?"

I blew back into the trailer once Marcus drove away.

"He just figured out I'm seventeen!" I said to Jen. She was standing in the middle of the room, dressed now, with a spatula in her hand. "He says he has to report it. It's his solemn duty or something."

"Can't you live alone at seventeen?" she asked. "I mean, if you kill someone at sixteen, you're considered an adult in North Carolina. So, why can't you live alone? That's insane."

"No shit." I was freaking out. I wondered if I could live with her. If she'd ask. But I'd have to let someone know where I was in case my mother was found.

"They'll make you go back to school," she said.

"And stick me in some foster home. Probably a group home with a bunch of nutcases. I won't go."

She turned off the burner under the eggs and sat down at the little table. "I think they can make you," she said.

"Like how? You mean physically?"

She nodded. "I think the cops can force you if you won't go on your own."

I dropped into the other chair. "What am I going to do?" I felt beaten down. I'd *die* in a group home. With my face, I'd be the one getting all the grief. Getting beat up. It was so stupid. I was *fine* in the trailer.

"I don't know, baby," she said, reaching across the table and running her fingers over my fucked-up left hand. "All I know is, somebody really turned your life upside down."

Chapter Thirty-Nine

Maggie

"I DON'T BELIEVE THERE ARE ANY GOOD PEOPLE IN THE WORLD," I said to Dr. Jakes. I was sitting on the edge of the leather chair and my voice was louder than usual. Too loud.

"What makes you say that?" he asked.

"I think people put on a show that they're good," I said. "Maybe they even start to, like, believe it themselves. But people are really...not *evil,* exactly, but they just care about themselves. They don't really care about who they step on. They just pretend like they do. You can't trust them. You really can't trust anyone."

He frowned at me. "Where's this coming from, Maggie?"

"From everywhere!" I said. I'd just told him about the depraved mess that was my family. Did he really need to ask me where my distrust was coming from?

"Can you be more specific?" he asked.

"Take Ben, for example," I said. "He was this sweet, wonderful guy. I would have trusted him with anything."

"You trusted Ben with your heart."

I rolled my eyes. "That sounds so melodramatic."

"But it's true, isn't it?"

"*Yes,* it's true," I said. "I trusted Ben, but he was just looking out for number one. Everything he said was a lie. And then there's my father, who was…" I gripped the arms of the leather chair. "God, I thought he was so amazing, and all the time he was cheating on my mother with Sara. And Sara is, like, this perfect supersweet kind of person, and she deceived my mother, not to mention her own husband. And my mother screwed my uncle when she was married to my father. And that brings me to my uncle, who was screwing his brother's wife. And all these people—you'd meet them and think they're, like, the best people in the world." I turned my hands palm side up. "See what I mean?" I asked. "There are no good people. Not really. My little brother's good, because he doesn't know any better, and even *he's* probably hiding something. Some dark side. There are no good people left."

"Left?" Dr. Jakes raised one eyebrow over his striped glasses. "That implies you think there *used* to be good people in the world."

"Left in my mind, I mean." He could be so literal.

"If all those people you mentioned are not good, are they bad?"

"Yes!"

"Your father was bad?"

I couldn't quite say it. I nodded instead.

"What about you?"

"I'm the worst of them all," I said.

He sighed and put down his pen. I didn't know why he always had that pad and pen on his lap. He hardly ever wrote anything down anymore.

"You're trying to paint things as either black or white," he said. "As either good or evil. It's never that neat."

I leaned my head against the back of the chair and looked up at his burned-out bulb. Was he ever going to replace that thing?

"Are you feeling some envy of Andy, Maggie?" he said out of the blue.

"Envy?" I lowered my head to look at him again. "No way. Why would I?"

"Well, now he has a living father and you don't."

"Oh, no. I'm really glad for him." I was. "He loves our uncle. Well...*my* uncle. His father." This was going to take some getting used to. "Of course, I wish my father was alive, but I'm not envious of Andy."

"You wish your father was alive, terrible person though he was." Dr. Jakes smiled at me.

"Right." I was annoyed by the *Gotcha!* tone in his voice.

"Why did your mother decide all of a sudden to tell Andy and you about Andy's paternity?"

I had to stop and think. So much had happened in the last couple of days. Then I suddenly remembered feeling Madison's light weight against my body.

"There was this little girl at the hospital," I said. "She's really sick and I... She's really sweet. Anyway, I was reading to her when this guy burst into her room and said he was her biological father. She didn't know anything about him. It was really traumatic." Not to mention scary as hell. Madison was home now, at least for a few days. Everyone knew she'd be back soon, that she would probably spend the rest of her too-short life in and out of the hospital. "So I told Mom I thought Andy needed to know the truth before he found out some other way."

"I hope they're getting that little girl counseling," Dr. Jakes said. He thought therapy was the answer to everything.

"I actually miss her," I said. "It's terrible to say that, because I know it's better for her to have some time at home than in the hospital, but..." I remembered watching Madison's concentration as she painted a lion. A bear. "Sometimes at the hospital, I forget about myself," I said. "I think about what those kids are going through and forget all about prison and the fire and just think about them instead."

"You empathize."

I looked at him. Laughed. "I have a tattoo on my hip," I said. "Do you know what it says?"

"Not *Ben,* I hope."

"Oh, God, no. I would have to have that one removed. No, it says *empathy.*"

"Really? That's unusual."

"My father had one on his arm. He got it to remind him to try to…well, to *empathize* with other people. I wanted to be like him so much that I got one, too."

"Why your hip?"

"So my mother wouldn't see it." I laughed again.

He smiled, then looked at his watch, and I knew our session was over. For the first time, I really didn't want it to end. I was just getting revved up.

"Time's up?" I asked.

"I'm afraid so." He nodded. "I'll see you next week."

I stood up and walked to the door.

"Maggie?"

I looked over my shoulder at him. He was still in his chair, but he'd taken off his glasses and was leaning toward me. "There *are* good people left in the world," he said. "And you are most certainly one of them."

Chapter Forty

Sara
A Morning by the Chapel
1996

It had been years since I'd babysat for Maggie at Free Seekers, and three years since I'd completed the cushions for the pews, yet I still spent part of nearly every day in or around the building because I could never get enough of the setting. Sometimes Jamie was there and sometimes not. While I loved seeing him, he was not the only thing that drew me to the chapel. I wanted some of what I experienced on Sundays to carry me through every day. That spiritual pull. It erased any negativity I might be feeling and left peace in its place.

With Keith in kindergarten, I'd taken an office job working for an accountant on the mainland, but I kept my schedule to three days a week so I would still have time for myself at Free Seekers. I didn't need to work. I had no rent. The two thousand dollars Jamie gave me every month easily covered my expenses, and when something unexpected came up, such as my own medical care or my car breaking down, he was quick to give me more. But I needed to feel productive, and I didn't want people wondering how I was managing financially without a job.

One morning in June, I dropped Keith off for his last day of kindergarten, then drove to the chapel. I sat in the sand behind the building, leaning against the cool concrete with my knees up to my chin, watching a sailboat cut through the inlet toward the ocean. I dug my fingers into the warm sand and shut my eyes.

"I thought I saw you walk past the window."

I looked up to see Jamie coming toward me. "Hey," I said.

"Is Keith glad it's his last day of school?" He sat down next to me.

"I don't think he understands yet," I said. "He can't conceive of a day without school."

"Ah, how quickly they forget." Jamie laughed. Keith had sobbed on his first day of kindergarten. I had sobbed myself, once I was out of my baby boy's sight.

"How are things going with Marcus?" I asked. After four years away from Topsail Island, Marcus had come back for the funeral of his and Jamie's mother. I knew that, while Jamie had been looking forward to seeing his brother, he also felt anxious about his return. They hadn't parted the best of friends.

"It's going really well, actually," he said. "The kids love him."

"And he's sober?"

"He told me he got sober even before he left the island. That he didn't tell me then because he… I don't know. I guess because he needed to be sure it'd stick."

"So it's been almost, what? Five years?"

Jamie nodded.

"That's fantastic."

"I think Marcus is Andy's father."

"*What?*" I leaned away from him, wondering if I'd heard him correctly. "Why would you think that?"

He rested his head against the side of the building, eyes shut. "Because," he said.

"Because *why?*" The morning sun was golden on his skin. His thick, dark eyelashes, so much like Keith's, rested on his cheeks. I turned my head back to the inlet. It did me no good to look at him too long.

"Way back when they were drinking together, I wondered about it," he said. "I wondered if they could be sleeping together, too. A couple of times, I picked up...*vibes* between them. It's hard to describe. It was just a feeling."

"You never said a thing about it to me back then," I said.

"Well, I didn't know for sure, and I didn't want to... I knew you weren't thinking too highly of Laurel to begin with. I didn't want to make you feel worse about her."

I laughed. "Jamie. I was your *lover*. I didn't have much room to throw stones."

He smiled at me. "Good point," he said. "Anyhow. As soon as Marcus showed up the other day, I saw how much Andy looks like him. Seeing them side by side. It just... It gave me a shock."

"Well, they *are* related," I said.

He shook his head. "Then I overheard him and Laurel talking. Just... I could be reading way too much into it, but we—all of us— were talking about him possibly moving back here for good. And after dinner, I heard him ask Laurel if she'd be comfortable with that."

"Probably because he was her drinking buddy," I said.

Jamie shook his head. "It was more than that. Laurel hushed him up." He let out a sigh. "Andy's not mine. I mean, in my heart he's mine. He always will be. But I'm not his father."

"You sound so sure."

"It all fell into place for me last night. I *am* sure."

I sat up tall so I could put my arm around his shoulders. "Are you okay?" I asked.

He nodded.

"Is Marcus going to move here? Would you be all right with that?"

"I'm encouraging it," he said.

"How come?"

"Because of you."

I lowered my arm and dug my fingers into the sand again. "You're not making a whole lot of sense today, Jamie Lockwood," I said.

"You still love me?"

"Do you need to ask?"

"I want you back," he said. "I want *us* back. We're great friends, but I want the rest of it. I want all of it."

I couldn't believe what I was hearing. I'd long ago given up on anything more than friendship with him. "Jamie, I don't understand," I said. "After Andy was born, you...you recommitted yourself to your marriage. In four years, you haven't even hinted to me that you wanted to start things up again."

"Oh, I've wanted to," he said. "But you're right. I made a decision to give Laurel and Maggie and Andy my all, and I did. But it's never felt...right. Laurel's wonderful, don't get me wrong."

"She's amazing," I said. She was. It was undeniable. In the three years since Andy was returned to her, Laurel had become a spokesperson on fetal alcohol syndrome in addition to being the best mom imaginable—at least to Andy. Maggie often seemed to get the short end of the mothering stick, which I have to admit bothered me. I still thought of Maggie as part mine.

"No argument from me on that," Jamie said. "She's become a dynamo. But I didn't marry a dynamo."

"She's grown," I defended her. It was easy to defend Laurel at that moment, because my pounding heart knew where this conversation was going. Finally. *Finally.*

"And growth is good," Jamie said. "But we've grown in different directions. With you, it's so much better. I mean, look at this!" He turned his hand palm side up, running it through the air next to my body as if using me for an illustration. "You come here even when you know I'm not around because you can't stay away from this spot any more than I can. You painted the damn place yourself. You made those cushions. You come to the service every week. When's the last time Laurel came to a service? You *understand*. You're a great mom to Keith—to our *son*—but you have another side to you, too."

I drank in his words. They filled up the huge empty place I'd tried to pretend was no longer inside of me. I was afraid I was going to cry.

"I don't want to hurt her," Jamie said. "I have to see how things play out with Marcus here."

"What do you mean?"

"He loves her. I'm sure he does. He gets all goo-goo eyes around her."

I laughed, brushing away the tear that ran down my cheek. "Really?" I felt almost giddy.

"Yeah," Jamie said. "I'm less sure how she feels about him. But..." He rested his head against the wall again. "I should have thought this all through better before talking to you about it," he said. "I saw you out here, and once I started talking to you, it just came pouring out." He looked at me. "What do *you* want? Do you want us back again?"

I nodded, but slowly. "Not sneaking around, though." I realized as I said that how my self-respect had grown since the end of our affair. I was a mother now, too. Keith needed a man who would be a real father to him. "I can't do that again, Jamie."

"I know," he said. "That's no good. Give me some time to think about how to do this, okay? I can't be far from any of my kids. I... That'd kill me." He looked toward the water. "I have something for you," he said.

"What?"

He reached in his jeans pocket. "I've been carrying this around since I got back from my parents' house." He pressed something into my hand.

I opened my fingers and saw a necklace. An *amazing* necklace. I lifted up the gold chain and watched the sunlight glitter on the nine stones. Four diamonds and four emeralds, with one teardrop diamond in the center. I didn't know much about jewelry. I wouldn't have known a real diamond from a rhinestone. But I knew beauty when I saw it.

"Jamie!"

"It was my mother's," he said, lifting it from my hand and undoing the clasp. "When my father made his first million, he bought it for her, but she just wasn't a diamond-and-emerald kind of gal. She never wore it, so you don't need to worry about anyone recognizing it."

I turned my head as his fingers worked the clasp at the back of my neck. I felt the light weight of the stones against my throat and shivered. "What if the clasp breaks and I lose it?"

"It's got this double clasp on it, so it's fine. You should get it appraised so you can insure it." He turned me toward him. "Let me see," he said.

He looked at my throat, where I could feel my pulse thrumming harder than it had been an hour earlier. "Beautiful," he said, smiling. "It's right where it belongs."

I wanted to kiss him. Just put my hand on his cheek, lean forward and let our lips touch. But that could only lead us down the path we'd just agreed to avoid. So I rested my head on his shoulder instead, and together we watched the choppy water in the inlet, our backs against the chapel we both loved.

Chapter Forty-One

Andy

WE WEREN'T SUPPOSED TO TEXT ANYBODY IN CLASS. MOST kids did anyhow. I got caught once, so I waited till lunch if I could stand it. If my phone vibrated in my pocket, though, I couldn't wait. It was always Kimmie texting me. How could I wait?

I was in my Life Management class, where I'm a very good student except for the reading part. My phone vibrated, and I put it on my lap so Mr. Drexler couldn't see.

R U going to call him Dad now? she wrote.

I told Kimmie about the whole birth-father thing on the phone last night. "That's so cool!" she kept saying. She meant it was cool we both had a birth father and an adopted father. "Now it's like we're totally equal."

I wnt 2 call him Uncle Marcus, I texted back. It would feel funny to change that.

The whole thing confused me. Maggie made me a chart. Not like the get-ready-in-the-morning chart. And not like Mom's stick-people chart. Maggie made a chart with lines and things, but she cut out pictures of Daddy and Mom and Uncle Marcus and Miss Sara and me and Keith and her and all the lines showed how we were related. I still didn't understand, though. I tried explaining it to Kimmie, but she was confused, too, and she was really smart. I couldn't wait to show her the chart. The important thing was Uncle Marcus was really my dad, though I could keep calling him Uncle Marcus. And Maggie was still my sister. She said that. She said, "Don't even *think* about that half-sister stuff." And Keith was my cousin. We had some of the same blood. That was hard to believe because we were totally different, but it was true.

The night before, I dreamed about the stick people Mom drew. There were zillions of them all running around the beach. The girl ones had those little stick-people dresses on. I was normal, though. Not a stick person. They were nice and we played volleyball and just ran around. Then I realized we were by Keith and Miss Sara's trailer. I looked over and saw a stick boy sitting on the railing of the deck. He was alone, watching all the people have fun on the beach. I knew it was Keith. My cousin. I felt sad he was alone. Miss Sara was gone. Maybe dead. Also, he was poor. I was rich, but I wasn't supposed to brag about it.

I wanted to tell Kimmie about my stick-people dream and how fun it was, except for the seeing-Keith-alone part, but that was definitely too much to text. I started to try anyway.

I dremt about stick—

"Andy?" Mr. Drexler said suddenly.

I was so surprised, I actually jumped and my phone fell on the floor.

"Put your phone away," he said.

I picked up my phone. I wanted to type later, but I didn't want to get sent to the office, so I put my phone back in my pocket. Kimmie would understand.

Mom drove me home from school since she was the elementary-school nurse today, and I told her all about the stick-people dream.

"What a happy dream," she said after I said about the volleyball and the nice people.

"Except then I saw a boy alone—he was a stick boy—on Miss Sara's deck. I think it was Keith. I mean, it wasn't *really* Keith because he was a stick boy, but I...I don't know how to explain it."

"In the dream," Mom said, "you sensed that boy was Keith. The stick figure represented Keith."

Mom always got what I meant. "Exactly," I said.

"We all feel sad about Keith," she said. "He's had a very hard year and a half, hasn't he?"

"'Cause Miss Sara disappeared," I said. "And because of being hurt in the fire. And because of finding out he's a cousin."

"Yes," Mom said. "That shook him up, too, I'm sure."

"I like having a cousin," I said. I never had one before and it was fun to say *I have a cousin* even if Kimmie was the only person I got to say it to so far. It was just too bad my cousin had to be Keith.

When we got home, I told Mom I was going for a bike ride and she said be home by dinner. She didn't like me to ride on the main road in the summer because of too many cars, but now was okay. I saw hardly any cars. I was a good biker because my legs were very strong from swimming. I rode to the bank in Surf City. I had my own ATM card and was allowed to take out twenty dollars at a time. But when the screen said how much do you want, it also said other numbers, including one hundred. So even though I wasn't allowed, I hit the button for one hundred. It came out all in the twenty-number bills. Five of them. Five times twenty was a hundred, so that was right. I got back on my bike and rode to Keith and Miss Sara's trailer. That was the totally spooky part. When I got close to the trailer, I saw Keith sitting on the deck, practically right where the stick boy had been!

His back was to me when I parked my bike by his car. I climbed up the steps to the deck. There he was, sitting like the stick boy on the railing.

"Hi, Keith," I said.

His body jumped a little like I scared him. "What are you doing here?" he asked.

"I had a dream you were on the deck."

He just shook his head. "You're so weird." He got off the railing and sat down by the table.

"I really did." I wouldn't get angry at him, even if he called me a retard. My brain was really thinking hard. If we fought on the deck, one of us could fall over the railing and die. "You were a stick boy," I said. "I mean, the stick boy repasented you."

He looked toward the beach. "What the hell are you talking about?"

"I brought you money." I moved closer to hold out the five twenty-number bills and he looked at them.

"Is that from your mother?" he asked.

"No. I got it from my savings account. You can get to it from the ATM."

"That's from *your* savings?"

"Yes."

"Why would you give me money?"

"Because you're my cousin and you need it."

"I don't want your money."

"That's stupid if you need it."

"Not as stupid as you are," he said.

I wanted to hit him so bad! *Stop,* I said inside my head. *Think. Act.*

"I've got to go," I said. "I have to be home by dinner."

I started walking down the stairs.

"Hey, Andy," he said when I was partway down.

"What?" I turned to look at him. His face was leaning over in a shadow and I couldn't see the scars.

"Thanks for the offer, dude," he said. "But I'm good."

"Okay."

I went down the stairs to my bike. I had a hand in my pocket and could feel the bills. I wasn't sure what to do with them now. I knew how to get them out of the ATM thing, but nobody ever told me how to put them back in.

Chapter Forty-Two

Keith

IT RAINED ALL DAY SATURDAY. NOT LIKE A DRIZZLE. MORE LIKE a downpour. I couldn't see two feet out the trailer windows, and it was cold enough that I thought about turning on the heat. Why not? Laurel was paying for it. But it seemed like a wimp thing to do. It was barely October.

I wasn't having a good day. One of the things about living in the trailer was that I couldn't hear myself think when it rained hard like that. Seriously. It was like somebody was firing rivets into my brain. Then there was the small matter of Marcus saying he was going to report me to DSS. So, had he done it yet? It'd been, like, twenty-four hours and nothing had happened, but I still worried that some social worker was going to show up at my door any second and drag me to a group home. Or even worse, to some foster home with smiley foster parents who'd be paid to be nice to me. I tried calling Jen to see if she could come over or vice versa, but she wasn't picking up. She had caller ID, right? Why wasn't she answering? I didn't like to think about her being with someone else. Maybe this day had her down, too. Those inside scars of hers. Maybe she just didn't want to see anyone.

It got so bad that I dug out this cassette tape my mother made for me while I was in the hospital. The counselor helped her make it, and it was supposed to help me relax. On the tape, my mother first talked about how much she loved me and how I should be strong and that kind of thing. Then she went into this bit about feeling my feet relax, my legs, and on up. First, I dug it out because I needed something to help me relax. But then I knew I really wanted to play it just to hear her voice. Big mistake. I could hardly take it, listening to her "I love yous" and all that. I hadn't said those words to her in a century or two. I could be such an asshole.

So, I spent the whole day like that—lying around the tin can with the rain shooting like bullets against the roof, feeling sorry for myself, missing my mother. Around seven, just after it got dark, I heard some car doors slam out front. I was on my bed, and I looked out my window. It was nearly impossible to see anything because of the dark and the rain, but then someone opened a car door, and in the light from inside I saw there were three—*three*—cop cars out there. I knew in my gut they weren't there about my mother. I knew they were there to drag me somewhere I didn't want to go.

For a split second, I couldn't move. Then I heard them on the stairs coming up to the deck, so I took off down the hall to my mother's room, where the trailer had another exterior door. That door was always locked and for a good reason: there was nothing on the other side of it. No deck. No stairs. Just an eight-foot drop to the ground.

My hands shook while I unlocked the door, and I didn't even think before I jumped. I landed hard on my left ankle. Maybe busted it, but I didn't care. I started running away through the darkness and the rain. I heard some shouts from the trailer and saw some flashlights bobbing around. I just kept running.

I gimped the three miles to Marcus's tower, freezing in my sweat-shirt and bare feet, going through the yards of vacant houses in case the cops were looking for me. I saw maybe two cars on the road the whole time. I was the only person desperate enough to be out in that weather.

The tower was dark when I got there, and the damn front door was locked. I walked around the back to check the sliding glass doors, but they were locked, too. I sat down on the steps of the deck. I was soaked through, ice cold, and my ankle felt like it was twice its normal size. I sat there for hours. *I could die here,* I thought, shivering. *Hypothermia could get me.* I didn't really give a shit at that point. I kept hearing my mother's voice: *now your calves are warm and relaxed.* The same damn sentence played in my mind, over and over again, and I knew I was really on the verge of losing it.

So when the lights suddenly popped on in the tower behind me, I was nearly too stiff and cold and crazy to get to my feet. But I managed to stand up. I hobbled across the deck and knocked on the sliding glass door. After a second, the deck lights came on, and the door slid open.

"Keith!" Marcus looked totally shocked at the sight of me.

I couldn't move. My teeth chattered and my arms felt like they were made out of concrete.

Marcus grabbed me. Pulled me inside. Put his arms around me like he could warm me up that way, and even though I was probably an inch taller than him, I lowered my head to his shoulder like I was a little kid, too tired to fight anymore.

"It's all right." Marcus rubbed my arms—gently—through my soggy sweatshirt. "It's gonna be all right, okay? Keith? Don't worry, buddy," he said. "We'll work it out."

Chapter Forty-Three

Maggie

FROM THE LIVING-ROOM WINDOW, I SAW JEN PULL INTO OUR driveway in her beat-up black car. There was a dent in the passenger-side door, and the paint had worn off in so many places that the car looked almost gray.

I grabbed my purse and headed outside. We were going to Sears Landing Grill for dinner. Jen had talked me into it. My first real public appearance on the island since I got home, and I was nervous about it. Sears Landing was the kind of place where everybody knew everybody else, and everybody would know me, that was for sure. I hoped it wasn't a totally stupid idea. Mom was psyched that I actually had a social life. "I'm so glad you're finally getting out!" she'd said. But I could tell that even she was worried about me making my post-prison debut.

"Hi," I said as I got into Jen's car.

She was leaning forward, looking through the windshield at my house.

"Is your family home?" she asked.

"Uh-uh," I said. "Maybe you can meet them when we come back." Mom and Andy were at a swim meet, and they were bringing Kimmie back with them. It was an at-home date for Kimmie and Andy. They'd eat pizza and watch a DVD. I had the feeling they'd be having a lot of at-home dates for a while as Mom guarded Kimmie's virtue. Uncle Marcus thought Andy and Kimmie were getting too close and needed better supervision. I thought he must have had a talk with Andy about sex, because he was really serious about it. Mom even called Kimmie's mother to tell her to keep an eye on the two of them. I couldn't believe Andy was thinking about doing it. Ben had been my first. Of course, I'd been seventeen and Andy would be seventeen in a few months, so maybe I shouldn't have been so surprised. But Andy couldn't possibly know what a can of worms he was opening once he took that first step.

Jen was still looking at my house. "I would seriously love a tour of your house," she said.

"Now? Or when we come back so you can meet everyone?"

"How about now, while it's still light out?"

"Sure," I said, getting out of the car again. "Let's go."

Jen was majorly into the house. I could tell she really had a thing for design. "Your mom has awesome taste," she said, admiring the furniture and paint colors and draperies and all the things I took for granted. She walked through the downstairs, checking it out like she was looking for a house to buy. Seriously, I expected her to start opening the kitchen cupboards any second. She loved the porch and stood for a long time staring out at the sound and our pier.

"How come you don't have a boat?" she asked. "I would, if I had a pier like that. I'd just go out my back door, hop in my boat and travel all over the place."

"My mother's not wild about boats," I said. "She said Andy can get a kayak, though. And Uncle Marcus has a couple of boats, so I think she's starting to loosen up about it."

"He's a fireman, right?"

"Yeah. Fire marshal. He and my mom are getting really *tight*. As in, romantically."

Her blue eyes widened. "But he's your uncle!"

I laughed. "My father's brother. Not my mother's. It's kind of cool, actually."

"Things work out for your family," she said.

What was that supposed to mean? "They're better than they were," I said. "Definitely."

"Your uncle doesn't live here, though, does he? I mean, you said about him having boats like he might dock them here."

"He just about has been living here," I said, "but now Keith—the son of that woman who went missing—"

"Sara Weston."

"Right. Her son is moving in with my uncle because he's only seventeen and he'd have to go to a foster home if he didn't. So I don't think he'll be over here quite as much." How had we all forgotten Keith's age? Mom felt absolutely terrible about it, but with the police saying he was eighteen, nobody stopped to figure it out.

Jen pushed open the porch door as if she wanted to go outside, but then she closed it again.

"Does your bedroom have a view of the sound, too?" she asked.

"Uh-huh," I said. "Come see." I walked back into the house, and Jen followed me, pulling the door closed behind her. "Do you want me to lock this?" she asked.

"Nah," I said. "They'll be home soon."

"It's nice living someplace where you don't have to worry about locking your doors," she said.

"Well, we do sometimes lock them now, since I'm not exactly Miss Popularity around here at the moment." There I was, talking about me and my life again. Tonight was the night I'd planned to ask her questions about herself. "Do you have to worry about that kind of thing in Asheville?" I asked.

"It's not bad," she said, following me up the stairs.

"I'll show you my mom's room first, because hers is the only one you're going to like." I laughed.

My mother's room was perfect, with blue walls and blue-and-brown bedding, and a view of the sound outside the big windows.

"I love that painting." Jen pointed to the massive painting of a flock of geese above the headboard. "The colors are perfect in here. It's awesome."

"Yeah, well, now I'll take you to the tasteless part of the house. My brother's room and mine."

I showed her Andy's room, which was actually in pretty good shape except that it still had that teenage-boy smell to it. I hoped it didn't gross Jen out.

"What's all this?" She walked over to Andy's corkboard wall and started reading one of my mother's charts.

"My mother makes charts to help keep him organized," I said.

"Do you get along with him?"

"Totally," I said. "He's easy to get along with."

"I remember seeing him on the *Today* show," she said, fingering the corner of one of the charts. "He was cute."

"You'll love him," I said. "You can meet him and his girlfriend when we get back from dinner. Do you want to see my room?"

She followed me into my very yellow room. The sun was sinking toward the sound and the sky and clouds were turning a purply pink. Jen stared at the sound the way she had from our porch, and I had the feeling she was drawn to water the same way I was. I wondered what it was like for her living in landlocked Asheville.

"You're so lucky to live here," she said.

"I know."

"You're so lucky," she said again. I could see the purple of the sunset reflected in her eyes. "You've got a great family and everything."

It was my invitation to ask her about herself, and I wasn't going to miss it.

"How about your family?" I asked. "What are they like?"

She turned to me with a scrunched-up expression on her face. "I don't really like to talk about my family," she said.

And that was pretty much the end of that.

I was so nervous as we pulled into the Sears Landing parking lot. Jen parked the car and opened her door, but I just sat there. She looked at me.

"Are you freaking out, or what?" she asked.

"Just mildly," I said. I was remembering the last time I was there, when Uncle Marcus told me about my father's affair with Sara. The waitress who served us was a girl I knew from high school named Georgia Ann. Did she still work there? I didn't want to see her. I'd thought I was so much better than her. Smarter. Prettier. Better off. I'm sure she wouldn't want to see me any more than I wanted to see her.

"Come on," Jen said. "It'll be fine."

Easy for her to say. I got out of the car and walked with her into the building. It was a weeknight, off-season, but the restaurant was still busy and no one paid any attention to us as we waited to be seated. One of the posters I'd made about Sara was taped to the counter in front of us. I pointed to it. "She's still gone."

"Yeah. I know. It looks really bad, doesn't it."

"I just don't get it," I said. "The police have all these bulletins out all over the East Coast looking for her car and nothing's turned up."

"I think she killed herself, like that other woman did," Jen said. "Maybe she did it out in the boonies so she and her car wouldn't be found."

"Oh, please don't say that," I said. I wanted Sara to be safe somewhere. I knew it looked grim. I hated—*hated*—the idea that she might have been down enough to kill herself.

One of the waitresses finally appeared and led us to a table. She smiled right at me as she handed me a menu. Didn't even bat an eye. Maybe this would be okay after all.

"See?" Jen said as she opened her menu. "No one's paying any attention to you."

"You're right," I said. "Sorry to be such a baby."

"No problem."

I was torn between keeping my face buried in the menu and looking around for Georgia Ann so that I could be sure to avoid her.

A different waitress showed up to take our orders. "Know what you'd like to drink?" she asked, and I could tell by the way she stared at me that this one knew who I was. I actually stammered as I ordered a Coke.

I watched the waitress walk back to the kitchen. "She'll probably spit into it before she brings it out to me," I said.

"You're really getting paranoid," Jen said. I thought she sounded a little annoyed, like my self-pity was getting to her. It probably *was* annoying.

I remembered what we'd been talking about before we were seated. Sara. Killing herself. I didn't want to go there again. But Jen didn't want to talk about her family, so I'd have to try something else.

"Well, update me," I said. "How's your college search going?" That always seemed to be a safe topic with her.

"Pretty good." She sipped iced tea through her straw. "The library's just not the same without you, though."

"Yeah, no spitting," I said. *Stop it,* I told myself, but she laughed.

"If I decide I want to go out of state," she said, "I have to move, like, *yesterday,* so I can become a resident wherever the school is. It's so much cheaper if you're a resident. That's the only way I could afford it."

"Uh-huh." I felt a big, thick, black cloud over my head at the thought of her leaving. I couldn't believe how attached I felt to her already. My one friend. "I hope you don't move," I said.

The waitress put my Coke down in front of me.

"Y'all know what you want?" she asked.

We ordered crab-cake sandwiches with fries, and the waitress didn't bother to write it down. Just slapped up our menus and took off for the kitchen.

Jen twirled her straw in her tea. "I'm not deciding anything about school yet," she said. "Life's too good here right now. I love getting to hang out on the beach."

"Your tan is awesome," I said.

"Mostly fake and bake," she said. "I use SPF 40 on the beach but I hate to be pale."

"Like me," I said. A year in prison could wash the color out of anyone.

"You'd be beautiful even if you were green," she said.

For the first time, I wondered if she might be a lesbian. I hoped not. That was all I needed. A few of the women in prison had come on to me, but I'd been able to avoid any major run-ins. Some guys, back when I was in high school, used to say I was pretty or hot or whatever. Ben's the only one who ever used that word: beautiful. But then I remembered Jen's birth control pills. Thank God.

"So how's the hospital?" she asked. "Still working out?"

"I totally love it," I said. "Everyone's really nice and the kids are...they're amazing and brave and they need me." Miss Helen said that all the nurses were talking about me after the incident with Madison and her "real" father. "You were cool, calm and collected," she'd told me.

"Hospitals give me the creeps," Jen said.

"I actually kind of like it," I said.

"Maybe you can find a cute doctor there to hook up with," she said.

"Uh," I said, smiling, "no, thanks. I'm not hooking up with anybody for a long time. Although there *is* this doctor at the hospital who reminds me of Ben."

"Ben...the guy you lit the fire for?"

"I didn't light it."

She rolled her eyes. "*Set* it," she said. "Whatever."

"Yeah. That's the guy. I can't stand that I'm attracted to someone who reminds me of him. I want to be totally over him. I *am* over him."

"I was only joking about hooking up with a doctor, you know," Jen said. "I mean, how old is this guy?"

"I don't know. About Ben's age."

"*Seriously?* How old was Ben?"

"Eleven years older than me."

"Get out!" She leaned back from the table to stare at me. "You're crazy!"

"I know."

"You better talk to your shrink about this before you do something stupid."

What did she mean by something stupid? Set a fire?

"I'm not going to do anything stupid," I said. "I'm in control." I was desperate to turn the conversation around to her. "So, how about you? Do you have a boyfriend? Have you met any guys while you've been hanging out on the beach?"

"Not really," she said. "Just to say hey to."

From the corner of my eye, I saw a woman approach our table, and I knew it wasn't our waitress because this woman wore a skirt. I was afraid to look up in case it was Georgia Ann.

"Maggie Lockwood?"

I braced myself and looked at her. She was middle-aged with short fluffy blond hair and blue eyes, and she looked familiar, but I couldn't place her. She stared at me, and I went stiff, ready to be spit at or worse.

"Yes." My hands tightened around the napkin in my lap. I thought Jen was holding her breath.

"I'm Lurleen Wright," she said. "Henderson Wright's mother?"

Oh, God. Henderson Wright was the boy killed in the fire. I remembered his picture blown up poster-size at the memorial service. He and his family had been homeless. They'd lived in a car.

"I'm so sorry." My tongue clicked against the roof of my mouth, it was so dry.

"I just want you to know that me and my husband forgive you," she said calmly. Her hands were folded in front of her, her purse dangling from them. "I know some people are still hangin' on to their anger, but we ain't."

My cheeks burned. I'd been so ready for an attack. An attack might've been easier to hear. This was like a gift I didn't deserve. I felt Jen's eyes on me.

"Thank you." It came out a whisper. "I'm still… I wish I could undo—"

"I know." She put her hand on my shoulder. "I know you do. You ain't evil. Jesus tells us to forgive others to find our own salvation."

I nodded. My neck felt like it was made out of wood.

"And listen," she said, "I know you're not religious. I remember your daddy's church from long ago…that seekers place?"

"Free Seekers," I said.

"Right. And I know that must've had a right terrible influence on you coming up. But if you want to come to *our* church with us some Sunday, we'd love to bring you. You'd find your own salvation there, Maggie. I'm sure of it."

"Thank you," I said again.

She reached into her purse and brought out a postcard. "We had these made up," she said, handing it to me. "You might want to have one."

I looked down at Henderson's face. Smiling. Not like the scared picture of him they used at the service. Beneath it, it said, God needed another angel. Henderson Emery Wright. 1992–2007.

"Thank you," I said again. They were the only words I seemed able to find.

"Okay, honey. You call me if you want to come to church. We're in an apartment now. In the phone book."

I nodded, and she walked away smiling to herself. I was paying for their apartment with the restitution money, I realized. Probably for their dinner here at Sears Landing, too. I was glad. That was the way it should be.

"*Bizarre,*" Jen whispered. Her eyes were wide.

"That was nice of her," I said. "I mean…I don't deserve it, but she's the first person to say anything like that to me."

"She wants to convert you," Jen said. "That's why. Would you go to church with her?"

SECRETS SHE LEFT BEHIND   307

I shook my head, although I felt drawn to that word she'd used.
Salvation. I remembered Dr. Jakes congratulating me for arranging
the job at the hospital myself: *This is the first step in saving yourself.*

"What did she mean about your father's church?"

"Daddy built a chapel at the north end of the Island before I was
born," I said. "He wanted people to be able to, you know…
worship…any way they wanted. So it wasn't connected to any
religion."

"Is it still there?"

I shook my head. "Just the foundation and a few of the walls."

All of a sudden, my mind suddenly leapfrogged from Daddy to
Ben to Dr. Britten. *Bam Bam Bam!* It hit me all at once. Ben was big
and dark-haired and cuddly. Like Daddy. Like Dr. Britten. I flashed
back to Uncle Marcus telling me long ago that Ben reminded him
of my father. And now Dr. Britten reminded me of Ben. It was all
one long chain.

"Oh…my…God," I said, leaning my head back to look up at
the ceiling.

"What?" Jen asked.

"I am *so* screwed up."

We pulled up in front of my house an hour or so later. All the
lights were on inside, and the house gave off the warmest, most wel-
coming glow.

"Come in and meet my mom and Andy and Kimmie."

Jen stretched her arms out over her steering wheel. "Not
tonight," she said. "I'm sleepy."

"Come on," I said, disappointed. "Just for a few minutes."

"Next time," she said. "But thanks for the tour earlier. It's a great
house."

"Okay." It would take her nearly a half hour to drive back to Serenity Point, and she *did* look tired all of a sudden.

I got out of the car just as Andy walked from the house onto the front porch.

"Maggie!" he shouted. "Kimmie's here!"

"Come here and meet Jen, Andy," I said, but before I even finished my sentence, Jen stepped on the gas and pulled away, the passenger-side door not even fully closed.

I stared after her, glad I'd at least been clear of the car when she took off. I felt suddenly worried about her, hoping she was okay to drive the fifteen miles home in the dark.

I didn't know it was really myself I needed to worry about.

Chapter Forty-Four

Keith

"Hangin' out with you is gonna kill me, buddy!" Marcus laughed as we carried our boards back to the tower after surfing. The surf sucked, so we'd only caught a few waves, but even though Marcus had to keep in shape because of being a firefighter, he looked totaled. "It's gotta be ten years since I surfed," he said.

I wasn't as good a surfer as I was before the fire, and my ankle was still sore from my escape from the police on Saturday night, so I figured we'd been about equal out there.

It blew my mind when Marcus told me he used to surf. I didn't know why I was so surprised, since he grew up near the ocean and everything. But I just couldn't picture it. When he dragged out his old board and I saw how dinged-up it was, I was convinced he'd actually used it a few times.

We peeled off our wet suits on his deck. He pulled a couple of bottles of water from an ice chest near the back door and tossed me one.

"Sit out here for a while, or is it too chilly?" he asked as he dropped onto one of the lounge chairs.

"It's good." I sat on the other lounge chair and stretched out my legs while I twisted the cap off the water bottle. Didn't have quite the same *snap* to it as twisting the cap off a bottle of beer, but it was only day three at the tower and I wasn't going to push my luck. And *luck* was the word of the day. We'd just heard from DSS that I could stay there. I was supposed to go back to school, but Marcus wasn't pushing me. At least not yet. I was starting to feel safe. I liked Marcus. I liked the dude a lot. I couldn't help it. He was on my side. I'd known him most of my life, but I realized now that I'd never really *known* him. He was just this older dude who was a bigwig in the fire department. But he had a story. I guess everybody did. People walked around with this thick dark film sticking to them and until you scratched it, you had no idea.

He took a pull on his water bottle. "How's your ankle?" he asked.

"Not bad." I looked down at my bare ankle. Just a little swollen. A little bruised looking. "It's okay."

"And how're your arms?" he asked.

"They suck," I said honestly.

"We'll get that pain under control," he said. He'd already made an appointment for me with a pain guy in Wilmington for next week. Till then, I told him I was cutting down on the Percocet, but that was only half-true. I was trying, but I needed that stuff.

"I could use a beer," I said, testing the waters, so to speak.

"You're seventeen," he said, like that was a logical response.

"So, how old were you when you started drinking?" I asked.

"Thirteen," he said.

"Whoa." Even *I* didn't start drinking till I was nearly fifteen, though I smoked dope when I was twelve. My lungs wouldn't ever be able to handle smoking anything again, thanks to my charming half sister. "Did you do drugs, too?" I asked.

"Not much. I just liked drinking. It was a nice escape."

"Tell me about it." The water bottle crackled when I took another swallow. "What did you have to escape from?"

"Small potatoes, compared to what you've been through," he said. "My brother—your father—couldn't do anything wrong. I couldn't do anything right."

I was stuck on the words *your father*. They sounded so strange to me. I'd known for over a year that Jamie Lockwood was my father, yet the words still got stuck somewhere between my ears and my brain.

"Your father was one of those genuinely righteous people," Marcus said. "You know what I mean? And, man, it could be rough having someone like that for a brother. He set the bar high. My parents thought he was the next Dalai Lama."

I wasn't totally sure who the Dalai Lama was, but I got the idea.

"I wasn't as smart," Marcus said, "or maybe I *was* as smart, but I was dyslexic—still am—and school came harder for me. And I wasn't nearly as nice. Plus, I didn't have goals. Ambitions."

"Did he?" I barely remembered Jamie Lockwood and I really knew next to nothing about him. I found out he was my father the same day as the fire, and the next year went into recovery, not into long talks with my mother about her adultery.

"Oh, hell yeah," Marcus said. "You know about the church he started?"

"Yeah."

"I think he was *born* wanting to start that church. He had lots of things he wanted to do and he just took them on, one after another. The chapel. Managing the Lockwood properties. Being a firefighter. Having a family."

"Or two," I muttered.

Marcus laughed.

"It's fucked up," I said.

"One way to look at it."

"So, did you hate him?"

"Jamie? Not at all. I had those complicated sibling emotions about him. I idolized him. Resented him. Wanted to be like him. Wanted to be nothing like him." He shrugged. "The usual."

"And he's why you started drinking?"

"Can't blame that on anyone but myself," he said, taking a final swallow from his water bottle. "I didn't feel good about myself, and I got in with friends who were into music and alcohol and drugs." He tossed his empty bottle into a recycling bin on the other side of the deck. Perfect shot.

"Two points," I said.

"So, how about you?" he asked me. "When did you start drinking?"

I felt a wall instantly go up between me and him, but I decided to take it down—for now, at least. "A little older than you did. My friends were all doing it."

"That makes it hard to know when it's a problem."

The wall came up again. Stayed up this time. "It's not," I said.

He looked at me, shading his eyes with his hand. "Be careful, okay? Your liver's taking a beating enough with the Percocet. Beer can only make that worse, and beer at ten in the morning like that day I came over to the trailer is not a good sign."

So much for the buddy-buddy chitchat. "That was unusual," I said.

"Glad to hear it," he said, like he didn't quite believe me.

"Why'd you stop?" I asked.

He didn't answer right away. "Long story. In a nutshell, I could see I was screwing up my life and I didn't want to. I got into AA."

"You go to those meetings and stand up and say, 'I'm Marcus the alcoholic' and everything?"

"I did. I don't go much anymore. Maybe a couple times a year to see old friends or to get someone else into it. But I went nearly every day the first few years. Sometimes twice a day."

"Shit. Could you drink now without becoming an alcoholic again?"

"I'm still an alcoholic," he said. "Always will be. And no, I couldn't drink again. Sometimes people think they can, that they have it all under control, and then they start slipping back into it. That'd be me. So it's better just to forget about it. It's not a part of my life."

"So...like, would it bother you if I kept some beer in the fridge?" I asked. "Just a six-pack?"

"Being around it doesn't bother me," he said, "but you, my friend...my *nephew*—" he grinned at me "—are not legal."

"Oh, dude, that's weak."

"No booze in the house," he said, and I knew he meant it. He got up and pulled another water bottle from the ice chest. Back in the lounge chair, he twisted it open and took a drink.

"So, Keith." He put the bottle on the deck and stretched his arms over his head. "Tell me about this girl."

Chapter Forty-Five

Andy

"This is the bedroom I stay in when I sleep over sometimes," I whispered to Kimmie. I wasn't sure why I whispered it. No one was home at Uncle Marcus's, because I planned it that way.

"Is the bed made?" Kimmie asked.

Anybody could see the bed was made. It had a dark blue bedspread on it, all tucked under the pillow like it was supposed to be. "Yes," I said. "That blue thing is the bedspread."

"No, I mean is it made *up.*" She pulled the bedspread down a little and I figured out she meant were there *sheets* on the bed. "Oh. Good," she said.

There were blue-and-white striped ones under the bedspread. I remembered when Uncle Marcus and I bought them. He said they were musculine sheets, or something like that. The room that Maggie stayed in sometimes had yellow sheets that were girlie. That was the room where Keith lived now, so maybe he got different sheets.

Kimmie sat on the edge of the bed with her hands folded up while I got the condom out of my pocket. I looked at the date again to be sure it was the same as before. I didn't know if I should open it now so it would be totally ready or not.

"Should I open it?" I asked.

She nodded. "I think so." Kimmie usually uses a lot of words, but not now.

The condom package was easy to open. Kimmie took it from me. She peeked inside and then put it on the corner part of the table.

People said I couldn't plan good, but I planned this out totally. Uncle Marcus was at work and Keith wasn't there because he was at a date. Mom said that. She said she asked him to come to dinner since Maggie was out late. Keith and Maggie don't like to see each other. Keith said he had a date, so I knew the tower house would be empty. I couldn't figure out how me and Kimmie would get there, though. Kimmie said, did Maggie have a bike? I was only thinking about *my* bike. I forgot about Maggie's. It needed air in the tires but we had a pump. Then I lied to Mom about how we were going for a bike ride. That wasn't a *big* lie because we did go for a bike ride. I just didn't say where to.

"Should we get under the covers or on top of them?" Kimmie asked. Usually she told *me* what to do.

It was pretty warm in the room. "On top," I said.

She took off her glasses and put them on the table. "Should we take off our clothes first?" she asked.

"I don't know," I said. Uncle Marcus gave me lots of rules but it turned out he didn't give me enough. The people in Max's magazines were already naked when I saw their picture. "I think so," I said.

She got on her knees to shut the window things. Then we started getting undressed. It took me, like, one second to get off my shirt and my jeans, but it took her, like, one whole minute to unhook the buttons on her shirt. I felt funny watching her. I sat on the bed and made like I was folding my clothes up neatly instead. I still had my boxers on. I didn't care about hiding my hard-on this time, because we were going to have sex.

She got off all her clothes and then I looked at her. She was so pretty.

"Don't stare," she said. She closed her arms over her breasts so I couldn't see them.

"I'm not," I said. She was right, though. I *was* staring. I really liked how dark and smooth all her skin was. She had way more public hair than me. Max said a lot of girls shaved theirs, but Kimmie didn't.

"I want to get under the covers now," she said.

"Okay."

She got under the bedspread while I took off my boxers. Then I got under the bedspread with her. I kissed her right away. I put my tongue in her mouth, but she didn't put hers in mine like she usually did. That was okay. I just wanted to get on top of her and put my penis in her. I started to get on top and then all of a sudden remembered the condom.

"The condom!" I said. I got it out of the pack and it went on perfect like it was supposed to because Uncle Marcus showed me a long time ago on a zucchini, which was so funny.

I got on top of Kimmie, then, but her legs were hooked together.

"You're supposed to put your legs apart," I said.

"I'm too scared," she said.

"Why?" I asked. "You said you wanted to do sex with me."

"I don't want to now."

I *had* to do it now. "Please, Kimmie!" I said.

She didn't answer me. I couldn't see her face very good, but I heard her crying.

I got off of being on top of her. She didn't exactly say no, but that's what she meant. Now I was supposed to go jerk off.

She turned toward the window. "I'm sorry," she said.

I rolled off the condom and tried to stick it back in the pack, but it wouldn't go. I was angry and sad and everything because I planned it so good and for nothing. I didn't even feel like jerking off.

I looked down at Kimmie. Part of the bedspread was down, and Kimmie's long hair was on top of the blue-and-white pillow. Her shoulders were jumping up and down, like when you cry. She was even sadder than me. I suddenly really, really got what Uncle Marcus meant about not pushing a girl.

I picked up her shirt from the floor and put it over her shoulder. Then I lied down behind her and put my arm around her. She turned and looked at me.

"Are you mad at me?" she asked.

"No." I wasn't mad anymore. I just didn't want her to cry or be sad.

"I just got scared," she said.

I wanted to ask her, *of what?* But that would be a kind of pushing her.

"That's okay," I said.

"Maybe we should go back to your house," she said. "I don't want to be here anymore."

"Okay."

We got dressed and walked down the metal stairs that went round and round to the living room. We were partway through the living room when a car door slammed.

"Uh-oh," Kimmie said. "Is that your uncle?"

It better not be. I'd be in a lot of trouble. We might have to sneak out the door by the deck. Or maybe we could hide on the roof. I went to the kitchen window and peeked out. "His car place is empty," I said. But then I saw Keith's car.

"It's stupid Keith," I said.

"Should we hide?" Kimmie asked.

I wasn't sure. Would Keith tell Uncle Marcus he saw us there? I took too long figuring it out, because all of a sudden Keith and a girl came in the front door. The girl was laughing and kind of hanging on him. Me and Kimmie froze perfectly still, like they wouldn't notice us if we didn't move. And for a minute, they didn't. Keith was too busy kissing the girl.

All of a sudden, the girl saw us and stopped kissing Keith. She pointed at us, and Keith turned around.

"What the hell are *you* doing here?" he asked.

"I wanted to show Kimmie the Operation Bumblebee tower," I said.

"Yeah." Keith laughed. "I bet that wasn't the only tower you wanted to show her."

I didn't know what he meant, but the girl laughed, too. She had gigantic eyes that were blue and black hair with a red plastic clip thing on her head. I knew her. When she turned her head, I saw that funny spot below her ear. Like a heart tattoo. I waved to her.

"Hi," I said.

She just smiled at me. She looked really different than the other time I saw her.

"This is Kimmie," I said. You're supposed to introduce people when they didn't know each other. Keith didn't introduce the girl, though. Probably because I sort of knew her already even though I didn't know her name.

"I'm going upstairs," she said to Keith.

"Right behind you," Keith said. He looked at me. "You'd better get out of here," he said.

I wanted to ask him not to tell Uncle Marcus me and Kimmie were there, but he was mean. Mean people sometimes did the opposite of what you asked them to.

"Okay," I said. "We're going."

We walked outside to our bikes.

"Will he tell?" Kimmie undid the kickstand on her bike.

"I don't know." I could get in so much trouble and we didn't even have sex. That would be totally not fair.

Kimmie put her hand on my arm before I could get on my bike. I hated that her eyes had water in them and her nose was red. "Will you still be my boyfriend after today?" she asked.

It was a crazy question. "I'll *always* be your boyfriend," I said.

She smiled and even though her nose was still red, I knew she was finally done crying for now.

Chapter Forty-Six

Sara
Losing Jamie
1997

JAMIE'D PROMISED ME THAT THIS WOULD BE THE WEEK HE'D tell Laurel he wanted a divorce.

A year had passed since Marcus's return, and I had done nothing to pressure him—although the thought of an ultimatum swept through my mind a few times. How could it not? A year! But if I told him it was now or never, that if he didn't ask Laurel for a divorce, I would take Keith and leave...well, he'd know I was lying. I'd never leave the island.

Granted, it had been a terrible year for him. For everyone, really. Hurricane Fran had swept across the island, demolishing homes and roads. It lifted my trailer up and spun it around, setting it down again on a sea of beach grass. Of course, we'd all evacuated, so we were safe, but it took months to get my home back where it belonged, and the Sea Tender, while still standing, was wobbling on its foundation of stilts. The Lockwoods would not be able to live in it much longer, so Jamie was building a gorgeous new house for them on the sound. As I tried to put my dented trailer back in order, I felt my envy of Laurel creeping back in. She still had it all.

Jamie wanted to talk to Marcus about the divorce before he said anything to Laurel, he told me. He wanted his brother to be ready to give Laurel emotional support, because he knew she was going to need it.

"I'm dreading telling him," Jamie'd told me.

"It'll be okay," I'd reassured him. I just wanted him to get this *over* with. I'd been waiting so long. He'd asked me months earlier why I never wore his mother's necklace, and I told him truthfully that I was saving it for our wedding day. He promised me that day would come soon. "Everyone's going to be shocked at first," I said, "but they'll be all right, Jamie. You know they will be."

Finally, that Friday night, Jamie called to say that he and Marcus were going out on Marcus's boat in the morning and he would tell him then. Then a quick "I love you." It was the last I'd ever hear.

In the morning, Laurel called me in hysterics. There'd been an accident on the boat. A whale lifted it into the air, she said, tossing Jamie into the water. He was gone. Lost. *Dead.*

I raced over to the Sea Tender to stay with the children, while Laurel joined Marcus at the police station. Maggie was eight, and she had some understanding of what was going on. Keith, at six, less so. And five-year-old Andy was in the dark, as usual. I took the children out to the beach and huddled there with them in the sand, thinking, *This has to be a mistake. It* has *to be.*

But in my heart, I knew it was not a mistake at all.

The memorial service was held at the chapel, and there were so many people that they spilled from the doors. A Wilmington minister Jamie'd respected performed the service, but everyone knew it was too flowery and regimented for a man like Jamie Lockwood. Afterward, Laurel and Maggie and Andy tossed Jamie's ashes into the inlet, while Keith and I—his second family, the one no one knew about—hung back with the others.

That was the hardest part of being the other woman, I thought in the days to come: grieving alone. While friends reached out to Laurel in huge numbers, no one said a word to me except a passing "Shame about Jamie Lockwood, isn't it?" In addition to my grief, I was fearful about what would happen when Jamie's will was read, remembering what he'd said about "making arrangements" in case something happened to him. Everyone would know about Keith and me then. But days passed and I never heard a word about anything being left to us. There was no call from Jamie's attorney. No outraged call from Laurel. And I knew that nothing had been left to us after all. Nothing to me, and nothing to Keith.

We were on our own.

Chapter Forty-Seven

Keith

WELL, ONE THING I HADN'T FIGURED OUT ABOUT KAYAKING was that I wouldn't be able to paddle with my screwed-up arm. That meant we had to rent a double kayak, and that Jen had to do all the paddling, which was humiliating, but she just kissed me and said she didn't care at all. Even after she discovered paddling wasn't as easy as it looked, she didn't complain. I felt like a total loser, though, just kickin' back while she did all the work. Adding to that was the fact that I'm not supposed to do sun, and of course, I didn't think about that, so I didn't have a hat or sunscreen. So Jen gave me her straw hat to wear and slathered her sunscreen all over my face and hands. Oh, and we had to wear these dorky life preservers. Dawn got Frankie to rent us the kayak for free. She probably paid for it, but whatever. Anyhow, Frankie said, no life preservers, no rental, so that's why we looked like total wusses as Jen paddled us through the narrow waters of the sound.

Except for all that, it was pretty cool being out on the water. You get so used to living someplace that you don't notice how amazing it is sometimes. We were so close to the birds in the marsh that we could practically see the pupils in the eyes of the blue herons. It was like I didn't have to think about all the shit in my life for a while. Jen was into the exercise part of it. She liked seeing how fast she could paddle.

"Where does that Maggie Lockwood girl live?" she asked, as Stump Sound widened in front of us. She was studying the houses along the shoreline. There weren't that many. "You said she lives on the sound, right?"

"Yeah. She lives in a little shack we should be coming up on soon." I looked to my left, but the world was totally different from the water and I felt disoriented. Finally, I pointed ahead of us. "That's it," I said.

"Wow," she said as we floated past the end of the Lockwoods' pier. "It must really piss you off to know she lives in a house like that."

"Royally." I couldn't even look at the place. My burned left hand had felt fine up until that moment, but suddenly I could feel the sun hitting it. Stinging it. I pressed it between my knees.

"Well." Jen sounded down all of a sudden. "My arms are telling me it's time to turn around."

I felt kind of depressed, too. It was like seeing Maggie's house had killed the fun we'd been having up till then.

Jen paddled us back to the boatyard, and we thanked Frankie and gave him our life preservers, then walked across the parking lot to Jen's car.

"Let's get a burger somewhere," she said, opening her car door.

"Cool." I took off the straw hat and tried to put it on her head, but she was already ducking into the car. The hat caught on the door frame and fell to the sand. When I bent over to pick it up, I saw something shiny beneath her seat. "What's that?" I asked, reaching for it. I wasn't sure what I thought it was, but the second I touched it, I knew. I pulled my hand away.

"What the... There's a *gun* under your seat!"

"Shh!" she said, although there was no one nearby to hear us. "Don't worry. It's not loaded."

I left the gun where it was and stood up straight. "Why do you have a gun?" I asked. I knew lots of people who owned guns, but it still shocked me that Jen was carrying one around in her car. I hadn't figured her for the gun type.

"If you were a girl, you'd understand," she said. "Driving alone at night and all that." She nodded toward the passenger seat. "Come on," she said. "Get in. I'm hungry."

I got into the car, leaning over to get another look at the gun, but with the doors shut, it was too dark to see it.

"Don't get obsessed," she said. "I told you, it's not loaded. I just like having it in case I need to scare somebody off."

"Where'd you get it?"

She didn't answer right away. "My father gave it to me," she said. "He'd take me to the range. Said if I was going to have it, I needed to know how to use it."

She'd never mentioned her father before, and I suddenly pictured this tall, skinny black-haired dude, teaching his daughter how to shoot a gun. I wanted to know more. Did he live in Asheville? Was she close to him? To her mother? Did she have brothers and sisters? I didn't know a thing about this girl except that she was dynamite in bed and the best thing that had happened to me in a long time.

"Is your father in Asheville?" I asked.

She turned to me with a smile. Pressed her fingertip to my lips. "Let's talk about where to get our burgers," she said.

Chapter Forty-Eight

Maggie

IT WAS DOWNRIGHT HOT FOR AN AFTERNOON IN EARLY OCTOBER, and Jen said to come over and we'd go for a swim. The front door of her cottage was unlocked, and I walked in when she didn't answer my knock.

"Jen?"

"Hey!" she called from upstairs. "I'm in the bedroom. Come on up."

I walked up the stairs. It was the first time I'd been to the house in the daytime and I was totally mesmerized by the view. At the turn in the stairs was a humongous window and it framed the beach and ocean like a photograph.

I walked into Jen's big, citrusy-smelling bedroom with its king-size bed, and found her standing near more huge windows that looked out over the water. She wore a bikini—tiny triangles on top and a string bottom—with little pink stripes of sequins sewn to the fabric. Pure Victoria's Secret, and the kind of bathing suit only a girl like her could get away with wearing. She had one foot up on the windowsill and was slathering lotion on her leg.

She lowered her leg when I walked in. "You're smokin' in that tankini, girlfriend!" she said, and I wondered how someone who looked as incredible as she did in her bikini could even notice how another girl looked. I *did* think I looked pretty good in the green-and-white tankini, though, especially since I lost my belly fat in prison, but if there were guys on the beach, it was no contest which one of us they'd be looking at. Not that I cared.

Jen held out the tube of sunscreen. "Want some?" she asked.

"I'm good," I said. I'd put some on before I left the house, though not her SPF 40, that was for sure. I was dying for some color.

"I've got towels for us downstairs," she said, "but I have to use the loo, so I'll be with you in a sec."

She disappeared into the bathroom, and I stood at the window for a bit. There was no one on the beach—at least not behind the cottage. The waves were smooth and low and I felt suddenly relieved. I hadn't realized until right that moment that, even though I'd agreed to Jen's suggestion like I was totally happy about it, I'd actually dreaded going swimming. I hadn't been in the ocean since the night of the storm, when Andy and I nearly drowned and the Sea Tender was destroyed. I used to love swimming in the ocean. I'd practically been raised in it. Now it seemed so...so *malicious* to me. Stupid.

I wandered into the attached sunroom and immediately noticed that something was different. The painting on the easel—the painting that had only sea and sky the last time I saw it—now had seagulls in the air. White froth on the waves. I lowered myself to the lounge chair and stared at it.

I heard the bathroom door open. "All set!" Jen called. "Where'd you go?"

"I'm in here," I said.

She came to the wide arched entrance to the room. I pointed to the picture.

"The picture's changed," I said.

I could see the wheels turning in her head. She opened her mouth to speak, then bit her lower lip. "Busted," she said.

"This is *yours?*"

She nodded.

"Why didn't you *tell* me? You're so good."

She crossed the small room and reached between the arm of the sofa and the wall to pull out another canvas. It was the same size as the one on the easel, but this painting was complete. It showed a girl sitting alone on the beach. She was looking at the water, so you could only see her from the back, and she wore a green tankini not all that different from mine and a wide-brimmed straw hat. Her hair was long and blond down her back. There was a tiny little crack where her tankini bottom didn't quite cover her butt. In the ocean, there were dolphins. In the sky, clouds were like cotton balls.

"Jen! I can't believe how good you are." I really couldn't. I was shocked.

"I'm not great at people," she said with a laugh. "Which is why I usually draw them from the back. Cheating, I know."

I pointed to the painting on the easel. "You told me this was done by the owner of the house. I don't get why you'd lie about something like that."

"Just…modest, I guess." Was she blushing? The light from the window was behind her and I couldn't really tell. "I hate…I don't know. The attention."

"But this is crazy!" I said. "You were trying to figure out what to study in school when it's totally obvious."

"This is just a hobby," she said. "I mean, how can you make any money as an artist?"

"Probably as easily as you can a fashion designer."

She shrugged. "Well, I don't have to figure it out right now," she said. "And I'm hot, even in here with the AC on. Let's swim, okay?"

The beach was very narrow behind the cottage, a scary sign of erosion I remembered from the Sea Tender. Or maybe it was just high tide and I was being paranoid. I saw a few people in the distance north of us, but behind Jen's cottage, it was deserted. The air was thick and muggy and I knew my hair was turning to frizz. We dropped our towels and headed into the chilly ocean. Jen was way ahead of me as we ran through the shallow water. Or rather, *she* ran. I walked like the water was made of glue. I understood phobias all of a sudden. How people got them. How they could suck you down. But I would *not* let this totally calm water have that power over me.

Jen was in the deep water now, stroking like crazy, and I dived in and started toward her. I'd gone swimming nearly every day in the pool at the prison, and once I was able to shake off the heebie-jeebies about being in the ocean again, I felt good and strong. Jen kept swimming, though, farther out than I ordinarily would have. She was from Asheville. What did she know about swimming in the ocean? Rip currents and undertows and all that? I didn't know why I felt such a need to keep up with her, but I did. I was relieved when she finally stopped stroking. She rolled into a sitting position, treading the water with her hands.

I started treading myself, turning to face the beach. When I saw how far we were from shore, it reminded me in one frightening nanosecond of the day Andy and I had been pulled out to sea. I suddenly shivered with panic, so far from the beach with nothing to grab on to. Except Jen, I reminded myself. If I needed to, I could tell her I was panicking and I knew she'd let me hang on to her. But I didn't want to be such a baby.

"I've been looking forward to this all day," she said. "She twirled a couple of times in the water. The sun shone on her glossy dark hair.

"You're a good swimmer." My teeth were chattering even though I wasn't cold. Just freaking out.

"You, too," she said.

"Well, I grew up on the water. You grew up in Asheville."

"I belonged to the Y, so I got to swim a lot."

I looked toward the beach, wishing we were a dozen or so yards closer to it. I'd feel so much better. I thought of telling her about floating out to sea with Andy, but decided that would make me feel even more afraid. I needed to talk about something entirely neutral.

"How long have you been painting?" I asked.

"Oh—" she tipped her head back and looked at the sky "—forever. Since I was a kid."

"And no one ever said you should pursue it seriously?"

She shrugged.

"Your parents had to know how good you were," I said, knowing I was fishing a little for information on her family. "Didn't they ever encourage you?"

She shot me a look that felt like bullets pinging off my cheek.

"Sorry," I said. "I forgot you don't like to talk about them."

"Damn straight." She did another twirl in the water again. "Sooo," she said, dragging out the word, and I knew she was looking for a way to change the subject. "What have you decided about that doctor at the hospital?"

"What do you mean?"

"Are you going to hit on him?"

"Of course not," I said. It bugged me that she thought I would. "He's married. And anyway, I told you I'm not interested in him. Or anyone. I was just briefly attracted."

"Oh. Right." She laughed like she didn't believe me.

I'd told Dr. Jakes about realizing that Ben reminded me of my father, and that Dr. Britten reminded me of Ben. Dr. Jakes thought that was "a major revelation." I thought it was just a wake-up call for me to watch my step. It also gave me the creeps that I'd slept with a man who reminded me of my father. Yuck.

"Do you think he's interested in you?" Jen asked.

"Jen!" I said. *"No!"*

"How do you think he'd...I mean, not just him... How do you think everyone at the hospital would react if they knew about you and the fire?"

The thought of Taffy and Miss Helen and Mr. Jim and Dr. Britten and everyone knowing the truth about me was so depressing I thought I might cry. I would *never* let them find out. "You saw what happened at the library," I said. "I think it would be all over for me."

"But the woman who took your application knows, and she was okay with it," Jen said. "Look how fast she gave you the job. And you said how much they respect you there now and everything. Couldn't you tell them now? Wouldn't it feel good not to have to worry all the time about being found out?"

I felt this slight pain in my calf. The beginning of a cramp? That was how people drowned, wasn't it? Cramps in their legs?

"I just can't tell people, Jen." I was going to drown any second and she was making it worse.

"They could find out, though. Wouldn't it be better if you told them yourself?"

She totally did not understand. *"Look,"* I said. "I'm not bugging you about your family, so please don't bug me about this!"

She looked shocked by my outburst. I was a little shocked by it myself, but she was pushing all the wrong buttons when I felt panicky enough to begin with.

"Sorry," she said. "I'm just thinking of you. You were able to tell me and I didn't freak."

My teeth chattered so hard, I wondered if she could hear them. "You...you're more accepting than most people," I said. "I'm afraid to tell anyone else."

She suddenly laughed. "I didn't realize you were such a chicken." She plowed her palm through the water to splash me.

"Hey!" I turned my head away. *"Stop."*

She splashed me again, still laughing like it was the funniest thing in the world. But when I looked at her face, there was something mean behind the laughter.

"Jen! Come *on.*" I outgrew splashing my friends when I was about ten. Next thing I knew, she'd start dunking me. I wasn't hanging around for that. "I'm going back," I said, and I started swimming toward shore.

She caught up to me, swimming close by my side. We matched each other stroke for stroke. For her, I guessed it was just a race. Some kind of competition. For me, my heart was pounding so hard, I felt like I was swimming for my life.

Chapter Forty-Nine

Sara
The Other Widow

A NOR'EASTER SWEPT ACROSS TOPSAIL ISLAND THREE MONTHS after Jamie's death. It demolished a few of the trailers in the trailer park. It tore the roof and steeple from the chapel and broke every one of the windows. It was not the first time weather had destroyed part of the building. In the past, though, Jamie'd been quick to make repairs, as he did after Hurricane Fran. Now, I knew no one would bother.

For a few weeks after Jamie died, people came to the chapel on Sundays, and a couple of them tried to re-create the spell he'd cast over the place with his questions about experiencing God, but no one's heart was in it. Or, as I thought, no one but Jamie had that sorcerer's touch. So people stopped coming to the chapel, and now that the roof was gone and the windows were gaping holes in the concrete walls, I knew the building would disintegrate bit by bit until it was nothing more than a memory. Just like the man who created it.

A few days after the nor'easter, I pulled into the trailer park after dropping Keith off at school and saw Marcus's pickup in front of my trailer. He was sitting behind the wheel, and he got out as I parked next to him. I hadn't really spoken to him since the service. I'd started working at a new coffee shop in Surf City, Jabeen's Java, and he came in there often because it was close to the fire station, but he didn't have much to say to me. So little, in fact, that I was certain Jamie must have told him about me before the accident happened on the boat.

I had nothing to say to him, either. There was some speculation that Marcus may have been involved in Jamie's death. A humpback whale in June? The investigators didn't think so. But they hadn't been able to pin Jamie's death on Marcus, and he'd walked. As for me, I didn't know what to think. Who to blame. Did Marcus love Laurel, as Jamie had thought? Did he love her enough to want Jamie out of the way? Or was a whale the actual culprit? Either way, Jamie was gone.

"What are you doing here?" I asked as I got out of my car.

"Just wanted to talk to you for a minute," he said. He was holding a large manila envelope in his hand. "I have something for you."

I hesitated, then nodded toward the trailer. "Okay," I said. "Come in."

I opened the blinds in the living room and let in the morning light. Marcus looked uncomfortable as he handed me the envelope. "That's for you," he said, sitting down on the sofa. "Really, for Keith. I was going to just leave it, but then I thought I'd better wait and give it to you in person."

I sat down and opened the envelope. Inside was a handwritten letter and a document.

"You don't really need the letter," he said. "Since I'm here, I can just explain it to you."

I held up a hand to stop him as I read:

Dear Sara,

I know that Keith is Jamie's son. He told me about it the morning he died. It's taken me some time for that to sink in and when it finally did, I realized how unfair it is that Maggie and Andy will always have plenty of money, but Keith won't. If Jamie had lived, he would have provided for him. So I started this college fund for Keith. I set it up so he can have the money for college whenever he's ready to go. If he doesn't end up going to college, he can get the money when he's twenty-five. I hope this eases your mind a little.

Sincerely, Marcus

I read through the document quickly, but thoroughly enough to see that Keith now had a college fund worth forty thousand dollars. Forty thousand!

I looked at Marcus. "Where..." My throat felt tight. "Where did this money come from?" I asked.

"It's mine," he said. "It's not a big sacrifice for me. I'm never going to need all the money I have. So, that's invested now." He motioned toward the document that shook in my hand. "It should be worth quite a bit more when Keith is ready for college."

"Marcus...I don't know what to say." I didn't want to cry. I was so, so tired of crying. "Thank you so much."

He nodded awkwardly. "How are you doing? Financially, I mean? I don't want to pry, but Jamie told me he was giving you a few hundred a month to help out."

I nearly laughed. "That's what he told you? A few hundred?"

Marcus nodded.

"It was quite a bit more than that," I said. "It was enough so that I was able to save some every month." I had a nest egg. It wouldn't last Keith and me forever. But if I could somehow continue to live rent-free in the trailer, plus earn a little extra at Jabeen's, we'd be okay.

"Oh." He looked surprised. "Well, I'm glad."

"I…I guess that all his money—all the property he owned—went to Laurel," I said.

"Yeah. That was pretty automatic. He had a living trust with everything he inherited from our parents in it, and Laurel was the beneficiary."

Son of a bitch, I thought. For the first time, I was truly, deeply angry with Jamie. "Well…I'm a little worried about one thing," I said.

"What's that?"

"This trailer. I know he owned this trailer park, and he let me live here without paying rent, which is how I could get by. But now, if Laurel owns the trailer park, I don't know what to do. Should I move out?"

"Hmm." He sat back on the sofa. "No. Don't move. Here's what I think. First of all, I'm sure Laurel would want you to stay here rent-free," he said. "She doesn't know anything about you and Jamie and she's never going to know anything about it, okay? You and I—as far as I know—are the only people who know about it. Is that right?"

I thought of Steve, but he was long out of the picture. "Yes," I said.

"I don't think Laurel will even give a thought to you living here. The truth is, she now owns so damn much property on this island, that she may not even realize—or care—that she owns this trailer park. It's a drop in her financial bucket."

I tried my best to hide my resentment. He didn't even seem to realize how hurtful his words were.

"Okay," I said.

Marcus leaned forward and I noticed how golden his brown hair looked in the light from the window. He really *did* look like Andy. "I know you and Jamie had plans," he said. "You know, plans for the future."

I pressed my lips together.

"You must feel like a widow, too," he said. "Only you're not supposed to act like one."

He understood. Tears welled up in my eyes. "Exactly," I said.

"Let me know if I can help, Sara," he said, getting to his feet. "I have to get back to the fire station."

I stood up, too. "Why do you work when you really don't need to?" I asked.

He shrugged. "Why did Jamie?" he asked.

"Because he loved it. He felt like he was doing something valuable."

"There you go." He pushed open the door and walked out onto the deck.

"Marcus?"

He turned back to look at me.

"Are you in love with Laurel?" I asked.

He raised his eyebrows, looking surprised. Then he smiled. "Only since I was sixteen," he said. Then the smile faded. "But nothing's going to happen there. She thinks I... She doesn't believe there was a whale."

I clutched the document in my hand. There'd been no need for Marcus to do this. No need for him to come here and offer his sympathy. I looked at him again.

"I believe there was a whale," I said.

Chapter Fifty

Keith

MISTER JOHNSON SHOOK MY HAND WHEN I WALKED INTO THE conference room at the police department that Friday night. Dawn and Laurel were already there, and Dawn slung an arm around my waist as we waited for Flip to set up the DVD player.

"How's my guy?" she asked.

"Hangin' in," I said.

"You doin' okay over at Marcus's?"

"It's good." I liked that she was so cool with me around other people. She made me feel halfway normal.

"I think Marcus likes the company." Laurel smiled at me.

I looked away from her. "Whatever," I said. Man, I could be a son of a bitch.

"Okay," Flip said as he stepped back from the DVD player. "Take a seat, everybody."

We all sat around a long table, Dawn between Laurel and me on one side, Flip and Mister on the other. Mister was dressed in a suit that didn't fit into the beach world in any way, shape or form. He looked like a rapper. Like if you took away that collar and tie, you'd find some bling.

"As I told the three of you on the phone," Flip said, "Mister filmed his interview with Sara's memoir teacher, and while he doesn't think there's anything much here, he wanted you to be present as we watch it."

Mister leaned forward on the table. "There's always a chance y'all might pick up on something I'd miss," he said.

"Right," I said. My mother'd been gone three and a half weeks, and I was ready for *somebody* to pick up on *something.* How long could this go on?

The interview was kind of creepy, and the creepiest part of it was the teacher himself. His name was Sean, and he reminded me of Reverend Bill—very tall and skinny—but he had spiky, bright red hair and pale skin. He shook Mister's hand, then sort of folded himself into a chair across from the P.I.

Mister asked the dude some basic questions, and we learned that the class met six times in a church meeting room. There were five women and two men. The only person my mother seemed to know was Dawn, he said, and as far as he could remember, she never talked much with the other class members.

"As in, not at all," Dawn said.

"I can't say if she ever got together with any of them after class or during the week, though," Sean said.

"Nope," Dawn said.

"How much of Ms. Weston's memoir did you read?" Mister asked him.

"Just the first few pages." The teacher waved his hand around when he spoke. *Gay,* I thought. "It was very well written, but she was the only student who wrote by hand. I asked her to type her entries in the future, but she said a) she didn't have a computer or typewriter and b) the memoir was for her eyes only. She just wanted me to see the beginning to be sure she was…I think she said 'doing it right.'"

"I told you," Dawn said. I had the feeling Dawn had been a wiseass as a kid who got in a lot of trouble at school.

"Do you recall the content of the pages you read?" Mister asked the teacher.

"Yes, because it was unique," Sean said. "She was in her early twenties, attending a church in North Topsail for the first time. The building was on the beach or...I don't recall precisely where, but it was at least partially surrounded by water and was pentagonal. She was taken with the minister and unhappy with her husband." He chuckled. "I have to admit, I wanted to know where her story was going. But not at the cost of my eyesight."

Thank you, Jesus, I thought to myself. If my mother was heading in the direction of telling all about her relationship with my father, I was glad she decided to keep it to herself. Out of the corner of my eye, I saw Laurel playing with her fingernails. I sort of felt sorry for her. She knew where that story was going, too.

"She never spoke during class," Sean said. "Everyone else wanted to read from their work, but Sara kept hers to herself. I once asked her if she needed any help, but she said she was doing fine with it. I honestly don't know how much she took away from the class. I don't think she missed any of them, though."

"Just one," Dawn said, and as if he could hear her, Sean sat up straight in his chair.

"Oh," he said. "She did miss one because of her son. He was one of the teenagers injured in that church fire in Surf City and he wasn't feeling well and she needed to stay home with him."

I wondered if that had pissed her off, having to miss the class because of me.

The interview went on a few more useless minutes. Then Flip turned off the video and Mister looked across the table at me and

Laurel and Dawn. "The fact that Sara was working on this...journal or memoir may mean nothing," he said. "But what interests me is that she was looking back into her past, and when someone does that, they sometimes try to get in touch with someone from that past. Laurel, Flip tells me you've known Sara the longest. Does any of this ring a bell for you?"

Laurel laughed. Man, I had to give her credit for that. Before she laughed, I thought the tension in the room was going to suffocate me. "Well," she said, "to begin with, the minister was my husband."

Mister's eyes widened. Dawn rubbed a spot on the table with her fingertip.

"He died in 1997," Laurel said, "so I doubt she was trying to get in touch with him."

"I see." Mister made a steeple with his hands on the table. "I think... Maybe you and I could speak in private later, okay?"

"Sure." Laurel nodded.

"As for the other gentleman mentioned in the memoir," Mister said, "I *have* met with your father, Keith."

It was my turn to look surprised. "That's a neat trick," I said.

"What do you mean?" Flip asked. I shook my head. Laurel was back to playing with her fingernails.

"So where is he?" I wondered what he was like, the man who had nothing at all to do with me coming into the world.

"In Minnesota," Mister said. "He remarried and has three daughters. He was sorry to hear that your mother's missing, but said he hasn't heard from her since they split up when you were a baby. Does that fit what you all know?"

The three of us nodded.

"He's paid no child support, but he said that your mother agreed to that arrangement, and I did find that to be the case when I read their divorce records."

"That's why I live in a tin can," I said.

Mister nodded. "It *was* an unusual arrangement," he said, "but I've seen stranger."

He put his hands on the table and got to his feet. "Well, I wanted you to see the interview." He starting doling out his business cards, like we didn't have them already. "Give me a call if you think of anything that might help later."

When I got back to Marcus's tower, the front door was locked. Marcus was really a pain in the butt when it came to locking the door. Three-quarters of the time, he didn't bother, so I got in the habit of not taking a key with me when I went out. Then he'd lock it, for no reason I could figure out. When I complained, he told me to put the key on my key ring, but I kept forgetting. So now I was locked out.

I didn't think he was at the fire station, which meant he was probably over at Laurel's, and you couldn't pay me enough to go over there with Maggie and the gang. I was about to call him to come home and let me in, when I remembered that there was a ladder attached to the side of the tower. It was a skinny little thing that ran straight up to the roof, maybe a foot across with rungs the diameter of my thumb. It stuck out a few inches from the wall, just enough to get a toehold. I asked Marcus about it and he said it was there when he bought the tower. Probably supposed to be a fire escape.

I walked around the side of the building and looked at the ladder. The moon was full, and the narrow ladder cast long sharp shadows against the side of the tower. No way, Jose. Even if I could get up that ladder, it would just put me on the flat roof that had no railing around it. But there was a door up there. A short, slanted door that I didn't think Marcus ever locked and that led to the circular metal stairway inside the tower.

I leaned against the building with a sigh. Looked at my watch: 9:07. I could call him, but it'd piss him off. He told me ten times about taking a key.

I grabbed the ladder and started to climb. Fast. If I did it fast, I wouldn't have to think about it. The ladder shook like it was going to peel off the wall any second. The rails were as thin as cigars beneath my hands, and my toes hit the side of the building with each step. *Don't look down,* I told myself. *Don't think about how this is screwing up your shoulder. Don't think, period. Just keep moving.*

I did. I climbed higher. Higher. And I was okay until maybe two-thirds of the way up. Suddenly, I froze. My body went stiff as a corpse, my hands locked around the cigar rails. I couldn't unclench my fingers to move my hands either up or down. I couldn't make my feet go up to the next rung or down to the one below it. I was fucking trapped on the side of the building, and not only couldn't I move a muscle, my head was starting to spin. I pressed my forehead against the ladder, keeping my eyes closed. I was gonna hurl any second.

Could I just jump? I thought of how I'd wrecked my ankle jumping the eight feet from the back door of the trailer. I had to be up at least twenty by now. I'd die. *That's why heights are scary, you asshole.*

I must have stood like that for five minutes. Finally, I unkinked my right hand. I forced it open, and slid it jerkily down the rail. Moved my right foot down a rung. Did the same with my left side. I felt uncoordinated, but I was moving and when I got about six feet off the ground, I let go and jumped to the sand.

By then, my body was made of Jell-O and I was ready to swallow my pride. No, I wouldn't go over to the house on the sound, but I *would* call Marcus to come save me again. He was probably getting used to it.

Chapter Fifty-One

Andy

I NEEDED TO TALK TO A GIRL ABOUT WHAT HAPPENED WITH me and Kimmie. Mom was a girl, but she'd say, "Where did this happen?" Then I'd say about the tower and she'd tell Uncle Marcus and I'd be in trouble. So I asked Maggie to come into my room. I closed the door and went, "Shh."

"What's up, Panda? Andy?" she whispered.

I didn't yell at her about calling me Panda because she fixed it.

"You can't tell anybody," I said.

She shook her head. "Okay." She sat down on my bed, cross-legged, like she always did.

I sat in my swively desk chair. "Me and Kimmie tried to have sex but it didn't work," I said.

Maggie didn't look mad or upset or anything. "What happened?" she asked.

"Don't tell anyone. Promise?"

"I promise. As long as nobody got...you know... Is Kimmie all right? Did she get hurt?"

"No!" I said. I forgot we were whispering. Mom was home, but she was downstairs so it was probably okay. "No. I wouldn't hurt anybody."

"I know that. Where were you?"

"At Uncle Marcus's. He wasn't home."

I waited for her to yell at me, but she didn't.

"Okay," she said. "And what happened?"

"We planned it all out. I had my condom and we went to that room I sleep in with the blue bedspread."

She nodded. She knew which room I meant.

"And…" I started feeling embarrassed. Maggie's someone easy to talk to. She's so nice. But I remembered how Uncle Marcus said you never talked to anybody about it. It was private. "This is private," I said. "But I don't know what to do."

"It's okay, Andy," she said. "You know you can trust me."

"I was ready to do it," I said, "but Kimmie started crying and wouldn't open up her legs."

"Oh." Maggie bit her lip. "What did you do?"

"I said okay. We didn't have to do it. And she was worried I wouldn't still be her boyfriend, but I will be."

Maggie smiled. "I love you, Panda Bear," she said.

That was a dumb thing to say that had nothing to do with what I was talking about! "Did you understand what I said?" I asked.

"Yes, I did. You really wanted to have sex, but Kimmie got scared at the last minute and changed her mind. You cared enough about her to not try to force her. And you're mature enough to know that sex isn't the most important part of a relationship."

"It's pretty important," I said.

"But not important enough to ruin what you and Kimmie have right now."

"What do we have?" I was getting confused.

"Your relationship. Your love for each other."

"Right. But I don't know what to do next time."

"You need to wait," Maggie said.

"I don't want to wait."

"You need to. You need to tell Kimmie that you'll wait until *she* feels ready."

Maggie wasn't giving me good answers. "That might be never."

"It might be a long time, that's true," Maggie said.

"Can't you tell me how to talk her into it?"

"No way," she said. "That'd be totally unfair to her."

"I don't want to be unfair to her," I said, "but I want to have sex."

"You are such a typical guy," she said.

"Why did you say that?"

"Look, Andy," she said. "Girls sometimes aren't as hot for it as guys are. They have more to lose."

"What can they lose?"

"They can get pregnant, for one thing, while guys can't."

"Not with a condom."

"Even with a condom, but definitely not as easy."

I didn't know that. I tried to picture Kimmie with a big baby growing inside her. No way.

"It can hurt the first time, too," Maggie said.

"Was that why she was scared?"

"Ask her, Andy. She's the only one who can answer that question. And just...you have to be patient."

"My condoms could expire by when she's ready."

Maggie laughed. "You can always get new condoms," she said. "A new girlfriend as pretty and cool as Kimmie is harder to find."

"*Oh,*" I said, getting it. I really *would* have to wait, because Maggie had finally said a very smart thing.

Chapter Fifty-Two

Keith

JEN WAS INTO THIS "DRIVING ON THE BACK ROADS" DEAL, which is why we were in no-man's-land on a pitch-black night coming back from the movies in Wilmington. She liked driving any time of day or night, which was okay with me. Saved me gas money. I didn't know what Jen's story was, moneywise. She liked eating out and she paid for the movies and even filled my tank the last time we used my car. But she didn't act like she was rolling in it. I didn't care what her story was. All I knew was that I liked being around Jen better than I liked anything else in my life. She was the only person—next to my mother and Dawn and now Marcus—I didn't feel like I had to hide my face around. She'd started helping me with my exercises, and even went with me to my last couple of PT appointments to learn the right way to do them. Gunnar fell all over himself to teach her what to do. Cracked me up.

It blew my mind that Jen never seemed embarrassed to be seen with me. At PT, it wasn't such a big deal since there were a lot of screwed-up-looking people there. But at the movies and in a restaurant where I knew people were staring at me, she treated me like I was normal. She'd hold my hand. Even kiss me. Her attitude was, like, "Who gives a shit what other people think?" That's how

I felt about whatever the hell her age was. With that little streak of gray covered up, she looked nineteen to me again, totally, but I didn't care one way or another how old she was.

When I was younger, before the fire, I'd told a few girls I loved them. A couple of times, I actually believed it. I didn't know what I was talking about. This thing with Jen was the real deal. When I could make her smile—no better feeling than that.

"I'm *starving*," she said now. "When we get back to my house, let's make some eggs and grits. I love eating breakfast late at night."

Whatever. That girl could eat eggs any time of the day. "Sounds good to me," I said. I'd just as soon skip the meal and take her straight to that king-size bed, but if she wanted food first, that was cool.

The movie tonight was one of those serious flicks where you know way in advance that very bad things were going to happen to very good people. Sort of like life. It made me think of my mother. She was the best person, and something very bad had happened to her. I had no doubt about that anymore. I had to wipe the thought out of my mind while I watched the flick, or I knew I was going to lose it.

Jen cried during the movie. She was quiet about it, but I held her hand to comfort her, thinking that crying was really an over-reaction to what was happening on the screen. I mean, it was sad, but not totally tragic. Not compared to *my* life, anyway.

Now, driving back from Wilmington, I thought again about those scars she'd said she had inside. Maybe she was thinking about *them* during the flick. I decided I should finally ask her.

We were going over the swing bridge when I figured out what to say.

"You know when you told me you had scars inside you?" I asked.

"Mmm." She pulled up to the only traffic light in Surf City. It was blinking red. Not another car in sight.

"What did you mean?" I asked.

She didn't say anything as we started moving again. "It'd burden you if I told you," she said finally. "I don't want that."

I turned toward her as far as the seat belt would let me. "You took on *my* burden," I said. "Let me help you with yours."

"It's totally different."

"How?"

"It just is." She glanced at me. "You really want to help me?"

"Yes," I said.

"Just keep lovin' me to pieces."

It was the first time either of us had said the L word.

"Cool," I said.

"You know——" she looked over at me "——maybe you should let Andy and his girlfriend use the tower to get together."

Wow, nothing like an abrupt change of topic. I liked the other one better. "Why?" I asked.

"You remember what it was like before you got your license," she said. "Wanting to have sex and having no place to do it."

"Whatever." I really didn't care where Andy had sex; I just didn't want a picture of him doing it stuck in my mind.

Jen turned onto South Topsail Drive and we went a ways without talking. It was so dark. If I'd been driving, I'd've turned on my brights, but she was going pretty slow so it was no big deal. Just before we came to the place where South Topsail runs into South Shore, though, this small dark blur flew out of the woods and into the road ahead of us, and I felt the thud as we hit it.

"Oh, damn!" she said, hanging on tight to the wheel. "*Splat!* I hate that." She kept right on driving.

"Aren't you going to stop?" I asked. I could see the blur in my memory. A raccoon? A cat? A small dog?

"No way," she said. "I don't want to examine roadkill in the middle of the night."

"Maybe it's not dead, though." Once, I ran over a rabbit in broad daylight. I could see it in my rearview mirror after I hit it. It was still alive, but writhing. Kind of flopping all over the road. I was shook up. I drove about a mile, but that stupid rabbit wouldn't get out of my mind, so I turned around and drove back. I wished I had a gun to put it out of its misery, but of course I didn't. I couldn't think of anything to do but run over it again. I'd never forget the feeling of my tire flattening that poor thing. I drove miles past my destination, trying to get any trace of him off my tire and out of my head.

"I really think we should go back," I said to Jen. She *did* have a gun. We could use it if we needed to.

"I'm hungry, Keith. We're practically to my house. I'm not turning around now."

"What if it was a cat or dog?" I asked. "Maybe it'd have tags and we could call—"

"It was only a possum or something."

"But what if it wasn't?" In my mind, the blur had turned into a black cat. Someone's pet. "Wouldn't that bother you? Wouldn't you want to know if your cat was run over?"

"Why are you making such a federal case out of this?"

I pointed to a driveway. "Just turn around here," I said. "You don't even have to get out of the car. I'll look. Do you have a flashlight?"

"I'm not turning around, Keith. You're being silly."

I stared at her. "*Man,*" I said, "you've got a real cold side to you." In fifteen seconds, she'd totally blown the stupid romantic image of her I'd been building up in my mind.

"It was a *possum,* Keith!" she said. "It's not like I hit a person. Not like it's your mother. Or my mother. Or any other human being."

I hated that she'd mentioned my mother like that, in the same breath as a squashed possum.

"We're going back," I said.

She stopped the car in the middle of the deserted street. "I do *not* believe you."

"Come on. Just turn around in the next driveway."

She made this huffing, annoyed sound, but she pulled into the driveway of an old cottage and turned around. We drove back to where she'd hit the animal, and we got out of the car and searched the road and the bushes in the light from her headlights. Nothing. Not even a clump of fur or a trail of blood.

"See?" she said. "It's probably fine. Just bruised. And I'm starving."

I wasn't ready to give up. I started walking back up the road, checking the ditch on one side of it and the bushes on the other.

"Keith!" she called after me. "You're driving me crazy!"

I hardly heard her. I picked up a stick and started pushing the tall weeds out of the way so I could see behind them. Then I started whacking the bushes. Whacking the street. And I knew I was losing it, that I wasn't looking for any injured cat or dog or possum. I was looking for my mother.

Chapter Fifty-Three

Sara
Healing Our Hearts
1998

KEITH WAS THE LIGHT OF MY LIFE. I DOUBT ANOTHER MOTHER ever loved a child more. He was handsome and bright, loving and lovable. I saw Jamie in him more and more each day, something that both saddened and comforted me. Since his birth, I'd been getting Keith's heart checked, as prescribed, every year at UNC in Chapel Hill. For the longest time, I thought we'd dodged the bullet. He seemed so healthy. So active and playful. His doctor thought he might be okay and that he'd never need surgery. Shortly after his seventh birthday, though, I began to see a change in him. He couldn't keep up with the other kids on the soccer field the way he used to, and sometimes I'd see him breathing hard just from his horseplay around the trailer. I tried to convince myself that he was fine. One day on the soccer field in Hampstead, though, I knew his doctor had been wrong.

Laurel was there that day. I was sitting on the lower bench of the metal bleachers, watching the last fifteen minutes of Keith's game when she and Andy sat down next to me.

"Maggie's team's playing next," she said, and I spotted Maggie with her teammates at the side of the field, wearing their blue-and-white uniforms. "What's the score?"

"Two-three," I said. "The other team's ahead."

We were coming up on a year since Jamie's death and much had changed. Laurel and I saw each other with some frequency, but always around the kids' activities. Keith and I often had dinner at her new house on the sound so the children could play together, but it was never the same without Jamie. Marcus, who'd usually been a part of those family get-togethers, was never around, either. I knew Laurel let him see Andy and Maggie, but she wanted nothing to do with him. Occasionally, she'd ask me to lunch when the kids were in school, but I always made up some excuse. I couldn't do it. I couldn't be alone with her, just the two of us. I didn't want to hear her talk about how much she missed Jamie. I didn't want to hear her talk about the designer she'd hired to put the finishing touches on the interior of her four-bedroom house. Should she go with a floral or a stripe for the draperies in the family room? Should she replace the fixtures in her brand-new bathroom because the finish on them didn't quite match the finish on the doorknobs? Her insensitivity to my own financial situation was galling to me. Sometimes I hated her.

"Is Keith all right?" she asked suddenly as we sat side by side at the soccer game.

I looked at my son. He was running with his teammates toward the goal, but he was undeniably sluggish, as if he was trying to run through mud. I bit my lip, wondering if I should pull him out of the game. Before I could decide, he stopped running altogether and bent over from the waist, fighting for air.

I was instantly on my feet, running toward him. "Keith!" I yelled.

A whistle blew when I ran onto the field. I reached him and only then realized that Laurel was at my side. Keith looked up at me with his big Jamie Lockwood eyes. He opened his mouth as if he wanted to say something, but couldn't find the breath to get the words out. Before I knew what was happening, Laurel had scooped him into her arms and was carrying him off the field, with me close on her heels.

She set him down in the grass near the bleachers. People brought us water and orange slices, but I knew he needed far more than that: he needed surgery to repair the hole in his heart. I fought back tears, running my hand over his hair as Laurel took his pulse and counted the number of times his chest rose and fell in a minute. Sometimes I forgot she was a nurse.

"Hi, Keith!" Andy walked over to us and sat on the grass next to Keith.

"Hi," Keith managed to answer. Was I imagining it, or were his lips a little blue?

Laurel let go of his wrist. "I think he's okay," she said, "but we should take him to the hospital just to be sure."

I felt grateful to her for saying "we" instead of "you." I needed someone with me.

She found another parent to watch Andy and arranged a ride home for Maggie, then she drove Keith and me to the hospital. I was a wreck. I kept turning around to touch Keith's leg. He stared out the window and I was terrified by the blank look in his eyes.

"Has this happened before?" Laurel asked, peeking at him in her rearview mirror. She spoke quietly and I knew it was so Keith couldn't hear.

I didn't answer right away. I felt like a bad mother, ignoring symptoms that never should have been ignored. "Not like this," I said after a while. "But I *have* noticed him getting winded more easily recently."

"When was his last cardio checkup?"

"October," I said. "His doctor seemed to think he was okay."

"Did they do an echo or what?"

"Just an EKG."

She looked over at me. "Maybe it's time for some more inten-sive testing," she said.

I pressed my lips together to keep from crying. Laurel reached over and squeezed my arm. "It'll be all right," she said. "I'll help you."

Laurel meant what she said about helping me. She went with us to Keith's appointment in Chapel Hill, and she actually held my hand as the cardiologist told me about the surgery Keith needed. He talked about cutting open his chest and about the heart-lung machine that would keep him alive during the hours it would take to repair the hole in Keith's heart. He described the weeks of recovery. My brain spun around and around inside my head, and it was Laurel who asked the questions I couldn't seem to formulate. What were the risks of the surgery? (Death, of course.) What were the risks of doing nothing? (Decades cut off his life span.) When the doctor left the room, Laurel took me in her arms as I cried, and I leaned against her, leaned *on* her, as I would in the months to come.

The surgery was scheduled for the second Tuesday in July. Laurel set up child care for Andy and Maggie because she planned to stay in Chapel Hill with me. She reserved a hotel room for us near the hospital, brushing away my weak protests about her footing the bill for it. Five days before the surgery, though, she invited me over for lunch, telling me there was something she needed to talk to me about.

"I want to show you something," she said when I arrived. She pulled me by my arm through the living room, where swatches of different-colored fabrics were spread across the sofa, and upstairs to the bedroom she used as a home office. "Have a seat." She pulled a second chair up to the desk where she had a computer with a connection to the Internet. I barely knew what the Internet was, but she was always talking about it.

"I've been doing some research ever since we saw the surgeon," she said. "I didn't want to tell you about it until I had to, in case I hit a dead end." She pressed some buttons on the keyboard and a document appeared on the screen. "This is an e-mail from a doctor in Boston," she said. "They're doing clinical trials of a less invasive way to repair atrial septal defects. I've been communicating with him and he thinks Keith might be a good candidate."

She leaned to the side so I could read the e-mail. Keith would need to be examined in Boston to determine if the procedure would be right for him, but from what Laurel had told him, the specialist thought it would be. Laurel used the mouse to go to a Web site where I read about the procedure itself. They'd go in through the artery in his groin and carry a tiny umbrella-shaped device up to his heart, where it would open up, lock in place and cover the hole. My own heart thumped as I read.

"That's it?" I asked. "They wouldn't have to open him up?"

"Right." Laurel smiled. "There's always a chance the procedure won't work, and then he'd have to have the surgery. But so far, they're having really good success with this. If you want to try it, we should go up there soon."

That *we* again. I knew how hard it was for Laurel to leave her children—Andy in particular—with someone while she was away. When Jamie was alive and could watch the children, she'd travel the country speaking to groups about fetal alcohol syndrome, but she never went away anymore. Here she was, though, ready to drop her own life to help my son.

Downstairs, my heart light with the hope she'd given me, I studied the swatches of fabric for her new sofa without a shred of bitterness or resentment.

"I like this yellow better than the green," I told her, and I meant it.

It turned out Keith was a perfect candidate for the procedure. We didn't even need to make a second trip to Boston. Laurel waited with me while they slipped the little umbrella into his heart and popped it open, telling me the whole time that it was going to work. She could feel it, she said. We had to stay up there four days to be sure the umbrella wasn't going to budge, and by that time, Keith was already breathing like a normal boy, bored by his confinement and begging to go home. Laurel and I played games with him in his hospital room, and when he slept, we talked about our own childhoods and our dreams for our children. In those hours, I grew to love her. We were like sisters, sharing everything about our lives.

Everything, that was, except the one deep pain we would always have in common.

Chapter Fifty-Four

Maggie

MONDAY MORNING, I WAS LOADING A MOVIE IN THE DVD PLAYER for the little boy sitting at the table, when Mr. Jim walked into the playroom.

"Can you come in the hall with me for a second, Miss Maggie?" he asked.

I started the movie and followed Mr. Jim into the hall.

"Madison's back," he said when we'd walked a little bit away from the playroom.

"Oh, no," I said. She'd been home for more than a week, and I'd hoped she'd had some kind of miracle.

"They think this is it," Mr. Jim said.

"You mean...she's dying?"

He nodded. "Her mother said that while they were driving in, Madison asked if you'd be here."

"She did?" I was so touched by that.

"I don't know if you want to see her or not," he said, "but I thought I'd tell you and let you decide. I know you felt a special...a connection to her."

Yes, I wanted to see her. Of course I did.

"Okay," I said.

He touched my arm. "You don't have to, honey. She may not even know you're there, so if you don't want to, you—"

"I want to," I said. "Can you watch the playroom?"

He nodded. "Taffy's her nurse today," he said.

I found Taffy, and we walked together toward the little girl's room. I had a lot of questions I wanted answered before I saw her.

"What about her father?" I asked. I didn't want to run into him again.

"I think he's locked up," Taffy said. "At least he was. Drunk and disorderly and a few other things."

"Is she awake?"

Taffy shook her head. "She's getting a lot of morphine to keep her comfortable. Her mama's in there with her and I know she's completely wiped," she said. "Would you be okay sitting with Madison for fifteen minutes or so to let her mother take a break?"

I nodded, but inside, my anxiety kicked up a notch. "What if she dies when I'm with her?"

"Well, I don't expect that to happen," she said. "But the truth is, sometimes kids—and adults—seem to wait until their relatives are out of the room to go. It's like they don't want to distress them more than they have to."

Oh, right, I thought. "Do you really believe that?"

She smiled. "I've seen lots stranger things than that happen, Maggie," she said.

Madison's mother, Joanna, her face ashy gray and her eyes red, sat in the recliner with the little girl on her lap. She handed her over to me as if Madison was a delicate flower. Silently, we sorted out all the leads and the clear plastic tubes that ran to this bag and that. Then Joanna smoothed her hand over Madison's head, and without a word to me, walked out of the room.

The recliner rocked, something I hadn't noticed the day I'd read to her in her room. I rocked her gently, knowing the motion was to soothe myself more than to soothe her. She was so medicated, I doubted she had much of a sense of anything going on around her.

I shut my eyes and rocked and rocked, and I didn't even open my eyes when I sensed Daddy in the room.

"I wanted a miracle for her," I whispered to him.

I know you did.

"She's too young."

She'll be fine.

I pressed my cheek to the warm skin of Madison's temple. Against my chest, she slept, barely breathing. She wasn't struggling, though. She didn't seem to be suffering at all. I wasn't kidding myself that *I* had anything to do with how calm she seemed. Anyone could have been holding her at that moment, and she would have seemed just as peaceful. But it wasn't just anyone. It was *me*. And I felt strangely lucky to be able to hold her life in my arms that way.

She'd felt light the last time I'd held her here in her room. Now she seemed to become lighter by the second, and it took me a moment to understand the reason: circled by my arms, she was already turning to dust.

Chapter Fifty-Five

Keith

I'D BEEN BACK TO THE TRAILER TWICE IN THE WEEK AND A HALF since I moved to Marcus's tower. The first time, I needed to dig up the name of the doctor who prescribed my Percocet. This second time, I needed to find the textbooks I'd never returned to the school. They were after me for them. Not only that, Marcus had it in his brain that he was going to get a tutor for me so I could try to get a GED since I refused to go back to school. I told him I didn't care if I finished high school or not, but he just kept saying "we'll see." That was what Marcus always said when he figured he'd get his way eventually. I was onto him. Jen was on his side. Though they still hadn't met each other, they were coming at me from different angles, pushing that damn GED. I knew I'd have to cave or else DSS would start making noise about foster care again, and that was the last thing I wanted.

I pulled up in front of the trailer and climbed the steps to the deck. A month had passed since my mother disappeared, and she was quickly dragging Mister Johnson's eighty percent success rate down toward seventy-nine. Even after all these weeks, it still felt weird to walk into the trailer and know she wasn't going to be there. Rationally, I knew it, but that didn't stop me from calling "Mom?" when I walked in the door.

Of course there was no answer, though I thought I heard a sound coming from her bedroom. I pulled a knife from the knife block and went into the room. Nobody there. Nobody in the whole double-wide except me. And somewhere, those damn textbooks.

I started hunting for them and found two of them—chemistry and this book of short stories—sticking out from under the sofa. I was pawing through the pile of stuff on the end table when I saw the blinking light on our answering machine. I dropped the books I was carrying and hit the play button, my finger jumping all over the place. The mechanical female voice said, "One message."

Mom, Mom, Mom.

I didn't even realize how hard I was hoping the message would be from her until I heard a stranger's voice on the tape. Disappointment raced through me so fast I felt like I was going to pass out.

"This is Barbara McCarty," the woman said, "and I'm trying to reach Sara Larkin."

Huh? Larkin was my mother's maiden name. I had no idea who Barbara McCarty was, and I thought that was all she was going to say, but then she kept going.

"Ms. Larkin, we have a three-bedroom available on the first in case you're still interested. I'll need to verify your employment at Western Carolina Bank, though, so if you can get back to me ASAP, that'd be great."

My brain was numb as I listened to the woman give her number, twice. I started dialing it on our landline, but my hand was shaking like crazy. What was going on? I unplugged the answering machine and carried it out to my car. The textbooks could wait.

Chapter Fifty-Six

Keith

I CARRIED THE MACHINE INTO THE FIRE STATION.

"Where's Marcus?" I asked the first person I saw, a new volunteer whose name I didn't know.

"In the garage," he said.

I put the machine down on the desk in Marcus's office, then went out to the huge garage where three of Surf City's fire trucks were parked side by side.

"Marcus?"

"Yeah!" His voice came from somewhere in the middle of the garage.

I walked around the first truck and saw him up on the second, doing who-knew-what with a piece of equipment.

"Gotta talk to you," I said.

He stood up on top of the truck and wiped his hands on a rag. "Can it wait?"

I shook my head, my voice suddenly stuck somewhere in my throat.

"Okay," he said. "Go in my office. I'll be right in."

In his office, I sat in the chair in front of his desk and stared at the machine like it might get up and walk out of there. He showed up a few minutes later with two bottles of Coke. He pulled a couple of tubes of peanuts out of his desk drawer and held one toward me.

"Want some?"

"No, man." I plugged the answering machine into his wall outlet. "This is from the trailer. You've gotta hear this." My hand looked like I had one of those shaking diseases as I pressed the play button again.

He was pouring the peanuts into his Coke, but when the woman started talking, his hand froze in midair.

"What the...?" he said.

"Exactly."

"Larkin?"

"Her maiden name."

Marcus frowned at the answering machine. "It's got to be the wrong Sara Larkin."

"Oh, right. And it's just a coincidence that this lady called our number."

"Good point." He let the peanuts fall, fizzling, into the Coke. "Does this make any sense at all to you?"

"Hell, no. And what's this employment-at-a-bank crap?" *And why was she keeping everything from me?*

"Was that area code 704?" Marcus asked.

"I think so." I could hardly remember my name.

He picked up the phone.

"You going to call the lady?" I asked.

He shook his head. "We need to get Flip over here." He held the phone between his chin and shoulder as he typed something into his computer. "Charlotte," he said.

"Charlotte what? The area code is *Charlotte?*"

"Did she ever talk about Charlotte?"

"Hell, no!"

"Hey, Flip? It's Marcus. Come over here, okay?"

* * *

Flip showed up in about three minutes. I must've said "I don't get it" about a hundred times by then.

"What's up?" he asked when he walked into Marcus's office. He saw me. "You okay, Keith?"

"Just listen." Marcus hit the play button, and Flip looked as weirded out as I felt.

"You wrote this down?" he asked Marcus when the McCarty woman gave her number again. I was starting to hate her voice.

"Got it." Marcus clicked off the machine.

"Let's do this on speakerphone," Flip said.

Marcus hit a button on his desk phone. "Ready for me to dial?" he asked Flip, who nodded. It was me who wasn't quite ready. My mother had a secret—one, at least—and I didn't know if it meant she was still alive or not. If we didn't talk to this woman, at least I could hang on to a little bit of hope.

The phone rang on the other end. Flip checked his watch.

"Failey Hill Apartments," a woman answered.

"Barbara McCarty, please," Flip said. "This is Philip Cates of the Surf City Police Department in North Carolina."

I rested my head on my arms on the top of Marcus's desk. The room spun, and I shut my eyes.

After a minute, that now-familiar voice came on the line. "This is Barbara McCarty."

"Hello, Ms. McCarty," Flip said. "I'd like to talk with you about the message you left for Sara Weston—Sarah Larkin—today."

"You're with the police?"

"Surf City. Yes, ma'am."

"What do the police have to do with this?"

"Ms. Larkin's been missing for four weeks, and we're investigating her disappearance."

The woman was quiet at first. "I don't know anything about that," she said finally.

"She was interested in renting an apartment?"

"Yes. But it's been months now. She... I'd have to check, but I believe she e-mailed us at least six months ago, looking for a three-bedroom. She must have asked to be put on our waiting list, which is why I called her."

I lifted my head. "What the..." Maybe it *was* the wrong Sara Larkin. This just didn't make sense.

"You said in your voice mail that you needed to check with Western Carolina Bank regarding her employment," Flip said.

"That's right. We always need to verify an applicant's employment."

"Why did you think she was working there?"

"She's not? She must have said so on her application."

"Can you fax or e-mail me a copy of her application?" Flip asked.

"It'll take me a few minutes to get my hands on it, but yes. Sure."

Flip gave her his e-mail address, while Marcus jotted something on a piece of paper and slid it across the desk to him.

Flip glanced at the paper. "And can you tell me how much the rent would be on a three-bedroom?"

"The one coming open is twelve hundred."

I let out a laugh. "Right," I said, and Marcus shut me up with a finger to his lips.

"All right," Flip said. "I'll watch for your e-mail."

Marcus clicked the button on his phone.

"It's gotta be the wrong Sara Larkin," I said. "Maybe Mom...for some weird reason...changed our phone listing to her maiden name and this lady looked it up and..." I shrugged.

"Why would she do that this long after divorcing your...Steve Weston?" Marcus asked.

I shook my head. "I feel like I don't know her right now," I said.

Flip looked at me. "What money did she have besides the thousand or so in her savings account?" he asked.

"Zilch," I said. We'd already been over this. Over and over. "She'd cash her check from Jabeen's and we'd live off that. She didn't even pay rent on the trailer."

"She didn't?" Flip raised his eyebrows. "For how long? Is there a chance the two of you were getting evicted?"

I laughed. "No way."

Marcus shook his head. "Long story short," he said to Flip. "Laurel owns the trailer park and she let Sara and Keith stay there rent-free."

"So there was no way she could pay this twelve hundred a month without a new job," Flip said. "Even then, that's a chunk of change for someone with only a thousand dollars in the bank."

I suddenly thought of my college fund. I looked at Marcus. "Could she have gotten into the money you gave her somehow?"

Flip turned to Marcus. "You gave her money?"

Marcus sighed. Looked at me. "You okay with Flip knowing?"

I nodded. "Why not? The whole world knows how fucked up we are now."

"Jamie was actually Keith's father," Marcus said.

"Jamie..." Flip looked totally confused. "Your *brother?*"

Marcus nodded. "So when Jamie died, I started a trust fund—a college fund—for Keith. It had forty thousand dollars in it at the time. I don't know how much it has in it now. Sara was the trustee, but she couldn't...can't...touch the money until Keith goes to college."

"We'll check on that and make sure it's still there," Flip said. "Keith, think hard. Did your mother talk about moving to Charlotte or applying for a job in Charlotte or anything like that?"

I tried to think back to conversations my mother and I'd had over the last year. The thing was, I didn't pay a whole lot of attention to what she talked about. I had two burned arms and one burned face and they'd occupied most of my time. I sure as hell would have remembered if she said she was planning to move to Charlotte, though. "So, do you think that's where she is?" I asked. "Maybe she *did* get a job there and found a different apartment." Maybe she'd deserted me after all. I watched Marcus take a swig of his Coke and peanuts and thought I might barf.

"None of this makes sense right now, Keith," Marcus said. "But it gives the police a bit more to go on."

"Right," Flip said, like everything was now fine and dandy. "We need to bring the P.I. into the loop. Let him know about this."

I leaned back and looked at the ceiling. "This is so lame," I said, getting to my feet. "I'm outta here."

"Hold on, Keith," Flip said. "We're going to have to go through the house again."

"You mean the trailer, don't you? The pile of rust she left me with while she moved into—"

"Why do you think she was looking at a three-bedroom apartment?" Marcus interrupted me. "Just for herself? I doubt it. I imagine you were in her plans."

I stared at him. "Then why didn't she let *me* in on those plans?" My brain was fried, trying to figure it all out.

I wanted to tell Jen. I wanted to crawl into bed with her and tell her everything. Lay it out. She wouldn't ask me a thousand questions. She'd just listen and then she'd hold me that way she did, like

I wasn't damaged goods. We could have sex, but I didn't even care about that right then. And that was really saying something.

I just needed to matter to somebody.

Chapter Fifty-Seven

Maggie

I STAYED LATE AT THE HOSPITAL THE DAY THAT MADISON died. I didn't want to go home. I wanted to stay in the peds unit with people who understood how I felt. Even after the shift change, when Taffy left, I stayed. I think Taffy'd taken some heat for letting me stay with Madison when she was so close to dying, and I tried to let everyone know I was okay. I honestly was. I was okay enough to be worried about Joanna. She fell totally apart when she realized that she'd left her daughter's side for fifteen minutes in the last twenty-four hours, and it was the wrong fifteen minutes. It shouldn't have been me with her. It should have been her mom. Yet it was nobody's fault.

Tony, one of the male nurses in the peds unit, came on duty after Taffy left, and when he found out what had happened, he called the social worker to come talk to me to be sure I was all right. She was a pretty woman in her thirties who'd been leaving for the day when Tony'd called her. She came to the playroom, carrying her purse and her sweater, and I felt terrible that I was causing her to stay late.

"I'm absolutely fine," I said, sitting down on the rocker at her request.

She sat on the playroom table, setting her purse and sweater next to her.

"Tony said you were supposed to leave at five," she said, "and it's now after six. Why don't you go home?"

"I just want to stay," I said. "There are a few kids here whose parents can't come in tonight. I can read to them or whatever."

"Who's at home?"

"What?" I didn't know if she was talking about my family or the patients' families.

"If you go home now, who will be there?"

"My mother and brother. Possibly my uncle."

"Are they supportive? Can you talk to them?"

"Oh, sure," I said.

"Then what do you think is keeping you here?"

"I told you. I can help out if I stay."

She smiled a little. "The people at home, no matter how loving and supportive they are, didn't know Madison," she said. "But everyone here did. Right?"

I hesitated. It wasn't as though everyone in the peds unit was talking about Madison or anything, but there was this *bond* I felt with them that I would lose the moment I walked out the door. "Right," I said.

"Have you cried yet today?" she asked me.

I shook my head.

"If you go home, do you think you will?"

Yes. I was sure I would. "I don't want to," I said.

She nodded, and I thought she understood exactly how I felt. She reached into her purse and pulled out a business card. Then she jotted a number down on it and handed it to me.

"I'm leaving for the day, but this is my cell number. If you feel like you need to talk tonight, call me. But right now, you need to go home."

I started to shake my head, but the expression on her face told me I wasn't going to win the argument.

"Yes." She stood up. "You need to go home, Maggie." I didn't budge from the rocker as she put on her sweater. "I've heard good things about you," she said. "I think it's great you're putting in so many hours here, and you've really earned the respect of the staff. But part of being a good, responsible health worker is learning how to take care of yourself in an environment like this one that can tax you to your core. It might seem like staying here until you're so tired you fall asleep sitting up is the way to do it, but it only puts off the grief. You'll need to figure out other ways of dealing with it. Okay?"

She reached out a hand and I stood up and shook it.

"Okay," I said. I still didn't want to leave. I didn't feel up to figuring out "other ways of dealing with it." But I knew she was right. I couldn't hide out in the peds unit forever.

I was getting my jacket in the volunteer office when I heard a commotion at the nurses' station. I walked into the unit and saw Madison's father, Rudy, bedraggled and red-faced, shouting as he waved his arms through the air. "It's a fucking scandal!" he yelled at Tony and Constance, the only two nurses in the station. "I'll *sue!* I'll sue your sorry asses."

I hesitated near the corner of the nurses' station, which was between me and the exit. I didn't know if I should try to zip past Rudy or duck back into the volunteer office. I could see that Constance, who was probably the oldest nurse in the unit, was on the phone. Calling security, I hoped. I felt sorry for Madison's father, but he scared me.

"Mr. Winston," Tony said, "please settle down so we can talk about this calmly, all—"

"Fuck that!" Rudy shouted. "My little girl is dead! Talking calmly's not gonna bring her back, and it's your fault. All of you!" He pointed his finger and his whole arm shook as he swept it in a horizontal arc in front of him. I took a step forward and saw that other nurses and parents were standing in the doorways of the patient rooms. A couple of them were on their cell phones.

"Don't you have any…any, like, screening?" Rudy shouted.

One of the parents, a huge, burly guy, walked from his child's room toward the nurses' station. "Sir," he said, "let's go outside. You're scaring the children." He reached for Rudy's arm, but Rudy jumped backward.

"What about *my* child?" he wailed. "My little girl! If I was you, I'd get my kid out of this hospital before it's too late." He looked down the hall at the other parents. "All of you! Get your kids out of here. They don't have no quality con—"

He saw me. His eyes burned into me and I stood paralyzed at the corner of the nurses' station. "You goddamn bitch!" He started toward me, but one of the security guards suddenly appeared, and between him and the burly father, they managed to hold Rudy back.

"Parents!" Rudy shouted, his arms twisted behind his back by the guard. "Listen to me! Do you know who this girl is?" He jutted his chin toward me. "Maggie Lockwood, that's who! Does that name mean anything to you? Remember her? The arson fire in Surf City! People killed and burned. She just got out of prison, and this back-water hospital hires her to take care of kids!" He kicked the wall of the nurses' station so hard I jumped. "Where's your brains?" he shouted toward Tony and Constance. "Maggie Lockwood was with my daughter today when she *died.* Joanna'd been with her every minute for days and she was *fine,* and in the five minutes this bitch is with her—" he jerked his chin toward me again "—she just happens to *die*. You think that's a coincidence? Huh?" He kicked the wall again. Once. Twice. I jumped each time, horrified by what he was implying. "How dare you let someone like that work with kids!" he shouted at Tony, as if he was responsible for me being there.

I leaned against the counter as a couple of police officers burst in the door. Thank God! Without missing a beat, they took the place of the security guard and the burly father. Rudy didn't even put up a fight, but he wasn't done shouting. "How *dare* you!" He kicked the wall again. "I'm suing the ass off this hospital, you better believe it!"

The cop slapped handcuffs on him. *Roughly.* Too roughly. "Let's go," the other cop said as he led Rudy toward the exit.

"You let her take care of my little *girl!*" Rudy wailed as he stumbled toward the door at the policeman's side. He sobbed, gasping for breath. "You let her take care of my little *girl!* My little—"

The door closed behind him, cutting off his words. Tony turned toward me, and only then did I realize I had my hands on the sides of my head like in that painting *The Scream,* tears pouring down my face.

"Is this true?" Tony asked.

I felt so many pairs of eyes on me. Nurses who didn't know me well because they didn't work the day shift. Parents, only a few of whom I'd met.

"Cathy Moody knew," I said quietly. "She knew everything. I told her when I applied."

Tony looked away from me. "Get out of here, Maggie," he said. "You've had a long day. Call Cathy Moody in the morning and…see what she wants you to do."

I walked past the nurses' station, my cheeks on fire, and I heard the whispering start behind me as soon as I opened the door.

I could hardly see the road as I drove home. Was this it? The end of my community service at the hospital? I wanted to stay there so badly. But maybe a criminal wasn't supposed to be able to do community service in a place she loved that much.

My car suddenly lurched to the left, the steering wheel vibrating so violently I could barely hang on to it. I wrapped my hands around the wheel and forced it to the right, holding on tight until I came to a stop on the shoulder. I got out, and although daylight was fading, I could see that my left front tire was nearly in shreds. *Damn.* Could this day get any worse?

Stay calm, I told myself. I'd changed a tire before, although not on the sloped shoulder of a four-lane road. I wasn't sure if I should pull forward or what exactly, and I decided the first thing I needed to do was check my spare. I opened my trunk and discovered I *had* no spare to check. Great. I couldn't believe Mom had let Andy drive around without a spare.

I got back in the car and dialed home, but there was no answer. I tried Uncle Marcus's cell number, then my mother's, and got dumped to their voice mail both times. I even tried Andy's, in case he was with them and had his phone on, but I remembered he had swim practice tonight. No doubt, my mother was with him.

Jen. I hadn't spoken to her since Friday, when she'd splashed me in the water. Even after we went back inside her house, I'd felt uncomfortable with her and left pretty quickly, trying to figure out why our couple of hours together had gone south so suddenly. We didn't speak all weekend, and now it felt strange to call her. But she was a friend, right? My *only* friend, actually.

I dialed her number.

"Hey." Her voice was quiet when she answered. A whisper, really.

"I've got a problem," I said. "I'm halfway home from the hospital and I have a flat. I tried calling my mom, but I can't reach her. Is there any chance you could come pick me up?"

Silence.

"I'll buy you dinner if you haven't already eaten." It was after seven. Of course she'd already eaten.

"I can't right now," she said.

She had someone there, I thought. A guy? Another friend?

"Can't you call a service station?" she whispered.

I felt myself tear up again. How was I supposed to find the name of a service station? And besides, I didn't have a spare.

"Could you do me a favor and look up a service-station number for me?" I asked.

"Are you crying?"

I bit down on my lip to try to stop the tears. "It's just been a crappy day."

"I'm sorry, but I can't help. You'll figure it out. You've got your phone, so you'll be okay."

I looked through the windshield at the darkening sky. I didn't feel okay at all.

"I have to go," she whispered.

"All right. Good—" I heard the click of her phone. I stared at my own phone for a minute, hoping she'd call back or that Mom or Uncle Marcus would get my message and come rescue me. Then I called information and asked to be connected to the nearest towing company. I was going to have to rescue myself.

Chapter Fifty-Eight

Keith

"Who was that?" I asked. I was half-asleep in Jen's bed, but I'd heard her whispering on the phone. I could tell she wanted to get rid of whoever it was and get back to me.

"Just a friend." She was sitting up in bed with her back against the headboard. "Go back to sleep, baby," she said. "You need it."

I didn't want to sleep anymore. When I first got to Jen's, I just wanted to shout and punch the walls and let out all my confusion on someone who'd listen. She *did* listen. Then she did more than that, taking me into her bed. Having sex with me so I'd forget for a little while what the hell was going on with my mother. Now, though, I was in radical pain.

"I need my drugs," I groaned.

"Are they in your pants pocket?"

"No. *Shit*." I suddenly pictured them on the kitchen counter in the tower. "I left them at Marcus's." I carefully raised myself up on one elbow and saw that she had her computer open on her lap. "What are you doing?"

"Just surfing."

"You have a wireless connection?" I hadn't seen her use her computer before.

"Oh, yeah. It's great," she said. "All over the house. I can even get online on the deck."

"Checkin' e-mail?" I felt jealous all of a sudden.

"No," she said. Then she looked down at me. "I Googled those apartments you said your mother was trying to move into."

She helped me sit up, then moved the computer to my lap. "Don't freak out, okay?" she said as she adjusted the screen.

There they were, the Failey Hill Apartments, looking like part of a resort in the Caribbean or something. The two-story building had arched balconies, tennis courts and a couple of pools in the courtyard, just waiting for the arrival of Sara Larkin without her pathetic son.

I stared. Couldn't speak. I was torn somewhere between fury and a gut-wrenching sadness. Jen stroked my neck with her fingers.

"I don't get what she was up to," I said when I could finally talk. I knew the whole bit about Western Carolina Bank was bogus. Flip checked. She wasn't working at any of their branches—not unless she'd changed her name one more time. "I mean, if she wanted to split, she could've at least waited until I was eighteen," I said. "It'd be bad enough then. But I just don't... This isn't like her."

"The fire," Jen said.

"What do you mean, 'the fire'?"

"It changed you, and it probably changed her, too. Maybe she just couldn't take it anymore. Maybe you didn't notice her changing because you were so involved in getting better yourself."

Of course it changed her, but not so much that she'd take off without me. Start a whole new life without me. I touched the blue water of the pool on the laptop screen.

"I hate my damn half sister," I said.

"I know. I don't blame you a bit, and I hate her, too, for what she's done to you." She lifted my messed-up left hand from the computer and pressed it to her lips. "You must wish you could hurt her the way she's hurt you."

"She's gonna show up at Marcus's one of these days when I'm there," I said, "and I swear, somebody's going to have to hold me back from kicking the shit out of her."

"That's too good for her," she said. "You'd give her some cuts and bruises and she'd heal up in no time, while what's happened to you...that's never going to go away."

"You're not making me feel much better." I didn't want to look at the apartments any longer. They were just bringing me down. I started to hand the computer back to Jen, but my shoulder suddenly seized up like a son of a bitch.

"Shit!" I squeezed my eyes shut.

"Oh, baby!" Jen set the computer on her nightstand and got out of bed. She leaned over and kissed my forehead. "I'm gonna get you a glass of wine and some Tylenol," she said. "Sorry, but that's the strongest stuff I've got. I'll be right back."

My eyes were still shut, and I was afraid to breathe. It felt like if I moved half an inch to the left or the right, I'd tear my arm clean off my shoulder. I listened to Jen racing down the stairs, hurrying to get something to make me feel better, and I remembered my mother screaming at the doctor in the hospital to give me something for the pain. I remembered how she'd sit with me, day and night, while I could barely move. Barely breathe. How she changed my revolting bandages and cleaned my butt and cried when I cried. I heard Jen down in the kitchen, opening the refrigerator for the wine, because she loved me, which made me feel like a shit for the thought that was running through my mind: I loved my mother more than I would ever love Jen, and my mother loved me more than Jen ever would. No matter how it looked to anyone else, my mother would never leave me. Not for all the ritzy apartments in the world.

Chapter Fifty-Nine

Sara
The Fire
2007

I LEFT JABEEN'S JAVA AROUND FOUR BECAUSE I WAS BATTLING a sore throat and Dawn said she could manage without me. All I could think about on the drive home was taking a couple of aspirin and crawling into bed. Keith was probably surfing—his usual Saturday activity—so I thought I'd leave him a note about the leftover chicken in the fridge before I conked out. I could quickly make some rice to go with it. I had it all planned out by the time I pulled up in front of the trailer.

It was dim inside, especially after walking in from the bright sunlight, and I jumped when I saw Keith sitting on the sofa in our little living room.

"Hi, honey," I said. "You surprised me. I thought you'd be surfing."

"What's this?" He held something out to me. A manila envelope?

"What's what?" I pulled open the curtains above the sofa to let in more light.

"*This.*" He rapped the envelope on his bare knee.

"I have no idea." I took it from him and looked at it, back and front. No name or address. "Where'd you find it?"

"Like you don't know." He could get so snarly sometimes, and I really didn't need one of his moods when I felt so lousy myself.

I sat down with a sigh and opened the flap on the envelope, pulling out the three sheets of paper inside. I saw the handwriting on the top sheet: *Dear Sara.*

Oh, no, I thought. *Oh, God, no.* What had Marcus written in that letter? I searched frantically through my memory, hoping there was some way Keith couldn't have figured out why he had a college fund.

"So, were you ever going to tell me Jamie Lockwood was my father?" he asked.

I looked at him. "Oh, Keith, I'm so sorry you found out this way."

He got to his feet. "You're sorry I found out, period, aren't you?" he shouted. "You weren't ever going to tell me. Don't you think I had the right to know?"

"Too many people would be hurt," I said.

"What about *me?*" he shouted. "What about *me* being hurt?" He stomped around the living room so hard, the trailer shook.

"Yes, you deserved to know," I admitted. I'd hated keeping that secret from him. I planned to tell him when he was older. He needed to be mature enough to handle the news without hurting everyone else in the process. "I know it wasn't fair."

"You put Laurel and Maggie and Andy ahead of me!" he shouted.

"No, I never—"

"They're rich! And I'm poor, in case you never noticed. Even that college fund. I can't have that till I'm twenty-five? What kind of crap is that?"

"You can use it for *college,* Keith." I sat forward. "You should be grateful for it. Marcus didn't need to use his own money that way."

"I deserve a hell of a lot more than that. The Lockwoods are zillionaires."

"I know you're upset, honey," I said. "I don't blame you. But you absolutely *mustn't* tell anyone about this. There's no point in dredging it up now. It would kill Laurel and her children."

"What about *me!*" he shouted again.

"You have to suck it up." I slid the papers back into the envelope. "The same way I've been sucking it up for the past seventeen years."

He stopped his pacing and glared at me. *"Bitch!"* he said. "I can't believe you're on their—"

"Don't you *ever* speak to me that way again!" I stood up myself and tried to stare him down. He was taller than me now and beginning to take on Jamie's thick build. "Sometimes you have to put your needs aside for the sake of other people," I said. "Laurel's been my best friend since you were little. You'd have a foot-long scar on your chest if it weren't for—"

"I don't care!" He stomped across the floor and out the door, slamming it shut behind him. From the window, I watched him grab his surfboard and wet suit and head toward the beach.

I pressed my hand to my forehead and sat down on the sofa again, shutting my eyes. Could I have handled that any worse? I was not a good mother. I'd failed him in so many ways. If only Jamie had lived! Keith would have had a father, and I would have had a partner to help me raise him better. Was that a cop-out, though? Laurel managed to raise two great kids without Jamie. Yes, she had money, but I knew it was more than that. I'd tried to give Keith my values, to teach him right from wrong, and he started out as such a lovable little boy. Yet now he was a lazy student with mediocre grades. He'd skipped school at least a few times. I knew he sometimes drank, and once he was caught with an ounce of marijuana in his pocket. I could blame it on peer pressure, but that seemed weak. He was right that he deserved more, and not just money. He deserved a more competent mother.

I looked at the letter from Marcus, still in my hand. How hurt Keith must have been when he read it! My heart broke just thinking about it, but he *had* to keep it to himself. I didn't trust him not to tell anyone, though. Not when he was this angry.

I called Marcus, but got his voice mail.

"It's Sara, Marcus," I said. "Call me back as soon as you get this."

I thought of going down to the beach to try to talk with Keith again, afraid he'd call Laurel from there, but then I spotted his cell phone on the kitchen counter. As long as he was at the beach, it'd be okay. I made myself a cup of tea with honey, but despite my aching head and sore throat, I didn't dare go to bed. I wanted to be up and alert when he came home. We needed to talk.

I was half-asleep when I heard him on the deck around seven-thirty. He came into the trailer, wet and sandy and flushed, and he walked right past me toward his bedroom.

"Keith," I said, sitting up straight. "Let's talk more about this, okay? Let's...order pizza and—"

"I'm going out." He walked into his room and slammed his door shut. I suddenly remembered he'd planned to go to a lock-in at Drury Memorial that night. I'd been happy about it. An all-night, chaperoned event sponsored by a church. I'd know right where he was and he'd be safe. Now, though, I didn't want him to go.

I knocked on his door. "Honey? Please stay home tonight. You're too upset and we need to talk about this."

He opened the door, but only to walk past me toward his bathroom. "The only thing *I* need is a shower," he said. "I'm getting picked up in fifteen minutes." He shut the bathroom door behind him.

"Who are you going with?" I asked through the door. "Who's picking you up?"

"Chick from school. Layla. You don't know her."

I leaned against the wall as I heard the squeak of the faucet. My head felt as though it was in a vise. All right, I told myself. He'll be away all night. Supervised and—hopefully—having fun. In the meantime, I'd talk to Marcus and we'd come up with a plan. Maybe Marcus could talk to him. Keith listened to other adults more easily than he listened to me. Maybe Marcus could settle him down.

An hour or so later, I was asleep on the sofa when my phone rang. The woman on the other end of the line was hysterical. "I'm Layla Schuster's mother!" she shouted. "There's a fire at the lock-in! It's on the news!"

I didn't bother with the news. Instead, I jumped in my car and drove the few miles to Drury Memorial and into a nightmare that would forever be a part of my life. Worse, it would forever—*forever*—be part of my son's.

The word *chaos* is inadequate to describe the scene at the church. I had to park a quarter mile away, yet I could smell the stench of the fire before I was even out of my car. I ran toward the smoking, flaming church, where people were screaming and shouting, out of their minds with terror. I searched faces in the darkness, looking for Keith. In my mind, he was not the snarly teenager from earlier that evening. He was the baby I'd once held to my breast, the toddler who took his first steps into Jamie's arms, the seven-year-old who submitted bravely to all sorts of frightening medical procedures.

"Sara!" one of the police officers hollered to me. He grabbed my arm and half pushed me across the street toward a taped-off area. "Keith was hurt!" he shouted in my ear. "Burned. They can tell you where they took him!" He gave me a shove toward the yellow tape.

The word *burned* played over and over in my mind as I ducked beneath the tape. I was surprised when I suddenly spotted Laurel among the crowd.

"Laurel!" I shouted. "Why are you here?"

"Andy's here!" She jockeyed her way closer to me.

Later, I realized how crazy it was that Andy was there—she never let him go *anywhere*—but that fact didn't have time to register because we suddenly heard this horrible cracking, groaning sound coming from behind us. We turned to see the roof of the church collapse in a horrific, thundering mass of flames and smoke. Laurel and I hung on to each other, scared out of our wits.

The next few hours were a blur. They told me Keith had been taken to New Hanover Hospital, but by the time I got there, they'd flown him on to the burn center at UNC. I made the three-hour drive in two, actually hoping a cop would stop me so I could plead my case for an escort. When I got to the hospital, they wouldn't let me see him. His condition was grave, they said. His lungs had been seared, his face and arms burned, and he was in a medically induced coma. I fell completely apart in the waiting area and someone took me into a little room where I could wail and cry. I wanted Laurel with me. I needed my best friend's support, but I knew she had her own fears about Andy. I would have to make it through this crisis alone.

In the burn unit, it was touch-and-go. I was allowed to sit with Keith in his extraordinarily hot room between the horrific treatments he needed to undergo. They kept him in the coma because it was the only way he'd be able to endure the pain. I talked to him constantly, keeping up a one-sided conversation just in case he

could hear me. I told him how much I loved him and apologized
for being a less-than-perfect mother. At night, I lay awake on a cot
in his room, wishing for some knockout medication of my own.
Laurel and Dawn left phone messages for me, but I didn't return
their calls. I was too wrapped up in Keith and the world inside the
hospital, and every ounce of my energy went into understanding
what the doctors told me about his condition. If I tried to speak to
anyone else, I knew it would be pure jibberish coming out of my
mouth.

Around the fourth day after the fire, I received a voice mail from
Marcus. He'd reserved a room for me at a pricey hotel near the
hospital. I could use it as much or as little as I wanted, and he added
that I should put any meals I ate in the hotel on my room tab. I was
so grateful to him. I needed a long soak in a tub and a real bed for
at least one night. I didn't want to be away from Keith, but his nurse
convinced me that I'd be doing him a favor if I took better care of
myself, so I moved into the hotel even though I still spent most of
my waking time at the hospital. As for those meals in the hotel restaurant, though, I didn't bother. Seeing Keith in his hot and airless
hospital room, wrapped in enormous bandages and hooked up to
IVs and a breathing tube, left me far too nauseated to even think of
food.

Laurel met me at the hotel for lunch one day after Keith had been
in the hospital nearly two weeks. I still had no energy to see anyone,
but I needed some clothes from home and she was willing to bring
them, so I agreed to meet her in the hotel restaurant.

It's amazing how much you can change in two weeks! I knew I
was an emotional wreck, but I hadn't realized what a *physical* wreck
I was until I saw myself through Laurel's eyes. We met at the

entrance to the restaurant and she looked absolutely horrified by my appearance. My clothes were hanging off me, and I hadn't bothered with makeup. I was known for always being neat and sort of tailored. No wonder she was so shocked.

She started crying, and I realized the reason I hadn't wanted to see her or anyone else from home was that I didn't have the energy to cope with *their* worries about Keith and me on top of my own.

She asked me questions about Keith's condition, and I tried to answer her as best as I could. I felt like I was in a dream—or a padded cell—removed from what was really going on around me. I could see Laurel's mouth moving, and on some level, I heard what she said and even managed to respond, but she and I were in two entirely different universes. Hers had two healthy children in it. Mine had one child whose life was hanging by a thread.

"You should talk to him," she said. "They think that people in comas might be able to hear even if they don't respond."

"I talk to him constantly," I said. "I tell him I love him and…I tell him I wish I'd been a better mother for him."

"Sara!" Laurel looked shocked. "You're a *terrific* mom."

"He gets in so much trouble, though," I said. "You're a single mother, too, and your kids are perfect." Well, Andy was hardly perfect, but Laurel knew what I meant. "Maggie's just a year older than Keith, but she's so much more mature."

"You and I both know it's Jamie who made her the way she is," Laurel said.

I suddenly remembered Keith finding that letter. How could I have forgotten about that? What would I do when he was better—he *had* to get better—and wanted to lay claim to being Jamie Lockwood's son? I couldn't even look at Laurel then. Instead, I pretended to study the menu.

The waitress brought our lunch. I'd ordered soup I knew I wouldn't eat.

"There's something I need to ask you," Laurel said suddenly.

I felt so *guilty* all of a sudden, as though she already knew about my affair with Jamie.

"What?" I asked.

"Are things all right between you and me?"

I had no idea what she was talking about. "Of course," I said. "Why would you ask?"

"We haven't spoken since the fire," she said. "You haven't returned my calls and...I feel distant from you, so I just wanted to be sure we're okay."

"I'm sorry," I said. "I've been so focused on Keith that I—"

"Of course you have been!" she said. "I'm just being paranoid." She dabbed at her chicken breast with her fork; she didn't seem to have much of an appetite, either. "You probably don't know this," she said, "but at the lock-in, Keith and Andy got into a fight. Keith called Andy a 'little rich boy.' I suddenly started worrying that you might resent the fact that my kids and I are...so comfortable finan-cially, while you and Keith... While it's harder for the two of you."

I smiled at her as though the difference in our finances meant nothing to me, even though I was trembling over the news that Keith had called Andy "rich." I hoped that was all he'd said. "That's never been an issue between us, silly," I said. "I can't believe you've been worrying about that."

But it *was* an issue, wasn't it? I loved Laurel with all my heart, but deep down, when she'd show off something new she'd bought for herself or the house or the kids, expecting me to ooh and aah over it, I *did* feel resentful. Now, though, wasn't the right time for that conversation.

I watched her cut her chicken, the wedding band she still wore sparkling on her finger, and I knew the right time for that conversation would never, ever come.

Chapter Sixty

Maggie

I WAS SO MISERABLE BY THE TIME OF MY THERAPY APPOINTMENT
Tuesday that it was all I could do to drive myself to Dr. Jakes's office.
When you screwed up as much as I did, it made sense to feel like
you didn't deserve anything good in your life. That meant you
didn't deserve people to treat you well, you didn't deserve a boyfriend, you didn't even deserve friends. And so, when everything
fell apart at the hospital because of Rudy, I was devastated, but I
felt like I deserved it. And when Jen didn't seem to really care when
I asked her for help, I felt like I deserved that, too. She didn't even
call to be sure I got home all right. I was so desperate for friendship that I built her into this great friend in my mind, never realizing that she didn't think of me that way at all. I wondered if I would
ever have friends again. How could anyone want to be friends with
someone who did what I did?

I was such a wreck after getting towed home the night before
that Mom insisted I call Dr. Jakes on the phone. I didn't want to,
but she put the phone in my hand and told me she wasn't letting
me out of her sight until I had him on the line. I told him everything about Madison dying and Rudy's meltdown and how my
friendship with Jen was tanking. I must have sounded truly awful,

because he asked me if I felt like killing myself. I didn't. I just felt horribly, inescapably, bad.

When I got off the phone after nearly an hour, Mom told me about the message on Keith's answering machine. That took care of my self-pity routine. Keith had it so much worse than me. My mother was standing right there in front of me, healthy and whole and loving me every single minute. I hugged her, thinking about Sara and how all the stuff about Charlotte raised more questions than answers.

I knew better than to go into the hospital this morning, but Cathy Moody called me before seven just to be sure I had no plans to come in. She said she'd need to talk to the hospital administrators to figure out how to proceed, and that I shouldn't come back until I heard from her. It wasn't a surprise, but I felt such a deep loss on top of everything else. I loved the peds unit. I was good with the kids. But I totally got what she was up against. I was sure she regretted ever giving me a chance.

I went back to bed, too depressed to do anything else, and Taffy left a voice mail while I was asleep. She said that, no matter what the hospital decided, everyone knew I had nothing to do with Madison's death. "That's insane," she said. "And as far as I'm concerned, you served your time for that fire in Surf City. I hope you get to come back. You were excellent and we really need you, and I just wanted to let you know how we feel." I wondered how many people were part of that "we." I hoped at least Miss Helen and Mr. Jim. And Tony. But I remembered how Tony'd sounded the evening before when he told me to go home. He'd taken the brunt of Rudy's anger, and I doubted very much that he was one of the "we."

* * *

"I'm glad you called last night," Dr. Jakes said as I sat down across from him in his office.

I nodded, but what I was really thinking was, *Thank you for being there and making time for me and for listening and caring.* I wasn't sure how I would have made it through the night before without being able to dump everything on him.

"Have you heard from the hospital?" he asked.

"No," I said. "I'm not optimistic."

"I'm sorry."

"I feel bad for that father, even though he really screwed things up for me." l could still hear Rudy wailing, *You let her take care of my little girl!,* and I knew that even though he was a jerk and a drunk and a bully, his heart was breaking.

"It was a tragic situation all the way around," Dr. Jakes said.

I sighed, rubbing the soft leather on the arms of the chair. "I loved it there," I said.

He nodded. "I think it was an excellent fit," he said. "Now you know that about yourself, whatever happens."

"What do you mean?"

"You know you like working in hospitals. You like working with children."

"Fat lot of good that's going to do me," I mumbled. I sounded so pathetic. "Sorry," I said. "I just feel…shitty."

Dr. Jakes didn't respond right away. I thought he was waiting for me to fill the silence, like he usually did, but then I heard him draw in a breath.

"What do you think would make you feel better?" he asked.

Daddy. He just popped into my mind. I hugged myself, pressing my fingers into my arms. My eyes suddenly filled with tears, but I held them in. Of all the things I'd lost—my friends, my freedom, my future—Daddy was the one loss that could instantly make me cry. No way could I explain how I felt about Daddy to Dr. Jakes.

"I don't know," I said. "I can't undo the fire. I can't undo what I did."

"Tell me about your tears."

Once he mentioned them, my tears spilled down my cheeks. I pulled a tissue from the box on the table beside me.

He leaned forward. "I tell you what I think," he said. "I think it's good you feel so alone right now."

"What?" I pressed the tissue to my eyes. "You're a *bastard,"* I said.

He smiled. "You were focused on Jen. And on the children at the hospital. They kept you from focusing on *you.* Now you're free to deal with yourself."

"Ugh. I don't want to."

"Why not?"

"I don't like myself."

He didn't say anything. I blew my nose. Stared up at his stupid burned-out lightbulb.

"What are you thinking, Maggie?" he asked finally.

I looked at him. "If I tell you, will you promise not to send me to a mental institution?"

"I don't believe you need to be in a psychiatric setting," he said. "I think you have amazing resources inside yourself you don't even know about. And, as we talked about when I first started working with you, what you tell me stays between us. The only time I would break that pact between us is if I feel you're a danger to yourself or others. It would be very important for you to tell me if you ever feel that way. But, Maggie, I don't think that's who you are."

He was right. I'd hurt a lot of people, yet I'd meant to hurt no one. And offing myself? I lacked the guts for that, even though there were times in prison when I felt like I wanted to die.

"So, can you tell me what you were thinking a few minutes ago? You looked like you were far away."

"I was thinking about my father." I twisted the tissue in my hands.

"You're angry with him."

I shook my head quickly, but then, without even thinking about it, I began to nod. "I told you about our old house," I said.

"The Sea Tender."

"Right. Well, I have these memories of my father being there. We'd sit on the deck together. He'd take me swimming in the ocean. He was the greatest dad." The tears started again, and it took me a minute to go on. I took a fresh tissue from the box. "It hurts to know he was…involved with Sara and had another kid and all that. But it doesn't change how great he was to me as a dad. And when the Sea Tender was still…before the storm washed it away, I used to go there sometimes at night and sit on the deck, and I felt like my father was with me. Not always. But sometimes I could get really still inside and…sort of *connect* with him. It was like I could really feel him there with me."

Dr. Jakes nodded like I'd said something perfectly normal. "I hear you," he said.

"Do you believe me, though?" I asked. "I mean, that he was really there? That I was actually connecting with him?"

"I don't know, Maggie." He took off his striped glasses and sat them on the table next to him. "They say some people have an ability to do that, but I don't know if it's real or just wishful thinking. No one can know that for sure. It's the great mystery, isn't it?"

"That we don't know what happens after we die?"

"Right. The thing is, it felt real to *you*. We—you and I—can't know if it *was* real, so we have to deal with the fact that it *felt* real. That's what matters."

"But…crazy people have delusions and hallucinations that feel real to them."

"We're talking about *you,* though. Not 'crazy people.'"

I managed a smile.

"What was special to you about those visits with him?"

"He loved me for myself," I said. "I mean, at the time, I was lying to my mother, hiding out with Ben, smoking weed and screwing up in school. And with Daddy, it was like he saw me on a different level. A deeper level or something, like none of those things I was doing mattered. Like it was just the fact that I was Maggie, the daughter he loved. It didn't matter what I did."

"He accepted you."

"Totally."

"What a great feeling that must have been."

"But the Sea Tender's gone, so I can't connect with him that way anymore. I've felt him with me a few times since, but he just sort of…appears. I can't connect with him on purpose, the way I used to."

"Well, I don't agree. I think you can connect to him anytime. Anywhere. Even in here."

"It's not the same. I won't feel him like I did there."

"I'd like you to try."

"Here?"

He nodded.

"No. I don't want to."

"I know you won't feel him the same way you did at the Sea Tender," Dr. Jakes said. "But I think you'll feel him in a *different* way. If you try."

I looked down at the wadded-up tissues in my lap. I'd feel like an idiot trying to connect with Daddy in front of someone.

"How would your father react if you told him what you did?" Dr. Jakes asked. "If you told him about the fire?"

I looked at him. "He'd understand me," I said. "I wouldn't even have to explain why I did it, and he'd get it. He wouldn't be angry with me."

"I remember he had that tattoo on his arm," Dr. Jakes said.

"Empathy. Right. And I got mine after the first time I felt that connection with him."

"I bet that felt good, to have that link to him."

I nodded.

"Maggie…close your eyes."

I did.

"Just breathe for a minute. Just focus on your breathing. Feel your breath at the back of your throat. How it feels coming in. How you can feel it going out through your nose."

I did what he said. I knew he was trying to get me to still my mind, and at first I thought, *This is ridiculous. I know exactly what he's trying to do.* But after a couple of minutes, I nearly forgot where I was.

"Tell your dad…tell him out loud, what you did."

"Daddy," I said, even before I made the conscious decision to go along with Dr. Jakes, "I set fire to a church. I mean, I laid the fire and it accidentally ignited. Some people died."

Where have you experienced God lately?

I laughed out loud, my eyes popping open. "Oh my God!" I said to Dr. Jakes. "That was so *Dad*."

"What do you mean?"

"My mother told me that when he used to have a service in his chapel, Daddy'd ask people 'where did you experience God lately?' And that's what he said to me right now. 'Where have you experienced God lately?' It was so bizarre."

"By your smile, I think it was a good sort of bizarre."

"I really could hear him."

"Maybe you should answer him."

I laughed again. "You're crazier than I am."

He smiled. Waited.

"Nowhere," I said.

Dr. Jakes raised his eyebrows again. "Do you think he'd accept that answer? Your father?"

I closed my eyes again. I let Daddy's question fill me up, and I suddenly remembered holding Madison on my lap. Feeling the light weight of her in my arms.

"Holding Madison in the hospital," I said. "The girl I told you about whose father had the meltdown last night." I opened my eyes. "She died while I was holding her."

Dr. Jakes looked instantly concerned. "Maggie!" He leaned forward in his chair. "You didn't tell me you were *holding* her when she died!"

"I didn't?" I'd spilled so much out to him so quickly the night before, I had no idea what I'd left in and what I'd left out.

"How did you feel?"

Dozens of words slipped through my mind. "Sad," I said. "Helpful. Good. Bad. Amazed. Horrified. Overjoyed." I smiled at how strange the rush of words felt coming out of my mouth. "I felt *lucky*," I said. "I don't mean lucky, as in 'I'm lucky to be alive and she's not,' but I felt lucky to be with her. To know her and to be able to hold her that way." I wrinkled my nose. "Does that make any sense?"

"Were you thinking about what a bad person you were then?"

I shook my head. "I wasn't thinking about myself at all."

"Maggie," he said, "that tattoo of yours is perfect. Over the weeks that I've gotten to know you, I've heard your feelings of empathy for so many people. You have empathy for everyone but yourself."

"That's because what I did is unforgivable," I said.

"How much of your day do you spend thinking about that?"

"It's always in the back of my mind. Even in my dreams. I dream about fires and I'm always the one who started them. Sometimes it's other...tragedies. The other night I dreamed I caused a car accident. That kind of thing."

"So even in your sleep, you're beating yourself up."

"There's nothing you can say that makes what I did forgivable."

"Perhaps that's true," he said. "But I'm going to say something completely different. I'd like you to consider this idea—you're being selfish by not forgiving yourself."

"I don't get it."

"It keeps you stuck. You just said it yourself. When you held that child, you were helping her by not thinking about what a terrible person you are. Instead, you were thinking of *her*. The more energy you spend beating yourself up, the less energy you have for other people."

"I can't automatically say, okay, I forgive myself," I said. "It doesn't work that way."

"What's standing in the way of you being able to forgive yourself?"

I knew the answer instantly, even though I didn't like it. "I haven't apologized to anyone I've hurt," I said. "Not even Keith. Especially not Keith. I avoid him. I hide from him. From everybody who knows. I can't face them."

"It would take courage to face them."

Chapter Sixty-One

Andy

ME AND KIMMIE RODE MY BIKE AND MAGGIE'S BIKE TO THE Topsail Island Trading Company in Surf City. We wanted fudge, and they had all kinds there. We both had exactly the same favorite kind: chocolate marshmallow.

"It looks like us," Kimmie said while the lady put some of it in a little box.

"What do you mean?" I didn't see how fudge looked like us at all.

"Black and white." She pointed to the big thing of chocolate-marshmallow fudge behind the glass. The dark part was not black at all. It was brown. But Kimmie is brown, too. If she said it was brown and white, that would make more sense. I almost said it, but Mom said I should pick my fights better. So I just said, "Yeah."

After we got the fudge, we put it in Kimmie's basket and started riding home. There were no cars except parked ones on the street since it wasn't summer or a weekend, so we could ride next to each other.

"There's your cousin," Kimmie said all of a sudden. She pointed to the new police station.

Keith was walking to the street from the police station. His car was parked ahead of us a little and I could tell he was walking to it.

I didn't want to talk to him, but we were going to crash into him, so we had to stop right in front of him. Maybe we could've gone around him, but it seemed funny not to say anything, especially since he's my cousin now.

"Hi," I said.

"Hey." Keith hardly looked at us. He just opened his car door.

"We bought some fudge," Kimmie said. "Chocolate marshmallow. Would you like some?"

I didn't want to give away some of our fudge, but me and Kimmie thought Keith didn't tell Uncle Marcus about us being at the tower. Uncle Marcus would've said. I was surprised Keith would be nice like that. That was why Kimmie was being nice back.

"No, thanks," he said.

"Do the police know any more about Sara? Miss Sara?" I asked.

He laughed, but it wasn't like when you laugh at something funny. "I think it's time they called in a psychic," he said. "That'd be just as useful as anything that's happening now."

I wasn't sure what a psychic was. After the fire, they had these psychic people come to my school to talk to us to be sure we were okay. They were like counselors. Maybe Keith needed somebody to be sure he was okay now.

"You mean, like somebody who can have a dream about where your mother is?" Kimmie asked.

Oh, I got it. Not like a counselor at all. Kimmie was the brains. I was the brawn.

"Right," Keith said. He looked like he was waiting for us to say something else. Maybe he was waiting for me to try to give him money again, but probably not, because of the pride thing. Mom said pride made him not take my money, but she said it was nice to offer it to him. Pride is one of those things I don't understand.

"It's like when you lose a race swimming," Mom said. "Sometimes you say, 'Oh, I don't really care,' even though you do. That's because your pride is hurt."

I totally didn't get what she was saying, but I pretended I did because she would go on forever about it if I didn't. After Keith didn't take my money, I couldn't figure out how to get it back in the ATM. I only knew the getting-it-out part. Mom took care of it for me, though.

"Look," Keith said as he sat down on his car seat. "About the tower. I know y'all don't have anyplace to go since you can't drive yet, so it's cool, all right?"

I was totally mixed up. I thought he meant it was okay for us to have sex in Uncle Marcus's house, but we didn't do it. We were waiting till we're more ready. I wanted to tell him that, but I didn't on account of sex being private.

One thing I *did* know was Kimmie was blushing. Some people didn't know when she was on account of her dark color, but I could always tell. I changed the subject so she wouldn't have to blush.

"Your girlfriend is pretty," I said. "Her hair's dark now like Kimmie's."

Keith looked up from his car seat. "What do you mean, 'dark *now*'?"

"You know," I said. "It used to be white. Yellowy white. Like Emily Carmichael's."

"What the hell are you talking about, Lockwood?" he asked.

"Why do you get angry at everything?" I felt flustrated. We were having a good conversation and all of a sudden we weren't. "I made a compliment!"

"Just tell me what you mean about Jen's hair being white."

"Yellowy white."

"Whatever! What do you mean?"

"Nothing." I was glad we were in front of the police station in case he started hitting me. "She just looks different than she used to. That's all."

He got out of the car and I moved my bike backward a little.

"How do you know what she used to look like?" he asked.

How *did* I? I tried to remember where I saw her. Maybe school? I just remembered being somewhere, looking at the heart-tattoo thing on her chin. "The bus, I think. Or maybe...the auditorium. I don't remember exactly."

"I think you have her mixed up with someone else," Keith said.

"Definitely I don't. I remember her, like, tattoo thing." I touched the pointy part of my jaw under my ear. "The heart."

"The birthmark?"

"What's a birthmark?" I asked.

"It's like a spot on your skin when you're born," Kimmie said. "It can be different shapes."

"I think she has a tattoo," I said.

"I'm hungry," Kimmie said. "Let's go eat the fudge."

"Look, Andy," Keith said. "Maybe you saw someone who looked like Jen or had a birthmark on her jaw like Jen or something."

"Where?" I asked.

"You..." He made kind of a growl sound. "You drive me round the bend, you know it?"

"Okay." I decided to not fight with him anymore since Kimmie wanted to go.

I started to get on my bike again.

"Do you really think you saw her before?" Keith asked all of a sudden.

"People…ladies, I mean…they dye their hair sometimes," I explained to him. "So one day they have red hair and another day they have brown hair. It doesn't matter," I said. "They're still the same lady."

Chapter Sixty-Two

Sara
Little Miss Perfect

IN THE BEGINNING, EVERYONE THOUGHT ANDY STARTED THE fire. That was practically the first thing out of Keith's mouth once they removed the breathing tube. He was in agonizing pain, half his face covered beneath layers of thick bandages. His arms were wrapped in gigantic tubes of gauze with surgical pins jutting from the bandage covering his left hand, and he kept saying, "Andy. Andy. Andy."

"Andy's all right, honey." I thought he was worried that Andy might have been hurt in the fire, too, and I was surprised that he cared more about Andy than he'd ever let on. He always acted as though Andy, who'd once been Keith's little buddy, was now a nuisance to him. An embarrassment. Now, with him calling out Andy's name, I wondered if deep down he still loved him.

"*No*," Keith said. "Not what...I...mean." He needed to take a breath between nearly every word, his lungs raw from the fire. "Saw...Andy...outside church," he said.

I understood what he was implying, even though I hadn't told him the fire was arson. I was afraid of setting him off with that news. But he seemed to know, to intuit somehow, that the fire had been intentionally set, and in his mind, Andy was the guilty party. I knew in both my head and my heart that couldn't have been the case. Andy didn't have a malicious bone in his body, nor did he have the brainpower it would take to set and ignite such a spectacular blaze. But Keith's suspicions, which he whispered to Reverend Bill during the minister's visit to the hospital, set something in motion that couldn't be stopped. The next thing I knew, they'd found traces of fuel on Andy's clothing and his fingerprints on a gas can. I heard all of this through the grapevine, because although Laurel was calling me to check on Keith, asking if she could visit him, I wasn't calling her back. In spite of all she was going through with Andy— the hearing, the possibility of him being tried in adult court, which was simply, horribly ludicrous—she was thinking of us.

I couldn't bring myself to return her calls, though. I wanted Keith back the way he was, his body whole and spirited and even willful. I wanted his mind to be healthy, with every memory intact, except for one: finding the letter from Marcus. I wanted that small detail to have disappeared from Keith's memory forever.

But a day or two after Keith came out of the coma, the memory was back, florid in his mind. He seemed to remember every word of the letter and our conversation that followed his reading it. My son and I held the secret I knew would destroy Laurel. I didn't dare let her visit Keith, and I pled exhaustion when anyone asked why I didn't return her calls. I was living a nightmare through my son, discovering prayers I never knew I had in me, crying tears from some bottomless well. I knew Laurel, along with Maggie and Marcus, was going through an entirely different sort of horror with Andy's situation. I didn't have the strength to support her when I could barely support myself, especially not with that huge guilty secret sitting there between us. Little did I know that she already knew the truth.

Keith had confronted Maggie with it when Maggie came to the hospital to visit him. Then Maggie, angry with Laurel over one thing or another, had laid the truth on her mother. But I didn't know that then.

Marcus appeared unexpectedly in Keith's hospital room one afternoon, a few weeks after the fire. It was the day of Andy's hearing, when the judge would decide if he should be tried in adult court, and by the expression on Marcus's face when he walked in the room, I thought I knew the outcome. He looked worn out, the muscles tight around his mouth. I'd been sitting next to Keith's bed, coaxing him to eat some soup, and I put down the bowl, stood up and wrapped Marcus in my arms. He was the one person from home I felt safe having there. He knew all there was to know. Nothing Keith said could shock him.

"What are *you* doing here?" Keith asked. He was still convinced of Andy's guilt, and that, in combination with his pain and his justifiable self-pity over being denied his share in the Lockwood fortune, had turned him against everyone with that surname.

"Is it bad news?" I asked, letting go of Marcus.

He motioned toward the chair I'd just vacated. "Sit," he said. "I need to talk to the two of you."

I felt suddenly frightened, all sorts of bizarre possibilities running through my mind. Things that didn't even make sense. Andy hanging himself in a cell. Laurel shooting the judge. Crazy thoughts that were an indication of how far gone I was after spending weeks in a ninety-degree room watching my son fight for life.

I returned to my seat and nervously slipped a piece of wayward gauze beneath the bandage on Keith's face.

Marcus stood at the end of the bed, holding on to the footboard. "First things first," he said. "How are you doing, Keith?"

"Fuck you," Keith said.

"Keith!" I didn't care what kind of pain he was in, some things were unacceptable. "Watch your mouth!"

"It's all right." Marcus sounded so tired. He let out a sigh. "Well," he said, "it's like this. Maggie was involved with Ben Trippett."

"You mean...romantically?" I asked, and he nodded.

I was stunned. Dawn was so in love with Ben. *The first actually trustworthy man I've ever been with,* she'd told me. "Poor Dawn," I said.

"Maggie thought he'd broken up with Dawn," Marcus said. "That's what he told her."

"Why are we talking about Maggie's pathetic love life?" Keith asked.

"Here's why," Marcus said. "Ben was having a hard time in the department because he got claustrophobic when he had to use the SCBA gear. The other guys were razzing him about it. Maggie wanted to help him. He was talking about maybe leaving the island if the situation didn't get better."

"What does this have to do with Andy's hearing?" I asked. Why *were* we talking about Maggie's love life?

"Andy's not going to have a hearing," Marcus said. He shifted from one foot to the other. "See, Ben thought he finally had the claustrophobia thing under control, but he needed a fire to prove himself. So—"

I gasped, suddenly understanding, although it was completely unbelievable. "You're not saying *Maggie* set the fire?"

Marcus nodded. His eyes suddenly glistened. "She confessed, but she never meant for the kids to be there. Remember the lock-in was supposed to be in the youth building."

This was ludicrous! "I just don't believe it!" I said. "I've known Maggie forever, and she's the most kindhearted girl ever. She must be trying to protect Andy." But even *that* didn't make sense, because as kindhearted as Maggie was, Andy was even more so. "She's protecting *Ben,*" I said. "Maybe he set it and she's taking the fall!"

Marcus shook his head. "She was so hooked on him," he said. "She wasn't thinking straight."

I gripped the side bar of Keith's bed. I thought I was going to pass out or scream or throw the bowl of soup across the room. Instead, I just stared dumbly at Marcus.

"She poured fuel around the church," he said. "Andy's prints were on the gas container because he helped her. He didn't know what he was doing. He thought he was pouring bug spray." He raked a hand through his hair and blew out his breath. "It's a long story."

"Little…Miss…*Perfect,*" I said. Reality was sinking in. I'd known that little girl as well as I knew my own name, but how well did I know the *seventeen*-year-old Maggie, really? I knew the side she showed me. The side she showed the world. Sweet-natured. Generous. Smart and studious. But something devious had been going on behind the scenes. Something cruel and crazy. How I'd loved that girl!

"I don't think she meant to hurt anyone," Marcus said.

"How can you *say* that?" I nearly shouted as I filled up with fury. I felt it explode in my chest and spill into my arms. "Look at Keith! Look at my son! She didn't just *hurt* people, Marcus. She *killed* people!"

"She swears she didn't actually start the fire," Marcus said. "She said once she saw the lock-in was moved to the church, she gave up the whole plan."

"Oh, right," I snapped. "Spontaneous combustion."

"I know." Marcus ran a shaky hand over his chin. "I know it doesn't make sense."

Keith suddenly sniffled, and I looked down to see his unbandaged cheek awash with tears.

"Oh, honey!" I grabbed a tissue and smoothed it over his face. He looked so helpless, his arms like useless blocks of wood at his sides. What must it be like for him to listen to all of this?

"I thought it was *my* fault," he said suddenly. "I thought *I* did it."

"What do you mean?" I asked. "How on earth could it have been your fault?"

He gulped air, and I could tell by the pain in his face how much each breath hurt his lungs. I wished I could take some of that pain away. I'd take it all away if I could.

Keith told us about going onto the back porch of the church to have a smoke. He lit the cigarette, and when he tossed the match on the ground, it ignited the fuel Maggie'd poured over every inch of the pine straw surrounding the building.

"Massive flames," he rasped. "*Massive.* They trapped everybody. I thought it was all my fault."

My heart broke for him, and I hugged him as he cried. "My poor baby," I said, barely aware that Marcus was still in the room with us. "It wasn't your fault, honey. Not at all."

As I held him, so awkwardly because of the bandages and the metal pole and the wires and tubes and all the apparatus surrounding him, I no longer cared...I no longer *gave a shit*...about protecting Laurel or her family. I wanted to hurt them. In that moment, I would have given my right arm to see Maggie burn in hell. I would have loved to be the person striking the match.

Chapter Sixty-Three

Keith

I DROVE STRAIGHT TO MY PT APPOINTMENT AFTER THAT RUN-IN with Andy, and I swear, I didn't even notice the pain when Gunnar put me through his usual torture. My mind was a thousand miles away in some really pissed-off place. What the hell was going on? My mother. Jen. I just wanted one damn thing in my life to feel normal and predictable. My mother had kept some honkin' big secrets from me. And the other woman I thought I could trust— Jen—well, most likely Andy was being his usual off-the-wall self, but he'd planted that annoying seed of doubt in my mind and I didn't know what to do with it. I wouldn't have believed him, wouldn't have paid any attention to what he said—except for that white-hair bit. I still remembered seeing the skinny stripe of light hair that morning in my bed. Was she playin' me? I couldn't figure it out. All I knew was that I was pissed off while Gunnar whipped my arm around, and I was still pissed off by the time I drove to her house that night.

I skipped the extra Percocet after PT, even though my arm and shoulder were killing me. I wanted to be sharp when I talked to her. Stay focused. Not get sucked in by how sexy she was.

When I got into the house, though, she literally jumped my bones. Didn't even say hi. She did one of those monkey leaps, locking her legs around me, kissing me. Like something out of the movies. Holding her up was wrecking my shoulder, but right then I didn't care. All the questions I had for her flew out the window. Screw it. I was going to get one last good fuck out of her if nothing else. We raced up the stairs to her bedroom and I don't know if she threw herself onto the bed or I threw her. All I knew was that my anger was coming through and the sex was kind of rougher than it should have been. She didn't seem to mind. She actually laughed. "You need this *bad,* baby, don't you?" she said when I was giving it to her. I tuned her out. Her question. Her voice. Time for questions later.

When we were done, she curled up next to me the way she liked to do, her head on my chest. I didn't put my arms around her, though, and not just because my shoulder hurt like a bitch. I didn't feel like touching her now.

"Who are you really?" I asked, once my breathing had settled down.

Thirty seconds must've gone by before she finally spoke. "I'm Jennifer Ann Parker. Who are you?"

"What's your real hair color?"

She sucked in her breath. "You know, you just don't ask a woman a question like that," she said. She leaned up on her elbow to look at me. "What's going on?" she asked. "We just had a great time, didn't we? So why are you being so weird all of a sudden?"

I decided to level with her. "I saw Andy Lockwood today. He said he saw you before. A long time ago or...I don't know when exactly, but he said you had white hair. He recognized you by this." I touched the heart shape on her jaw.

She laughed, flopping back down on her pillow. "You told me Andy's not all there," she said. "There's your proof."

"I saw...one time I saw your roots. I thought they were gray, but maybe they were really—"

She smacked my chest with her palm, hard enough that it stung. "You're going to believe that kid over me?" she said. "What have I done to you except love you, huh? I thought you'd treat me better than the other guys. I thought you'd get what it's like to be hurt."

She suddenly got out of bed, turned on the light on the nightstand and pointed to her dark pubic hair. "Does this look like white hair to you?" she asked. "Son of a bitch." She grabbed her pile of clothes from the chair in the corner and ran out of the room.

Crap. I put my arm over my eyes, wincing from the pain in my shoulder. Damn it all. I'd found something good and now I was screwing it up. Story of my life.

Still, something didn't feel right. I knew Andy could be off the wall, but he also didn't just make stuff up. He wasn't all that creative. How many chicks had a heart-shaped birthmark on their jawline? I got out of the bed, aching all over, and I couldn't help feeling spooked while I got dressed. I remembered the gun in Jen's car, and I pictured one of those movies where this unsuspecting guy walks down the stairs and the girl's standing there with a gun ready to blow his head off.

When I got downstairs, I saw Jen outside in the moonlight, sitting on the top step of the deck with a blanket around her shoulders. I opened the sliding glass door and walked onto the deck. If she had her gun, I was done for. I almost didn't care. I sat down next to her. She was shaking hard and her eyes glistened. I put my arm around her and pulled her close to me.

"Sorry," I said. "It's just that when Andy started talking, I realized I don't really know much about you. Just that you're from Asheville and you're amazing in bed."

She laughed a little, brushing a hand across her eyes. I kissed her shoulder through the blanket. Smelled the oranges in her hair.

"You're right." She sighed. "I don't think Andy ever saw me before that time at your uncle's house," she said, "but I haven't been totally straight with you about me. I just don't like talking about myself. My life has kind of sucked."

I moved the blanket off her shoulder and kissed her skin. "Tell me," I said.

She let out a long breath. "I don't get along with my parents at all," she said. "They divorced when I was little and they just… My father was Mr. Tough Guy. I was this major disappointment to him. He wanted me to hunt and fish and I wanted to paint and do my nails." She raised a bare foot out in front of her, and the moonlight landed on her dark toenails. "And my mother was—is—mentally ill. A real fruitcake, so it was like my brother and I raised ourselves."

She had a brother? Man, I really knew nothing about her.

"And here's the thing, Keith. Don't be mad. I'm afraid you'll hear this the wrong way and be mad."

"What?"

"I love my brother a lot. He was in his chemistry class last year when some kids played around with a bunch of chemicals and started this explosion. My brother got badly burned, so I understand about living with the…the scars and everything. And when I saw you in the grocery store, I wanted to…I just wanted to make you feel good."

I stood up, so pissed off all of a sudden, I couldn't stand it.

"So what's this been, Jen?" I shouted. "A series of mercy fucks?"

Her eyes were huge and shiny. "Not at all!" she said. "No, no, no! At first, I just wanted to help you. I understood what you were going through. But once we got together and I got to know you…I really *care* about you, Keith." She reached for my hand and pulled me back onto the step again. "I'm in love with you. That's the honest-to-God truth." She put part of the blanket over my shoulders so our arms were touching. She was shivering and I took her hand. Held it between mine. I felt kind of humiliated, but it made sense that there'd been some good reason for her to come on to me in the store the way she did. Maybe it wasn't such a terrible reason. I reminded her of her brother. Someone she cared about.

"I wish you'd told me the truth right from the start," I said. "I don't get why you didn't."

"I was afraid you'd think exactly what you just thought. That I wanted to be with you out of pity."

I turned her head toward me and kissed her lips. "We have a lot of shit in common," I said.

"Right," she agreed. "And now you get why I hate Maggie Lockwood, too," she said. "I hate anybody who plays with fire."

Chapter Sixty-Four

Sara
Life Sentence
October 2007

"It could have been so much worse," Gunnar Stephensen said the first time he worked with Keith at the physical-therapy clinic in Jacksonville.

If I heard those words one more time, I was going to hit whoever said them.

I watched Keith squeeze his eyes shut in pain as Gunnar stretched his left arm straight. He didn't make a sound, although the tears that forced their way between his eyelids and down his cheeks said it all. I felt his pain—a searing, ripping agony—in my own arm. *It could have been so much worse.* Yes, it was true that Keith was alive when others had died. And it was true that he would "recover," if you didn't count the physical and emotional scars, but that didn't make his current suffering any easier to bear.

He'd spent three months in the burn unit in Chapel Hill, then another two months in a rehab facility. Finally, I had him home with me, but he'd be spending plenty of time in the physical-therapy clinic.

"Now, once I've finished assessing him," Gunnar said, "I'll show you how to help him with these exercises at home. But you'll be bringing him here every day for a couple of months."

I nodded. I'd been warned to expect that. I would take him wherever he needed to go for as long as was necessary.

"It's absolutely critical that you don't skip a day at this point," Gunnar said. "He misses a day, he loses a week of progress."

Keith opened his eyes. "I can't take this every damn day," he said.

"Hurts like a bitch, doesn't it," Gunnar said.

"How would you know?" Keith practically barked at the poor man.

"Keith," I scolded him, though I was thinking the same thing. Keith was a very angry boy, and I wasn't sure if he'd been that way all along or if his anger had been magnified by the fire. It had certainly magnified *my* anger. I was filled with a hatred and fury I'd never known before. That was one reason I started taking the memoir class with Dawn, because she said it would help to write my feelings down. It helped her deal with her anger toward Ben, she'd said. It wasn't working for me, though, in spite of the fact that I wrote like a madwoman. I wrote nearly every spare minute of the day. Sometimes, I'd feel a smidgen of peace start to work its way into my heart, but then I'd catch a glimpse of my bandaged, scarred and aching son and that peace would vanish.

"After a couple months," Gunnar continued, "we can cut it back to a few days a week, as long as he's doing the exercises faithfully at home. Of course, you need to keep up with the compression bandages and scar massage." He looked at me. "I can tell you've been doing a great job with that. Not much in the way of adhesions in this arm at all. Work on his hand, though. Especially right here." He rubbed the skin between Keith's index finger and thumb.

"Shit!" Keith shouted. "Not so hard."

"Sorry, Keith," Gunnar said. "It's gotta be hard to do the job."

"How often should he be doing the stretches?" I asked.

"As often as possible," Gunnar said. "You can't do them too much."

On our way back from Jacksonville, I pulled into the parking lot of the Food Lion.

"Why are we stopping here?" Keith asked. He was slumped in the front seat, the unbandaged part of his forehead furrowed with pain from the PT session.

"I need to pick up a few things," I said as I unbuckled my seat belt. "Do you want to come in with me?"

"No way," Keith said. He wasn't ready to be seen with those compression bandages on his arms and face.

"Okay. I'll be back in a jiff."

Inside the store, I grabbed a cart and starting filling it with things I knew Keith loved. His favorite cereal. Tangerines. Oreos. I was reaching for a carton of Ben & Jerry's when I heard a voice behind me.

"Sara."

I closed my eyes. I could have kept on walking. Just ignored her. I never thought it would be possible to live on Topsail Island and be able to avoid someone, but I'd managed to avoid Laurel since Maggie went to prison, and that had been for the best. Maybe Laurel'd been trying to avoid me as well, so that between the two of us, we'd never been at the same place at the same time. It was bound to happen at some point, but why did it have to be a day when I had Keith in the car and just wanted to get home and take care of him?

I sighed, turning around. "Laurel," I said.

She looked as wrung out as I felt.

"I...I can't tell you how many times I've picked up the phone to call you," she said.

I was glad she hadn't called. I wouldn't have been ready to speak to her. I wasn't sure I could speak to her even now.

"How's Keith?" she asked. "Marcus told me he can come home soon."

I knew Laurel and Marcus were finally together, and I felt no joy at all for them. Once again, she had everything she wanted. "He came home yesterday," I said.

"Oh, I'm so glad!"

"He has a long road ahead of him," I said sharply. "PT every day. Compression bandages. Scars you'd never want to see on a child you gave birth to."

"Oh, Sara. God. I'm so sorry." She reached out to touch my arm, then seemed to think better of it. A wise decision. "Will you let me help?" she asked. "Any way I can. Financially. Or taking him to appointments or running errands for you. Anything."

"I don't want your help," I said. "Your daughter gets out of *her* prison in eleven months." One lousy year! That's all she got. "My son's in *his* prison for the rest of his life."

"They are...they're half siblings," Laurel said.

I felt like smacking her. "They have the same father," I said. "That's all they've ever had in common."

"They're young, though, Sara. Maybe someday...in spite of everything...maybe their relationship will be important to them."

"I doubt Keith will ever want to be related to her, frankly. Even if he wasn't one of her victims, she burned down a church full of kids!"

"I know. And she's paying for it."

"Oh, good Lord, Laurel!" I said. "A year in prison with all of her skin intact and her life ahead of her." *Little Miss Perfect*. I couldn't believe Maggie was the same girl I'd taken care of when she was a child. I'd even felt sorry for her when Laurel lavished ninety percent of her time and attention on Andy. The truth was, everything had been handed to Maggie on a silver platter. Even her prison sentence.

"She made a terrible mistake," Laurel said.

"I can't talk to you." I pushed my cart past her, pushed it all the way down the aisle to the rear of the store, where I hurried inside the restroom. I locked the door and leaned against it, biting back tears.

I'd been at Maggie's sentencing, along with family members of the other victims and people from Drury Memorial. I watched Maggie's shrewd, callous lawyer twist the facts to get some of the charges dismissed and others reduced, so that Maggie would spend only one tiny fraction of her life behind bars. Some people yelled in outrage. Many cried. I just gritted my teeth. I was used to Laurel winning while I lost. I'd had years of practice at it that the other families didn't have. I would still be working at Jabeen's when I was eighty, while Laurel would be taking trips around the world with her scar-free kids and grandkids.

Two weeks after that run-in with Laurel, I woke up with the flu from hell. Groggy and feverish, I turned off my alarm clock and fell back to sleep and only woke up again when Keith knocked on my bedroom door.

"Mom?" he said. "It's almost time to leave. Are you up or what?"

I tried to roll over to check my clock, but the aching in my back and head took my breath away.

"What time is it?" I managed to whisper.

"What?" He opened the door a crack, then all the way. "Whoa. You sick?"

I shut my eyes. "Don't come in here," I said, although with all the massaging I'd done of his scars and all the hands-on stretching of his arms, I knew he was already well exposed to whatever I had. That's all he needed.

He stood in the doorway. "I'll skip PT today," he said. "No big thing."

"Uh-uh," I said. "I'm getting up. You know what Gunnar said about skipping."

"Gunnar's full of it."

"Go on and get ready. I'll be out in a minute."

My body ached as I got out of bed and walked into the bathroom. I took my temperature as I sat on the toilet. One hundred and two. I managed to swallow two aspirin before the room started spinning. I headed back to bed, moving the waste can next to the nightstand in case I got sick. I couldn't possibly drive Keith anywhere.

I reached for the phone and dialed Dawn's number, but got her voice mail. I stared at the phone a long, long time before I punched in the number I hadn't called in months.

"Hello?" Laurel answered right away, and I wondered if my number had come up on her caller ID.

I shut my eyes and pressed my aching head into the pillow. "Hi, Laurel," I said. "Did you mean what you said about helping me any way you could?"

Chapter Sixty-Five

Maggie

I WAS ON THE DEBATE TEAM IN HIGH SCHOOL. MR. FARMER took me aside one day and said I could be anything I wanted to be, but he'd love to see me go into politics or law because I could always make my case without getting flustered. I was always so calm, he said. My swim coach said the same thing, that I might not be the best swimmer on the team but I never choked at a meet.

I was never really all that calm, though. I was just good at faking it. Since the fire, I couldn't even do that. Now, I sat in my car in front of the New Drury Memorial Church—that was actually on its sign, *New Drury Memorial*—and shook all over. I had to find the courage to come out of hiding, Dr. Jakes had said, and I knew he was right, as usual. Keith was the person I most wanted to hide from, but after Keith came Reverend Bill, who was probably in the church right at that moment. Even before the fire, he'd made me uncomfortable. He never smiled and he was weird and he hated my family. Now, when I knew he had to hate me more than he'd ever hated anyone, I was going to have to face him.

I got out of my car slowly, like invisible arms were trying to keep me inside. I shut the door quietly because I felt paranoid. Maybe Reverend Bill was watching me from inside the church. The windows were stained glass, though, so he probably couldn't see me even if he was looking. I tried the front doors of the church, but they were locked and I felt relieved. I tried, right? Nobody home. But I could already hear what Dr. Jakes would say if I told him I gave up that easily. So I walked along the sidewalk that circled the brick building until I came to a door at the rear. I turned the knob, hoping that door would also be locked, but it opened easily. Didn't even squeak on its hinges.

I was in a hallway, a men's room on my left, a ladies' room on my right. On the wall next to the ladies' room was a photograph of the old church. It caught me by surprise and I looked away from it quickly, but I could still see the pretty little whitewashed building in my mind. I remembered the pine straw around it, how it crunched beneath my feet as I poured the fuel. I remembered thinking that pine straw would catch quickly and what a great fire it would make for Ben to fight. *Damn.* I really, truly couldn't stand myself sometimes.

I wanted to turn around and leave, but I saw the partially open door next to the men's room and read the wall plaque next to it: Reverend William Jesperson. I'd come this far. I had to do it.

There was a window in the door and I could vaguely make out Reverend Bill's reflection in the glass. I knocked softly.

"Come in."

Ugh. I remembered that voice. I forced myself to walk inside.

He looked up from his desk. If he was surprised to see me, he didn't show it, but he leaned back in his chair and put down the pen he'd been holding.

"Miss Lockwood," he said.

"Can I talk to you?" I asked. My voice came out high-pitched, like a little girl's.

He motioned to a wooden chair and I sat down, resting my hands flat on my lap.

"I'm here because I wanted to tell you I'm sorry for what I did," I said.

"It's about time," he said. "You got out of prison when?"

"Five weeks ago."

"Five weeks and this is the first time you've come to me," he said. "And all those months in prison, I didn't hear a thing from you, either, did I?"

"No, sir." He wasn't going to make this easy on me. Why should he?

"What are you doing now?"

"You mean..." I didn't know if he meant right that minute or what. "I'm doing...I've been doing community service at Brier Glen Hospital." I couldn't tell him I might never be able to work there again. I just couldn't.

"Three hundred hours," he said. He had my sentence memorized.

"Yes."

"You think three hundred hours is enough?" he asked. "You think that year in prison was enough for what you did?"

"No, Reverend. I know it's not."

He picked up his pen again and leaned over the notepad on his desk, ignoring me. His long face had taken on a ruddy color and all of a sudden I felt his *fury* at me. It radiated out of him, like a force in the room. I didn't blame him for it. He was an unlikable man, but I'd hurt him and his church in a terrible way.

"I'm sorry," I said again as I stood up. He wasn't going to say anything else, so I started for the door.

"Feel better now?" he asked suddenly.

"What?" I stopped and looked at him and instantly wished I hadn't. I could have handled seeing a typical ugly Reverend Bill sneer on his face or even the red-faced fury, but his eyes were damp, his lips quivering. That I couldn't take.

"Who was that apology supposed to help?" he asked. "Me, or you?"

I turned my hands palms up in a helpless gesture. "Both, I think. It's... I really meant it, if that's what you're asking." I couldn't take this. Couldn't take seeing Reverend Bill look human for a change.

He returned to his writing, and I had the feeling he wanted to hide that naked sadness in his face. "You can do community service here, you know," he said, his pen moving.

"What...what do you mean?"

He didn't look up. Kept writing, writing, writing. "We still have a lot to do to the interior of the church," he said. "We sponsor a food program on the mainland and run a day care in Hampstead. I could go on and on. We do more for the community than you could ever guess. There's plenty you could do."

Oh my God. Work for him? Never.

"Okay," I said. "Thanks for letting me know."

I nearly ran back to my car. I wanted to get away from the church and away from him. I didn't want to think about his quivering mouth, or about his question: Who was that apology supposed to help? I knew the answer. My apology had been sincere and totally heartfelt, but I'd finally gotten around to making it in order to help myself.

Which was why I couldn't go straight to Marcus's tower to see Keith, like I'd planned. I needed a break first. Talking to Keith wasn't going to go well. I knew it. He hated me as much as one person could hate another, and I was so afraid of his anger. Not that he'd hit me or anything, but that he'd yell and find a way to hurt me with words. I was most afraid to see the physical damage I'd done to him. I wasn't sure I could take seeing him like that, knowing I was responsible. The bottom line was, like Reverend Bill had implied, apologizing to Keith would be for *me*. To help *me*. Like I'd be using him to clear my own conscience.

Or was that just a cop-out?

Whatever. I wasn't going to go to the tower without a break.

I drove home, and as I was pulling into the driveway, I saw a yellow kayak docked near the end of our pier. Did Andy get his kayak? Then I spotted a woman—*Jen?*—running up the pier toward the boat.

I put my car in Park and jumped out.

"Jen!" I called, walking across our side yard toward the pier. It *was* Jen. That shimmery dark hair and skinny body were unmistakable. "Jen!" I shouted, louder this time.

She stopped and turned around. Waved. Then started walking back up the pier toward me. I felt *joy* at seeing her. All that stuff about her not coming to pick me up when I was stranded and her splashing me in the ocean was instantly forgotten.

"Hi!" I said as we met in the side yard near the pier. "Did you get a kayak?"

She glanced back at the boat where it rocked gently next to the pier. "A rental. I just felt like trying it out."

"Cool," I said.

"I stopped by to make sure you were okay," she said. "I felt bad about the other night. Not coming to get you."

"That's all right," I said. "I got towed."

"Excellent." She shook her head with a roll of her eyes. "It was stupid. I had a guy there. I always hate it when girls shaft their female friends because of a guy. Sorry I did that to you."

I practically loved her for saying that.

"I get it," I said. "How'd it go with him?"

She shook her head. "It was okay." She glanced back at her kayak again. "I've got to get going. I just wanted to be sure you were all right."

"Come in for a while," I said. I didn't want her to leave. I wanted so much to get back to the pedicure-and-movie feel our friendship had in the beginning.

She shook her head and started moving backward toward the pier. "Can't," she said. "Not today. But I'll call you and we can get together, okay?"

"Okay." I watched as she turned and ran up the pier toward her boat again, wondering where she had to run off to in such a hurry.

I walked into the house through the unlocked porch door and instantly smelled it: citrus. Oranges or lemons or whatever it was, and I knew that Jen had been inside the house. *Just to see if I was there,* I told myself. Probably poked her head inside the door from the porch and called my name. But even as I made up reasons for why she might have come inside, I stood in the middle of the room, breathing in her scent, feeling strangely chilled to the bone.

Chapter Sixty-Six

Sara
Here and Now
April 2008

AMAZING! I'VE CAUGHT UP TO THE PRESENT IN THESE NOTE-
books! It shocks me to realize how much I've written, how many
notebooks I've filled in the past six months, and—yes—how much
better I feel. Maybe it's simply the passage of time that's helped, but
I think it's the writing. Self-indulgent, I know. Especially all I wrote
about Jamie. Remembering him. Wallowing in those ancient
memories. Oh, he was so imperfect! Just like everyone else. But
writing about him made me remember all that I loved about him. The
joy I felt back then was intense. The grief, equally so, but I don't regret
a minute. If I'd never had Jamie in my life, I wouldn't have my son.

We just passed the one-year anniversary of the fire. Physically,
Keith is doing much better. He still wears the compression
bandages, but they'll come off sometime during the summer. From
an emotional perspective, though, I'm afraid his anger and bitterness are boundless. I forced him to go to a therapist a couple of
times, but he won't go back, and there isn't much I can do to make
him. His anger comes out in all sorts of ways and while it's often
aimed at me, I know its true target is Maggie. All the Lockwoods,
actually.

During my weeklong bout with the flu back in October, Laurel took time off from work to drive Keith back and forth to physical therapy in Jacksonville every day, in spite of the fact that he refused to say a word to her. For a while, I let her be my personal slave. She bought our groceries and picked up Keith's prescriptions and paid for repairs on my car, and I felt justified in letting her do all of it. After a while, though, it no longer felt right. I think my anger was starting to fade. I didn't want to be her friend again—I doubt that will ever happen—but I also didn't want to abuse her, and that's what I felt like I was doing. She was no more responsible for Maggie's actions than I was for Keith's smoking marijuana or skipping school. So I apologized to her, and although she said she sincerely *wanted* to help, I stopped calling her. We haven't spoken in a couple of months, although I see her here and there. It always feels strained. We're cordial to one another, nothing more.

Here is what I worry about now: In September, only five short months away, Maggie will get out of prison. It's one thing to bump into Laurel from time to time; it will be another to bump into Maggie. It will be *unbearable* for Keith to see her flitting around the island, free as a bird. I try to remind myself that she's Jamie's daughter, and I know that, deep down, a part of me still loves a part of her. Yet Keith is first in my heart and always will be, and I worry that seeing Maggie free is going to tear him apart.

For a while, I seriously considered moving. So seriously, in fact, that I did some job hunting, using the computer in the waiting area at the PT clinic while Keith was in with Gunnar. I needed a job that would pay better than waitressing, and it had to be in a location near good medical facilities for Keith. There were several opportunities in Charlotte—training positions in banks and that sort of thing. I applied for one of them at Western Carolina Bank under my maiden name, deciding that if we moved, I'd make it a truly fresh start. I got so excited about the possibility that I looked at apartments online as well. I stumbled across a gorgeous apartment complex with two- and three-bedroom units, plus both indoor and outdoor pools I was sure Keith would love. I filled out the application online, but I knew I was dreaming. The bank salary might cover the rent, but little else.

I thought about the necklace Jamie gave me so long ago, the one I intended to wear on our wedding day. I pay thirty dollars a year for the safe-deposit box it's in, and I haven't once looked at it since I put it in there. I fantasized about selling it so that we could live in one of those apartments. The way Jamie talked about the necklace, I think it might be worth five or even ten thousand dollars, although I've heard you can never sell jewelry at its true value. I found this high-end auction house online where you can sell jewelry at a good price and keep seventy percent of what they get for it. Seventy percent of, say, ten thousand dollars, along with the salary from the bank, would have made one of the two-bedrooms manageable, at least for a while. But even though I never wear the necklace, I like knowing it's there. Jamie gave it to *me,* not to Laurel. I doubt I'll ever be able to part with it.

As I waited to hear from the bank and the apartment complex, I lay awake every night imagining our new life in Charlotte. The more I thought about it, though, the less appealing the fantasy. I didn't want to do it. This is *my* island, too, not just Maggie's or the Lockwoods'. I may not own property all over it, but it's mine in my heart, and it felt so unfair that I should have to give it up. So by the time the bank called to say they had a trainee position for me, I'd changed my mind about leaving.

That means that in late August, as long as Keith continues to do well physically, he'll return to school. He'll be a year behind his friends—his *former* friends, since most of his old friends seem to have disappeared. Kids can be so damn fickle. I'm worried they'll also be cruel. I guess what I'm really worried about is that I made a mistake turning down that job. Was I being selfish?

A calendar hangs on the wall above my dresser, and I keep lifting the pages to see how quickly September is creeping up on us. I picture Maggie checking her own calendar, looking at the same date with happy anticipation that is the flip side of my dread.

Oh, God.

Was I being selfish?

Chapter Sixty-Seven

Keith

I WAS WORKING OUT ON THE ELLIPTICAL TRAINER IN MARCUS'S bedroom, watching this dude jog on the beach with his Jack Russell terrier, when the doorbell rang. I kept pumping away on the elliptical. I was going over to Jen's later, so I knew it wasn't her at the door, and anybody else would be for Marcus. But the bell kept ringing and I started thinking maybe Marcus locked himself out, or maybe it was Flip Cates with news about my mother. So after about five minutes of listening to the bell ring, I got off the elliptical, slung a towel around my neck and went downstairs. I pulled open the front door and was really sorry I bothered: Maggie.

Without even thinking about it, I turned my head to the left to hide the scars. "What do you want?" I asked. I could've happily gone the rest of my life without seeing her.

"To talk to you," she said.

I'd seen her those couple of times on the news since she got sprung, but I hadn't realized how skinny and pale she'd gotten.

"No, you don't," I said. "'Cause if you start talking to me, I'll start talking back, and you won't want to hear what I have to say."

"It's okay," she said. "I mean, I do. I want to hear what you have to say."

"Go away." I started to close the door, but she put out both hands to stop it.

"Please, Keith," she said. "I know you don't owe me anything but—"

"Damn straight."

"I know that, but please. Let me in."

I couldn't say why I caved, but I turned away from the door and let her walk into the house behind me. I flopped down on the sofa and folded my arms across my chest. I wished I wasn't wearing a T-shirt. I felt like one big walking scar.

"So, go ahead," I said.

She leaned against one of the chairs and stared out the window toward the beach, and I realized that the last time she saw me, I was in the hospital, covered in bandages. This was her first real glimpse of her handiwork. First time was always a shock. She pulled it together finally, though, and looked right at me.

"I'm really sorry, Keith," she said. "For the fire. For your injuries. They're all my fault. I'd give anything to be able to change what happened."

"You're not the only one." Man, I hated that girl. She sort of slid from leaning against the chair to sitting in it, like she was inching her way closer to actually being in the room with me.

"How are you doing?" she asked. "Uncle Marcus says your PT's going pretty well, but you dropped out of school."

"That's my business."

"I know," she said.

She was just trying to start up a conversation, and I felt kind of sorry for her. The weird thing was, she had the same eyes as me. I'd never noticed it before, but they were *exactly* like mine. The shape of them—kind of abnormally round. The brown color that was practically black. The fat eyelashes that looked good on a girl but were too fem for a guy. So, maybe it was because she had my eyes that I felt like I could see behind them. I could see she was scared, being there with me. I didn't want to feel any sympathy toward her, but when someone has your eyes and you can see right through them, you can't help but feel some of what they're feeling. I was glad when my phone rang and I could pull it from my pocket to look at the display instead of her eyes.

It was Marcus.

"Hey," I said.

"Hey, Keith." The way he said it, I knew something was wrong. I sat up. "What is it?" I asked.

"Your mom's car's been found."

"Is she... Is she with it?"

"Your mother?" Maggie leaned forward in the chair.

"I'm sorry, Keith," Marcus said. "She... It looks like she had an accident. She ran off Route 74 outside of Charlotte, and her car was deep in the woods. It probably happened that first day she went missing. They think she was probably killed instantly. I'm at the police station. They need you here. Do you want me to come get you?"

I couldn't speak right away. I couldn't get enough breath in my lungs to say a word.

"Keith? Let me come get you."

"No," I said. I'd known it from the start, didn't I? That she was dead? "I'll be there in a few minutes."

I got up, turning off my phone. I ignored Maggie as I headed to the kitchen for my car keys.

"They found your mother?" Maggie watched me grab my keys off the counter, then followed me to the door. "Keith? Did they—"

"*Yes,* they found her." I spun around to stare her down, smacking my fist against the wall. "She's dead!"

"Oh my God!" She covered her mouth with her hand, tears already in her eyes. "I'm so sorry."

"So what's the score now, huh, Maggie?" I asked as I yanked open the door. "Five for Maggie Lockwood? Congratulations! You have another victim."

She followed me out the door, practically tripping over me, she was so close.

"Are you going to the police station?" she asked. "Let me drive you."

My car. Her car. Both of them a blur in front of the tower. Why was it getting to me like this, when I'd known all along she was dead? My chest muscles squeezed tight around my windpipe.

I pounded the hood of my car. Once. Twice. "Fuck!"

Maggie took my arm and led me to her car. I let her. It was like I had no fight in me. I let her open the car door. My legs shook, from the elliptical or from freaking out or both. I fell into the seat.

Maggie got in behind the wheel and turned the key.

"Damn it!" I said when we pulled into the street. "Why Charlotte? Why without me? Why didn't she fucking *tell* me?"

"I don't know," Maggie answered, like I'd actually been talking to her and not myself. "Could she have been going to a job interview, maybe? Uncle Marcus told us about the apartment and the bank and—"

"Your uncle should keep his trap shut."

"We're *family,* Keith."

"Cut me a break," I snapped. "You and I might have some of the same blood in our veins, but that's where it ends. I don't want you for a sister. Get it? I don't want *shit* to do with the Lockwoods."

That shut her up. She sniffled and wiped her eyes with her hands, but we didn't talk for the rest of the way to the station. When we got there, she walked right into Flip Cates's office with me, like I'd invited her to tag along. Marcus was there, too, and if either of them was surprised to see Maggie and me together, they didn't say anything.

Flip stood up from behind his desk. "I'm sorry, Keith," he said. "This wasn't the news we were hoping for."

Marcus walked over to hug me, but I wasn't having any of it. "Where's my mother?" I kept my arms at my sides. "What did they do with her?"

"She's at the medical examiner's office in Charlotte," Flip said.

"Why? What does a medical examiner do?" It was one of those things I probably should have known, but I needed an answer and didn't feel like faking it.

Marcus leaned back against Flip's desk. "They'll figure out how long ago she died and the probable cause of death," he said.

I didn't want to think about what my mother looked like when they found her. Decomposed and everything. I didn't want that to be the last image I had of her in my mind.

"They'll probably want to do an autopsy," Flip said.

"Why?" Crap. Now they wanted to cut her up.

"To try to figure out if there was a medical condition or...possibly alcohol or another substance in her system that might have led to her losing control of the car."

"She didn't take any drugs," I said. "And she hardly ever drank. I already told you that."

"Maybe a deer ran out in front of her car," Maggie said.

"Very possible, Mags." Marcus nodded.

"There were boxes and some other things in the car with her."

Flip looked at a notepad lying on his desk. "The police will turn them over to you. When you're ready, you'll have to go up to Charlotte to get them."

"I can do that for you if you want, Keith," Marcus said. "Or at least go with you."

"Or I could," Maggie said.

"They can just throw it all away," I said. "I don't want it."

"Well, I think you need to get it in case there's something important." Marcus folded his arms. "The police said there were a lot of papers. Bank statements. That sort of thing. Then some books. Some clothing. A suitcase. Probably the one you thought might be missing."

"I never said I thought one was missing," I said. How many times had I told them I didn't even think she had a suitcase?

"One of the boxes had a pan on it, like Andy Lockwood said he saw her carrying," Flip said. "But it was an old box and just had toiletries in it."

"Like she was moving," I said.

"We don't know that."

"Without me."

"Her car was totaled," Marcus said, "but you should be able to get insurance money for it."

"Whoop-de-do," I said. "That should keep me going for another month or two." The walls of Flip's office were closing in on me, getting dark around the edges. My legs started shaking again and I sat down on one of the chairs by the desk. Flip and Marcus and Maggie were all staring at me, and I felt so *alone*. All those weeks my mother'd been missing, with me knowing deep inside she must be dead, and I'd never felt that horrible, scary, suffocating *aloneness* until that moment.

"What am I supposed to do now?" I asked. My voice cracked on the "now," and I was pissed at myself for sounding afraid.

"You don't have to make any decisions right away," Marcus said. "Let's take this one step at a time. The first thing is to just...let this sink in. I'll go back to my house with you and we'll chill for the rest of the day, all right? Then we can start planning a memorial service for her."

"I don't know how to do that shit."

"You'll have plenty of help," Marcus said. "Dawn and Laurel, for starters."

"I can help, too, Keith," Maggie said.

I snapped my head toward her. "Don't you get it, Maggie?" I asked. "I don't *want* your help. This whole mess wouldn't have happened if it wasn't for you."

"Mags," Marcus said. "Why don't you go home. We can talk later."

"All right." She nodded. "I'm sorry, Keith," she said for the zillionth time.

I waited till I was sure she was far enough down the hall that she couldn't hear me. "You don't need to come home," I said to Marcus. "I'm gonna call Jen to come get me." I needed to be with Jen. With her screwed-up family, she was the one person who'd get how I was feeling.

"You sure?" Marcus asked. "Why not let me take you home. Give you some time to process all this."

"I want to be with my girlfriend, okay?" I stood up, wobbling a little. Marcus reached out an arm to steady me, and I let him. "I'm all right," I said. "I'm not going off the deep end or anything. I'll come back to the tower later."

Chapter Sixty-Eight

Maggie

I NEEDED AN EXTRA SESSION WITH DR. JAKES THE MORNING of Sara's memorial service because I so didn't want to go. I wanted to hide in my room. Mom would have let me stay home. She was scared for me. She didn't say so, but I could tell by the way she kept checking on me as I got ready, and I finally told her what Dr. Jakes had told me: "Today is about Sara, Mom," I said. "It's not about me."

Keith and Uncle Marcus would be driving together to the service. Uncle Marcus told me that Keith had a girlfriend now, and she'd probably be coming with them. He said he'd been seeing her for a while, but Uncle Marcus hadn't met her yet. I was amazed that Keith had a girlfriend. It made me happy. He needed somebody to care about him, especially since he was pushing all of us away.

There was a line of cars parked on the road by the northern tip of the island, and we pulled right behind Marcus's pickup. Mom and Andy and I held hands as we walked toward the windy spit of land by the remains of Daddy's chapel. Apparently, Sara once told Dawn she'd like to have her ashes scattered in the inlet by the old chapel, so Dawn suggested the service be held there. I wished she'd picked someplace—*anyplace*—else. It had to be so hard for my mother. I held her hand tight as we got close to the twenty or thirty people milling around near the old chapel walls. Mom probably thought it was because I was freaking out with all the people there, but I just wanted to comfort her the way she'd been comforting me all year long.

The sky was that bright, bright blue you saw on the island sometimes. As things got going, I stood between Mom and Andy, and Marcus stood next to Keith. No sign of his girlfriend that I could see. Dawn was there, and she stood in front of everybody since she was in charge of the service. It was the first time I'd seen her since I got out of prison, and I couldn't look straight at her. I guessed the guy standing closest to her was her boyfriend, Frankie. He was short—a lot shorter than Dawn—and he had that blond-and-tan surfer look.

Dawn talked about Sara—what a good friend she'd been and how much she'd loved working with her at Jabeen's. I could hear her because I was close enough, but I was sure some of the other people just saw her mouth moving as her words were blown out to sea. Then Mom went up in front of everyone and talked about what a great mother Sara had been to Keith. A few other people spoke, but I was spacing out, thinking about how Dr. Jakes was wrong. This *was* about me. I'd changed the island. I'd done more damage than a hurricane. Keith with his scars. Sara dead. There was nobody to blame but me, and every single person there probably had that thought going through his or her mind. Some of the people hated me, for sure. Keith certainly did. Dawn. So many others. Even people who didn't know me still knew what I did and hated me for it. As long as I lived on Topsail Island, every time I'd be in a group of people, it would be about me. Someday I'd have to leave. If I ever wanted a normal life, it couldn't be here. But there was a difference between leaving and running away. I wouldn't go until I was sure which one I was doing.

When everyone was done speaking, Keith carried the urn out to the inlet, Marcus at his side. The wind blew Keith's dark curly hair all over the place and whipped at his shirt. I couldn't see what was happening, but he was struggling with the urn and Marcus had to help him. I watched Sara's ashes suddenly explode in a gray puff of smoke before they were swallowed by the wind and the water. It was incredibly quick. That's really when it hit me, and when I started to cry. She was actually *gone*. The woman I'd loved for most of my life. My second mother when I was little. In less than a second, she was gone.

People followed us back to our house afterward, where this caterer Mom knew was setting up sandwiches and coffee. I went straight up to my room. Mom had told me not to worry about socializing, and I was relieved that she understood how hard that would be for me. My courage had its limits.

I sat on my bed, looking out the window at the sound. Even though the window was closed, I could hear the squawking of the gulls that flew over the water. The activity going on downstairs was a steady thrumming sound, and my bed seemed to vibrate with it.

I noticed someone walking across our sandy yard, heading for the pier, and it took me a minute to realize it was Keith. He was kind of hunched over like an old man. I was sure he didn't want to mingle with the crowd downstairs any more than I did. My tattoo burned and I rubbed my hip as I tried to blink away the image of Sara's ashes disappearing in a puff of gray. As shocking as that moment had been for me, it must have been a thousand times worse for Keith.

I wanted to help him. To do things for him. I'd gone to Charlotte with Uncle Marcus the day before to get the things that had been in Sara's car. That's when Uncle Marcus told me about the girl-friend, and I felt kind of angry at her for not being with Keith today, when he really needed her.

I got off my bed, put on my sneakers and walked quietly down the stairs and out the front door. A few people saw me and probably thought I was the biggest coward, but I didn't care. I walked through the side yard and out on the pier, where Keith sat with his legs dangling above the water. He glanced up as I walked toward him, and I saw a look of disgust cross his face.

I sat down next to him. For a minute, neither of us spoke.

"Do you know that your mom's ashes were scattered in the same place as our father's ashes?" I asked after a while.

He was quiet. Finally he said, "Weird."

"I guess it's nice in a way," I said, trying not to think about my own mother. "Nice for them."

He picked a splinter off one of the boards and tossed it in the water. I was sitting on his right side. Looking at that part of his face, you wouldn't know there was anything wrong with him. He reminded me of pictures of Daddy from when he was young.

"Sometimes I talk to my father," I said. "And I think he hears me. Sometimes he...communicates with me."

"What is this?" He smirked. "True confessions?"

"No. I just wanted to tell you that. I know your mother's...gone from Earth, but that doesn't mean you can't talk to her."

He laughed. "I *know* I can talk to her," he said. "I just don't believe she'll be listening."

"Maybe or maybe not."

"Whatever." He looked toward the horizon, squinting. "You know, Maggie," he said, "I came out here because I wanted to be alone."

I nodded and got to my feet. "Okay," I said. "That's all right."

I walked back up the pier toward the house, hugging my arms against the wind. I wished I could really talk to him. I wanted to tell him that he didn't need to be alone, ever again. I wanted to tell him that I had an amazing mother and an amazing uncle and a totally wonderful little brother, and that we would always be there for him—whether he wanted us to be or not.

Chapter Sixty-Nine

Keith

"I STILL FEEL TERRIBLE ABOUT NOT BEING WITH YOU THIS morning." Jen held my hand as we walked from her house to her car. We were going to drive to the mainland to rent a movie. I was pretty desperate for a comedy. One of those really stupid lame ones like *Animal House* that forced you to laugh in spite of yourself.

"That's okay," I said. It really *wasn't* okay, though. I'd told her it was no big deal, but man, I'd wanted her there with me. She had to go to Durham. A cousin's wedding or birthday or who knew what. Something she said she couldn't get out of. She told me the whole story, but all I heard was that she couldn't come with me. Why not? Would missing her stupid cousin's stupid wedding have been so terrible? I would've felt a lot less pathetic having her there with me.

Maybe it was just as well, though. She wouldn't have fit in. It was a Topsail Island thing. A *Lockwood* thing. I'd felt like a Lockwood for the first time in my life, even though I resisted feeling that way with a passion. But it was the Lockwoods who were holding me up. Laurel asking me a thousand times if I was all right. Marcus actually helping me spill my mother's ashes into the inlet because my arms were shaking so hard. That whole spectacle stank. I hated it. When Maggie told me that's where my father's ashes had been scattered, though, it started making sense and I knew it had been the right thing to do. It was what my mother wanted.

We got into Jen's car and I sniffed the air.

"I smell gas." I wondered if she heard the panic in my voice. I'd pulled out the seat belt but didn't latch it. I was ready to bolt.

"Oh, I know," she said as she pulled onto the road. "I just filled it up. It always smells like this afterward." She rolled down her window. "Open your window and it'll go away."

I opened the window but still didn't latch the seat belt. I was already picturing the car exploding. Us trapped in it. Trapped in a fire. I thought of saying maybe we should go back and take my car, but I'd sound like a wuss and the video store wasn't that far.

"So how was your cousin's…thing?" I asked.

"Baby shower," she said. "It was okay." She glanced at me. "I *had* to be there, Keith. I was in charge of the whole thing, but I left as soon as I could get away. I hope you understand."

"It's okay." Right then, all I could think about was the explosion that was going to happen any second. My left hand hung on to the seat belt, while my right hand was on the door handle.

"Maybe I could help you go through your mother's things? That's got to be so hard, sorting through…you know." She glanced at me again when I didn't answer. "Or would you rather do that alone?"

"I haven't thought about it," I said. Marcus and Maggie had driven the five hours to Charlotte and back again to get the stuff from the car. There was a lot of it, and now the boxes were stacked up in my mother's bedroom in the trailer. I didn't even want to *go in* that room, much less go through the things she'd been taking to her new life in Charlotte. Marcus said I should go through it soon, though, in case she left a will. I doubted it. She wasn't the will-making type. Plus, she had nothing to leave anyone.

We pulled in front of the video store and I let go of the seat belt. Jen leaned forward to get a good look at me.

"You okay, baby?" she asked.

"Yeah, I'm all right." Images from the morning were coming back to me: the crowd of people by the ruins of that chapel. People saying things I wasn't really listening to about my mother. Trying to open that damn urn. Everyone back at Laurel's, politely nibbling little sandwiches and pretending not to stare at me. I'd needed to get out of there in the worst way. "Maggie was there, of course," I said.

"Of course."

"She gave me all this crap about how she talks to her father and he talks back."

"Really!" Jen opened her car door. "She sounds like a nutcase."

"Yeah," I said. "She's totally whacked."

I got out of the car and followed Jen into the store, trying not to think about how Maggie's eyes were exactly like mine.

Chapter Seventy

Sara
Maggie's Latest Victim
August 2008

It's 3:00 a.m., and i can't sleep.

This morning, I took Keith to PT, as usual.

"Do you need me here?" I asked Gunnar as he began working on Keith's shoulder. Lately, I have the feeling Keith doesn't want me hovering over him during his physical therapy. He says I ask too many questions. I think he likes having the time alone with Gunnar. An older guy for him to relate to. I just get in the way.

"We're fine," Gunnar said as he slowly stretched Keith's left arm over his head. Keith is really gaining mobility in that shoulder. I can tell when we do the exercises at home, and watching Gunnar work with him, it's even more evident. Gunnar isn't as afraid as I am of taking that arm to the limit. "I'll come get you if we need you." Gunnar glanced up at me.

"Okay," I said. "I'll see you in a little bit, Keith."

"Whatever," Keith said, his face knotted in either pain or concentration or both.

I sat down at the public computer in the waiting area to catch up on my e-mail. I spotted one from an unfamiliar address, EMatthews. Ellen Matthews? Jordy's mother? The subject line caught my eye: New Lockwood Victim. Those words shook me up. I clicked on the e-mail and saw dozens of addresses in the header. If it was from Ellen, I thought, she sent it to everyone in her address book. I quickly read the two lines.

On the news tonite, you can learn about Maggie Lockwood's latest victim. Be sure to watch.

Oh, no, I thought. Another child died? This long after the fire? I bit my lip. I always think of Keith as being the worst injured of the children who survived, but I know several of them suffered severe lung damage from the fire. Keith himself would always have to be careful with his lungs. I felt devastated for whatever family had lost its child, and I hated the cryptic and insensitive way Ellen was letting people know. I had to excuse her, though. Ever since losing Jordy, she'd been teetering on the edge of mental illness, and everyone knew it.

I saw her in Jabeen's a few weeks ago and barely recognized her. She'd aged five years since the fire, but I figured she could be thinking the same thing about me. I walked around the counter to give her a hug. Although I didn't know her well, all the parents of the victims became instant family the night of the fire.

"How is Keith?" she asked as I made her tea. "Is he in terrible pain?"

"It's a lot better than it was," I said. "The worst part is that he's embarrassed." I handed her the cardboard cup. "He doesn't want anyone to see him. He has to go back to school in the fall, and my heart breaks for him." I suddenly realized my terrible, *unforgivable* faux pas and my hand shot to my mouth. "Oh, I'm sorry, Ellen!" I said. "*Yes,* he's injured, but he's alive. I'm so sorry I said all that! I still have him. I know how lucky I am." I was stumbling over myself to apologize.

"It's all right," she said. "I'm glad he's doing well."

I thought she tried to smile, but I was so devastated by my stupidity that I really couldn't say any more, and she left without another word.

I put the e-mail out of my mind as Keith and I drove home. We stopped at the pharmacy in Sneads Ferry. Or at least, *I* stopped there, while Keith waited in the car.

"Please come in, Keith," I said as I picked up my purse from the floor between our seats. He still refused to be seen in public and I was getting increasingly worried about it. "You can't hide from the world forever," I said.

His eyes were closed as he listened to his MP3 player, but I knew he heard me in spite of the earbuds.

"At least I can hide from it for the next fifteen minutes," he said.

"Okay." I didn't push him. Maybe I should start to, though, I thought. School was just a few weeks away. I didn't know how he was going to manage.

I picked up a couple of prescriptions, then got back in the car. Keith was still hooked up to the MP3 player, humming, his eyes closed. I pulled out of the parking lot and turned toward the high-rise bridge that linked Sneads Ferry to the island. At first, the road was clear, but as we started over the part of the bridge that rises above the marshland, I saw the long line of cars ahead of us.

"Damn summer traffic," I said.

Keith opened his eyes. "Cops ahead."

I saw the flashing red-and-blue lights. Police cars. Ambulances. A fire truck. "Must be a bad accident," I said.

Keith sat up straight, pulling out his earbuds, craning his neck to see over and around the line of cars.

I looked in my rearview mirror. Was it too late to back up and get out of this mess? I could take Old Folkstone Road to the swing bridge and cross over to the island there. But already, cars were lined up behind me. I was good and stuck.

Keith put his earbuds back in and slumped down in the seat. I tapped my fingertips on the steering wheel for a moment, then put the car in Park, got out and walked to the side of the road to try to see better. A couple of old men, fishing poles in their hands, stood by the railing.

"Do you know what's going on?" I asked.

One of the men, his gray beard neatly trimmed, looked at me. "Car went over the side of the bridge," he said.

"We seen it happen," the second man said. "Went real fast, caught on the guardrail and flipped smack up in the air and over." He used his hand to demonstrate.

"How horrible!" I leaned over the railing. I saw a couple of Coast Guard boats in the water, just beyond the marsh. There was no sign of a car, though, and I pictured it sinking through the murky water to the bottom of the sound. Teenager on summer break, I thought. Too much to drink. I hugged myself, thinking of the phone call someone would have to make to those parents.

I looked back toward my car. I couldn't quite see it from where I stood, but I pictured my own son inside it and was once again grateful that he was alive. I doubted the person who flew off this bridge had been so lucky.

"You could turn around like them folks're doing." The man with the beard pointed to the line of traffic.

I looked behind me. People were jockeying for space so they could make U-turns and head back toward the mainland.

"Oh, good," I said. "Thank you!"

* * *

I went to bed about ten and, as I did every night, I watched the news on the small TV on my dresser. I'd completely forgotten about Ellen's e-mail, and I started to drift off during the first story, which was about a murder in Wilmington. Suddenly, though, the high-rise bridge appeared on the screen and I remembered the accident. I sat up quickly, hoping that whoever had flown off the bridge had survived.

"A woman was killed today when her car fell off the high-rise bridge in Sneads Ferry," the newscaster announced.

I hugged my knees beneath the sheet as a reporter started interviewing a marine police officer. He stood on the Sneads Ferry side of the bridge, the long span behind him.

"Witnesses reported seeing the white Toyota suddenly pull into the westbound lane, then pick up speed as it cut across the eastbound lane," he said. "When it hit the guardrail, it went airborne, flipped over the rail and fell into the water. Our divers were able to get the body of the driver from the vehicle. As best we know, there were no other passengers."

"Do you know the identity of the driver?" the reporter asked.

The officer rubbed his temple. "What I can tell you is that the victim is a woman in her early forties," he said. "She's a Hampstead resident, and we're withholding her identity until her relatives can be notified."

I sucked in my breath, then sank back on my pillow. Ellen. *Maggie Lockwood's latest victim.* Before I realized it, I was crying. I finally pulled out this notebook and began to write. It's as though I can't rest until I write things down these days. It helps me think things through.

I know why Ellen killed herself. It's more than the pain of losing her daughter. It's that in a few weeks, Maggie will be back and Ellen couldn't bear to see her return to normal life while Jordy would never have that chance. I understand. I picture Maggie stretching her arms above her head with painless ease, breathing in clean air with her perfect, healthy lungs. How can I expect Keith to stoically witness her return? It will hurt him so much, and I feel every speck of his pain—physical, emotional—a thousand times over.

I'm not sure how either of us is going to be able to bear it.

Chapter Seventy-One

Andy

THE DAY AFTER MISS SARA'S MEMORY SERVICE, MOM SAID MY room was a wreck and I wasn't allowed to go anywhere till it was clean. Me and Kimmie had a plan to go to Uncle Marcus's tower again. She was ready to have sex. Finally! But I couldn't go till my room was clean, so she was helping me clean it. I was doing things really fast. Putting clothes under my bed, even, which was totally against the rules.

"It's just as fast to hang them up," Kimmie said when she saw me push a shirt under the bed. She really did sound like Mom sometimes. She pulled the shirt out and stuck it on a hanger in the closet.

I was worried that when we finally got to the tower, Keith might be there. That would mean no sex because Kimmie said it would give her the creeps to do it with somebody in the house. I didn't care. I would've done it right there in my bedroom with Mom downstairs.

My desk had all this stuff on it. A book I was supposed to be reading. My tape measure. A bunch of pens and pencils. Eyedrops. My iPod. Some cables. I opened the clutter drawer of my dresser, got all the stuff from my desk and dropped it in the drawer.

"It's never going to close," Kimmie said.

"Yes, it will." I could always get that drawer closed, but this time, it only went in halfway. I moved stuff around and tried again. It still wouldn't close.

Kimmie made a sigh sound. "Let me work on it," she said. "You hang up the rest of your clothes."

I looked at the pants and shirts and things in the laundry basket on my desk chair. She was wrong about how everything should get hung up. "Some of them go in a drawer," I said. I started folding my T-shirts while she pulled the clutter drawer totally out of my dresser and put it on my bed.

"You need little boxes in here to organize stuff better," she said as she started moving things around. "I think you have things from when you were in diapers in here."

"No, I don't," I said. I didn't even *have* that dresser when I was in diapers.

"What's this?" She held up the mail for Keith I'd stuck in there. I'd forgotten all about it. It was kind of crumpled now.

"Just mail for Keith," I said. "His mother told me to give it to him, but I forgot."

"You should give it to him," she said. "It might be important."

I should've just thrown it away. "Okay," I said. I could take it over to the tower and leave it in the kitchen. That way he didn't have to know it came from me.

Kimmie shoved things around in the drawer some more. Then she stuck it back in my dresser and it closed right up. I folded the two last T-shirts real fast and stuck them in a different drawer. Finished!

I patted my jeans pocket for the condom and the key to the tower. "Let's go!" I said.

We rode my bike and Maggie's bike over to Uncle Marcus's. When we were a block away, I could see Keith's car wasn't there.

That made me smile really big and I hoped Kimmie was smiling, too. She was ahead of me, so I couldn't see.

We parked our bikes by the side of the tower so nobody would steal them. Most of the time, Uncle Marcus didn't bother locking his door, but today it was locked. I was really smart to bring the key.

We walked inside and there was Keith! He was sitting right there in the living room, watching TV.

"What are *you* doing here?" I asked.

"I happen to live here," he said. "The real question is, what are *you* doing here?"

"But your car's not here," I said. I actually felt like crying.

"I parked on the street because Marcus and Flip were here earlier and took up both spots out front," he said. "Not that it's any of your business. So what do you want?"

I wasn't sure what to say.

"We found a letter that belongs to you." Kimmie kind of knocked me with her elbow, and I pulled the letter out of my pocket. I walked over and handed it to him.

"Miss Sara told me to give it to you when I was sick," I said.

Keith stared at the envelope. "When were you sick?" he asked.

"It was the day she disappeared," Kimmie said. "I'm really sorry about her."

Keith tore open the envelope and unfolded the paper inside. Money fell out of it. Two dollars, or maybe they were bigger than just dollars. I couldn't tell from where I was. I thought we should leave. I knew Kimmie wouldn't have sex with him there. Keith was reading reading reading while I tried to figure out what me and Kimmie should do.

All of a sudden, he jumped off the couch. "You *asshole!*" he shouted. He waved the paper around and I could see lots of writing on it. "You total fucking loser!"

"Don't talk to him that way!" Kimmie shouted.

I should've been angry for him calling me names, but I was more scared because he looked real mean. He walked toward me. I wanted to run out the door so he couldn't hit me, but I had to stay there and protect Kimmie. Keith walked right past us, though. He grabbed his key-ring thing from the counter and opened the door.

"Can we stay here?" I asked.

"I don't care what you do!" he shouted. Then he slammed the door so loud my ears hurt.

Chapter Seventy-Two

Keith

I WAS GOING TO EXPLODE.

I laid on the gas all the way to Jen's house and burst in the front door without even ringing the bell.

She was in the kitchen, and she twirled around, her hand at her throat like she expected me to be a crazed rapist. I was crazed all right.

"She wanted me to go with her!" I reached across the counter and handed her the letter. My heart thudded in my temples as I watched her read it. I already knew it by heart.

Dear Keith,

First, I'm sorry to spring this on you, but I made the decision this morning. The more I thought about Maggie getting out of prison today, the more I knew I had to do something. Please trust me that this is the right thing for us. Unfortunately, I have Andy L. here at the moment—I'll explain about that later. That's putting a crimp in my schedule, but it will all work out.

You know how much I love this island, but I've been getting increasingly anxious as the time comes for Maggie to get out and upset over the thought of you having to live so close to her. I know you're concerned about it, too, and we both know how impossible it will be to avoid

*her. I also know that going back to school with kids who knew you be-
fore the fire hasn't been easy for you. They compare the boy you used
to be with the boy you are now, not realizing you're still the same inside.*

*So I've decided we're moving to Charlotte. I've thought about this
for quite a while, and thought it would be in the future and you and
I'd have time to talk about it, but frankly, I can't bear the thought of
us being here a single day with the possibility of you bumping into
Maggie. I have a good chance at getting a trainee job at a bank in
Charlotte. It may take a little while, but I'll have the money to tide
us over till then. I'll explain about that when I see you tonight. I'm
rushing right now because I have a lot to get done and having Andy
here isn't helping. Here's what I want you to do: pack up the things
you can't live without. Use the enclosed money to fill your gas tank.
Then head toward Charlotte. I'll get there before dark and find a motel
for us, so call me around eight or so and I'll tell you where we can
meet.*

*I know you probably think I'm out of my mind, but trust me, I've
been thinking about this for a long time. Keep your cell phone on,
pack whatever you need and get on the road as soon as you can.*

I've got to run! See you tonight.

Love, Mom

Jen looked up from the letter, blinking. "Oh my God," she said.
"I'm so pissed off at that loser!"

"Why did he have this?"

"He was sick, so my mother was watching him that day, and she
told him to give this to me and he's such a retard that he forgot. He
forgot!"

"How did you get it?" She held the letter in the air.

"He and his girlfriend brought it over a few minutes ago." I grabbed the letter in my fist. "If I'd had this, the cops would've found my mother so much earlier. They would've had some idea where to look, anyway. Maybe she would've still been alive when they found her. Maybe they could have saved her."

"Keith——" Jen leaned across the counter toward me "——I know this must be really upsetting, but remember? They said she probably died instantly."

"They still could have found her sooner."

"Where's Andy now?"

"Andy? Probably screwing his girlfriend at the tower. Why?"

She shook her head. "No reason."

I smoothed the letter out on the counter. "I should call Marcus or Flip about this," I said.

"Don't go," she said. "Let's just have a quiet night together. You have the most important question answered, and that's that your mother wanted you with her. She wasn't deserting you." She walked around the counter and took my hand. Lifted it to her lips. "The letter's not going to bring her back, baby," she said, putting her arms around my neck. "Here's what I think we should do. You turn on the hot tub and let it heat up. I'll run out and get us some takeout from the Beach Grill." She ground her hips against mine, making me forget for a second about the letter and my stupid cousin. "Then we can have some dinner and then some time in the hot tub and then..." She kissed me, and I reached between us to unbutton her pants. She pulled away with a laugh. "See?" she said. "You're feeling better already."

I smiled. She could always make me smile.

She buttoned her pants again. "One thing at a time," she said. "What do you want from the Beach Grill?"

My brain wasn't thinking about food. It was stuck somewhere between my mother's letter and Jen's body.

"Um...shrimp," I said. "Fried."

"You've got it." She kissed me quickly. "I'll be back. Don't go anywhere. And, Keith..." She turned to face me, walking backward toward the door. "Your mom loved you. It's awful she died, but she was happy about her plan for the two of you. Remember that. At least you know she died happy. That's more than a lot of people can say." She glanced down at her side to grab the doorknob. "And also," she said as she opened the door, "you're beautiful. Inside *and* out. I know you don't think so, but you are. I really, really mean that. Remember that, too."

She left the house and I stared at the door for a minute, frowning. It was weird, her saying all that stuff the way she did, out of the blue. I couldn't say exactly why it bothered me. All I knew was that by the time I went out on the deck to turn on the hot tub, my woody'd completely disappeared.

I stretched out on the couch to wait for her, rereading my mother's letter in the light from the floor lamp. On the kitchen counter, my cell phone rang, and I got up to answer it. Halfway to the counter, though, I realized that *my* cell was in my pocket. The one on the counter was in Jen's purse, which she forgot to take with her. Damn! She'd drive all the way to the Beach Grill and discover she had no money.

Her cell kept ringing. I pulled it out of her purse and looked at the caller ID. Local number. I had no idea whose it was. I stared at it a minute before flipping the phone open.

"Jen's phone," I said.

"Oh." It was a girl. "Is Jen there?"

I knew that voice. "Maggie?"

"Who's this?"

"Keith." This was totally screwy. Why the hell would Maggie be calling Jen?

"Did I dial the wrong..." Maggie hesitated. "No, that doesn't make sense. I don't even *know* your cell number. How come you're answering Jen's cell phone?"

"How come you're *calling* her?"

"She's a friend."

"Of *yours?*"

"Why do you have her phone?"

"She's my girlfriend," I said. My heart started that thumping in my temples again. Something was very wrong with this picture.

"She's... I don't get it," Maggie said. "How long have you known her? She never mentioned—"

"How long have *you* known her."

"About a month."

Man, with all the physical pain and emotional agony I'd been through the last couple of years, nothing felt as bad as the knife that sliced through my heart right then.

Memories zipped through my mind in vivid, half-second flashes.

That cold, who-gives-a-shit attitude the night she hit an animal on the road.

Splat!

The smell of gas in her car.

I just filled it up.

Andy talking about Jen's hair.

It used to be white. Yellowy white.

"Keith?" Maggie asked. "Are you still there?"

"Hang on." I held the phone between my chin and collarbone as

I fumbled through Jen's purse for her wallet. I found it, opened it. Dug through the pockets until I found her driver's license, and shook my head in disbelief at the picture. Pretty girl. Platinum blonde. I looked at her name. Jennifer Matthews? *Matthews?*

You must want to hurt her the way she hurt you.

"Oh, shit, Maggie!" I said.

Where's Andy now?

"*Shit!*" I snapped the phone closed and headed for the door.

Chapter Seventy-Three

Maggie

Why'd he hang up on me? If it hadn't been for that *Oh, shit!*, I would've thought the line went dead.

I was driving home from the Food Lion, and I redialed Jen's number one-handed, my other hand on the steering wheel. It rang four times, and he didn't pick up. What was going on?

I was totally confused. Was that why Jen had backed away from our friendship? Because of Keith? It sounded like he didn't know about me any more than I knew about him, though. But why would Jen lie to both of us?

I drove over the swing bridge, wondering how to get back in touch with him. Maybe he was at Uncle Marcus's. I started to dial Uncle Marcus's home number, but then realized how close I was, so I turned left off the bridge and headed for the tower.

Chapter Seventy-Four

Andy

SEX WAS REALLY FUN. IT WAS FASTER THAN I THOUGHT IT WOULD be, though. I only just got my erection inside Kimmie when it was over. She said ouch when I did it, but I didn't stop. Saying *ouch* wasn't like saying *no*.

"Why did you say ouch?" I asked after I rolled off of her. It was dark by then. Good thing our bikes had lights on them.

"It hurt," she said.

"It *did?*"

"Yeah, but it's supposed to hurt a girl the first time. It'll be better next time."

"I'm sorry," I said. I didn't mean to hurt her.

"Did you hear that?" she whispered.

"What?" I didn't hear anything. Actually, my ears were kind of ringing. "What did you hear?"

"Shh!" She put her finger on my lips.

I did hear something then. Somebody was walking around downstairs.

"We better get dressed!" I whispered. I got up real fast and tried to find my clothes in the dark.

"I can't find my underpants," she said.

I reached onto the table thing and turned on the light. Kimmie was naked in the bed and she looked so pretty I wanted to do it all over again, but then I heard some thumping downstairs.

We got dressed and opened the door. We started down the stairs that went around in a circle. I was trying to figure out what I would say to Uncle Marcus if it was him down there instead of Keith. All of a sudden, there was a big *whoosh* sound and I saw everything downstairs turn gold. Then I heard a big loud pop, like a firecracker.

"It's a fire!" Kimmie grabbed my arm.

It *was* a fire! "Stay calm!" I said.

I heard crackling noises and smelled smoke. It was just like at the lock-in, only there wasn't a boys' room at Uncle Marcus's. Just bathrooms and I didn't think they had air-conditioner boxes outside them. I could use a different window, maybe, but we were on the stairs and there were no windows there at all.

"We need to call the fire department!" Kimmie said. "Do you have your phone?"

My phone was up in the bedroom, but smoke was starting to fill the air up there. Smoke was all around us. We needed a window to get out of. From where we stood, I could see the window in the sliding back door downstairs, but there was a big fire in front of it. There was fire *everywhere*.

I put my arms around Kimmie. She was crying and shaking.

This wasn't like the lock-in at all.

Chapter Seventy-Five

Keith

I SPOTTED THE GLOW OF THE TOWER WINDOWS FROM HALF
a block away. On my way there, I'd convinced myself I was getting
worked up over nothing. The tower was made out of *concrete,* for
Christ's sake. It wasn't going to burn. But as I screeched to a stop
in front of the building, I knew that Jen had done her damage
inside. I only hoped Andy and Kimmie had left before she got
there.

The front door was halfway open and I could see a wall of yellow
flame inside. I dialed Marcus's number at the fire station. "Your
house is on fire!" I shouted when he answered.

"What?"

"Seriously. *Hurry!*" I hung up, then stood in the street by my car.
No way was I getting any closer than that. Man, I hoped Andy was
gone. I got back in my car and pointed the headlights at the front
of the tower. No bikes. Good. I moved my car to the street so
there'd be room in the driveway for the fire truck. I started to turn
off my lights, but my hand froze on the switch. Illuminated against
the side of the house, end to end, were two bicycles. *Shit!* I turned
off the lights and jumped out of the car.

I ran around the back of the tower, but the fire was even worse
in the rear of the building. It had blown out the sliding glass doors

and was lapping at the deck. I felt the heat on my face and I backed away from the tower. *Maybe they got out,* I thought, pressing my back against the wall of the house next door. *Maybe they took off running and just left their bikes here.* But Jen wasn't that dumb. She wouldn't go to all this trouble and let Andy escape.

The ladder! I ran a few yards toward the beach so I could see the roof. If they could get to the roof, they could climb down the ladder.

I cupped my hands around my mouth. "Andy!" I screamed toward the tower, but I knew he couldn't possibly hear me. The only sound now was the fire. It even drowned out the breaking waves behind me.

I ran toward the side of the building. I was going to have to do this. No choice. No fucking choice.

I should've left my car lights on. The side of the house was in darkness, the only light the sickening orange glow from the windows. I felt along the wall until my hands hit one of the skinny metal rails. *I can't do it,* I thought, but I was already grabbing the sides of the ladder and had a foot on one of the rungs.

"Keith!"

I was a few yards off the ground when I heard Maggie call my name. I glanced down just long enough to see her standing at the foot of the ladder, glowing in the flickery orange light. The world spun around me and I quickly shut my eyes, hugging the thin rails of the ladder.

"Oh my God!" she shouted. "Don't go up there!"

"I think Andy and Kimmie are inside!" I managed to shout.

"Andy?"

I felt her grab the ladder beneath me and start to climb.

"Stay down!" I shouted. I wanted to tell her the ladder wouldn't hold both of us—it was shaking and creaking—but I felt like if I opened my mouth to speak again, I'd puke.

"Go! Go!" she yelled.

I forced myself to put one foot above the other while the smoke rose around us. *That smell.* Oh, God. I'd forgotten about that smell. I kept feeling blindly above me for the roof. *Come on! Come on!* All my hands touched was the wall of the tower. Up and up and up. It went on forever, and my lungs hurt as bad as my shoulder. Finally, I saw where the pale wall of the tower met the black of the sky. I scrambled onto the flat roof on my hands and knees, every muscle in my body quivering. I half crawled, half ran to the center of the roof to get away from the edge, dry heaving all the way. Then I got to my feet and ran over to the slanted door.

I felt it for heat, scared shitless to pull the door open and find that flaming yellow dragon on the other side, waiting to finish me off.

"Is it hot?" Maggie was suddenly next to me.

"No." I pulled it open and we raced down the metal stairs, shouting for Andy.

We got to the first landing. The fire was right below us. I felt the heat of it on my scars. Smoke filled the stairwell. It caught in the back of my throat and I started to cough.

"Andy!" Maggie shouted from behind me. She tried to move past me on the stairs, but I grabbed her.

"You can't—"

"Maggie?" He was here. Not far from us.

"Andy!" I shouted. "Come this way. Come to the stairs!"

"We can't go down!" Andy said. "There's too much fire."

"Come *up!*" Maggie shouted.

I saw the two of them then. They were so close together, they looked like one person as they moved toward the stairs. I reached down my hand.

"C'mon!" I tried to shout, but it came out as a croak.

Andy grabbed my hand, and I pulled him and Kimmie onto the stairs.

Maggie tried to reach for him, but I gave her a shove. "Up! Up!" I shouted.

I was coughing and choking as we staggered up the winding stairs. At the top, I pushed open the door to the dark roof, and we fell together in a mound, my arms around Maggie and Andy, hanging on to them with all my strength. That's when I heard one of the most beautiful sounds in the world: sirens.

Chapter Seventy-Six

Maggie
Two Days after the Fire

I MISSED THE HOSPITAL. I FELT SO USELESS, JUST SITTING AROUND the house. I had to keep my leg up, so Mom rented a recliner and I sat in the family room watching TV and movies and playing games on my laptop.

I wasn't sure how I got injured. I had this big bloody gash on my leg that I didn't even know was there until they got us to the hospital. They treated Keith and Andy and Kimmie for smoke inhalation, and I was thinking how lucky I was to be fine, when a nurse asked me why my jeans were all wet. Blood. Ugh. Twenty-two stitches.

Nobody else was hurt, thank God—except for Jen. They found her body by the back door of the tower. At first, they thought she'd trapped herself when she lit the fire. That sliding glass door was always tricky to open, and I didn't like to think what it must have been like for her as she tried to escape. I was angry at her for betraying me, and beyond furious that she'd tried to hurt Andy, but I still didn't want to imagine her struggling with that door. Then they discovered she'd shot herself. Keith said she'd kept a gun in her car. Wow. That girl had some secrets.

They found lots of paintings in the bedroom at the house where she was staying, and most of them had that blond girl in them that was probably her sister, Jordy. Jen was crazy with grief over her sister and mother. It didn't excuse what she did, but it explained it. All I knew was that I wasn't the right person to judge someone else's temporary insanity.

I was in the middle of watching *You've Got Mail* when the doorbell rang. Mom answered it, and I almost jumped out of my chair when Reverend Bill walked into the room. Mom left to get him something to drink, and he sat down on the sofa and folded his hands on his knees.

"I heard you got hurt," he said.

"My calf," I said. "I'm supposed to keep it elevated."

He stared at me in that creepy way he had. "Always some kind of drama with you Lockwoods," he said.

It was an insult, but I had to admit it was also the truth. "I guess," I said.

"I thought you could start out with our visitation program."

"What?" What was he talking about? "I don't know what you mean."

"Visiting sick parishioners. Making sure they have the resources they need. Three meals a day, extra help around the house. That sort of thing."

"Reverend Bill, I don't—"

"You're coming to work for me," he said with that hideous, un-flinching, unsmiling look he was so good at. "You'll do your community service for me."

I knew the hospital was never going to take me back. Cathy Moody had called yesterday to tell me as much. But work at Drury Memorial? That was nuts.

"I'm not religious."

He smirked. "I'm well aware of that," he said.

"Wouldn't your…your parishioners… Would they even let me inside the church?"

"They'll adjust."

I frowned. "But you *hate* me," I said.

He rubbed his chin like he needed to think about that for a minute. "Help me get over that, will you?" he asked.

I stared at him. Then I started laughing. He may have smiled. With Reverend Bill, it was very hard to tell. All I knew was that I had my new community service placement, and it was going to be the hardest one yet.

I was halfway through the movie when Keith showed up at the house.

"Hey," he said to me as he carried a box of stuff into the living room. "Marcus asked me to drop this off. Where should I put it?"

"By the stairs, I guess," I said. Uncle Marcus was going to store some of his things with us while his tower was being gutted. "How's the cleanup going over there?" I asked.

He shook his head. "Fire sucks, you know that?" He coughed as he lowered the box to the floor.

"Yeah," I said. "I wish I could help."

I wanted to talk to Keith about Jen, but the right moment hadn't come up. Maybe this was it.

"Why don't you take a break," I said. "Stay here and watch a movie with me. I'm totally bored."

"And *I'm* totally busy." He headed back to the door. "I'm not going to desert Marcus just 'cause you're bored."

"Right," I said.

He opened the door. "'Later," he said.

Through the window, I could see him get into his car. So, today would not be the day I talked to him about Jen. One of these days, maybe. I understood how he felt. I'd thought I had a friend in Jen, but *he* thought he had a girlfriend, somebody who accepted him, scars and all. He was probably torn up over losing her—or at least what he thought he had with her. He lost the person he thought she was. Someday I'd tell Keith that I knew how it felt to be duped like that. To lose someone you never really had in the first place.

But Keith was never going to be all that easy to talk to. He was not exactly the receptive type. The night of the fire at Marcus's, though, I saw his soft side. Until then, I didn't know he had one. Uncle Marcus said Keith was afraid of heights, and of course he was terrified of fire. He could have stayed on the ground and let me climb that shaky metal ladder to the roof alone, but he was determined to get to Andy. That surprised me. Maybe it even surprised *Keith*. Now, two days later, he had his don't-get-too-close-to-me armor back on. That was okay. Keith was never going to be the nicest guy on the island, but after that night, I definitely knew what he *was:* part of my family.

My other brother.

Chapter Seventy-Seven

Keith
Three Days after the Fire

AT THE TRAILER, I STARTED GOING THROUGH THE THINGS FROM my mother's car. Plenty of people offered to do it for me. Dawn. Laurel. Marcus. Even Maggie. But I wanted to do it myself. Alone. I knew it was going to totally suck, and I didn't want anyone around me if I lost it.

But I didn't lose it.

I went through the papers first, because Marcus was badgering me about them. There could be a will, he said. Maybe a bank account I didn't know about. Something important. So I dug through the box of papers. There weren't all that many, and nothing important. Just bank statements and the information about my college fund and my health-insurance stuff and some other things that didn't mean much to me.

Then there were the notebooks. The so-called memoir. I went into Mom's room with the stack of them, laid down on her bed and started reading, and it was like having her there with me. I could hear her voice. I was probably the only person in the world able to read her handwriting, and that was just as well. I learned more about my mother than any boy should know.

Some things were really shockers. It was weird reading about always-in-control Laurel Lockwood as a total wreck. Same with Marcus, although he'd pretty much prepared me for that revelation. I had no idea my mother'd had a baby before me. My older half brother, Sam. I could really tell how lonely she was, not being able to talk about Sam to that Neanderthal, Steve Weston. She needed somebody to open up to. She needed my father.

I read the parts about Jamie Lockwood over and over until I finally felt as though I knew him. I loved him and I hated him. I supposed that if he'd lived, that's exactly how I would have felt about him. Sort of normal for a teenager, that love-and-hate thing. That's the way it'd been with my mother and me. I'd put her through hell the last few years. Some of it wasn't my fault, but a lot of it was. And she never stopped loving me. I got that. The notebooks were full of me and what I meant to her.

I was closing the last notebook, thinking about my mom and wishing I'd had the chance to really know my father, when something I'd read suddenly clobbered me over the head.

She had a safe-deposit box? And a *ten-thousand-dollar necklace?*

Chapter Seventy-Eight

Andy
Two Weeks after the Fire

A REPORTER LADY CAME TO THE HOUSE, AND MOM ASKED IF
I wanted to talk to her. I said, "Sure!" So the lady came in the house
and me and her sat in the living room with Mom.

She asked me all the regular things, like was I scared in the fire
at Uncle Marcus's and stuff like that. She asked me if I thought Keith
was brave to go into a burning house after already being messed up
by a fire. I told her, "Definitely, yes!"

Everybody knows that Keith is a hero now. He's going to go on
the *Today* show with me and Maggie. The *Today*-show people say
things have come full circle, but I don't remember what that means,
even though Mom explained it to me.

"Why were you and Kimberly Taylor in your uncle's house when
the fire broke out, Andy?" the lady asked.

"Marcus had asked them to organize his CD collection," Mom
said before I could answer. Which was a good thing. I kept forgetting about the CD-collection thing Uncle Marcus made up, because
it was a lie. I think Mom knows the truth, though.

I had to explain to Uncle Marcus why I was in the tower when
the fire happened. Even though he was very sad about his house
burning up, he laughed when I told him.

"Why are you laughing?" I asked.

"People always remember their first time," he said to me. "And in your case, you're going to have a whopper of a story to tell."

I didn't get it. I wasn't supposed to tell anybody on account of sex being private. He must've forgot he told me that. I was happy he was laughing, though, so I laughed, too.

"You must have been so relieved when you saw Keith and your sister on the stairs, ready to lead you to safety," the reporter said.

"Yeah," I said. "That was definitely the best part."

She asked me another question, but I wasn't listening. I was thinking how I was wrong about that being the best part.

"I thought of an even better part," I said.

"Better than knowing you were going to be rescued?" the reporter asked.

"Yeah," I said. "After we ran up the stairs, we popped out the door onto the roof and we kind of fell in a pile and everybody had their arms around everybody."

Mom leaned forward on the sofa. "That was the best part, sweetie?" she asked.

"Definitely."

"I don't understand," the lady said.

Mom smiled and leaned back against the sofa again. "It's a family thing," she said.

"Yeah." I remembered Keith's arm around me even though he was coughing and choking. He didn't let go of me even when we heard the sirens coming. "Keith's last name is Weston," I said to the lady, "but that doesn't matter. He's a Lockwood, whether he wants to be or not."

Chapter Seventy-Nine

Sara
The Lioness
September 15, 2008

SHE WAS TIRED AND VERY, VERY ANXIOUS.

She'd barely slept the night before, thinking about Maggie getting out of prison sometime the next day. Long before sunrise, she heard Keith's alarm go off. He had to go in early for a makeup exam. She got up in the darkness and made pancakes dotted with frozen blueberries. Keith's favorite. He stumbled into the kitchen, looking surprised, and—she thought—pleased, by the platter of pancakes. He grabbed a couple of them in his hand and headed for the door.

"Thanks, Mom," he said as she handed him a napkin.

"Love you," she said, and he grunted something past the food in his mouth as he pushed open the screen door with his good shoulder.

She watched him drive off, his headlights picking up the sea oats before he turned onto the dark, empty main road toward the bridge. Then she walked, still barefoot in her robe, down to the beach and sat in the sand to watch the sunrise bleed into the sky.

Walking back to the trailer a short time later, she spotted three vans on the sandy road in front of it. As she got closer, she saw the network logos on the sides of the vehicles. She started to run, and by the time she reached the trailer, six reporters, some of them wielding cameras, had gotten out of their vans and were descending on her.

"Has Keith left for school yet?" one of them asked.

Her face burned with anger. She ignored the reporters as she marched toward the deck of the trailer.

"We'd like to talk to him about Maggie Lockwood's release today from prison," another said, close on her heels.

"How do *you* feel about her getting out today?" a third asked as she climbed the steps.

"Can you ask Keith to come out to speak with—"

"No!" she shouted, turning toward them from the deck. "No, I will *not* ask him a thing about Maggie Lockwood, and neither will you! Get out of here!" She pointed in the direction of the mainland, the sleeve of her robe ballooning in the breeze.

"Is he upset that—"

"Don't you think he's been through enough?" Her voice sliced through the pink morning air, echoing off the other trailers. "Don't you dare…don't you dare…go near my son. *Ever*. Do you hear me? And don't you fucking *dare* go near his school, either!"

The reporters stared up at her, jaws hanging open. Some of them knew the mild-mannered Sara Weston. This woman was someone different. A lioness protecting her cub. They must have realized she would kill for him.

Sara's hands were knotted up in fists. "Don't you dare, or I *swear* I'll come after you all. Every one of you!"

She ran inside the trailer, slamming the door behind her, sinking to the living-room floor as her trembling legs gave out. She pressed her face into her hands. Thank God he'd had to go in to school early today! Though maybe she shouldn't have let him go at all. Maybe she should have hidden him inside with her. She'd been trying to treat this day like any other, but she hadn't counted on the damn media. They would hound Keith. They'd show his scars on TV. He'd never be able to take the public exposure. The *exploitation*. He was holding on to his sanity by a thread.

She knew all at once she'd made a grave error by not moving away when they had the chance. Her unwillingness to leave the island had kept them there, and now it was too late.

Or was it?

She got to her feet, suddenly energized, and began to formulate her plan as she tossed the leftover pancakes in the garbage. She had no appetite for them now.

The phone rang, and she stared at it a moment, answering it only because it might be Keith.

"I'm so sorry to ask you this." Laurel sounded breathless. "I don't know where else to turn. Andy was sick during the night, and Marcus and I need to pick up Maggie. Is there a chance you could just keep him at your house for a few hours? I'm desperate, Sara."

For a moment, Sara could think of nothing to say. How dare Laurel ask a favor on this day! Was she completely dense?

"Please, Sara," Laurel pleaded. "I'm sure it's just a twenty-four-hour bug. I know it's a huge favor to ask, but I can't leave him alone. It'll only be for a few hours."

Sara thought of all Laurel had done for them after Keith got out of rehab. She remembered the way she'd used her, taking advantage of Laurel's guilt, and she heard the rare panic in her old friend's voice. Could she really say no to her now?

"What time will you be back?" she asked.

"We should be able to pick him up by one. One-thirty at the very latest."

One-thirty. That would be all right. She could pack while Andy was there. He wouldn't have a clue what she was doing, and she didn't need to take much. She'd come back in a few weeks to get the rest of their belongings. The important thing was getting away from the island now. *Today.*

"All right," she said. "But I need to run an errand and I won't be back until about ten-thirty. Will that still work?"

"Yes, yes!" Laurel said. "That'll be fine."

"All right," Sara said. "I'll see you then."

She was at the bank the second it opened. She didn't look inside the jewelry case, not wanting to see the necklace or to remember Jamie fastening it around her neck. She slipped it into the box she'd already prepared for it, then rushed to the post office and mailed it to the online auction house—insured for a thousand dollars. She would have felt conspicuous insuring it for any more than that.

She raced home just in time for Andy's arrival. He was groggy and wan, and she parked him on the sofa and was glad when he quickly fell asleep.

She left a message on Keith's cell to come straight home after school and to ignore any and all reporters. She thought about waiting to leave until she could explain everything to him in person, but he might argue with her. He was going to be shaken up by the whole thing, and she wouldn't have time for a lot of back-and-forth with him. It would probably take her five hours to get to Charlotte, and she needed to get there early enough to find a decent motel in the daylight. She had a few hundred dollars in cash, which would get them through a couple of days before she'd need to hit an ATM. Tomorrow, she'd call Western Carolina Bank to see if they had any new job openings. She'd look for a place to live. They wouldn't be able to start out in that grand apartment complex, but that didn't matter. Maybe someday.

Andy woke up, and she gave him some ginger ale and hooked him up with Keith's video games, so he barely knew she was in the trailer, much less that she was packing.

Suddenly, though, the plan began to unravel.

Laurel called to say they'd be late. Four-thirty or five. Sara was livid. She'd have no choice but to leave before they returned. Andy would be fine. He was sixteen, for heaven's sake. She wrote the note for Keith, explaining everything, then she told Andy she was going to the store. She left the trailer, got into her car and drove away. With her, she had some clothes, some toiletries, the notebooks she'd never get the chance to write in again and the cell phone she always forgot to charge.

She made it over the bridge before she started crying. Turning the car around in a parking lot, she headed back the way she came. She wasn't going to her trailer, though. No. Instead, she drove to the northern tip of the island.

She parked at the very end of the road. Then she kicked off her sandals and walked across the sand until she reached the crumbling concrete walls of the chapel, all that was left of Free Seekers.

Did tourists who walked out to this slender bit of sand speculate about the remains of the chapel? Of the five walls, only two still stood, and even they were nothing more than jagged remnants of concrete. They rose a few feet above the sloping sand dunes that had formed around them over the years. Any sign of the chapel's roof, pews and flooring had long since disappeared. Visitors probably thought the remains had something to do with Operation Bumblebee, maybe debris from one of the old towers. They probably wondered why a tower would have been built in that spot, surrounded on three sides by water, but they'd shrug off the question a moment later. Who cared? Who, besides Sara, cared about this barren spit of land? She'd come often to this spot over the years, the place where Jamie's ashes had mixed with the water and the sand. Sometimes she could swear he was there with her.

She sat down on the sand, resting her back against one of the remaining chapel walls. She thought about all the days she'd spent inside the small building. Painting the walls the color of wet sand. Sewing yards and yards of fabric for the pew cushions. Taking care of Maggie. *Oh, Maggie.*

The turbulent water of the inlet blurred in front of her. Digging her hands into the sand, the full impact of what she was doing hit her. Her soul was tied to this place. How could she leave?

She thought of how different her life would have been if Jamie'd had the courage to leave Laurel and marry her early on. He never would have been on Marcus's boat. He'd still be alive, still a part of her future as well as her past. But it was stupid and pointless to think about what might have been. She had to focus on what was best for Keith. She thought Jamie would approve of her plan for their son.

Getting to her feet, she lifted her face to the sky and drew in air from the ocean and inlet and Intracoastal all in one breath. She would never stand there again. She was losing this, letting go of one more fragile thread that connected her to the man she'd always loved.

Bending over, she scooped up two handfuls of sand and folded her fingers carefully around the grains. There had to be some container in the car that would hold them. She could keep the sand forever, she thought as she walked away from the chapel ruins. She'd take this small part of the island, this small part of Jamie, with her.

But as she walked, she felt the sand spilling from the crevices in her fists. The tighter she held on to it, the more it slipped through her fingers, until by the time she reached her car, her hands were nearly empty...but not quite. Opening her hands, she looked at the thin layer of powdery sand coating her palms. She studied the grains of sand for a moment, those beige and white and brown bits of her past. Then lifting her hands close to her face, she leaned forward and blew them away.

Chapter Eighty

Keith
One Month after the Fire

I LIKE HOW I CAN SIT IN THE SAND WITH MY BACK AGAINST the old concrete wall of Jamie Lockwood's chapel and no one can see me. My mother's service was the first time I'd ever been to that end of the island, even though I'd lived less than ten miles from it all my life. I could see why someone—why my father—would pick that spot for a church. Peaceful and quiet and surrounded by water.

It's pretty cold, sitting here, though. The breeze is blowing hard off the ocean, but I came prepared with a blanket to wrap up in. I wanted to think about maybe building a house on this spot. I have money now. Lots of it. Three hundred fifty-five fucking thousand dollars, to be exact. Mister Johnson tracked the necklace down to this online auction house. They'd been trying to find my mother, but she'd gotten a new e-mail address to use with them and no one knew about it. I'm probably as rich as I'm ever going to be, and Laurel said I could pick some Lockwood land to build on if I want. But sitting on this bit of land where the chapel had been, with the wind practically blowing me away, I know this won't be it. First storm that hits the island, my house would be toast. My father must have been a crazy man.

I was spending my days since the fire helping Marcus with the tower. It was still a wreck inside, but we were making progress. The first day after the fire, Marcus asked me to start the cleanup in the living room. When I hesitated, he told me to go upstairs instead. He knew without me telling him that I didn't want to be in the room where Jen had been found. I didn't want to think about her or talk about her or ever hear her name again. Man, I'd been played for the fool before, but not like that. She'd handed me that story about her parents being divorced and her father who wanted her to hunt with him and her brother getting burned in chemistry class. All cock-and-bull. Flip put the truth together from talking to her friends: She was a twenty-year-old, very blond art major at UNC in Asheville. Her father left when she was a baby. Her mother, of course, drove off the high-rise bridge. She had one sister—Jordy— who'd wanted to visit her at UNC the weekend of the lock-in. Jen was hung up on some guy and wanted to be with him, though, so she told Jordy she couldn't come, which was why Jordy was at the lock-in and why she died. I guess Jen had a problem living with that guilt. Andy must have seen her at the memorial service for the fire victims, since the victims' families all sat in the front row and he was up there for being "the hero" and all.

I keep remembering Jen's last words to me as she walked backward out of her house the night of the fire. How I was beautiful. How I should remember that. She said it like she meant it, and I've decided to believe she did.

A small yacht is sailing into the inlet from the ocean in front of me. I watch it move from right to left, and I can see a couple of guys inside the cabin. Lucky bastards. Not a care in the world. Maybe I should buy a boat and skip the house idea?

I can see the wake from the yacht lapping against the sand a few yards from where I'm sitting. I think, *My mother's ashes are in that water.* I remember what Maggie'd said about my father's ashes being scattered in the same place. My mother really loved him. I could tell that from her notebooks. She'd never gone out with anybody since he died. I hadn't given it all that much thought—I never wanted to know about my mother's love life—but maybe she never went out with anyone because no one measured up to my father, at least not in her mind.

Man, I love reading those notebooks. I understand who she was when I read them. I even understand who *I* am.

When I was about three years old, I stopped crying over things. I toughened up, I guess. Probably some dude told me my mother needed me to be a man, and I took it to heart and never let anything get to me enough to make me cry. During the year and a half after the lock-in fire, though, I cried a lot. My life sucked, and it would catch up to me, and I'd just crack.

But I haven't cried about my mother. Not even when I read the notebooks. I feel really okay. I feel good. My mother didn't mean to, but she left me an awesome gift, and I'm not talking about the necklace. The money. What she left me is a whole lot better than that.

She left me her story.

Acknowledgments

Many people pitched in as I wrote *Secrets She Left Behind,* helping me understand everything from the juvenile justice system to the plight of a family when someone "goes missing" to the geography of Topsail Island.

For answering my many questions about the police response to a missing adult, my thanks go to Sergeant Art Cunio and Chief Mike Halstead of the Surf City, North Carolina, Police Department. My fictional police department will never measure up to yours!

For helping me understand the impact on a family when a loved one disappears, thank you to Project Jason founder Kelly Jolkowski and Project Jason volunteer Denise Gibb. You two give families hope.

For their unflagging support, thank you to my favorite booksellers, Nancy Olson of Quail Ridge Books in Raleigh and Lori Fisher of Quarter Moon Books in Topsail Beach.

For always being there, ready and willing to brainstorm at a moment's notice, thanks go to my Scribbler buddies: Mary Kay Andrews, Margaret Maron, Katy Munger, Sarah Shaber, Alexandra Sokoloff and Brenda Witchger.

For allowing me to use their Topsail Island homes for my research trips, thank you to Susan Rouse and Dave and Elizabeth Samuels.

For writing *Topsail Island: Mayberry by the Sea,* my favorite book about the area, thank you, Ray McAllister.

For their various contributions, I'd also like to thank Jean Beasley, Ken and Angie Bogan, Sterling Bryson, BJ Cothran, Evonne Hopkins, Kate Kaprosy, Lottie Koenig, Holly Nicholson, Glen Pierce, Adelle Stavis and Roy Young.

For listening patiently to my story ideas, reading first drafts, being my resident photographer, smoothing my furrowed brow when I hit a snag in the plot and cooking when I'm on deadline, thank you to John Pagliuca.

As always, I'm grateful to my editor Miranda Indrigo and my agent Susan Ginsburg. I'm lucky to have you two in my corner!